TYRANT

VALERIO MASSIMO MANFREDI is the professor of classical archaeology at the Luigi Bocconi University in Milan. He has carried out a number of expeditions and excavations at many sites throughout the Mediterranean, and has taught in Italian and international universities. He has published numerous articles and academic books, mainly on military and trade routes and exploration in the ancient world.

He has published nine works of fiction, including the 'Alexander' trilogy, translated into twenty-four languages in thirty-eight countries, whose film rights have been acquired by Universal Pictures.

He has written and hosted documentaries on the ancient world transmitted by the main television networks, and has written fiction for cinema and television as well.

He lives with his family in the countryside near Bologna, Italy.

Also by Valerio Massimo Manfredi

VALERIO MASSIMO MANFREDI

TYRANT

Translated from the Italian by Christine Feddersen-Manfredi

PAN BOOKS

First published 2005 by Macmillan

This edition published 2005 by Pan Books
an imprint of Pan Macmillan, a division of Macmillan Publishers Limited
Pan Macmillan, 20 New Wharf Road, London N1 9RR
Basingstoke and Oxford
Associated companies throughout the world
www.panmacmillan.com

ISBN 978-0-330-52676-0

Copyright © Valerio Massimo Manfredi 2005
Translation copyright © Macmillan 2005

First published in Italian 2003 as *Il tiranno* by
Arnoldo Mondadori Editore S.p.A., Milano

The right of Valerio Massimo Manfredi to be identified as the
author of this work has been asserted by him in accordance
with the Copyright, Designs and Patents Act 1988.

1 3 5 7 9 8 6 4 2

A CIP catalogue record for this book is available from
the British Library.

Typeset by SetSystems Ltd, Saffron Walden, Essex
Printed and bound in Great Britain by
CPI Mackays, Chatham ME5 8TD

Visit **www.panmacmillan.com** to read more about all our
books and to buy them. ou will also find features, author
interviews and news of any author events, and you can sign
up for e-newsletters so that you're always first to hear
about our new releases.

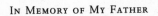In Memory of My Father

MEDITERRANEAN SEA

Eryx
Drepanum
Panormus
Solus
Thermae
Motya
Segesta
Lilybaeum
Halicyae
Entella
Selinus
Heraclea Minoa
RIVER HALYCUS
Acrag[as]

Sicily

0 — MILES — 50

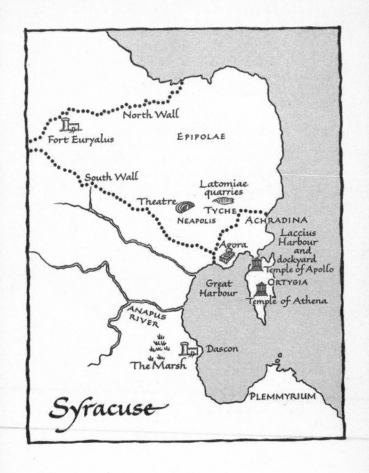

North Wall

Fort Euryalus

EPIPOLAE

South Wall

Latomiae
quarries

Theatre

TYCHE

NEAPOLIS

ACHRADINA

Agora

Laccius
Harbour
and
dockyard
Temple of Apollo

ORTYGIA

Great
Harbour

Temple of Athena

ANAPUS
RIVER

Dascon

The Marsh

PLEMMYRIUM

Syracuse

There is no doubt, in fact, that the gods
use certain men for the purpose of punishing
the evil of others, turning them into slaughterers,
before they, too, are destroyed.

Plutarch

PROLOGUE

CORINTH, 342 BC

The man arrived a little after dusk when the shadows were beginning to lengthen over the city and over the harbour. He walked at a quick pace with a satchel over his shoulder, glancing around him with a certain apprehension. He stopped near a shrine and the lamp burning before the image of the goddess Persephone lit up his face: the greying hair of a man past middle age, his straight nose and thin lips, high cheekbones and hollow cheeks bristly with a dark beard. His nervous, troubled gaze still held a trace of dignity and reserve that contrasted with his worn clothing and shabby appearance and hinted at a high-born provenance.

He turned down the road that led to the western port and walked towards the docks, crowded with taverns and inns frequented by sailors, merchants, longshoremen and soldiers from the fleet. Times were prosperous in Corinth and both of her ports were thronging with vessels carrying wares to and from all the countries on the internal sea and on the Pontus Eusinus. Here in the southern district where the wheat storehouses were located, every variety of Sicilian rang out around him: the colourful accents of Acragas, Catane, Gela, Syracuse . . .

Syracuse. Sometimes he thought he'd forgotten, but then a little nothing would send him back to the days of his childhood and his youth, swamping him in the lights and colours of a world long transfigured by nostalgia, but above all by the bitterness of a life inexorably marked by defeat.

He'd reached his tavern and went in, after taking a last look around.

The place was beginning to fill up with regulars who had come for a bowl of hot soup and a glass of strong wine, swilled straight as only barbarians and poor wretches were wont to do.

When the weather was fine, people would sit outside under the trellis to take in the two seas, one dark already, prey to the night, the other red with the last gleam of dusk, and the ships hurrying to harbour before the night set in. But when the winter wind of Boreas descended from the mountains to chill men's limbs, they crammed inside in an atmosphere dense with smoke and stifling odours.

The tavern keeper poked at the fire in the hearth, then took a bowl of soup and set it down in front of him on the table. 'Dinner, maestro.'

'Maestro . . .' he mumbled back, with a faint grimace.

The spoon was on the table, tied with a string so it wouldn't be carried off. He picked it up and began to eat, slowly, savouring the simple, tasty broth that warmed his aching bones.

The girls were arriving as the customers, dinner over, continued to drink or were already drunk, with the excuse that it was cold and that wine was what they needed to keep them warm.

Chloe was not especially beautiful, but her eyes were deep black and her proud expression was so absurd for a young prostitute that she reminded him of the women in Sicily. Perhaps she was Sicilian after all.

Yes, perhaps she reminded him of someone, a woman he had loved in his youth in his native land. That was why he glanced at her now and then, and smiled at her; she smiled back without knowing why. Her eyes were wide and a bit mocking.

He suddenly found her at his side; he was surprised at first, but then gestured at the keeper to bring over another bowl of soup. He pushed it over to her, putting a few coins on the table as well.

'Not enough to fuck with, maestro,' she said, with a glance at the money.

'No, I know that,' he said calmly. 'I only wanted to offer you something to eat. You're thin, and if you get any thinner they won't be keeping you around for the customers any more; they'll send you to the millstone. But . . . why did you call me that?'

'Maestro?'

The man nodded and continued to eat his soup.

The girl shrugged. 'That's what everyone calls you. They say that people pay you to teach them to read and write. I don't think anyone knows your real name. You have a name, surely?'

'Just like everyone else.'

'And you won't tell me what it is?'

The man shook his head, dipping his spoon back into the soup. 'Eat while it's hot,' he said.

Chloe brought the bowl to her lips and noisily gulped down the broth. She wiped her mouth with the sleeve of her tunic. 'Why won't you tell me?'

'Because I can't,' said the man.

The girl looked across at the satchel slung over the back of his chair. 'What's in there?'

'Nothing that concerns you. Eat, your customers are here.'

The keeper approached. 'Get over to the room,' he said, pointing at a door at one end of the tavern. 'Those two bold men of the sea are looking for a good time. They've already paid me. Make sure they leave happy.'

The girl took another swallow of soup, and whispered into his ear as she was getting up: 'Careful, that bag is bound to attract attention. People want to know what's in it. You didn't hear that from me.' Loudly, she added, 'Thank you for the soup, maestro. It warmed my heart.'

*

Chloe had been turned over to a couple of foreigners already reeling from their drink. Big, strapping, filthy. The kind who had to hurt a girl to get their thrills. The man heard her scream. He got up and moved towards the door at the end of the tavern; the keeper spotted him and shouted: 'Where do you think you're going? Stop, blast you, stop!'

But he'd already thrown open the door and was lunging into the small dark room, yelling: 'Leave her alone! Let go of her, you bastards!'

Pandemonium ensued. The two of them grabbed him and shoved him back out into the tavern, but he managed to seize a chair and waved it around wildly as the tavern-goers crowded around the brawlers, goading them on in loud voices. A third man crept up from behind and tried to slip off with his satchel, but he knocked him over the head with the chair and then backed up, panting, shoulders to the wall.

He was surrounded. Distressed at his own daring, he was dripping sweat and trembling as his adversaries closed in threateningly.

One of them lurched at him and punched him in the stomach, hard, and then in the face. As the other was about to jump in, three brutes that no one had ever seen before burst into the room and knocked the two men senseless, laying them out on the ground with blood spouting from their noses and mouths. Their aggressors vanished just as suddenly as they had appeared.

The maestro made sure that he still had his satchel and wove his way then through the awestruck crowd and out the door.

A gust of cold wind blasted him and sent shivers down his spine. He felt the effects of the blows he'd taken all at once as the tension that had propelled him began to wash away. He staggered, put his hands to his temples as if to ward off the dizziness that was pulling the ground from under his feet, groped around for a support that wasn't there, and tumbled into the middle of the road.

He did not come to his senses until much later, when it started to rain and the icy water dribbled down his face and back. After a little while, he felt someone dragging him to the side of the road under a shed where some asses were tethered.

He opened his eyes, and the light pouring out of the tavern window revealed the face of an old, bald-headed beggar without a tooth in his mouth.

'Who are you?' he muttered.

'Who are you, that's what I want to know. I've never seen anything like it! Three monsters show up out of nowhere, beat those creeps to a pulp . . . and then disappear! That's a lot of fuss over a tramp, I say.'

'I'm not a tramp.'

'Damned if you aren't.' The old man pulled him up a little against the wall and covered him with a few handfuls of straw. 'Hold on, big man,' he said, 'maybe I've got a little wine left. It's my pay for watching these asses all night. Here, drink some of this, it'll warm you up.'

He watched him as he gulped down a few swallows of wine.

'If you're not a tramp, what are you then?'

'I earn a living teaching people to read and write, but I . . .'

'You what?'

His mouth twisted into a grimace that might have been a smile. 'I was the lord of the wealthiest and most powerful city of all the earth . . .'

'Yeah, sure. Right. And I'm the great king of Persia.'

'And my father was the greatest man of our times . . . Give me a little more wine.'

'Are you going to get on with this story, then? And what have you got in that satchel that you're always clutching so tight?'

He took another couple of long draughts, then cleaned his mouth with his sleeve. 'Nothing that's worth stealing. It's his story . . . my father's story. The story of a man who became the lord of almost all of Sicily and much of Italy. He defeated the barbarians in countless battles, invented machines of war the likes of which had never been seen, deported entire populations, erected the greatest fortress in the world in just three months, founded colonies in the Tyrrhenian and Adriatic seas, married two women on the same day. There's never been anyone like him among all the Greeks.'

The old man reached over with the flask of wine again, and then sat down next to him, leaning up against the wall. 'By all the gods! And just who is this phenomenon, this . . .'

A flash of lightning brightly lit up the rain-spattered road and the maestro's swollen face. Thunder pealed through the sky but he did not move. He clasped the sack to his chest and said, emphasizing each word, 'His name was Dionysius. Dionysius of Syracuse. But the entire world called him . . . the tyrant!'

1

A HORSEMAN APPROACHED at breakneck speed, lifting a storm of white dust on the road from Camarina, directed towards the city's western gate. The officer on duty ordered him to stop. 'Halt!' he shouted. 'Make yourself known!'

His order proved unnecessary. The horse collapsed to the ground suddenly at less than two hundred feet from the walls, sending his rider rolling in the dust.

'Open the gate!' ordered the officer. 'Hurry, go see who it is and bring him in.'

Four guards ran out and reached the horseman, who was sprawled out in the dirt. The horse lay panting in agony.

The man screamed out in pain when they tried to turn him over. His face was disfigured from the strain, sullied with dust and with blood.

'Who are you?' asked one of the soldiers.

'I've come from Selinus . . . take me to your commander! Hurry, I implore you.'

The soldiers looked each other in the eye, then put together a litter with their spears and shields, lifted him on to it and carried him inside. One of them hung back to put the horse out of his misery; he gave a last shudder and expired.

The little group soon reached the guardhouse. Their officer approached, carrying a torch, and the messenger looked up at him: a handsome, sturdy youth with pitch-black, wavy hair, black eyes and full lips.

'My name is Dionysius,' he said. 'I'm the commander of the guards. What has happened? Speak, for the gods' sake!'

'I must report to the authorities. It's a question of life or death. The Carthaginians are laying siege to Selinus. There are thousands and thousands of them, they are attacking us with huge, incredible machines. We cannot hold out alone . . . we need your help! Now, in the name of the gods, you must leave now!' Then, in a lower voice, 'Give me water, please, I'm dying of thirst.'

Dionysius handed him his own flask and barked out quick orders to his men: 'You, find Diocles and tell him to meet us at the prytaneum; tell him it's a matter of the utmost urgency.'

'But he'll be sleeping at this hour . . .' objected the guard.

'Get him out of his bed, by Heracles, move! And the rest of you,' he said, turning to the others, 'go wake up the members of the Council and have them gather at the prytaneum. They must listen to this man. You,' he said to the last, 'go call a surgeon and tell him it's urgent.'

The men hurried off to do as they had been ordered. Dionysius had his second-in-command, a friend named Iolaus, replace him on guard duty, and he escorted the soldiers carrying the litter through the dark streets of the city, lighting their way with the torch he held in his hand. He'd glance back every now and then at the man stretched out on that rough litter, his features twisted into a grimace of pain at every jerk and jolt. He must have broken bones when he was thrown to the ground.

When they reached their destination, the council members had already begun to show up. Half asleep and in a foul humour, they were accompanied by their lantern-carrying slaves. Diocles, the commander-in-chief of the armed forces, arrived nearly immediately, but scowled when he saw Dionysius. 'What is all this rush? Is this any way to—'

Dionysius raised his hand sharply to cut off the complaining. He was only twenty-two years old, but he was the strongest warrior in the city: no one could match him in the use of arms; his resistance to fatigue, hardship and pain had already become legendary. He was fearless and had no tolerance for discipline. He had no respect for those who were not worthy of it, be they gods or men. He despised those who preferred talk over action. He believed that only a man who was willing to put his own life on the line deserved to command, and that a commander had to prove his nerve and his courage on the battlefield. And he always looked a man in the eye before he killed him.

'This messenger has done in his horse and shattered his bones to get here,' he said, 'and I say we need to listen to him immediately.'

'Let him talk, then,' snapped Diocles impatiently.

Dionysius drew close and helped the man into a sitting position. The messenger began to speak. 'They attacked us suddenly, arriving from the north, from where we would have least expected a raid. And they got all the way to our walls! We have been doing all we can to withstand their attacks, but they've been battering our walls day and night. They've got moving towers, fitted with swinging rams. Huge trunks of wood with solid iron heads! Archers posted at the tops of those tall towers are picking off our defenders on the battlements.

'Their commander is called Hannibal, son of Gisco. He's obsessed; they say he descends from that Hamilcar who died immolating himself on the altar of Himera seventy years ago, when you Syracusans wiped out the Carthaginian army with the help of the Acragantines. He has sworn to vindicate his forefather, they say, and he will stop at nothing to get revenge.

'We've managed to hold out for three days running, but the only thing that is keeping us in the fight is the hope of seeing you show up with reinforcements. Why have you done nothing? The city cannot resist much longer; we are short of food and water and we've lost a great many men. We've had to put sixteen-year-old boys and sixty-year-old men on the front lines. Our women are fighting at their sides! Help us in the name of the gods, I beg of you . . . help us!'

Diocles looked away from the anguished Selinuntian messenger and turned around to examine the faces of the councillors sitting in the hemicycle. 'Have you heard him? What do you decide?'

'I say we leave immediately,' said Dionysius.

'Your opinion has no importance here,' Diocles hissed. 'You are merely a low-ranking officer.'

'But those people need us, by Heracles!' snapped back Dionysius. 'They're dying; they'll be butchered if we don't get there in time.'

'That's enough!' said Diocles. 'Or I'll have you expelled.'

'The fact is,' spoke up an elderly councillor named Heloris, 'that we can make no decision before tomorrow, when a legal number of councilmen can be summoned. Why don't you let Dionysius go in the meantime?'

'Alone?' asked Diocles sarcastically.

'Give me an order,' said Dionysius, 'and before dawn I'll have five hundred men ready in fighting order. And if you give me a couple of ships I'll be inside the walls of Selinus in two days' time.'

The messenger listened anxiously to their debate: every passing moment could be decisive in his city's being saved or annihilated.

'Five hundred men,' said Diocles. 'Now you'll tell me where you're going to get five hundred men.'

'The Company,' replied Dionysius.

'The Company? I'm in charge here, not the Company!' Diocles shouted.

'Then you get them for me,' replied Dionysius coldly.

Heloris broke in again. 'I don't think it matters much where he gets them, as long as they can set off as soon as possible. Is there anyone against it?'

The councillors, who could not wait to crawl back under their covers, unanimously approved the expedition, but without allowing him to take the ships; they would be needed to transport the bulk of the troops later.

The surgeon arrived at that moment with his instruments in hand.

'Take care of this man,' said Dionysius, and left without

waiting for Diocles's orders. He soon reached his friend Iolaus at the guardhouse. 'We're leaving,' he said.

'When? Where for?' asked the youth, alarmed.

'At dawn, for Selinus. We're the vanguard. The others will arrive with the fleet. I need five hundred men and they must all be members of the Company. Spread the word, immediately. I want them here, fully armed, with enough rations for five days. And an extra horse every three men. Within two hours, at the most.'

'We'll never pull that off! You know the Company holds you in great esteem, but . . .'

'You tell them that now is the time to prove it. Move.'

'As you wish,' replied Iolaus. He whistled, and was answered by whinnying and the pounding of hooves. Iolaus jumped on to his horse and sped off into the darkness.

*

On the fourth day, one of the battering rams managed to open a breach in the walls of Selinus. The Campanian mercenaries hired by the Carthaginians rushed through the gap, driven by the desire to stand out in their commander's eyes, but above all by their greed, since he had promised them the sack of the city.

The Selinuntians crowded around the breach to defend it, walling out the attackers with their shields and their chests. They succeeded in driving back their assailants and slew a great number of them; the rest of the barbarian troops made a disorderly retreat, trampling the bodies of their fellow soldiers.

The next day, Hannibal gave orders to remove the rubble and had protective roofing built so that his men could work to clear a passage. From up high on the assault towers, his archers continued to keep the defenders in their marks, forcing them away from the breach.

On the sixth day, the passage was clear; the rams further widened the gap, opening the way for the assault infantry of Libyan, Iberian and Campanian mercenaries, who poured into the city, howling fearsome war cries.

The Selinuntians were expecting them; they had worked all night to erect barricades at the entrances to each of their streets, isolating the districts behind them. From these shelters they counter-attacked ceaselessly, pushing back the enemy and killing off as many as they could. But although their valour was beyond any imagining, their strength was waning with every passing hour. The strain of building the barricades, their lack of sleep and the exertion of endless battle made them a poor match for the fresh hordes of rested enemy troops.

On the seventh day, the rams opened a second breach at another point of the walls, and the attackers flooded through, raising cries so loud that the city's defenders felt the blood freeze in their veins. The second wave surged over the barricades like a river in full destroys a fragile bank. The obstacles were overrun and the Selinuntian warriors were forced back towards the market square, where they regrouped shoulder to shoulder in a last, desperate attempt to resist.

The bravery of their women was extraordinary. They climbed to the rooftops and threw everything they could get their hands on at the enemy: roof tiles, bricks and wooden beams. Even the children realized what fate they were in for, and did the same.

In this way, the Selinuntians managed to prolong the agony of their city for one more day, in the hopes that every hour won was an hour gained. The night before, light signals had been seen on the inland mountains, and they were convinced that their rescuers would soon appear. But the next day, their last attempts at resistance were overwhelmed. Exhausted by the strain of long days of combat, the men disbanded and the battle broke up into thousands of individual clashes. Many found themselves defending the doors of their own homes, and the shrieks of terror of their sons and daughters managed incredibly to squeeze a final spasm of energy from their worn bodies. But their obstinate resistance only served to increase the rage of the barbarians who, having finally gained the upper hand, abandoned themselves to the bloodiest massacre ever seen in the history of man. They mercilessly killed even the smallest children, slashed the throats of infants in their cradles. By that evening, many of them were proudly displaying dozens of severed hands, strung together as trophies, and spikes topped with the heads of their dead enemies.

Horror reigned. The cries and screams of the wounded and dying echoed everywhere.

But it was not over.

For two days and two nights the city was at the mercy of its pillagers. Women, girls and young boys were deliberately given over by Hannibal as prey to the violence and raping of the mobs of soldiers. What those wretches suffered was indescribable; the few who survived and were able to talk about what they had seen said that there was no prisoner who did not envy the fate of those who had died honourably with their swords in hand. There is nothing worse for a human being than to fall into the hands of another.

Selinus was destroyed two hundred and forty-two years after her founding.

Sixteen thousand people were killed.

Six thousand, nearly all women and children, were sold into slavery.

Two thousand six hundred survived by escaping through the eastern gate, because the barbarians were so glutted by their pillaging that they were oblivious of their flight.

Dionysius, at the head of a squad of fifty horsemen, met up with the straggling column in the dead of night. He was about an hour ahead of the rest of his contingent, while the bulk of the Syracusan troops would be landing at the mouth of the Hypsas river the following day.

Too late.

At the sight of the horsemen, the surviving warriors warily circled around the women and children, fearing that they had fallen into an ambush and that death had spared them only to reserve an even more bitter end. But when they heard them speaking Greek, they dropped their shields to the ground and fell to their knees sobbing. They had marched that far driven on by the sheer force of despair and now, finally saved, they were overcome by their memories of the disaster. The butchery, assaults and atrocities they had seen washed over them like the waves of a stormy sea.

Dionysius dismounted and inspected those sorry warriors. In the light of his torch, he could see that their shields and helmets were badly dented. The men were spattered with blood, dirt and sweat, their eyes were bloodshot with weeping and fatigue. They all wore the same haunted expression; more ghosts than men. 'Which of you is the most highly ranked officer?' he asked.

A man of about forty stepped forward. 'Me. I am a battalion commander, my name is Eupites. Who are you?'

'We are Syracusans,' was the reply.

'What took you so long? Our city has been destroyed—'

Dionysius raised his hand to interrupt him. 'If it had been up to me, our army would have arrived two days ago. But a people's assembly had to be called in Syracuse, and once they had come to a decision, our commanders had to discuss what line of action to take. I left alone, with this vanguard, as soon as your messenger reached us with the news that the city was about to fall. You're not out of danger yet; we must get you to Acragas before the barbarians set off in pursuit. Bring forth your wounded now; I'll have litters prepared for those who can't walk. Line up the women and children in the middle, the warriors at the fore and rear. We'll guard the sides.'

'Wait,' said Eupites.

'What is it?'

'Your name.'

'Dionysius.'

'Listen to me, Dionysius. We are grateful to you for being the first to come to our aid. We are humiliated and ashamed of the state we are in, but there is something I must tell you.'

As he spoke, the other Seliuntian warriors had picked up their shields and were crowding around him, their shoulders stiff and their hands gripping their spears.

'As soon as we have garnered our strength, we will return to rebuild our houses and our city, and if anyone, whoever he may be, should ever want to wage war against the Carthaginians, we will be ready to march with him. Revenge is our only reason for living.'

Dionysius raised his torch to illuminate the man's face and his eyes. He saw more hate there than he had ever seen in the expression of any human being. He passed the torch under the faces of the others; in each one of them he saw the same fierce determination. 'I'll remember that,' he said.

*

Dionysius sent a couple of men to signal to the rest of his contingent that they should turn back, for there was nothing more to be done for Selinus. They then resumed their march and walked the whole night long until they came upon a group of villages where they found some food. As the exhausted refugees stretched out under the trees of an olive grove, Dionysius rode back some distance to make sure they weren't being followed. It was then that his attention was attracted by a splash of white in the middle of a field. He spurred on his horse and went closer. A girl was lying there, apparently lifeless, on the grass. Dionysius dismounted, raised her head and brought his flask to her lips. She seemed no older than sixteen. Her face was so smoke-blackened that he could barely make out her features. Except for her eyes: when she opened them, they shone with an amber light. She must have collapsed during the night-time march without anyone noticing. Who could say how many of those poor wretches had yielded to fatigue?

'What's your name?' he asked.

The girl took a sip of water and said: 'You think I tell my name to just anyone who happens to come along?'

'Just anyone; me! You dolt, I'm the one who's saved your life. The mongrels would have started in on you in no time. Come on, get up. I'll take you back to the others.'

The girl struggled to her feet. 'Get on that horse with you? I wouldn't dream of it.'

'Stay here then. And when the Campanian mercenaries catch

up with you, they'll make you wish you'd been a little less stubborn.'

'My name is Arete. Help me up.'

Dionysius helped her on to his horse and jumped on behind her, spurring him into a trot. 'Do you have family among the refugees?'

'No,' replied Arete. 'My family are all . . . gone.' She spoke in an absent tone, as if she were referring to someone she didn't know.

Dionysius fell silent. He handed her his flask again. She drank, then spilled a little water on to her hands and washed her face, drying it with the hem of her dress.

A youth on horseback rode by at a clip, then pulled up short. Light eyes, balding at the temples. His receding hairline and well-trimmed beard made him look older than his years. He gave the girl a look over and then turned to Dionysius. 'So here you are!' he exclaimed. 'You could have said something. We thought you'd vanished into thin air.'

'Everything's all right, Philistus,' replied Dionysius. 'I found this girl who had fallen by the wayside. Go back to the village and fetch some food for her. She probably hasn't eaten anything for days. She's skin and bones.'

The girl glared at him and Dionysius was struck by the beauty of her dirt-streaked face and her lovely amber eyes, framed by long dark lashes. The horrors she had lived through had left her weary and bewildered, but she was still quite graceful, her fingers were long and slender and her hair preserved its violet highlights and its scent. After a while, Dionysius felt her adolescent's body shaking with sobs. She was weeping in silence.

'Cry,' he said. 'It will help you to get over the memories. But try not to dwell on them. Your pain will not bring the loved ones you've lost back to life.'

She said nothing, but Dionysius felt her leaning her head back on to his shoulder in a kind of grievous abandon.

Arete started as they came into view of the villages where the other refugees were eating and resting.

Dionysius slipped his hands under her arms and lifted her, setting her down effortlessly as if she were a feather. 'They are giving out food down there,' he said. 'Go now, before it's all gone.' But the girl did not move, and he gestured to Philistus to bring her something as he had asked.

He arrived with a piece of bread and a slice of sheep's cheese and handed them to the girl, who began to eat. She must have been starving.

And yet, as soon as she had swallowed a mouthful, her attention was drawn to a child who sat alone crying under an olive tree. She went over and offered him the bread. 'Are you hungry?' she asked. 'Have some of this.'

But the little boy shook his head and continued to weep his heart out. He covered his face with his hands as if he could not bear to see such a horrible world.

A group of refugees who had lagged behind the others appeared. One of them particularly struck Arete: a young warrior struggled forward under the weight of an emaciated old man who must have been his father; with his other hand he pulled along a child of seven or eight who stumbled behind him, whimpering.

Arete drew closer to the little boy under the olive tree and pointed to the group of three. 'Look at them, over there. Don't you think they look like Aeneas with his father Anchises and his little son Iulus?'

The boy stopped crying to take a look at the youth, the old man and the child who were just then walking in front of him.

'Do you know the story of Aeneas? Have something to eat, come on, I'll tell you the story . . .' she began. 'Aeneas, the Trojan prince, remained alone to defend the walls of his city after the death of Hector. But Troy fell as he slept, just like all the others. He had no choice but to go into exile. Someone must have taken note of him just then, as he was leaving his city, and we shall always remember him thus: leading a child by the hand and carrying an old man, paralysed, on his back. A defeated man forced to flee with the only treasure left to him: his hope.

'And so Aeneas has come to symbolize the refugee, for

thousands, millions of people who have shared in his fate, under every sky, in every land, among peoples whose existence he could have never even imagined . . .'

The little boy seemed to calm as he listened to her words, and he began reluctantly to chew a bit of bread. Arete continued her story, as though she were thinking out loud: 'Camped out in the dust, or in the mud, fleeing on their carts, with their asses and oxen, refugees like these are the very image of Aeneas, who lives still and will live in eternity. Troy burns, burns now and for ever . . .'

'Heavy going for such a little boy, wouldn't you say?' Dionysius's voice rang behind her.

'You're right,' replied Arete without turning. 'I guess I was talking to myself. I'm so tired I don't know what I'm saying.'

'What you said was beautiful,' replied Dionysius. 'Heartbreaking. I cannot resign myself to this disgrace. I can't bear it. I'm ashamed of my fellow citizens, who lost precious time in useless discussions, in endless tirades, while you were fighting against such cruel enemies and trusting in our help until the very end. Seventy years ago, when Himera was besieged by the Carthaginians, just one man was in charge in Syracuse. Our army marched to Himera in three days and three nights and defeated the enemy in a memorable battle. That same day the Athenians defeated the Persians at Salamina.'

'That man was a tyrant,' objected Arete.

'That man was a man!' roared Dionysius. 'And he did what had to be done.'

He strode off, and Arete watched as he stopped to give orders to his comrades. He mustered the Selinuntian warriors and urged them not to lose heart and to continue their march.

The refugees hadn't rested for more than an hour when they rose to their feet, collected their things and resumed their procession. Many of them had lost their sandals and they stumbled over the stones on their path, leaving bloody footsteps in their wake. What kept them going? Dionysius knew, and that was why he had convinced them to persevere in their journey: he knew that no one is stronger than a man who no longer has anything to lose.

They went on for hours, stopping only to drink when they found a spring, or to pick some green fruit along the road to calm their hunger pangs. The children no longer even had the strength to cry, but they gave a show of incredible courage; they took example from their parents and companions and trudged along, desperate not to cut a sorry figure.

It wasn't until evening of the next day that aid arrived: carts drawn by oxen, donkeys and mules, loaded down with abundant provisions. The old and the invalid, the women and the children were helped to climb on to the carts, and the warriors were able to unburden themselves of their shields.

After three more days of journeying, they arrived within sight of Acragas as dusk was descending.

The magnificent city, illuminated by the setting sun, seemed a vision of wonder. Built up high on a hill, circled by a mighty ring of walls ten stadia long, she proudly displayed multicoloured temples, statues and monuments. Acragas's city sanctuary stood up at the very top of the acropolis, its gilded acroteria shining like gems.

A trumpet blared loud and long through the valley and the gates opened. The refugees filed between the monuments of the necropolis and made their way towards the western gate. They entered the city amidst a stunned, silent throng. The signs of the disaster they had survived were evident: thin and wasted they were, with wounds, bruises and burns covering their bodies, filthy, ripped clothing, bleeding feet, hair clotted with blood and dust. As they proceeded through the most beautiful city that had ever been built in the West, emotion coursed through the surrounding crowd and many of them could not hold back their tears at such a miserable sight. Those unfortunates were the living proof of the vicious cruelty of their enemies.

Aware of the devastating effect that the sight of the refugees had had on the townspeople, the city authorities ordered that they be brought to the market square, near the big artificial pond, so their wounds could be seen to. There they were given food, water and clean clothing; lots were drawn using shards of pottery with numbers scratched on to them so each of the survivors would be assigned a family with which to stay until homes could be found.

Dionysius approached Arete and said: 'You'll be safe here. This city is rich and powerful; her walls are the strongest of all Sicily. I have a small house here myself, with an almond grove and a vegetable garden. I would be honoured if you and the boy accepted my hospitality.'

'Don't you want to wait until the lots have been drawn?' asked Arete.

'I never wait,' replied Dionysius. 'Destiny is blind, but I never close my eyes completely, not even when I'm sleeping. Will you accept?'

Arete smiled. 'Which way is it?' she asked.

'This way. Follow me.' Dionysius set off, leading his horse by its reins. But just then they heard a shout: '*Krisse!*' A woman ran towards them, calling out that name.

The child raised his head, shook free of Arete's hand and ran towards that voice, shouting 'Mama!' They embraced in the middle of the square, under the moved gazes of the onlookers.

'He's not the first,' said Dionysius. 'Other children have found fathers or mothers who they had imagined dead. Husbands have found their wives, brothers their sisters. Their joy is so great it wipes out the thought of all they have lost.'

'I'm a little sorry,' said Arete. 'I was growing so fond of him. So now you want me in your house alone? I don't know if I can trust you.'

'Of course you can trust me,' replied Dionysius. 'You're too skinny for my teeth.'

Arete shot a peeved look at him, but Dionysius's teasing smile dispelled any feelings of irritation. She'd been charmed, all right, as much by his looks as by his personality: he was taller than average, with dark hair and eyes as black and shiny as the sea at night. His sun-bronzed skin was stretched over the powerful muscles of a fighter, shot through with turgid blue veins on his arms and the backs of his hands.

He had led her fellow townspeople to salvation; he'd been the first to come to their aid and perhaps Selinus would not have fallen had he had his way.

Selinus . . . the name sounded sweet even in the extreme bitterness of her exile, in the loss of everything she had imagined belonged to her and could not be taken away: her home, her family, the childhood games she had so recently set aside, the girlfriends with whom she would go to the temples on the acropolis, bringing gifts to the gods for the prosperity of her city and her people. She remembered the big market square full of people and of goods to sell, the processions, the walks through the fields, the river bank where she'd go with her friends to do the washing and hang the linens in the sun so they'd absorb the scent of the wind, fragrant with poppies and wheat.

'What could smell sweeter than a field of wheat in flower?' she mused as they climbed upwards towards the high part of the city.

'That's silly,' replied Dionysius. 'Wheat doesn't flower.'

'Of course it does, when it's still green, in May. The flowers are really tiny, a milky white colour, inside the head. But their scent is so sweet that it mixes in with the smell of spring itself. You know when people say "it smells like spring" but the roses haven't bloomed yet, and the violets have withered? That's what wheat blossoms smell like . . .'

Dionysius looked at her closely, with a touch of tenderness. 'You know a lot of things, girl . . .'

'You can call me Arete.'

'Arete . . . where did you learn them?'

'Looking around. I've never as now understood the value of the treasures that surround us and that we don't notice. Like the wheat flowers . . . understand?'

'I think so. Are you tired?'

'I could lie down on these cobblestones and fall into the deepest sleep.'

'Better go inside, then. That's my house down there.'

Dionysius tied his horse to a ring on the wall, opened a wooden gate and entered a little courtyard shaded by an almond tree and a blooming pomegranate. He took a key from under a stone and opened the door. It was very simple and plain inside: a table with a couple of chairs, a bench along one wall, a sink and a clay water jug on the other. At the end of the room, opposite the entrance, was a wooden stair that led to a second floor. She lay down in the only bedroom and he covered her with a light blanket. Arete fell asleep almost instantly and Dionysius stayed to watch her for a little while. A neighing startled him and he went back downstairs to take care of his horse.

2

Arete awoke and was gripped by panic for a moment, not realizing where she was. The room was sunk in darkness and not a sound came from outside. She got up and went to the window that opened on to an inner garden. She saw the pomegranate and almond with its still tender leaves and remembered. She must have fallen into a deep sleep for many hours; evening was falling. She found a basin filled with water and was relieved to be able to wash and put on a fresh gown. Curious now, she looked around; a stair with a dozen stone steps led up to a landing and she walked up barefooted without making the slightest noise.

When she reached the terrace, she was confronted by a spectacle that left her amazed and moved: all of Acragas stretched out before her, the lamps being lit now in each of the houses. To her right, on high, she could see the Athenaion on the top of the acropolis, a wisp of smoke rising, perhaps from the altar. To her left, scattered over the hill which faced the sea, were the other temples of the gods: one was right on top, another halfway up the slope, a third a little further over at the same distance. They were painted in bright colours, adorned by friezes and sculptures, with beautiful trees and gardens all around. At the bottom of the hill, in the western part of the valley, was a gigantic building still under construction, a temple the likes of which she'd never seen. So tall that it towered over any other structure, the entablature was held up by stone colossi at least twelve feet high and the pediment was animated by huge statuary groups bulging with heroes involved in titanic struggles. She could see the walls surrounding the whole city, with armed sentinels marching back and forth on the battlements and, beyond them, the plain that stretched out to the sea, already the colour of iron. Two more temples arose in the distance towards the west, white with stucco work and glittering with the gilded edging on the pediments and acroteria.

Dionysius was sitting in an armchair, contemplating the sight in the last faint light of sunset. To his right, hanging from one of the arbour posts, was his armour; his shield and spear were leaning against the parapet. He was wearing only a chlamys over his nude body and he must have bathed, for as Arete drew closer, she could smell none of the stink of horse sweat that had made it hard to distinguish him from his steed.

'The most beautiful city of mortal man . . .' said Dionysius without turning.

Arete couldn't understand how he had sensed her presence since she'd come up in absolute silence, but she imagined that the long vigils he'd kept in war must have honed this sense of alertness. 'It's enchanting,' she answered, continuing to let her gaze roam over the stunning countryside.

'That's what Pindar said in one of his poems. Do you know his work?'

'Of course, although he's not my favourite. I like lyric poetry better.'

'He composed an ode to celebrate the victory of Theron, the lord of Acragas, in the chariot races of Olympia seventy years ago.'

'They must have paid him well. He certainly couldn't say anything bad about the place.'

'What a foolish thing to say. Money can't buy inspiration, and the spectacle you see before you has no equal in Sicily, or anywhere else in this world.'

'Unforgiving, aren't you?' observed the girl in a resigned tone. 'Everyone says stupid things sometimes. And I still have the splendour of my lost home in my heart . . . can't you understand that? I look at all this, and can't help but think that the city I loved has become nothing but a heap of ruins.'

'Not for always,' replied Dionysius without turning. 'We'll go back and build it up again.'

'We'll go back? You're not Selinuntian, you're Syracusan.'

'I'm Sicilian. A Sicilian Greek, like you, like all the others. The bastard race of the sons of Greece and the native women. "Half-barbarians", that's what they call us in our so-called motherland. But look what we've accomplished, we half-barbarians. Look at that temple down there, held up by a host of giants: it's bigger and grander than the Parthenon. Look at that artificial pond in the middle of the valley that reflects the colours of the sky in the middle of the city. Look at the porticoes, the statues, the monuments. Our athletes have made their challengers from the continent eat dust. The sons of the emigrants have won all the games of Olympia. Do you know the story of Euenetos?'

'The charioteer, the Olympic champion?'

'That's him. When he returned to the city after his victory in the chariot races, the young Acragantines greeted him with a procession of one thousand two hundred chariots. One thousand two hundred, understand? Two thousand four hundred horses. There probably aren't so many chariots in all of Greece these days! Here they make monuments to horses. They bury them in luxurious sarcophaguses, as if they were heroes. Look, there's one down there, see, with the Ionic columns?'

'I think so . . . but there's so little light now. Tell me about that tall temple down there, the one held up by the giants.'

'It's dedicated to Zeus of Olympia and it will be finished next year. That's a battle of the giants on the pediment. Zeus wins over the giants, and they are condemned to holding up the architrave of his temple in eternity. The scene on the other pediment represents the fall of Troy . . .'

'Oh, gods, why? Why choose such a theme for the tympanum? It's a sad story.'

'I know,' nodded Dionysius. 'Perhaps to ward off a similar fate; who knows? Or perhaps the Acragantines have such an intense sense of death . . . because they love life in such an extreme, exaggerated way. See? They are a strange lot: they make monuments as though they were going to live for ever and they live each day as though it were the very last of their existence.' He hesitated a moment, then added: 'Those aren't my words. It was Empedocles, their greatest philosopher, who said that.'

'They are beautiful and terrible words,' said Arete. 'I would like very much to see it when it is finished.'

'You will, I promise. I'll come to get you, if need be, wherever you are. When you've visited that marvel you'll forget everything you've suffered.'

Arete sought out his eyes in the darkness. 'Will you come and get me even if I'm so thin?'

'Silly girl,' said Dionysius. 'Silly, silly girl. Of course I'll come. I didn't save your life so someone else could have you.'

'If we were in another situation, I'd say you were making fun of me. But you found me in such a miserable state, deprived of my loved ones, my homeland . . . you've got to be sincere! But if you are, why haven't you kissed me yet?'

Dionysius got up, drew her close and kissed her. She could feel his nudity under the light chlamys and she pulled away, but kept talking: 'I'm glad you did that. As soon as I first saw you, mounting that splendid black horse, in your armour like Achilles, I thought, won't the girl he chooses be lucky! And then I thought that even the girl who got a kiss from you would be lucky. It's not that you can have everything from life.'

Dionysius shook his head. 'What a talker! Aren't you hungry?'

'Of course I'm hungry, but it's not good manners to say so.'

'Then let's go to dinner. We have an invitation.'

'From who?'

'We're going to call on one of the wealthiest men of the city. His name is Tellias. You'll have dinner with his wife and her friends.'

'I talk so much because if I don't, I feel like crying.'

'Your answers always come late, and never at the right moment.'

'No, it's not that. I'm afraid I won't make a good impression on your friends. I am trying to react, but it feels as though I'm just struggling to keep my head above water so I won't drown. I won't be good company.'

'You can't stay here alone in the dark; it would only be worse for you. Wait for me downstairs, I'll dress and be with you in a moment.'

Arete went down the stairs and waited in the little patio, listening to the sounds of the evening: the carts clattering over the cobblestones, the cadenced step of the patrols making their first rounds, the voices of mothers calling their children home. She had just wiped away her tears when she heard Dionysius's footsteps on the stairs.

'Tellias was a friend of my father's,' Dionysius began to explain, 'and when my father died in the great war against Athens, he took our family under his wing. I've always been his favourite. They've never had children of their own, you see, and I think he would have liked a boy. He's one of the richest men of the city, as I told you, and since this is probably the richest city in the world, you can guess what that means. The wealthy are usually swine who think only of getting fatter. Not Tellias; he's as rich as Croesus and as fat as a pig, but he's both wise and generous, an extraordinary man. Just think, once he was just standing under the portico of his house, watching a storm, when a Geloan cavalry squad rode by. Those poor lads were soaking wet, chilled to the bone, and he invited them all in to drink and warm themselves. Can you believe it? An entire squad of horsemen! He had them sit down and gave dry clothes to everyone, and as much to eat and drink as they wanted, until the weather had changed and they could set off again.

'Another time the city sent him to Rhegium with a legation, and the Rhegines invited him to speak at the theatre. But when he opened his mouth, with that scratchy, silly voice he has, small and plump as he is, someone started laughing and before you knew it, the whole theatre followed suit. The whole place was rocking with laughter.

'So what do you think he did? Got angry? Flew into a rage?

Not at all. He waited until they had finished, then said: "Laugh all you like; I'm not handsome, nor imposing, and I certainly don't have a commanding voice. But, you see, that's how it is where I come from: they send the handsome, vigorous, eloquent ambassadors to important cities, and the little fat ones with the funny voices like me to worthless places like this." No one felt like laughing after that!'

Arete laughed despite herself, amused. 'I'd like to meet him.'

'You will. He's a charming host, even with the ladies. Wait to speak until he's spoken to you, though, and after I've introduced you, take your leave and go to the women's quarters. I'll have you called when it's time to leave.'

They had reached the entrance to Tellias's home: a portico with a wooden door that led to a house with whitewashed walls, framed by creeping rose bushes on both sides which gave off a sweet fragrance in the evening air. A servant had them enter and took them to the atrium, where Tellias came to receive them.

'Dionysius, my boy! I've been so anxious since I learned that you'd set off with just fifty men to face the entire Carthaginian army!'

'Well, at least you still feel like joking,' replied Dionysius. 'If you had seen what I'd seen, you'd have lost your taste for it.'

Tellias gestured for both of them to come in. 'Do not scold me, son, I just meant to say that you were mad to set off with just a handful of men in such a dangerous situation.'

'At least I was able to help the survivors. We escorted them along a safer route and kept them off the more frequented roads where they could have met with trouble.'

'You are a headstrong young lad, but I must admit you're always right in the end. It's uncanny, really. And who, may I ask, is this gentle dove? She's beautiful, although I would have said a bit thin for your tastes. Where did you find her? She's certainly not from Acragas. What father in his right mind would allow you to wander around with her after dark like this? In any case, that lovely long hair of hers tells me that she is a free woman—'

Dionysius cut him short: 'She's from Selinus.'

Tellias's expression suddenly darkened. 'Oh, poor dear,' he said, lowering his eyes. 'Poor little thing.' He led them along the atrium, which was illuminated by two rows of bronze candelabra, each with four lamps. 'We respect tradition in this home,' he said to Arete, 'and so you'll dine with my wife and her friends. They are very agreeable and I'm sure you'll enjoy their company.' He gestured to a servant who was just entering with a tray of flat bread. 'She'll take you upstairs, to the women's quarters.'

The servant set the tray on the table and Tellias beckoned for her to come closer. He whispered something into her ear. When she had gone up the stairs with Arete, he turned to Dionysius: 'I asked her to tell the women not to trouble her with tiresome questions. Who knows what pain the poor girl has suffered.'

'Her whole family was exterminated by those barbarians. If any of them had lived, they would have envied those who died.'

'Was it so terrible?'

'I didn't see Selinus. I found the refugees at about ten stadia from the city. But I've listened to their stories. I've never heard of such horrors in all my life. Many of the women have totally lost their minds. There's one of them, a woman of about thirty, who must have been very beautiful. I noticed her that first evening because she was swinging her head back and forth and chanting a kind of dirge. Always that sing-song voice and her eyes staring off into nothing, for hours and hours. The day after, I sat down in front of her and tried to talk, to convince her to eat something. But I realized she couldn't see me. Her pupils were dilated and her eyes were a bottomless abyss of darkness. No one could get her to eat anything. She'll surely die, if she hasn't already.'

'How many were saved?'

'I don't know. Between two and three thousand, I'd say. But many more will die from their injuries and from the torture they've suffered.'

A servant brought a jug and a tray and poured water over the hands of the two table companions, handing them a linen cloth to dry them with. Other servants brought the dinner – roast squab with wild apples, sesame bread and red wine from Sybaritis – and the two men began to eat, sitting at a single table placed on the floor between them. Tellias had had the table set in this way because he considered his guest a dear, intimate friend.

'And now? What do you think will happen?' he asked.

'The surviving Selinuntians want to return to their city and exact revenge. They are full of hatred and bitterness, and thirsting for vengeance.'

'And Syracuse?'

'Syracuse is the most powerful city on the island. She will assume her responsibilities.'

'It doesn't seem that she has done until now.'

'You're right. We got there too late; we wasted time in useless debating. That's democracy, isn't it? To be fair, it was difficult to imagine such a determined assault, with a similar deployment of means. The city fell in nine days. Nine days, understand? That's never happened before, as far as anyone can remember.'

'You're right. It took ten years for Troy to fall ... Wars are entirely different now. It's machines that make war these days, not men.'

'The refugees told me that the assault towers were at least twenty feet taller than the walls and that they were assembled there, on site. They unloaded the numbered parts from their ships and transported them to where they would be used. There were iron-headed battering rams hanging from wooden frames that swung back and forth—' Dionysius stopped suddenly, got to his feet and drew a long sigh. 'There's something I haven't told you about the girl.'

'Let's hear, if you think I'm worthy of your confidence.'

'She's not from Selinus.'

'What?'

'She's the daughter of Hermocrates.'

'That's impossible!'

'No, I'm sure of it. She doesn't know, but I recognized her. I found her among the refugees, more dead than alive.'

'Gods of the heavens! No less than the daughter of Hermocrates. But what was she doing at Selinus?'

'You know the way things have been going lately in Syracuse. Hermocrates was off commanding our fleet in the Aegean, backing the Spartans against Athens. But Diocles managed to set the people against him by claiming that he was aspiring to personal power, that he was a danger to the democracy and other similar nonsense. With the help of his henchmen planted here and there and well represented in the Assembly, Diocles succeeded in ruining the man's good standing while he was far away and could not defend himself. Hermocrates became so blameworthy in the eyes of the people that they decided to oust him with an order of the Assembly. At that point, a warship was sent off with the order of dismissal and a summons to appear before the Council to make a full report and answer to the accusations that had been made against him.'

'Did he do that?'

'He was wise enough not to. As soon as he read the message, he put out to sea with his combat unit and disappeared. No one knows where he is now.'

'I'm beginning to understand.'

'You're thinking what I am. Hermocrates must have realized that his family were in danger and he had both his wife and daughter transferred to Selinus, where I believe he had trusted friends. He could not have imagined what would happen.'

Dionysius fell back into silence. The two men rapidly exchanged glances. Tellias was struck by an appalling suspicion: 'You can't be thinking that . . . ?'

'That the government of Syracuse deliberately delayed sending help so that Hermocrates's family would be wiped out in the fall of Selinus? Hard to say, but if you imagine the worst, you're rarely wrong. I can't rule it out. Those sods, they're nothing but a bunch of conniving demagogues! They're capable of anything, believe me.'

'You're exaggerating now. Tell me what your intentions are.'

'I don't know. I've kept her with me because I can't trust anyone. But I must return to Syracuse tomorrow and I cannot take her there with me, as much as I would like to. If anyone recognizes her, it would surely mean trouble for her. And for me as well. I don't want anyone to know anything about what I think, or about whose side I'm on. They need me; I'm one of their best combatants and that's all they need to know for now.'

'Right. And then?'

'I don't even want her to know that I've recognized her.'

'Why not?'

'She would have told me herself had she wanted to. She doesn't trust me enough yet, and I can't blame her. She's all alone, frightened. Anyone would be in her situation.'

'Go on.'

'Would you keep her here with you?'

Tellias seemed to hesitate.

'Please,' insisted Dionysius.

'Of course. How could you doubt it? She's a fine girl, and she's been through so much. We'll be happy to have her, if you feel she'd be happy here with us.'

Dionysius smiled in relief. 'I've told her all about you. I've said that you're fat as a pig and rich as Croesus, but that you're a good man despite all that . . . the best I know.'

Tellias shook his head, embarrassed, then pushed the tray towards his guest: 'Eat, you must be famished.'

*

Arete spent the evening with the women of the house, who dutifully tried at first to avoid asking her questions about her ordeal, but the massacre of Selinus was such an enormous event that it couldn't be kept outside the walls of their home or their conversation. The girl's curt answers made it clear that what she had experienced could not be the subject of idle chatter. But one of the women could not hold back. 'Is it true,' she asked at a certain point, 'that all the women were raped?' Clearly, in her cruel curiosity, she wanted to know: 'Were you raped as well?'

Arete answered: 'The women suffered like all our people did. Even worse, seeing their children and husbands killed before their eyes. You can't imagine how atrocious it is for those of us who

32

have survived when these memories surge up or someone forces us to remember.'

The women fell silent in chagrin and Tellias's wife broke in: 'That's enough, my friends. Let's leave her in peace. She needs tranquillity to begin a new life. Think of how you would feel if you had lived through such atrocities.'

Arete tried to lessen their embarrassment by asking them about their city; was it true that horses that had won important competitions were buried in monumental tombs, and that there was even a cemetery for the songbirds that kept the ladies company in their living quarters?

'Oh, heavens!' replied Tellias's wife. 'Who knows, perhaps once or twice. But I can assure you we don't have a necropolis for goldfinches! Just silly stories, my girl, that you needn't believe.'

After dinner, Arete was accompanied back to the ground floor where Dionysius sat alone. 'Where's the master of the house?' asked Arete.

'He's gone out a moment. Sit down.'

'I thought we'd be going home.'

'No,' said Dionysius. 'You're staying here.'

'Why?'

'Because tomorrow I'm leaving for Syracuse before dawn and I can't take you with me.'

'I don't need to go anywhere with you. I can take care of myself.'

'No you can't. A woman can't travel alone unless she's accompanied by a relative. You wouldn't know how to get around, how to find a place to sleep for the night. Syracuse is a dangerous place these days. Be patient. As soon as I can I'll come back for you, I promise.'

'Why should you?'

'Because . . . because I said that I'll be back and that means that I'll be back,' he said sharply.

'When will you come back for me?'

'As soon as I can. You'll be safe here and happy, my friends can give you anything you need.'

33

Arete bowed her head and was quiet.

'And I won't have to worry about you,' Dionysius added.

The girl stood up at those words and looked deep into his eyes. 'Will you stay away from danger at least?'

'No.'

'And will you give me a kiss before you leave me?'

'Yes,' said Dionysius. He pulled her close and kissed her on the lips. Then, without waiting for Tellias to return, he opened the door and walked out.

3

DIONYSIUS AROSE AT cockcrow thinking of Arete. That frightened, proud girl, brazen yet tender, as fragile as a vial of perfume, had awakened a feeling in him that he didn't want to admit or accept. He'd admired her since the first time he'd seen her long ago in Syracuse, at a procession during the festivities dedicated to Athena.

The daughter of Hermocrates, his idol and his model. He knew that she, the daughter of an aristocrat, would never have deemed him worthy of a glance; he could never have imagined that the day would come in which her survival would depend on him. He was rather annoyed at himself for having fallen for her so completely. No, it wasn't compassion that motivated him, although he would have liked to think so at first.

The evening before, he'd lingered to look at her after she'd fallen into a deep sleep. He had contemplated her every feature in the lantern light: her face, the soft curves of her body, her little sore-covered feet. Then he had returned to the terrace under the arbour to watch the sun sink into the sea.

He put a loaf of bread into his satchel and filled his flask with fresh water. He prepared his horse and walked down towards the market square, leading him by the reins.

His men were waiting for him with all their gear; they were having breakfast and tossing bits of bread to the fish teeming at the surface of the pond. They set off almost immediately. When they had exited the eastern gate and descended into the valley, they turned around to gaze upon the magnificent spectacle of the morning rays striking the Temple of Athena on the acropolis before slowly descending to illuminate the sides of the sacred hill.

Towering walls surrounded the hill on every side; thousands of mercenaries had joined the city's troops to guard the mighty barricade.

'Too big,' observed Dionysius as he took in that marvellous scene.

'What did you say?' asked Philistus, who rode alongside him.

'The circle of walls is too big. It could become indefensible.'

'What nonsense!' Philistus exclaimed. 'What are you thinking? Acragas is impregnable. The walls are too high for any siege towers, and the city is so rich she could take any steps necessary to ensure her defence.'

Dionysius kept up his grumbling. 'Too big, I'm telling you.'

They passed the camp of the Syracusan contingent that had been sent to assist Selinus; they were there waiting for orders but none were forthcoming. Dionysius and his men continued at a walk that whole day. They journeyed five more days after that, and on the sixth, towards evening, they came within view of Syracuse. The city was like a gem, set between land and sea. Her heart, Ortygia, lodged on the rocky island where their ancestors had first set foot; they had come from beyond the sea with nothing but a handful of dirt from their homeland and the flame they'd taken from the sacred brazier that burned on the acropolis.

The founding fathers had chosen a perfect place, both for defence and for trade. The city had two ports, in fact, one at the north called Laccius, sheltered from the south-west wind, and another at the south, sheltered from Boreas. This ensured that contrary winds could never isolate Syracuse, and made besieging the city almost impossible.

This was a lesson that the Athenians had learned at their own expense after trying repeatedly and futilely to take Syracuse by force. They suffered long months in the noxious swamps at the mouth of the Anapus, tormented by the heat, by fever and dysentery, watching their proud triremes slowly rotting at anchor. Although he was just a boy then, Dionysius remembered the procession of chained prisoners making their way to the *latomiae*, the horrible stone quarries where they would spend the rest of their days without ever again seeing the light of the sun. They were marked on their foreheads, one by one, using a branding iron for horses, and were left to waste away in that immense dark cavern from which the clang of their chisels sounded obsessively, ceaselessly, where the air was a dense cloud of dust that blinded the eyes and burnt the lungs.

The only men who were spared were those who could recite by heart the verses of Euripedes's *Trojan Women*, which sang praise to peace. It couldn't be said that the Syracusans were coarse or ignorant! And yet the city of Syracuse had ended up copying the institutions of her sworn enemy: like Athens, she approved a democratic constitution that drastically reduced the power and political influence of the great landowners and the nobility.

As they drew nearer, they could see the causeway which connected the island of Ortygia to the mainland, where a new district was expanding. On higher ground – on Epipolae, the plateau which loomed behind the city – were a number of guard posts facing the inland regions.

They passed the Arethusa fount, the nearly miraculous spring that flowed just a few steps from the sea. It gave forth the purest waters; it had allowed the city of Syracuse to be born and to exist, and her people venerated the spring as a divinity.

Dionysius stopped to drink, as he always did when returning from a journey. He wet his eyes and his forehead, thus allowing the lifeblood that flowed through the hidden, secret veins of his land to flow over his body.

His city, his homeland.

He loved her with a possessive, jealous love. He knew all the stories and legends which dated from the very day of her founding. He knew every wall and every stone, the discordant noises of the market and the ports, the intense odours of the land and the sea. He would be able to cross the city blindfolded, from one end to the other, without faltering. He knew the magnates and the beggars, the warriors and the informers, the priests and the hired mourners, the craftsmen and the thieves, the street prostitutes and the most refined courtesans from Greece and Asia. He had always lived on the streets, played on the streets as a boy with his brother Leptines, challenging rival gangs to stone-throwing fights.

All this was his city to him: an indivisible union, not a multitude of distinct individuals with whom to talk or quarrel or clash. And she was born to be the greatest, the strongest, the most powerful city in the world: more so than Sparta, who had helped them during the great war, more so than Athens, who still mourned her sons, fallen in the plague-ridden swamps of the Anapus and on the scorching banks of the Assinarus.

As he advanced at a walk, leading his horse by the reins and nodding at all those who greeted him, he continued his brooding, furious at the fate of Selinus, which could have been avoided if Hermocrates had been present. He was indignant over Syracuse's treatment of the valiant admiral: they had shamefully stripped him of his position and his rights and forced him to flee in order to save his life. And whom would Dionysius soon be reporting to regarding his failed mission? None other than Diocles, the man he considered the primary culprit in Hermocrates's exile, the man who – had fortune not assisted her – had likely plotted Arete's death as well.

Diocles received him, along with Philistus, in the council hall at the hour in which the market was most crowded. He knew that Dionysius was loyal to Hermocrates, but he was also well aware of what fame Dionysius enjoyed among the people for his courage and daring, for his untiring spirit of self-sacrifice, for his impulsive temperament and for the combative zeal that he never turned against the weak, but always against bullies and deceivers. What's more, he was a favourite of the women, and this was not to be overlooked.

'So it was a massacre,' he began as soon as Dionysius entered the room.

'Except for the two thousand six hundred people who escaped, all the others were killed or taken slaves. The temples were sacked, the walls destroyed. The city is in ruins.'

Diocles bowed his head, and for a moment it seemed that the catastrophe weighed on his soul and his conscience.

Dionysius held his tongue because talking would have been useless; it was clear what he was thinking from his expression, and Philistus's hand gripped his arm as if he could thus restrain his reactions.

Diocles sighed. 'We've arranged for an envoy to meet with Hannibal as soon as possible.'

'You're going to negotiate?' asked Dionysius, utterly shocked.

'We'll offer a ransom. Slaves can be bought, can't they? We can be buyers like anyone else. I've ordered them to offer a higher price than what they can get on the market, to free as many people as possible. The legation has already left in the hopes of reaching the Carthaginian before he moves on. Empedius is leading the mission.'

'That spineless worm!' Dionysius burst out. Philistus dug his fingers futilely into his arm. 'That barbarian will spit in his face and kick him in the ass.'

'So you have a better solution?' asked Diocles, irritated.

'Certainly. We should use the money to recruit mercenaries, who cost much less than slaves. We'll storm the Carthaginians when least they expect it; we'll butcher them and sell off the survivors as slaves. We'll use the money to compensate the prisoners so they can rebuild their homes and the walls of their city.'

'Sounds easy, to listen to you.'

'It is easy if you have guts.'

'And you think you're the only one who does?'

'That's what I'd say, seeing it was just me and my men who made it out there. My unit was the only one ready to move.'

'What's been has been. If this mission goes well, I'll be satisfied with the results.'

'It's a question of how you see things,' broke in Philistus, who hadn't opened his mouth during their exchange. 'I hope we're not going to loaf around and wait for that barbarian to move in for the slaughter. If we allow him to destroy the Greek cities one by one, we'll end up alone. And then there will be no way out.'

'Our army is on the alert.'

'Fine, then,' shot back Dionysius. 'And don't say I didn't warn you.' He turned to Philistus. 'Let's go, there's nothing more to be said here.'

They walked out into the street and towards Dionysius's house in the southern part of Ortygia. The narrow, shady streets of the old city teemed with people, and the attendant buzz announced the nearing of the noon hour, the busiest time of day, with people bustling around to settle their affairs or finish their chores. The catastrophe of Selinus seemed as far away in space and time as the fall of Troy. Only the thought of Arete seemed real, and Dionysius would have done anything to be able to see her, if only for a moment.

*

Empedius reached Hannibal at the camp he'd set up between Selinus and Segesta, and he asked to be received, with his interpreter. He was not kept waiting long; the two men were escorted through the area where the prisoners were being held, and they saw such scenes of despair that they were wholly shaken by the time they were brought before the general. To think that just a few days before these people were living free and prosperous in comfortable homes, wearing clean, elegant attire! Here they were lying in their own excrement, feeding on scraps which were thrown into their pens as if they were animals. Some of them shrieked out, babbling meaningless words. Others shouted even louder to shut them up.

Some realized that the man being escorted by the guards was a Greek, and they ran along the confines after him, crying out pitifully for help. They begged him in the name of all the gods to have pity on them, to free them from their miserable plight. He answered that he was there for just that purpose, that soon they would all be free. His soul swelled with pride and satisfaction as he spoke, so sure was he that his mission would be successful. The Carthaginians were merchants, not warriors: why would they refuse a good deal?

'Take heart,' he told them. 'I've come all this way to liberate you. Have no fear; we'll ransom you all! Your suffering will soon be at an end.'

Hannibal, the Carthaginian commander, was an elderly man, well over seventy; his skin was dark, his hair and beard white, his eyes a deep, cold blue. Some Berber woman from the Atlantic tribes must have been among his ancestors. He received Empedius and the interpreter in his tent, a pavilion of white wool cloth supported by cedar-wood poles; the ground was covered with coloured mats and Numidian rugs. The golden cups and plates on the table looked like plunder from one of the temples of Selinus.

Such ostentation did not promise well, thought Empedius, but he nonetheless made his offer, speaking on behalf of his city and his government: 'We admit that the Selinuntians have erred against you by attacking one of your allies, but you'll surely agree that they have already suffered the worst of punishments. We are here to offer a ransom for them: one-third more than their price on the market, in silver and coins.'

Hannibal arched an eyebrow at the thought of the mountain of money that this man was willing to spend, and he listened attentively, without allowing his expression to betray was he was thinking. He then replied: 'The crime that the Selinuntians committed against us deserves no pardon. They challenged me, although they had been given the opportunity to surrender, causing the death of many of my men. It is only right and fitting that they live in slavery for the rest of their days. As a sign of my generosity of spirit, I will free any of your relatives who may be among the prisoners. Consider this my gift to you; you need not pay me for them.

'My informers tell me that a certain number of them fled the city. I shall allow the survivors, if they so desire, to return and rebuild their homes, to cultivate the fields and to live in their city, as long as they do not reconstruct the walls, and pay an annual tribute to our tax collectors. I have no intention of discussing these decisions.' Having said thus, he dismissed the envoy.

Empedius declared that some of the prisoners were his relatives, and they were duly released: a young couple with two children were the only ones among six thousand prisoners who he was able to bring back to Syracuse with him. But even such a meagre result had given meaning to his undertaking, and he felt that he had not acted in vain. On his return journey, he stopped at Acragas to inform the Selinuntian refugees about the outcome of his mission and of the conditions laid down by Hannibal should they want to resettle in their city.

None of them accepted, and their hate mounted beyond measure when they heard about the cruel sufferings of their fellow citizens and relatives, condemned to perpetual slavery, outrage and humiliation. The insolence of that barbarian! He had dared to refuse the ransom which he was bound to accept in accordance with the will of the gods and the rights of the people.

The surviving heads of family assembled in the temple of the chthonic gods – the faceless divinities who rule over the gloomy world of the dead – and swore that they would live only for revenge, and that when the moment came, no Carthaginian would be spared: not a man, nor a woman, nor a child. They promised the heads of their enemies to the infernal gods, and laid a curse upon them that would endure from generation to generation until that abhorrent race was wiped off the face of the earth.

Empedius returned to Syracuse then, to report to Diocles.

In the meantime, Hannibal had turned east and it was soon clear that he was headed for Himera, the city where his grandfather Hamilcar had perished seventy years before. His army was sixty thousand men strong, and they were joined by contingents of natives, lured by the promise of plunder and slaves. Terror spread rapidly, and the Himerans readied to defend themselves to the death. Selinus's fate left no doubt as to the intentions of the enemy, and their only hope lay in their bravery and their arms.

The high command met in Syracuse with Diocles at their head. They decided to send an expeditionary force to assist Himera. If Himera should fall, the other Greeks of the West would lose all faith in Syracuse, and their cities would be wiped out as if they had never existed.

This time as well, however, Hannibal moved faster than the

government of Syracuse, and before Diocles's decision could be finalized, his army was already at the gates of Himera. He pitched camp on the high plains overlooking the city, to ward off unexpected sorties, and he set his moving towers and rams to work on the city walls. Twenty thousand of his assault troops laid siege to the city, reinforced by a numerous contingent of seasoned, belligerent native Sicels and Sicans.

Himera was a symbol for the Greeks of the motherland and the colonies because, seventy years earlier, as the Hellenes of the continent were defeating the Persians at Salamina, the Greeks of Sicily were likewise winning their battle against the Carthaginians and would soon defeat the Etruscans as well in the waters of Cumae. It was later said that the three battles were fought on the very same day, month and year, symbolizing the fact that the gods had willed the triumph of the Greeks on all fronts against eastern and western barbarians.

But for Hannibal, son of Gisco, the city was cursed. His grandfather Hamilcar had found defeat there and had killed himself after having seen his entire army destroyed. From dawn to dusk, throughout the entire battle, he had sacrificed victim upon victim, imploring his gods for victory, but as the sun fell and he had to watch his men routed and hunted down like beasts, fleeing in every direction, he threw himself on to the pyre, screaming out promises for revenge amidst the flames.

Hannibal's own father had been defeated there as well, and sentenced to exile. He was the third of his family to attempt the endeavour and he had a burning desire to exact vengeance for the downfall and disgrace of his forebears; he would redeem their honour and his own.

Diocles managed to put together three thousand men in all, calling up the contingent stationed in Acragas as well. He set off towards Himera to save her, if he could, from the bitter fate that had befallen Selinus.

The Carthaginians had meanwhile positioned their assault towers at various points of the walls, and the rams battered relentlessly from daybreak to nightfall, continuing after dark at times. They found that these walls could not be demolished as easily as those of Selinus. The Himerans had, in fact, built them by embedding great blocks of stone both horizontally and transversally.

Seeing that the rams were largely ineffective against these fortified walls, the Carthaginians withdrew and resolved to dig a mine. They worked ceaselessly day and night, in shifts, until they had opened a tunnel under the walls, which they reinforced as they went along with pinewood timbering that they had harvested from the surrounding forests and saturated with liquefied resin. Working by night, so as not to be seen by the city's defenders, they dug ventilation chutes, both to give air to the miners and to feed the fires they would soon be setting.

They finished just before dawn on a cloudy night. A group of raiders made their way through the tunnel to the opposite end and set the timber aflame. The blaze spread like wildfire as the incendiary substances the wood had been soaked with burst into flames. The sentries up high on the walls could see a row of red eyes lighting up in the plain: the glow of the fires burning below, visible from the ventilation shafts. Whirlwinds of flames and smoke soon roared out of the holes and twirling sparks rose to the sky, spreading an acrid, scorched smell throughout the countryside. The timbering was reduced to ash in no time and a stretch of wall, deprived of its foundations, crumbled to the ground with a resounding crash, taking the defenders with it into a heap of ruins.

Even before the dense cloud of smoke and dust could clear, the bugles and war horns sounded and the Libyan, Mauritanian and Sicilian infantry of Hannibal's army launched their attack. The rest of the army drew up, ready to rush in as soon as the attackers had opened a passage; they would overwhelm anyone who tried to resist.

But that screaming horde were no sooner at the base of the breach than the passage was already teeming with defenders. None of their actions had passed unobserved and nothing they could do would be unexpected. Every man capable of carrying arms had taken them up. Their outrage over the atrocities committed by the barbarians at Selinus was so strong that not only were the Himerans ready to die to the last man rather than surrender, but they hurled themselves at their assailants with such violence and loathing that no one could doubt their resolve.

They were at the base of the breach even before the attackers arrived, and they formed ranks in phalanxes, in a single battle line at first and then in two or even three lines, as new combatants arrived; they drew up in a curved front to prevent any access to the breach. Then, at a signal from their commanders, they surged forward, holding their spears high in clenched fists, as the men and women remaining inside the city rushed to repair the damage, bringing all sorts of material that could be used to close up the breach.

The impetus of the Himerans was so forceful that the assailants wavered and began to retreat. At that point Hannibal, who had remained with his crack troops on the hills, gave orders for reinforcements to be sent in, and the reserves who were already waiting on the plain entered the fray. The battle continued for hours, with neither of the two sides giving up a span of ground. Only the onset of darkness put an end to the combat. Hannibal's mercenaries dug themselves trenches in the plain and the Himeran warriors returned to the breach where they joined their families. The oldest soldiers, who had been held back as reserves, guarded the bastions in fear that the barbarians might attempt a surprise attack under the cover of night.

The women gave ample proof of their mettle as well. The young and old alike, who had worked all day bringing arms to the defenders and stones to close the breach, without pausing a moment to eat or drink, rushed now to their men returning from the battlefield, blood-spattered and grimy. They helped them to remove their armour and they tended to their wounds and their wearied spirits. They brought hot water, clean clothing, food and wine to refresh and restore.

Wives, mothers, daughters and sweethearts gave a show of strength even greater than that of the warriors. They showed their men they were not afraid, did not fear death, actually preferred death to slavery and disgrace. They praised their bravery, stirred their pride, never wavered in their faith in the favour of the gods and in the trust that the warriors' courage and abnegation would bring them victory. They held the valour of their husbands and sons up as an example to their younger children not yet of fighting age, and taught them that no sacrifice was too great to defend their freedom.

The evening breeze from the sea brought a little relief from the oppressive heat. The darkness and silence that followed the blinding light of that day and the screams of battle led many of the men to seek a little rest.

The old men, too feeble to carry out any other task and too anguished to sleep, stood vigil. Joined under the porticoes of the agora, they reminisced about the wars they had fought in their youth and the risks that they had run. They sought any pretext to take heart, found the words to console those among them whose sons had not returned from the battlefield. They told stories of episodes of the past where men given up for dead had miraculously reappeared, knowing full well that bad luck is much more frequent than the good kind. And yet they encouraged each other with the promise that reinforcements were on the way; they wouldn't be long now.

The low murmur of their conversation was interrupted by a clanging of arms, by loud voices in the dark, by sudden and unexpected commotion. They instinctively huddled together against the wall, already prepared for the worst, when a voice rang out: 'It's the reinforcements! We're saved!'

The veterans ran towards the point where the voice had come from and thronged around a lad of about fifteen, firing questions at him:

'Reinforcements? Are you sure?'

'Who are they?'

'Where did you see them?'

'How many of them are there?'

'Who's leading them?'

'What direction are they coming from?'

The boy raised his hands to quiet them down. 'It's just twenty men for now . . .'

'Twenty men? Are you joking?'

'About twenty,' confirmed the boy. 'They're being led by a Syracusan officer who has passed the enemy lines. He said that down there, somewhere down in the plain, there's an army of three thousand men headed by Diocles. He's talking with our commanders.'

The old men hastened towards the eastern gate where fires had been lit to illuminate the area of the breach. The commanders were grouped around the new arrivals, led by a young man armed with only a sword and a dagger. His long hair was tied back with a leather string, and he looked no older than twenty. They drew closer so they wouldn't miss a word.

'Diocles wants to enter the city tonight, under the cover of darkness, and attack without warning tomorrow with all the forces at his disposal.'

'Enter the city?' asked one of the officers. 'How?'

'Nearly all of the barbarians are at the camp. There are just a few sentinels posted around those campfires you can see down there. There's a dune stretching along the coast that's high enough to hide anyone walking along the waterline from view. Our men will come in that way, but you'll have to draw up a contingent to guard the northern gate and ensure that it stays open. If you agree, we can launch the signal right now.' He gestured to one of his men, who neared the fore with a tow-wrapped arrow.

'Just a moment,' said one of the Himeran commanders. 'Who can tell me this isn't a trick?'

'I can,' replied the young man. 'I'll stay here as a hostage with all my men.'

'And just who are you?' asked another officer.

'Dionysius,' replied the young man. 'Son of Hermocritus. Now let's get moving.' He took the bow from the archer's hand, ignited the arrow and let it fly high.

Far away, on the dune ridge, two sentinels saw the small

meteor streak through the dark sky and exchanged a relieved look.

'The signal,' said one of them. 'He did it again. Tell the commander.'

4

BEFORE THE SUN had set, the Syracusan squadron, twenty-five triremes strong, appeared offshore. They had dismasted and were advancing by oar; it was clear that the commanders were on the alert for any unexpected occurrences.

Diocles was camped on the beach, hidden from view by the long coastal dune that stretched towards the interior. He was preparing the contingent that he had brought to assist the besieged Himerans. The navarchs were instructed to stand by and remain ready to intervene if the ships were needed. Diocles waited until night had fallen to give the signal for departure; the password flew from one unit to the next.

The column began to march along the waterline without making a sound, their steps muffled by the damp sand. Diocles was at their head, followed by the companies and the battalions, each led by its own commander. Sentries crouched on the top of the ridge to keep an eye on the plain and ensure that the barbarians remained unaware of the fact that an entire army was marching at a short distance from their camp in the dark in silence, like a multitude of ghosts.

When they had neared their objective, Diocles sent out a couple of scouts who approached the Himeran troops guarding the northern gate. Before the garrison commander could challenge them, they identified themselves: 'We're the vanguard of the Syracusan army.'

'May the gods bless you,' said the commander. 'We thought you'd never get here.'

The man whistled and the army moved forward, four-across,

through the northern gate. In cadenced step now, their nailed boots rang out against the walls and porticoes. As soon as they began to enter, the news spread that reinforcements had arrived and the inhabitants of the city left their houses and thronged along the street that led to the agora. Such was their joy at seeing them that they would have liked to shout and applaud those young men who had come to risk their lives to help them, but they remained silent, each one of them anxiously counting the files that passed. Their hopes for salvation grew as each unit was added to the one that had preceded it and had disappeared up ahead, towards the entry colonnade of the main square.

'Three thousand,' said an old man when the last file had passed before him.

'Not many,' commented another with a disappointed tone.

'You're right,' replied the first, 'but they're crack troops. Did you see how they march? Like a single man. Those men there, when they're drawn up in line, they're like a wall, I tell you. Each one of them counts for three.'

'Let's hope so,' responded the other, 'because I don't think any more help is on the way.' He walked off into the darkness.

Diocles held council in the agora with the Himeran officers. 'I will take supreme command, if you have nothing against that,' he began.

No one spoke.

'How many men can you draw up?' asked Diocles then.

'Seven thousand,' was the answer. 'Counting youths of eighteen to men of fifty.'

'There are three thousand of us. That makes ten; ten will be enough. Tomorrow we'll leave the city in combat formation. A two-thousand-man front, five deep. A long line, but it'll hold. We'll be on the front line, because we're fresh and none of my men are older than thirty. Each one of them has sufficient rations for four days; you'll only need to supply water.'

The most highly ranked Himeran officer stepped forward. 'I want to thank you and your men for having come to our aid. Tomorrow we'll show you that you won't regret it.'

'I know,' answered Diocles. 'Let us get some rest now. We'll attack tomorrow at dawn, in silence, without bugles. We'll wake them up in person.'

The warriors settled down under the porticoes where hay had been laid out, and soon the whole city plunged into silence. Diocles checked that everything was under control, and then got ready for the night himself.

Dionysius appeared just then, as if from out of nowhere. 'It's all gone smoothly, I see.'

'That's right,' replied Diocles, 'and tomorrow we'll settle our score with those barbarians down there on the plain.'

'There are more of them on the hills. You know that, surely?' retorted Dionysius.

'I don't need you to tell me anything.'

'That's a relief. Yet I don't understand all this hurry to attack.'

'It's evident, isn't it? The less time we stay away from home, the better for us.'

'Haste is a poor counsellor. I would have tried to understand the situation better, the placement of the enemy forces. Hidden traps.'

'You're not in charge here.'

'No, unfortunately,' replied Dionysius, and walked away.

★

They left at dawn, as Diocles had ordained. Rested and refreshed, they marched for nearly a stadium before the war horns echoed from the enemy camp. The Punic army soon appeared on the open field: there were Libyans wearing light-coloured tunics with iron plates on their chests defending their hearts, their bronze helmets and shields painted with their tribal colours, Sicels donning long, ochre-tinted garments of raw wool with leather helmets and cuirasses, Sicans bearing wooden shields adorned with images of their totemic animals, Iberians wearing white tunics edged in red and embossed greaves decorated with tin; their leather helmets had neckguards which extended over their shoulders and were topped with a red tin crest to give them the look of magical creatures. Then there were the Balearics who whipped their slings, whistling them through the air, and the Mauritanian horsemen with their dark, shiny skin and thick heads of curly hair. They rode fiery steeds from the Atlas mountains barebacked, and carried long spears and antelope- and zebra-hide shields. Infantry and cavalry from many nations, all obedient to a few Carthaginian officers, were fitted out in the Oriental style with conical helmets, heavy leather cuirasses decorated with vivid colours, and green and ochre tunics with red and yellow fringes.

All of those warriors must have joined the ranks with empty stomachs, but they let out loud war cries nonetheless, jumping about and waving their weapons with threatening gestures. Their excitement grew visibly as the ranks swelled; it was their way of winning over the fear that grips a combatant before the moment of the attack. They filled their bellies with ferocity in anticipation of the clash.

The Greeks instead marched in absolute silence and perfect order, and when the sun rose, their mirror-polished shields flashed with blinding light and the ground trembled under their heavy cadenced steps.

The Balearics let loose with their deadly slings, but the hail of shots crashed against the wall of shields without doing any damage. They were too close for the archers now, for Diocles had ordered the Greek phalanx to close the gap between the opposing fronts at a run. The two formations collided with such violence that the shouts of the Punic mercenaries turned into screams of agony. The pressure from the enemy's back lines had pushed the men in front, mostly Libyans, Sicels and Mauritanians, against the levelled spears of the Greeks, and they were mowed down in great numbers. The light arms of the mercenaries were a poor match for the heavy shields and thick metallic breastplates of their adversaries.

Dionysius, drawn up on the left flank with his soldiers from the Company, drove his spear into the chest of the Mauritanian chieftain he found before him – a Berber from the Atlas mountains with reddish hair and brilliant blue eyes – and ran his sword through the comrade who had lunged forward to avenge him. Even though the forces they were facing seemed to be wavering, he continued to shout out to his men: 'Hold the line, men! Stay together!' He used the tip of his sword to strike the shields of those who were pushing too far forward, to remind them to remain within the ranks.

The resistance of the Punic army, who had thought they would be fighting the desperate, battle-weary Himerans, was quickly worn down in the prolonged clash with the rock-solid Syracusan hoplites; when their commander fell and was trampled under the hobnailed boots of the enemy, the Carthaginians fled in utter disarray.

Diocles, sure of victory now, launched his men after them in pursuit without worrying about keeping them in formation. For the Himerans above all – for whom every dead Carthaginian meant a greater hope for the survival of their city – this was a licence for slaughter, with no thought to maintaining discipline. Drunk on the carnage, they did not see Hannibal loosing his troops to their right, down the side of the hill.

Dionysius saw, and ordered a bugler to sound the retreat. Diocles, who imagined that victory over the enemy camp was already in hand, fell upon him furiously, shouting: 'Who told you to sound a retreat? I'll have you arrested for insubordination, I'll have you thrown . . .'

Dionysius did not allow him to finish the phrase: he punched him full in the face and sent him rolling to the ground. He put his sword to the throat of the bugler who had stopped blowing, and calmly gestured for him to put the instrument back to his lips.

The horn blared out the order to retreat, as more buglers fell in to echo the first. The warriors attempted to reform under the standards that Dionysius had had amassed at the centre of the field under the protection of the members of the Company, but many of the men were surrounded and slain before they could get safely back into their ranks. Even Diocles, realizing the extent of the disaster, did everything in his power to save what he could of the situation, and in an hour's time had succeeded in drawing up his formation and retreating towards the city.

The people of Himera, ecstatic at first over the supposed victory, were forced to watch helplessly from the towers and bastions of the city as Hannibal ambushed and decimated their sons. When the army re-entered through the eastern gate, the sad spectacle that always accompanied the return of soldiers from the battlefield was repeated: fathers, mothers, wives and sweethearts thronged along the road trying anxiously to pick out their own loved ones. It was terrible to see hope snuffed out on those faces little by little as the survivors filed past them, without their helmets so as to be more easily recognized. Their despair contrasted with the joy of those who had spotted a son or husband safe from harm.

The battalion commanders read off the roll in the agora. At the end, the city magistrates counted three thousand fallen on the field of battle. The best of their youth had been wiped out and the bodies of these their sons lay scattered over the plains at the mercy of the barbarians and the dogs. Every name called without an answer met with a shrill wail, and the weeping of the mothers grew until it became a mournful chorus. In many cases, both father and sons had been lost, and entire families were forever deprived of descendants. Three hundred and fifty men of the Syracusan expeditionary force were also missing at the roll-call.

Dionysius volunteered to go in person and negotiate the restitution of the prisoners, had any been taken, and the truce that would allow them to collect their dead. Diocles had to swallow his pride and admire the man's courage; he consented to Dionysius's request.

He left through the eastern gate between two magistrates on horseback, unarmed and bare-headed, although he still wore his breastplate and greaves. He advanced to where Hannibal had had a pavilion built for himself in the middle of the plain. Perched on a high seat, he was distributing awards to those among his mercenaries who had most distinguished themselves in battle.

The Carthaginian general received him with an air of contempt, and, before Dionysius could open his mouth, had an interpreter tell him that he would not grant any truce; that he was there to avenge the memory of his ancestor Hamilcar and that there would be no peace until the entire race of the Himerans was totally annihilated.

Dionysius got as close as he could and pointed in the direction of the battlefield, saying, 'Down there among the dead lie four of my friends, members of my Company. I must reclaim their bodies: we are sworn to do so. If you allow me this, I shall spare your life when the moment comes.'

Hannibal couldn't believe his ears when the interpreter had finished translating. 'You . . . you will spare my life!' he exclaimed, bursting into laughter.

'I shall,' confirmed Dionysius without batting an eye.

'I'm sorry,' he answered, 'but I will make no exceptions. Be content to return safe and sound to the city. I want them to hear from your lips what awaits them.'

'So be it,' said Dionysius. 'Know that you will meet a disgraceful end. He who has no mercy for the dead does not deserve the mercy of the living. Farewell.' He mounted his horse and returned to report the unhappy outcome of his mission.

He found the city in an uproar, seized by extreme agitation. Some of the passers-by even railed against him, shouting, 'Traitors! Cowards!'

'What are they saying?' Dionysius asked the two magistrates at his sides, but they could only shrug, unable to explain such an attitude.

'Pay no attention,' said one of them. 'They've lost their minds. War is a terrible thing.'

Dionysius did not answer, but he was sure that something strange had happened. He had his explanation when he arrived at the Syracusan headquarters near the agora. The Himeran commanders were just leaving, cursing furiously.

'What has happened? Speak!' demanded Dionysius.

'Ask your commander!' replied one of them before walking off in disgust. They were so angry that they hadn't even asked him about the outcome of his mission.

He found Diocles surrounded by the city elders, who were crowding around him, shouting and beseeching. 'What is happening?' asked Dionysius loudly. 'Will someone tell me what is going on?'

The shouting died down a little; one of the old men recognized him and said: 'Your commander has ordered the evacuation of the city!'

'What?' exclaimed Dionysius in amazement. 'What did you say?'

'You heard him,' broke in Diocles. 'The city must be evacuated.'

'You're crazy. You can't do that.'

'I'm your commander, I demand respect!' shouted Diocles in a fit. His right cheek was clearly swollen with the punch he had received that morning.

'You have to deserve respect,' retorted Dionysius. 'These people have fought with superhuman courage: they deserve our support and we're still capable of winning. Hannibal lost twice as many men as we did. We can call in the navy infantry and . . .'

'You just don't understand, do you? Hannibal's fleet is heading for Syracuse. We have to return immediately after having secured whatever we can here.'

Diocles stared at him with an incredulous expression. 'Who told you such a thing? Who?'

Dionysius seemed to hesitate, then said: 'Someone who arrived after you had gone.'

'Someone? What does that mean: "someone"? Did you see him? Did you talk to him? Do you know his name? Does anyone in the city know him?'

Diocles snapped at his insistent questions. 'I'm not obliged to account to you for my decisions. You are my subordinate,' he shouted, 'and you must only obey my orders!'

Dionysius got even closer. 'Yes, I'm your subordinate, here, in time of war and under wartime laws, but once we get back to

Syracuse I become a citizen again, and while you can accuse me
of punching you in the face, I can have the Assembly incriminate
you for high treason. I assure you that all my friends in the
Company will uphold the charge.'

Diocles struggled to curb his anger: 'The city has become indefensible, understand? We've lost a third of our forces, and it's more
than likely that Hannibal's fleet is sailing towards Syracuse, taking
advantage of our absence. Everyone is saying so; it must be true.'

'You are taking on an enormous responsibility,' replied Dionysius. 'The fate of this city and the blood of this people will be on
your hands.' He turned and made to leave, but Diocles stopped
him.

'Wait! Stop, I say! And the rest of you as well, listen to me.
Call back your commanders, convince them to listen to my plan.
You'll realize yourselves that it's the only sensible way to proceed.'

It took hours before the Himeran commanders could be
convinced to return. Dionysius and the other Syracusan officers
were present as well when Diocles began to speak.

'I know what you're feeling. I know that you've sworn to
defend the city to the very end, but think about it: what good will
this sacrifice do? Why give up your lives if you cannot save those
of your wives and your children? What solace will you have,
dying, to know that they will be enslaved and at the mercy of a
cruel enemy? Heed my words; listen to the plan I've prepared.
We will evacuate the city in three stages. There will be a new
moon tonight; the darkness will allow us to take the women and
children aboard the fleet. Our ships will take them to Messana,
where they will be protected by a navy infantry unit.

'Phase two: another group will follow us to Syracuse by land,
along the coastal dune that hid our approach.

'Phase three: the fleet will return before dawn and take aboard
anyone still in the city. If there is not enough room on the ships
for everyone, those remaining can scatter through the countryside
or try to reach us in Syracuse, where we will provide them with
help. When Hannibal orders the attack, he'll find the city deserted.'

A deadly silence fell over the council hall, and no one dared speak: the mere thought of abandoning the city where they were born and had lived was more terrible than death. After a while, one of the Himerans arose and spoke for all of them.

'Listen to us now, Syracusan. We've decided to resist at any cost because that barbarian out there is a bloodthirsty beast and he has sworn to exterminate us for offences we are not to blame for. We readied for combat because you had promised to help us, whereas now you force us to surrender, for we both know full well that we could never succeed alone. This plan of yours is folly, and you are well aware of that. You have twenty-five ships out there, but they are certainly not merchant ships. They are war vessels. How can you think of transporting so many people? You know full well that many of us will be left behind, defenceless, to await a horrible death.

'We are asking you, Syracusans, to reconsider. Remain here with your soldiers and fight at our sides! We will repair the breach, and we will resist until the very last drop of sweat and blood. You will not regret it if you decide to stay. We implore you to remain. Do not abandon us, in the name of the gods!'

'I am sorry,' replied Diocles. 'The city is indefensible. Return to your homes, gather together your women and children. Your time is running out; dusk is upon us.'

'Traitors!' shouted out a voice.

'Cowards!' shouted another.

But Diocles did not blink an eye; he walked off in the direction of the eastern gate. Dionysius felt those invectives branding his skin like fire, but he could neither do nor say anything.

*

The sad exodus began as soon as night fell. The women could not bear to let their arms fall from their husbands' necks, the children wept pitifully, calling out their fathers' names. They had to be compelled to leave the city by sheer force. Dionysius's task was to accompany them to the beach and see to it that they boarded the ships. The rest of the Syracusan army, escorting about one thousand people, began their march along the coastal dune, trying to distance themselves as quickly as possible from the walls of the condemned city. The soldiers marched in silence and their ears were filled, all night long, with the soft, harrowing laments of the women and children who were abandoning their homeland.

The fleet reached the confines of Messanian territory at the third hour that night. Dionysius disembarked the refugees along with about fifty of his soldiers who would escort them to Messana. He turned back with just a few of his men, who grimly took up the oars at the rowers' sides, in an attempt to reach Himera before dawn.

An unfortunate westerly wind greatly delayed their return, despite the concerted efforts of the crews, and when they finally came within sight of Himera, they were forced to witness a horrifying spectacle.

Hannibal, in utmost secrecy, had had a second mine dug under the city walls. A vast stretch of the walls came crashing down just as the Syracusan sailors were approaching the bay. The Punic mercenaries raged through the city, massacring all those they found and capturing a great number of others.

Dionysius, on board the flagship, was devastated; he ran to the navarch, who stood at the stern. 'Quickly, put ashore,' he said, 'we'll land all the available forces. The barbarians are scattered and intent on their plunder: if we fall upon them in a compact attack, we can turn around the situation and . . .'

The navarch cut him short. 'Don't even think of it. My orders are to bring the population to safety and return to Syracuse as soon as possible, not to engage in combat. There's no one left here to save. Those poor souls are done for; there's nothing we can do for them any more.' He turned towards the helmsman. 'Turn the bow east,' he ordered, 'and hoist the sails. We'll head for the Straits.'

The big trireme made a wide semicircle towards the north before sailing back in the direction of Messana; the others followed suit one by one, slipping off along the coast. The soldiers on board tried to turn their eyes away from land, but the wind carried to their ears the shrieks – muted by the distance – of the dying city.

The three thousand prisoners taken were tortured one by one with the most atrocious of methods, with no regard for either age or sex, and then slaughtered on the stone where Hamilcar, the grandfather of the Carthaginian leader, was said to have died. The walls were demolished, the city destroyed, and the Temple of Nike, raised to commemorate the great battle won seventy-two years before against the Carthaginians, was razed to the ground.

Himera perished two hundred and thirty-nine years after her founding. In the end, having satisfied his desire for vengeance and victory, Hannibal son of Gisco returned rich with plunder to Panormus where he boarded the ships that would take him back to Carthage. The threat of the fleet attacking Syracuse had never existed, except in the imagination and duplicity of the same high command which had allowed Selinus to perish, preparing the way for the barbarian to enter the very heart of Sicily.

Philistus finished dictating, and the scribe placed the quill back into its case. 'That's enough for today,' he said. 'The story we've told is sad enough.'

His servant bowed and left the room. Philistus neared the papyrus scroll, still wet with ink, and let his gaze fall on the few lines that summed up the martyrdom of one of the most beautiful and glorious Greek cities of the West. He sighed and put a hand on his forehead as if to suppress the destructive force of those images. From his window he could see a warship entering the northern harbour; the sailors were just dropping a rope for mooring. The sun was setting on the horizon, making the acroteria sparkle on the Temple of Athena in Ortygia. The cries of the gulls mixed with the calls of the swallows returning to their nests under the roof of the great sanctuary.

He called a servant. 'Run down to the port and see if the ship that's just about to dock is carrying any news; come back and let me know immediately.'

The servant hastened out and Philistus continued to pace back and forth in his study, wondering what had become of Dionysius, of whom he had heard nothing for quite some time. News of the massacre of Himera had shaken the city, and the arrival of Diocles with thousands of despairing refugees in his wake – added to the survivors of Selinus who had been evacuated to Acragas – filled the people with an oppressive sense of anguish. Until just a few months earlier, Carthage had been nothing more to them than a far-off city that maintained a small base in an island of western Sicily. Now Carthage was a looming threat, a monster that was gobbling up the Greek cities one after another, wiping out entire populations.

Besides all this, the fact that Diocles had abandoned the fallen bodies of the Syracusan warriors and their allies, leaving them without burial under the walls of Himera, had caused deep pain and consternation to hundreds of families in the city, where just about everyone knew each other.

Many other warriors were missing, and Philistus asked himself whether Dionysius was among them. He was one of the most fearless, one of the strongest, always the first to cross blades with the enemy and the last to leave the battlefield. Men like him were more prone to suffer the blows of fate.

The servant returned after sunset with an important message. 'One of the officers aboard the trireme is a member of the Company. He wants to meet you in private under the portico of the Temple of Apollo, at the sounding of the first guard shift.'

'What did you tell him?'

'Knowing you, master, I replied that you would be there. And that if you weren't, you would send me to set up another appointment.'

'Good man, I knew I could trust you. Now fetch me my cloak, and go have dinner in the kitchen.'

'Don't you want me to accompany you with my lantern, master? It will be dark soon.'

'No, that won't be necessary. The light of the moon will be sufficient.'

He set off as soon as he heard the bugle up on the bastions sounding the first change of the guard. He entered the maze of narrow curving roads of the old city. As he neared the square in front of the temple, he scanned the porticoes but saw no one. He waited a little before coming out into the open, then crossed the nearly deserted square and walked up the steps that led to the front portico.

A man slipped out from behind a column almost immediately and approached him. 'Are you Philistus?' he asked.

'I am. And who are you?'

'My name is Chabrias. I'm from the Company and I know Dionysius,' replied the man, showing him the leather bracelet wrapped around his wrist: it bore the figure of a dolphin.

Philistus pulled back the sleeve of his tunic to show the same.

'I have a message from Dionysius,' said Chabrias.

'I'm listening.'

'He says that he is well, but that he would rather have died than witness such an atrocity.'

'I understand. What else?'

'He is in Messana, but he has no intention to return to Syracuse. He wants your help.'

'Speak.'

'He needs money . . .'

'I imagined as much. Here it is,' said Philistus, laying his hand on a purse which hung from his belt.

'He also wants you to deliver this letter to a girl named Arete who is living in Acragas as Tellias's guest,' the man added, passing him a small leather cylinder.

'She will receive it within three days at the most.'

'If the girl decides to remain at Acragas, you can return home without any further ado. If she decides to set off on a journey, Dionysius asks you, in the name of the friendship that binds you, to find her an escort so she runs no risks.'

'Tell him not to worry; I shall see to the whole matter myself.' He gave the man the money and turned to go.

'There's something else,' said the man, beckoning with his finger.

'I'm listening,' replied Philistus, not without a certain apprehension.

'Hermocrates landed in Messana the other night with ten warships and several hundred mercenaries.'

'Are you serious?' asked Philistus incredulously.

'It's the absolute truth. This is why Dionysius hasn't returned. You must pass word on to everyone in the Company and tell them to stay on guard. They may need to use their fists.'

'Their fists,' nodded Philistus. He was thinking of how many young members of the secret society were raring to fight at Dionysius's side. 'Listen . . .' he said then, but the man who called himself Chabrias had already vanished.

5

Dionysius to Arete, Hail!

What I have seen and heard of late cannot be described. In part, you'll be told what has happened by the person who brings you this letter, and the rest you will learn from my own words, I hope. I need only tell you that in my whole life I have never suffered such horror or felt such humiliation. The disaster of Selinus, which you lived through yourself, was repeated in an even more frightful and cruel way with the fall and destruction of Himera.

In the midst of so much misfortune and shame, one reason for hope remains: ships and men have been gathering in Messana, all of us truly determined to avenge the massacre perpetrated by the barbarians. I've joined these men with a select group from the Company and I've declared my willingness to take on whatever mission they shall entrust me with.

I know that by doing so I will be cutting off any chance I have of making a name for myself in my own city, of building myself a future in politics or even as a simple citizen, and yet I am asking you to join me here, to unite your destiny with mine: to become my bride. As I've said, I have nothing to offer you but myself, and I think that a wise woman would refuse the offer of a man like me; I own no property and I have no prospects but that of becoming, perhaps, a bandit and an exile. But I hope that you will show no wisdom and that you will set off to meet with me. The person who has delivered this letter to you is willing to make your transfer as comfortable and as safe as possible, given the circumstances.

If, on the other hand, you decide not to accept my

proposal, I will not think ill of you and you should not consider yourself beholden to me for any reason. What I did for you, I would have done for anyone I found in your conditions.

I want you to know that I have been thinking of you for all this time I've been away, and that I long to see you again.

Arete folded the letter and looked the person she had in front of her in the eyes: 'I've seen you before,' she said.

The man smiled. 'Yes, in that village between Heraclea and Acragas. Dionysius had just found you. You were in a terrible state. You look much better now.'

'What's your name?'

'Philistus,' replied the man.

'And you're a friend of Dionysius's?'

'More than a friend; I'd follow him to the underworld if necessary. Well, what have you decided?'

'I will go to Messana.'

'I hoped as much, and I've already prepared everything we'll need for the journey. When do you want to leave?'

'Now,' replied the girl.

'Now?' repeated Philistus in surprise.

'The man I've always dreamt of is waiting for me in Messana. Why should I wait?'

'What about me?' asked a voice behind her. 'I don't count for anything?'

'Tellias!' exclaimed the girl, spinning around. 'You know how much I care about you, even though you've always kept me locked up in the women's quarters!'

'So that's why you're so eager to leave now!' said Tellias, smiling. 'Dionysius entrusted you to me and I've always kept an eye on you, like grapes when they are ripe.'

'I think we'll leave tomorrow,' said Philistus. 'We'll go by sea, on the same boat that brought me here. It will be the safest way, but we have to wait for the morning's light, and for a favourable wind.'

'Do you know anything about what happened at Himera?' asked Tellias.

'I know what I've been told,' replied Philistus. 'And it's enough to make the disaster of Selinus pale in comparison.'

Arete bowed her head. She was ashamed of the joy she'd felt at the idea of joining Dionysius, thinking of all those poor wretches that the war had created, of the infinite grieving that so many people – close to her by way of blood, language, customs and traditions – would yet have to bear.

Tellias fell silent as well, as the singing and teasing of a group of youths accompanying a bride to the house of her groom could be heard outside. Little street urchins ran after them, calling out gleeful obscenities.

'There's always someone celebrating in this city,' commented Tellias with a sigh. 'Celebrations for religious feast days, for good harvests and for bad ones as well, because they could have gone worse. We make merry when a child is born, or even a pony, for engagement parties and weddings, for victories in athletic contests, even for funerals: the living must be consoled for the loss of their loved ones!'

'I don't see anything wrong with that,' said Philistus. 'Acragas is a wealthy city: people feel that they can enjoy life.'

'That may be so, but sometimes I have the impression there's something else behind it. As if they knew their end was near.'

'Oh, come now, Tellias!' scolded the girl. 'If the barbarians won, it's only because they caught us by surprise. Now we're all ready to defend ourselves . . .'

Neither Philistus nor Tellias spoke, and in the silence of the night the wedding song could be heard – sung by a solitary voice now on the hill of the temples – spreading through the valley all the way to the agora, carried by the sea wind.

Tellias's wife appeared soon afterwards, descending the stair: 'Come,' she said, 'you must see this spectacle!'

They all got up and went up to the high terrace, from which almost the entire city could be seen, with the stunning temples that stood tall on the hill along the circle of walls. At that moment, midway up the slope, right in front of the groom's house, a huge fire was being lit. And soon after, as if obeying a signal, other fires were lit at various spots, both on high and down in the valley, on the acropolis and at the base of the walls. It was a beautiful and moving sight. The bonfires continued to multiply until it seemed that the whole city were prey to the flames.

'Phaillus of Megara, the father of the bride, gave every shop-keeper in the city a stack of wood,' explained the woman, 'with an order to light up at his signal, at the very moment in which the groom would be taking the bride to their wedding chamber. Those fires reflect his wishes for an ardent, everlasting love.'

Arete took in the breathtaking scene and felt profoundly moved.

Tellias looked at his wife, then at Arete: both had tears in their eyes. He shook his head, muttering: 'Women!' But despite his teasing banter, it was clear that his mind was occupied by distressing thoughts.

Philistus took his arm and said: 'I hear that the best wine in all of Acragas is to be had at your home, but I haven't been offered a drop yet!'

'Oh yes, of course,' said Tellias. 'Let's leave the women here to enjoy the celebration, and we'll break out an amphora of the good stuff. We could have dinner in the garden. It's quite pleasant to sit out, even this early in the season.'

They sat under the portico and the host had a jug of his best wine brought to while away the time until dinner was served. Philistus watched him attentively as he appraised the colour and fragrance of the precious liquid, swirling it on the bottom of a finely crafted cup, a true jewel of antiquity decorated with black figures of dancing satyrs. And when Tellias raised his cup to toast his guest and put it to his lips, his every gesture showed just how much he appreciated all the fruits of civilization.

The servants brought out the tables, with fresh bread, meat and legumes, and the two men began to eat.

'There's no need for you to worry,' said Philistus, after he'd had a few sips of the wine himself.

'No, I'm not worried at all, not at all. I'm just sorry about

Arete leaving us: she's a treasure, a true delight. I'll miss her boldness, her spontaneity, her charm. Did you see how quick she was to speak her mind about a political issue, certainly not a suitable subject for a woman, let alone a young girl?'

'You don't have children, do you, Tellias?'

'No, in fact. I have no children.'

'It's a pity. You would have been an excellent father.'

'I would have been terrible! I'd have spoiled them as I have that cheeky little thing out there!' He had another sip of wine and began to eat with quite an appetite. When they had finished, he had another platter brought out, with boiled eggs, cheese and olives. 'I eat too much!' he sighed. 'And I keep getting fatter.'

'That's not what worries you, though, is it?'

'The Carthaginians will be back.'

'I don't think so. Why should they? They've had their revenge, taken their plunder. They're merchants, they want to return to their trading. They can't wait to dismiss all those mercenaries. They're costing them a mint!'

'Acragas is the border city now,' continued Tellias as if Philistus hadn't spoken.

'That does not mean they will attack.'

'Yes, it does. Tell me: what do you think Dionysius is doing in Messana?'

'He's helping the refugees, as he always has done.'

'Perhaps, but he's certainly getting himself into trouble as well. Word has it that many of the survivors are regrouping for a counter-attack. If they manage it, you can be sure that Dionysius will be among them. He's a hothead; he's bold, he's reckless, he's not happy unless he's picking a fight with someone . . .'

'A man of courage, a dreamer, a patriot, perhaps . . . a hero?' suggested Philistus.

'The Carthaginians will certainly react if they are provoked.'

'True enough; that can't be excluded, but it's not a foregone conclusion. Wars cost money, as I've already pointed out.'

'What time will you be leaving tomorrow?' asked Tellias.

'Early, at daybreak.'

'Fine. I'll be there, even though I detest farewells. I've had a bed prepared for you. The servants will accompany you with a lantern. Goodnight.'

'Goodnight, Tellias,' replied Philistus, getting to his feet and following one of the servants, who led him to his quarters.

Tellias remained alone under the portico, watching in silence as the wedding fires went out one after another, until the city was totally in the dark.

*

They said goodbye at the door. Arete threw her arms around Tellias's neck and hugged his wife; she seemed loath to leave them. 'If you could see what I feel in my heart right now,' she said, 'you would know how much I care for you and how grateful I am to you for having treated me like a daughter. I would give anything to be able to repay your generosity!'

'Just getting rid of you will be a nice gift on its own: you are the most impertinent, petulant . . .' grumbled Tellias in an effort not to break down.

Arete went from tears to laughter. 'That's just why I'm going! Be good, my pot-bellied friend!'

'You too, little one,' replied Tellias, his eyes shining.

'I'll keep you informed,' said Philistus in parting.

He accompanied the girl to the southern gate, which was already open at that hour. They continued past the monumental tombs that flanked the street. Arete pointed them out to her companion, telling him about the famous athletes, philosophers and rulers who were buried there, all things she had learned during her stay in the city. Every now and then, they turned around to contemplate the acropolis, illuminated by the rays of dawn, and the acroteria of the temples that stood high above the walls. The shrill notes of a bugle on the tallest tower saluted the sun's rising.

The view was even more glorious from the ship, as it began to pull away from the coast. The temples on the hill, and the Temple of Athena on the acropolis, rose up over the city as if the hand of a god were lifting them up to the sky. On the west side, they could clearly see the still unfinished sanctuary of Zeus: the grandiose pediment crowded with despairing figures, the giants bearing the immense rooftop on their shoulders.

'Do you really think the city is in danger?' asked Arete.

'No, I really don't think so,' replied Philistus. 'Acragas is invincible.'

'Then why is Tellias so stricken?'

Philistus looked away for a moment so she would not notice his apprehension. 'He was sad about you going away, that's all. And a little worried, too: a voyage by sea is always risky.'

Arete fell silent, watching as the most beautiful city that man had ever built slowly faded into the distance and vanished over the ridge of the waves that washed against the ship as the wind carried it away. She suddenly said, as if speaking to herself, 'Will we ever see her again?'

Philistus pretended he hadn't heard, this time.

*

They reached Gela as night was coming on and they dropped anchor at the mouth of the river from which the city took her name, represented on her silver coins as a bull with a human face. The city had been built on a rocky cliff which stretched out both to the east and to the west and was defended by formidable walls made of huge blocks of grey stone. Gela was the metropolis of Acragas, and had been founded by colonists from Rhodes and Crete nearly three centuries earlier. The city had also been the birthplace of Gelon, he who had won over the Carthaginians at Himera, unleashing such undying hate and thirst for vengeance in Carthage that three generations later she had struck back.

There in the city of Gela slept Aeschylus, the great tragic poet, and Arete wanted to visit his grave before darkness fell. It was a modest tomb, topped by a slab bearing a brief epigraph:

Here lies Aeschylus, son of Euphorion of Athens,
having died at Gela of the rich harvests.
His valour can be vouched for by those who beheld it:

the Mede of the flowing tresses
and the Sacred Forest of Marathon.

Arete was moved as she read the inscription. 'Not a word about his glory as a poet!' she commented. 'Only about his valour in war.'

'They don't make his kind any more these days,' observed Philistus.

They set off again the following morning before dawn, after having refurbished their water supply, and sailed towards Camarina, where early that afternoon they spotted the Temple of Athena emerging from the red rooftops of the city.

'Camarina has always been hostile to Syracuse, even during the war against the Athenians,' Philistus explained to Arete. She was leaning against the ship's railing, watching the city sparkle in the bright sun.

'The cities of the Greeks are like seagulls' nests perched on the cliffs along the coast,' observed Arete, 'surrounded by lands inhabited by barbarians who do not understand our language or worship our gods. We should unite and help each other in time of need, and yet our cities are often at odds. Sometimes we even act as mortal enemies! We consume all our energies in continual conflicts, while the true enemy is looming at the horizon and there's no one capable of stopping him . . .'

Philistus was once again impressed and surprised by the girl's observations. It was unusual for a woman to be on such familiar terms with political topics. Perhaps that was the aspect of her personality that had won Dionysius's heart. He answered: 'It's their very nature that makes it difficult for them to understand each other, much less to form a true alliance. You said it well: they are scattered settlements, established by communities who have come from many different places. They only unite when they are forced to do so by a danger so great that it threatens their very existence. But by then it's often too late. It's a pity, because when the Greeks of Sicily have joined together they have achieved great victories.'

'Do you think unity is still possible?'

'Perhaps. But what we need is a man who is capable of convincing all these cities that unity is essential for survival. Using every means possible, even force, if necessary.'

'Such a man would be a tyrant in his own city, and would be seen as such by all the others,' objected Arete staunchly.

'There are times in which people must give up a part of their own freedom if life itself is at stake, and the survival of entire communities. Can't you see that? There are situations in which the people themselves are willing to grant exceptional powers to a man who is truly worthy.'

'You seem to be thinking of someone in particular as you're saying those words,' said Arete, without looking away from the little city that was disappearing amidst the foaming waves.

'I am. That man is already among us, and you have met him.'

'Dionysius! Are you thinking of Dionysius?' exclaimed Arete, finally turning to face him. 'But that's absurd. He's only a boy.'

'Age doesn't mean anything. What counts is courage, intelligence and determination, and those are qualities he possesses to the highest degree. You can't even imagine the enormous sway he holds over people, and how many men not only admire him but would be willing to do anything for him.'

'I can imagine it very well, actually,' replied Arete with a smile.

*

It took them two more days to reach Syracuse, where they docked on the southern shore of the Great Harbour. Philistus sent a couple of men into the city to buy food at the market and get water. He himself stayed on board with the girl, knowing that Dionysius expected constant and prudent attention on his part. He noticed that Arete seemed unnerved when she first saw the city, and could not hide a marked agitation.

'Do you know someone here?' Philistus asked her.

'I spent my childhood here,' replied Arete, trying to control herself.

'Really? Then perhaps I know your parents.'

'I don't think so,' replied the girl, and went to sit at the aft deck to put an end to the conversation.

Philistus said nothing else, and occupied himself with the provisions. He gave orders for dinner to be eaten on board; no one was to go ashore.

Before the sun set, she sought out her escort again. 'Can you see his house from here?' she asked.

Philistus smiled and pointed at a spot in front of him. 'Look straight up there, above Achradina, where the theatre is. Now follow an imaginary line to the causeway of Ortygia. See the terraced house with the trellis, about halfway down the road?'

'Yes, I do.'

'Well, that's where Dionysius lives.'

'Are his parents there?'

'They're gone. His father, Hermocritus, died during the Great War, when the Athenians were laying siege to Syracuse. His mother followed him to the tomb just a short time later; she died of an incurable illness. At sixteen he found himself having to care for his little sisters, who are all now married in other cities, and his brother Leptines.'

Arete asked nothing more, but never took her eyes off the red roof tiles and the trellis until the sun vanished over the horizon.

Two more days passed before they came within sight of Mount Aetna, still hooded with snow. So tall, with its curl of smoke. The gulf was a wonder, set against a coastal plain full of olive trees and grapevines that were just starting to sprout tender springtime leaves.

Naxos stretched out along the coast. The first colony of the Greeks in Sicily, her biggest temple still stood on the spot near the beach where the city's fathers had touched land, led by Tucles, her founder. Philistus explained that an altar to Apollo, Leader of Men, stood in the agora; he was the god said to guide colonists leaving their homeland in search of fortune on distant shores. All of the delegations sent to Greece to consult the Oracle of Delphi set off from that very altar, the oldest sacred place on the entire island.

'No one would ever attempt to migrate,' pointed out Philistus, 'without the assistance of the Oracle. The voice of the Oracle indicates the place where the emigrants should found a new homeland, and the best time to take to sea. That's why you'll find an altar to Apollo in many colonies; sometimes even a temple, like at Cyrene in Africa . . .'

'Have you ever visited Cyrene?' asked Arete, her curiosity piqued.

'Certainly. It's a marvellous city. There's a huge inscription, right in the main square, that reproduces the oath of the colonists. Do you know the story of the founding of Cyrene? One day I'll tell you all about it; it's a fabulous adventure, full of extraordinary happenings.'

'Why don't you tell me the story now?' asked Arete.

'No, another time,' replied Philistus. 'The closer we get to our destination, the more I can tell that your mind is occupied by other thoughts. It's only right, and I can imagine why.'

'It's not easy to keep anything hidden from you,' said Arete.

'I've dedicated my life to studying man's nature and actions, and I hope I've learned something. And yet I can tell that you're going to surprise me, sooner or later. There are many things in you that I still can't understand.'

'When will we get to Messana?' asked Arete, changing the subject.

'This evening, if the weather stays good. Our journey is almost over.'

They entered the great sickle-shaped harbour of Messana at sunset and Arete was as excited as a little girl to see the Straits that divided Sicily from Italy. Rhegium, on the other side, seemed close enough to touch with a hand. 'What a magnificent place!' she exclaimed. 'It's hard to imagine that Scylla and Charybdis were here.'

'What seems like such a marvellous place to you now, with beautiful cities on both sides, looked wild and treacherous to the first navigators that ventured into these waters. The strong current of the Straits tossed their fragile vessels against the rocks this way and that. The sight of Mount Aetna with its rivers of fire, the rumbling that shook the earth, the cliffs towering on the east, the dark forests . . . it all seemed monstrous and threatening. And so they imagined that Odysseus, the wandering hero, had ploughed these turbulent waters long before they had, managing to defeat the monsters, overcome the Cyclops, trick the sirens, elude Circe's sorcery . . .'

Arete turned towards the Sicilian shore and gazed at the beautiful harbour swarming with vessels; the sea had turned the colour of lead and the distant clouds were reddened by the last rays of the sun. Even the plume of Mount Aetna was tinged with unreal colours, and she understood what Philistus's words meant. 'I could listen to you for days and days,' she said. 'It's been a privilege to spend this time with you.'

'As it has been for me,' replied Philistus.

Arete dropped her eyes and asked with a blush: 'How do I look to you? I mean . . . don't you think I look too skinny?'

Philistus smiled. 'You look beautiful to me. But look, there's someone coming this way, and I'd say he can't wait to get you into his arms.'

Arete glanced over at the dockyard and was struck dumb: Dionysius was running towards her like a young god, dressed only in a light chlamys, his hair curling over his shoulders. He was shouting out her name.

She would have wanted to run and shout as well, or maybe break down in tears, but she could do nothing. Still and silent, she gripped the ship's railing and looked at him as if he were a vision from a dream.

Dionysius sprang from the edge of the wharf and grabbed the ship's railing from the other side. He hoisted himself up on his arms and pushed himself clear over the railing. She found him standing in front of her.

She could only gasp: 'How did you know that . . . ?'

'Every evening I watch the mouth of the harbour hoping to see you arrive.'

'You haven't changed your mind? Are you sure that . . .'

Dionysius cut off her words with a kiss as he pulled her close. Arete threw her arms around him and felt herself melt in the heat of his embrace as she abandoned herself to the fiery words he whispered in her ear.

Dionysius stepped back and said to her, smiling: 'Now we have to respect tradition. Come on, I've got to ask for your hand in marriage.'

'What do you mean . . . ask for my hand? Ask who? I'm all alone, I'm . . .'

'Ask your father, little girl. Hermocrates is here.'

Arete looked at Philistus and then again at Dionysius, saying: 'My father? Oh gods in heaven, my father?' Her eyes welled up with tears.

6

HERMOCRATES HAD BEEN told only that Dionysius had asked to be received and that he would have a person with him who wanted to see him. He suddenly found the daughter he had thought dead standing in front of him.

He was a hard man, tempered by the vicissitudes of an adventurous life, a proud, austere aristocrat, but he was thoroughly shaken by the sight of her. Arete did not dare run to him, in keeping with the respect she'd been taught to have for her father since she was young. She took a few timid steps in his direction, without daring to look him in the eye. He had always been more of an image, an idol, for her than a real parent, and the sudden, dramatic intimacy of such an extreme situation made her feel panicky and light-headed. Her heart was beating so hard she thought she would suffocate. But her father rose to his feet as soon as he had got over his shock and he ran to her, holding her close in a long, emotional hug. She burst into tears as all her tension dissolved and she clung to his neck. She stood there without moving, in the middle of that plain, bare room, wrapped in the warmth of an embrace that she had always desired.

It was Dionysius's voice that shook her to her senses: '*Hegemon* . . .'

Hermocrates seemed only then to notice his presence. He looked at him with a quizzical expression, not understanding how that young warrior could have brought him the daughter that he had thought lost to him forever.

'Father,' said Arete, 'it's to him I owe my life. He found me nearly unconscious along the road. He helped me up, he comforted me, protected me . . .'

Hermocrates shot a suddenly dark, suspicious look at the young man he had in front of him.

'. . . and respected me,' concluded Arete.

Hermocrates released her and turned to Dionysius. 'I thank you for what you have done. Tell me how I can reward you.'

'I've already had my reward, *hegemon*. Meeting your daughter was the greatest fortune that has ever befallen me. The privilege of talking to her and listening to her words has changed me profoundly—'

'It's all ended up well,' Hermocrates cut him off. 'I'm very grateful to you, boy, more than you can imagine. When I learned about the fall of Selinus and found no way to have news of my daughter, I was tortured by the thought that she might be a prisoner, dragged who knows where in slavery, exposed to brutality and violence of every sort . . . The uncertainty of her fate was even more painful for me than if I had learned of her death. There is no worse torture for a father than not knowing the destiny of his daughter. My properties and my wealth have been confiscated, but I still have something hidden away. Let me pay you back.'

'There's no price for what I'm about to ask you, *hegemon*,' said Dionysius with a firm voice, looking him straight in the eyes, 'because I intend to ask you to give me the daughter I've just returned to you.'

'But . . . what are you saying . . .' stuttered Hermocrates.

'I've fallen in love with him, father,' Arete broke in. 'As soon as I saw him, as soon as I opened my eyes. And from that moment I've wanted nothing but to be his bride and live with him every day that the gods shall grant us.'

Hermocrates looked like he'd been struck by lightning, and couldn't say a word.

'I know, I'm a man of humble birth,' continued Dionysius, 'and I should never have even raised my eyes to her, but the love I feel for her gives me the courage to dare so much. I will prove myself worthy of your daughter and of you, *hegemon*. You will not regret having granted me so great a treasure. I'm not asking for her hand because I want to have a family and ensure my progeny, nor in order to bind myself to one of the most illustrious houses of my city, and certainly not to take the credit for having brought her back to you. I would have tried to save anyone I found in those conditions. I'm asking you for her hand because without her there would be no joy in my life, because I want to love her and protect her against any harm or danger, even at the cost of my own life.'

Hermocrates nodded solemnly without saying a word, and Arete, realizing that he had consented, hugged him tightly, whispering in his ear: 'Thank you, father, thank you ... I'm happy because I'm with the only people in the world who mean something to me.'

*

Their marriage was celebrated the following day. Since Arete had no friends who could accompany her to her husband's house, and since her husband had no house of his own in Messana, the noblest families of the city offered Dionysius a home, and their virgin daughters accompanied the bride to her wedding chamber to loosen the belt of her gown. Arete thought of the fires of Acragas and of the solitary song of the poet on the hill of the temples as she made her way to the house where Dionysius was waiting for her. He was a hero to her; the man who most resembled her father, the love she'd dreamt of since she was a child, when she would listen to fanciful stories on her mother's knee.

The procession was festive, the young people along the way shouted and teased, the children chanted the traditional nursery rhyme that wished offspring of both sexes upon the couple.

> The swallows are back again
> And the crow is on his way
> Carrying a little boy in his beak
> Or a pretty little girl!

The maidens who accompanied Arete sprinkled wild rose petals before her. They were all lovely, dressed in their best peplums, but no one could match the splendour of the bride. Her happiness made her even more luminous: she had cast aside all her worrisome thoughts to think only of the young man who awaited her at the threshold of a modest home at the foot of the hills.

The sun was setting behind the mountains when she came within sight of the house. Dionysius stood at the door dressed in an elegant white floor-length chiton embroidered with silver palm leaves; certainly some wealthy friend had lent it to him! At his side was the priest who united their hands with the sacred ribbon and blessed the bride.

The girls then accompanied Arete to the bridal chamber, chanting the wedding hymn and lighting the torches they held in their hands from the oil lamp in the atrium. They loosened her hair and combed it, then untied the belt that graced her gown. They undressed her and lay her down on the bed, under the white linen sheets.

Then they scampered down the stairs with mischievous little yelps. Dionysius waited until everything was tranquil and quiet, then went upstairs and neared the bedroom door. He strained his ears, and finally heard the serenade that he had requested for his bride that night. Down in the street, a Messanian singer, accompanied by a flute and a string instrument, had struck up his song: a moving love story where a poor boy falls in love with a princess after having seen her pass only once on her sedan chair.

He gently pushed the door open just a crack, and saw with surprise that the bed was empty. Alarmed, he entered the room: it was empty as well! His heart pounding, Dionysius tried to calm down. He closed the door behind him and started. Arete had been hiding behind the door and was now standing proudly naked in front of him, backed up against the wall, with a naughty, amused smile on her face.

Dionysius shook his head and came close. 'You know that a

young bride should wait timid and trembling under the sheets? Does this seem the time to play games?'

Arete smiled: 'Do you still think I'm too thin?'

'I think you are very, very beautiful,' replied Dionysius. 'And that I was completely wrong.' He held out his hand to caress her cheek and she kissed it gently, barely grazing it with her open lips. He slid his other hand down to caress her breasts and stomach. He saw Arete close her eyes and felt her flesh quiver under his fingertips.

He suddenly lifted her in his arms with a natural, gentle gesture, as if she were as light as a feather, and laid her on the bed. He undressed, and to Arete he looked like the statues of the Olympic athletes in the squares and of the gods on the temple pediments. The last rosy reflections of the evening sifted in through the window and alighted on Arete's skin like the gaze of Aphrodite. The serenade was more distant now, and softer, so much like the melody she'd heard in Acragas, accompanied by the mellow notes of a flute and the silvery warble of strings.

Dionysius lay down next to her and he was drawn in by her warmth and her fragrance; he saw her slowly transfigured by the pleasure he was able to arouse in her virginal body. Her eyes were gleaming with a golden light, her lips swelling, her face relaxing into an almost glassy transparency. She responded to every kiss with equal ardour, gave herself over to every caress with innocent abandon. It was she who drew him into her body, dissolving the reserve of the warrior with the burning intensity of her gaze, enthralling him with her immaculate breasts, gripping his flanks between her thighs like an Amazon. They made love for as long as the flame flickered in the lamp, until they fell back exhausted, immersed in a state of numb, humid bliss. They slipped from love to dream without realizing it: the pearly light of a watery dawn found them still embracing, covered only by their beauty.

*

Hermocrates desired nothing more than to return to his home-land. He contacted friends who still lived in Syracuse to see if they might petition the Assembly to pass a bill recalling him from exile. Dionysius sent messages to Philistus as well, asking him to mobilize all the members of the Company to vote in favour of Hermocrates' return. He sent others back to Syracuse just so they could take part in the vote. But after the shameful defeats at Selinus and Himera, Diocles feared that Hermocrates would totally overshadow him if he were to return: the commander's prestige and his ardent rhetoric would inflame the mob and incite them to insurrection. He worried that Hermocrates would drag the city into another long, bloody war, and that the democratic institutions would not hold up against such a powerful personality. In a series of stormy meetings, the opposing factions clashed harshly in the Assembly, but by the end it was clear that the people imagined that Hermocrates's return might give the aristo-crats the chance to seize power again, and the motion that proposed his recall from exile was rejected by a small margin of votes.

It was Dionysius himself who brought the news to Hermocra-tes; scowling, he received the younger man in the shadowy atrium of his home, drawn up like a vexed divinity. His body and spirit were still at the height of their vigour, and his gaze emanated a fierce, threatening intensity that struck fear even into the heart of his friends.

The newly acquired kinship with him had not changed the sense of reverential respect that Dionysius had always had for him, and he continued to call him *hegemon*, as would any of his soldiers.

'So they've refused,' said Hermocrates, barely restraining his wrath.

'It was a very small majority,' Dionysius offered in an attempt to console him.

'In a democracy, it makes no difference if you're defeated by one vote or by a thousand.'

'You're right. What will you do now, if I may ask?'

A long silence followed, then Hermocrates spoke: 'It was not a thirst for power that motivated my desire to return; I simply wanted to lead the uprising against the barbarians.'

'I know, *hegemon*.'

'Seeing that my city does not want me, I will lead the war nonetheless from here.' He stood, and the tone of his voice rang out powerfully, as if he were haranguing the Assembly. 'Let the refugees who are still in Messana know that we're going back to Selinus. We will reoccupy the city. Tell them that the days of their humiliation are over. Tell them it is time to gather together all the survivors, wherever they may be; we will help search for them ourselves. I will write a proclamation that will circulate in hundreds, in thousands of copies, a proclamation to rally all the vanquished, all those who have lost their families and their homes, all those who still hear the agonizing cries of their butchered children and raped wives in their ears. I shall call on them to pitch camp among the smoking ruins of their demolished city, I shall return their weapons and their honour to them. We will restore the images of our gods in their temples; the sacred symbols of our religion will be returned to their rightful homes. And then we will attack. We will rout out the enemy wherever they may be, we will hunt them down without respite and without mercy. Go, now!'

Dionysius assented with a barely perceptible nod of his head and left to muster up his comrades and inform them of Hermocrates's intentions. In less than seven days, one thousand Himerans and five hundred Selinuntians were ready to march at his orders.

Arete would have followed Dionysius wherever he went, but she could not oppose the will of both her husband and father, who wanted to send her back to a safe place in Syracuse to shield her from the perilous military campaign and the strain of forced marches. She was so furious at being excluded that Dionysius could barely get her to listen to him when he came to inform her of their decision.

'You are a bastard, and a son of a bitch,' she shouted in a fit of anger. 'What have I done to you to make you treat me like this?'

'Say that again and I'll slap you till your face is as swollen as a wineskin!'

'Just try it!'

'You bet I'll try it! I'm your husband, by Zeus!'

'You'll be sorry you sent me away!'

'What is that, a threat?'

'Take it however you want!'

'I'm not sending you away, sod it, I'm sending you home!'

'That's all? What do you need a wife for anyway, just for fucking? Find yourself a whore then, or better yet, stick it up the arse of one of your friends.'

Dionysius raised his hand to slap her, but she glared back without batting an eye, openly challenging him. 'I'm leaving,' he muttered, then turned and strode towards the door.

'Dionysius . . .'

Her voice stopped him before he could go. He did not turn.

'I tried,' said the girl.

Dionysius did not answer.

'The truth is that I'm miserable without you, while you're just fine without me, and it drives me crazy.'

'It's not true.'

'What's not true?'

'That I'm fine without you. I'll be counting the days and the hours that separate us and every instant will seem endless.'

'You're just saying that so that I'll go without making a scene.'

'I'm saying that because it's true.'

'Really?' She was very close now, and he could smell the scent of her skin and the violet fragrance of her hair.

'Really,' he replied, and turned. She was standing in front of him, cheeks flushed with annoyance and emotion.

'Then take me to bed before you go, you bastard. Your men can wait. They'll have you for who knows how long. I won't.'

He took her into his arms like he had the night of their wedding and carried her up the stairs to their bedroom. 'Where did you learn to talk that way?' he asked as he unbuckled the breastplate and greaves he was already wearing. 'You're the daughter of a nobleman, an aristocrat; I thought that—'

'At camp with the warriors. My father would let me come and stay with him for a few days. Sometimes even a month or more. And now,' she said, letting her gown fall on to the floor, 'make this good enough for the whole time you'll be away.'

*

They marched for eleven days towards the interior of the island along the steep ridge of the mountains. No one ever dared to challenge them, or even to approach, although sometimes they would spot a man on horseback watching them from the high ground that flanked their path before he raced away at a gallop. Hermocrates marched tirelessly at the head of the column, always the first to awaken and don his armour, and the last to sit down alongside the campfire for a frugal meal. Before he took his rest, he made sure that everyone had eaten enough and had a blanket to shelter from the cold, still fierce at night at that altitude, like a father with his sons.

On the evening of the twelfth day they came into sight of Selinus and the warriors drew up stone-still to behold her. It seemed impossible that such a great and beautiful city had been completely destroyed and her people cruelly massacred and dispersed.

Hermocrates dismissed the men, and the Selinuntians drifted through the city, roaming like ghosts around the crumbling walls, down the roads crowded with debris, among the remains of carbonized bodies. Each was looking for his own home, redolent of freshly whitewashed walls in the spring and of rosemary and mint in the summer, the homes where they had grown up, where they had gathered with their families for so many years to eat their dinners, to laugh and joke, to talk about what they had done during the day. The rooms which once rang with the voices of children playing no longer had roofs, invaded now only by the sigh of the wind blowing down from the mountains.

When they found what they were searching for, they would wander around the empty shell, touching, almost caressing, the door jambs and walls. Weeping, they would pick up a memento of the life they had led, holding on to it like a precious talisman: the fragment of a dish, a little ornament for an arm or ankle, a pin that had once gathered the hair of a beloved person.

Here and there, in what had been their gardens and orchards, pomegranates had managed to bloom, but the vermilion petals, once a festive sign of spring, now seemed nothing more than stains of blood on the fire-blackened walls. Vine shoots snaked over the ground, intertwining with the brambles that had sunk their roots everywhere.

Only once evening had fallen did the Selinuntian warriors emerge from the maze of ruins, one after another, heading towards the flickering fire that had been lit in the agora. Hermocrates awaited them there, along with the Himerans and the Syracusans who had joined him.

They ate mostly in silence, overwhelmed by their memories, and yet, as night drew on, the heat of the blaze and the food they had eaten together, the sensation of being animated by the same emotions and the same determination, the reflection of the flames on the facades of the deserted temples restored a sense of pride to the men, of territory reconquered, of ground reconsecrated.

The next day they collected the remains of their dead and buried them in the nearby necropolis, then divided into groups according to the tasks they'd been assigned. Some went down to the sea to fish with their bows and arrows since they had no nets, others scattered through the fields in search of plots of land that could be cultivated. Several of them set about identifying the least damaged houses and began to clear away the debris and repair them. Still others went into the wood to chop down trunks which could be made into beams for the roofs, boards for doors and windows, planks for building ships. The city soon took on a different appearance, at least in the area around the agora.

The villagers up on the hillside would see fires flickering in the city at night and shadows roaming among the ruins, breeding all sorts of stories. They were rumoured to be the shades of the dead who wandered restlessly among the wreckage of the destroyed city, and the fires were said to be their spirits which blazed with hate for the enemies that had deprived them of life. Not even the shepherds ventured as far as the walls any longer, fearful of making ghostly encounters. But before long, these rumours dissipated as the truth became evident and spread to the three corners of Sicily and beyond.

Hermocrates's proclamation had had the desired effect and volunteers began to pour in from all over the island, mostly Selinuntians and Himerans. Hundreds, at first, and then thousands of them came on foot and on horseback, from every direction, even from the sea. One man had even managed to escape from slavery and cross the African sea with a kind of raft that he had built from palm trunks. They found him on the beach one morning, more dead than alive; when he came to his senses and saw hundreds of warriors training in the agora with their spears and swords he began to shout that he too wanted his armour and that the time had come to invade Africa. Calming him down took quite some effort.

In just a couple of months' time, six thousand warriors had assembled and were ready for anything; they were perfectly trained and blindly faithful to their commander. Dionysius had become the second-in-command and was in charge of leading raids into enemy territory to seize food and forage. But the little army's activity soon became much more massive and aggressive. Hermocrates led a couple of actual expeditions over the summer, attacking Lilybaeum and Panormus by surprise and inflicting severe losses on the garrisons of mercenaries in the service of the Carthaginians. They even made an assault on the island of Motya at night, setting fire to a couple of dry-docked warships. The detachment of Carthaginian soldiers patrolling the territory was intercepted and wiped out. Although both Hermocrates and Dionysius attempted to curb the violent instincts of their troops, they could not prevent the men from committing every sort of atrocity, thus rekindling the hatred and rancour of the enemy.

Philistus constantly sent news from Syracuse through friends in the Company, like Biton, Doricus and Iolaus, who had been Dionysius's childhood friends. They thus learned just how worried Diocles had become about these military sorties, which he feared would provoke a huge Carthaginian reaction, but even more so about the enormous popularity that Hermocrates and Dionysius himself were gaining at home as news of their exploits spread, especially among the young. The same messengers brought Dionysius ardent letters of love from Arete, unfailingly ending with pleas to join him as soon as possible.

He managed to see her in secret several times during the following winter, taking advantage of any pause in military operations, but it was never possible for them to enjoy more than a couple of days together for fear of being found out. He was forced to spend his time inside the house, to the great delight of Arete, who wanted him all for herself.

At the beginning of the following spring, Hermocrates made a decision destined to cause a great stir. He crossed western Sicily at the head of his army and marched all the way to Himera. He wanted the meaning of his gesture to be quite clear: the Greeks of Sicily must unite in a single powerful alliance, muster an army of unprecedented size and banish the enemy from the entire island. It was at Himera that the war against the Carthaginians had been fought and won seventy years before under the leadership of Syracuse, and it was from Himera that the counter-attack would begin.

It was because of that very defeat, however, that the enemies' revenge had been so fierce: the vision of what remained of Himera was even more devastating for the survivors than the ruins of Selinus had been. Here the fury of the barbarians had gone totally unchecked: they had demolished the city house by house, torn down the walls, set fire to the temples, toppled and disfigured the statues and tortured to death anyone they found with a weapon in hand. Their dismembered corpses were still scattered among the ruins and at the site of the final massacre; on the great stone that had been their sacrificial altar, the sight was so horrendous that one of the younger warriors fainted outright. The bodies were piled up in the thousands and the ground beneath them was still black with their blood.

Hermocrates himself was completely overwhelmed. Pale with rage and indignation, he circled around that heap of horrors growling words from clenched teeth that no one could understand.

He ordered that funeral rites be celebrated, with immediate burial for those miserable remains. He sent other men out into the fields, where the last bloody battle had taken place, with instructions to gather the bones of the Syracusan soldiers fallen during the unfortunate attempt to succour Himera, the bones of the men that Diocles had abandoned on the battlefield. Stripped of their weapons and anything else of value, they were still recognizable by the bracelets – made of a willow branch split in two lengthwise and carved inside with the warrior's name – which they wore braided on their wrists like the soldiers of Sparta.

He had a pinewood coffin made for each one of the fallen warriors with his name branded upon it, and sent them back to their homeland for proper burial. It was a momentous gesture, and not only from an ethical point of view. Hermocrates was certainly aware of its political impact on the people of Syracuse, from whom he still expected an official decree recalling him to his city. This act made the differences in moral stature between him and his adversary Diocles, their democratic leader, appear clamorous. On one hand, the exiled leader – never defeated, and stripped of command exclusively for political reasons – had vindicated the honour of Syracuse and of all the Sicilian Greeks by bringing their sons fallen in battle back to the city which had humiliated and disclaimed him. On the other hand his rival Diocles was disgraced by his failure to stop the barbarians from annihilating two of the most illustrious cities of Sicily. What's more, Diocles had ignominiously fled the battlefield, abandoning the allies to the most ferocious retaliation. And he had left the bodies of his soldiers unburied, allowing their desecration, condemning their troubled souls to wander perpetually at the threshold of Hades.

The news that Hermocrates was bringing home the remains of their sons who had fallen in combat aroused intense emotion in the people of Syracuse, who gathered in Assembly to decree a solemn public funeral. The proposal was advanced that Hermocrates's civic rights be immediately restored.

Diocles, who had kept at a distance until then, aware of what a wretched situation he found himself in, stepped forward as the matter was being discussed and asked for the floor.

A hush greeted his unexpected appearance: a tomblike silence fell over the Assembly.

—

7

'Syracusans!' began Diocles. 'I know what you are feeling. I too had friends who fell at Himera and yet I did not stop to collect their bodies . . .'

'Because you're a coward!' exclaimed one of the men present.

'Silence!' commanded the president of the Assembly. 'Allow him to speak.'

'I did not stop,' continued Diocles, 'because it would have meant risking the lives of other comrades who were still alive. I wanted to bring them back to you safe and sound. And in doing so I saved the lives of many refugees who would have otherwise been slaughtered . . .'

'But how many others did you abandon to their destiny?' shouted another. 'People who believed in us, who trusted us. You dishonoured us all!' He pointed his finger at him as he pronounced those words, and Diocles saw that the bracelet on his wrist bore the symbol of the dolphin, worn by those of the Company which Dionysius belonged to.

The president of the Assembly called those present to order, and Diocles continued his speech. 'I had no choice, believe me! The city was lost: no one and nothing could have saved her from the assault of sixty thousand men. That bloodthirsty barbarian would not have raised the siege until every last Himeran was exterminated. At least I saved their women and children, and many men as well. But I have not come here to defend myself from your accusations. I acted in good faith and I fought courageously. My comrades can testify to this. I am here instead to exhort you not to allow Hermocrates to enter the city . . .'

A murmur of disapproval ran through the Assembly. Some cursed, others called out insults.

'I know that at this moment he seems like a hero to you. A valiant man who has challenged the barbarians, who has camped among the ruins of Selinus, who has brought back the bones of your sons. And perhaps he is a hero. But he is also an adventurer, a man whose only aim is to take power. Syracuse is a democracy, and democracies have no need of great public figures, of heroes. Democracies need ordinary people, they need citizens who do their duty every day and who serve their homeland. If Hermocrates's exile is revoked, will our free institutions survive? He is followed by Himerans and Selinuntians, along with a group of Asiatic mercenaries he pays with Persian gold; these men are loyal to him, not to a city or an institution, and they're prepared to do anything for him. If his only purpose was to restore our dead to us, why has he brought along thousands of warriors?'

'Because he's assembling an army to drive the Carthaginians out of all Sicily,' echoed another voice, Philistus himself this time.

'I know whose side you're on!' thundered Diocles. 'And we know well that your friend Dionysius has married Hermocrates's daughter.'

'I am Dionysius's friend and I'm proud of it!' exclaimed Philistus. 'He is a courageous man who has always fought without regard for his own life, exposing himself to danger and to death on the front lines. Can anyone be called to blame for remaining faithful to his friends?'

Diocles did not answer, and resumed his speech to the Assembly. 'Have you perhaps forgotten the arrogance of the aristocrats? If you allow Hermocrates to enter the gates of this city, you may be sure that he will bring your old masters back to power; those who had you whipped if you did not work their fields like beasts from dawn to dusk, those who didn't even deign to look you in the face if they met you on the street, those who only married into each other's families as if they belonged to a different breed of men!'

Philistus reacted. 'Do not heed his words, citizens! They are only meant to distract your attention from his ineptitude, from the dishonour he has cast upon us by leaving our allies at the mercy of the enemy, fleeing by night like a thief, abandoning the bodies of your sons unburied, prey to dogs and vultures. I am asking you instead to welcome Hermocrates between the walls of this city. He was unjustly dismissed from his charge while he was fighting far from home at the head of our fleet; he was denied return to his city although he had committed no crime. Hermocrates is the only hope for this land, the only leader capable of expelling the Carthaginians from the island, the only man who can avenge your sons!'

His words stirred the crowd. Many of them rose to their feet shouting at Diocles: 'Get out of here! We want our dead! You're only envious of a better man!'

Many of the others remained in silence, however. Diocles's speech had had a certain effect on them.

In the end, the magistrates decided to put the order of the day to a vote. Two points were to be decided: the celebration of a public funeral at State expense to honour the dead brought back to their homeland, and granting Hermocrates permission to return to the city.

The first motion was approved, the second rejected, once again by a small margin of votes.

A group of citizens proposed a third motion that sentenced Diocles to exile for his incompetence in leading the army and his pusillanimity in facing the enemy. The proposal was approved by a wide margin, as if the citizens felt guilty about denying the most valorous of the sons of Syracuse the right to return and sought to somehow compensate by banishing his main adversary.

Hermocrates had been rejected by his city once again, in such a short span of time; the fact that Diocles had been condemned to exile gave him no joy. He was brought the news by a delegation from the Assembly, and the man who spoke in the name of his fellow citizens did so reluctantly, with profound discomfort, and he felt even worse when Hermocrates did not answer, but simply nodded his head in silent scorn.

It was Dionysius who spoke. 'You can take the coffins with the remains of your fellow citizens and give them the funeral honours they deserve. The sooner you go the better.'

The convoy departed then and there and reached the city in less than an hour. The coffins were lined up in the agora so that each family could identify their kin. When the man's willow bracelet had been found, the name of the fallen warrior had been branded on to the wooden coffin. When it had not been possible to give a name to the body, the word αγνωτος 'unknown' was written instead. When a single coffin collected the limbs of several persons, the word πολλοι 'many' had been marked on the wood.

The return of these remains intensified the suffering of the parents and relatives, and every corner of the city was filled with wailing and lamentation that whole night. The next day the funeral was held. Pyres were lit outside the city, to the south, and when the fire had consumed what the dogs and predators had spared, the bones and ashes were returned to the families so they could be deposited in their tombs.

Arete participated in the funeral, alone, because among the dead was a cousin who had always been very dear to her. As she set off for home, just as darkness was falling, she became aware that someone was following her, and she picked up her pace.

She suddenly realized that only a slave or a prostitute would be out walking alone on the street at that hour. Without turning, she began to walk even faster, nearly breaking into a run in her anxiousness to reach the door of her home and close herself in. The footsteps following her became quicker and heavier, like the pounding of her heart. Then, all of a sudden, they disappeared.

Arete stopped and finally looked back. No one. She drew a breath and turned quickly to the left, but as soon as she had rounded the corner she bumped into a dark-cloaked figure and could not help but scream.

'Sshh! *Siopa!*' threatened a commanding voice.

'Dionysius!' gasped Arete, recognizing him.

His head and face were covered by a hood and he said: 'Keep going and don't stop. I'll be behind you until you reach home.'

She hurried along the roads of the Achradina district until she reached the house with the trellis. The grapevines had already come into leaf and so had the fig tree that was practically growing out of the wall next to the door. Arete took the key from her bag, opened the door and let her husband in. She double-locked the door behind her and threw her arms around his neck in a long embrace. He held her tightly without saying a word.

'Do you want dinner?' asked Arete.

'I'm really not hungry.'

'How did my father take it?'

'Badly. What did you expect?'

'What will he do now?'

'I think we'll return to Selinus. There's no other place we can settle.'

'This time I'm coming with you. It makes no sense for me to stay here.'

'Yes it does.'

'What do you mean?'

'Your father wants you to stay here in Syracuse.'

'So what? I'm a married woman. I don't have to listen to my father. It's your permission I need, not his.'

'I agree with your father. As long as we're in Selinus, it's too dangerous.'

'You are a bastard,' said Arete with tears in her eyes. 'You don't love me, not even a little bit?'

'Let's not start fighting again,' replied Dionysius in a conciliatory tone. 'You know very well that you're the person I love most in this world. And that's why I've decided that you can't come with me. But listen ... there's something that I shouldn't be telling you, but I'll say it anyway: I don't think we'll be staying far away for long.'

'Why?' asked Arete, drying her tears.

'Your father is returning to Selinus but I'll only be following him in the first part of the journey. I have to meet some people who will help me prepare for his return to the city.'

'His return? But how?'

'It's better that you don't know. Believe me, it's just a question of days, less than a month, surely. And after that, we'll never be separated again. You'll grow bored with me, I promise.'

Arete shook her head.

'You don't believe me?'

'I do believe you,' she replied, 'and that's why I'm afraid. Returning like this has to mean blood.'

'No, that's not said. We'll arrange it so that it's all over with quickly. Your father doesn't want bloodshed and the city has already seen heavy losses. But it's his right to come back: the decree that sentenced him to exile was unjust. What's more, Syracuse is without a leader at the very moment that the Carthaginians are preparing a new invasion.'

'How do you know that?'

'We have our informers.'

'In the city they're saying that if the Carthaginians come back it's your fault, because you've installed an army at Selinus and have stirred them up by carrying out acts of war.'

'What do you think?'

'That they may be right, at least in part.'

'We've only done what we had to do, and I'm amazed that you of all people, who witnessed the horrors they're capable of, are saying such a thing.'

'Women think differently than men do. You men only think of revenge, of honour, of showing your bravery as warriors, but all you're doing is perpetrating hatred and encouraging ill will. You seek glory, we grieve our sons, our brothers, our fathers and mothers. I dream of living in peace in this house with you, of seeing friends and cooking for them under the trellis on summer evenings, watching the ships entering the harbour. I dream of raising children, and seeing our grandchildren one day. I know they're not important dreams, but it's all that I hope for.'

Dionysius grasped her by the shoulders and looked into her eyes. 'The women of Selinus and Himera had dreams too, didn't they? And someone turned them into bloody nightmares. And even the refugees who have been spared their fate have a dream:

to return to their homes and live there the rest of their lives. All of our cities are on the coast, and they've been founded in the only suitable places for living. If they are destroyed, we have no alternative: we will vanish as though we never existed. Is that what you want, Arete? Do you want the Greeks of Sicily to disappear like phantoms? Do you want our cities to be reduced to heaps of debris, dens for wild beasts?'

'No . . .' Arete replied weakly. 'I don't want that. But I'm tired of living in anxiety. In the fear that every time there's a knock on the door, there will be someone there to give me the news that will break my heart.'

'Then we have to drive the barbarians off the island. It's the only way we can live in peace and build a future for our children. Your father and I will lead the uprising from Selinus. But time will have to pass before that happens and we can be together and enjoy life a little . . . and love.'

Arete's eyes welled up again. 'I know that there's nothing that I, or anyone else, can say that would make you change your mind; you or my father. It's incredible that the only men who count in my life agree on everything that makes me miserable . . . it must be my destiny.'

Dionysius smiled: 'If you want to know the truth, it's not quite that way this time.'

'What are you saying?'

'Your father still knows nothing about my plans.'

'I . . . don't understand.'

'He'll be told in due time.'

'That scares me even more. It sounds like utter madness.'

Dionysius touched her cheek. 'Don't worry, I know what I'm doing. When the time comes, it will all be over in a few hours.'

Arete stared at him in dismay; there were a thousand things she had to tell him, reasons to dissuade him, doubts, anxieties, fears. She managed only to say: 'Shall I make you some dinner, then?'

'Dinner?' repeated Dionysius.

'Yes or no?'

'No,' he replied. He took her into his arms and carried her upstairs to the bedroom.

*

Hermocrates struck camp three days later, and many Syracusans drew a sigh of relief when they learned that the column was headed west. No one noticed Dionysius breaking away from the others, later, on horseback. He was directed towards a place in the interior where he had arranged to meet some men from his Company. His most trusted friends were among them: Iolaus, Doricus, Biton and Philistus.

Diocles had already left Syracuse, obeying the Assembly's orders. He disappeared without leaving a trace and was never heard from again. Perhaps he was content with his success in keeping Hermocrates out of the city, or perhaps he was overcome with shame and wanted to live out his years like any ordinary man in some obscure place.

Hermocrates and his men marched for nine days until they came within sight of Selinus, where many other warriors awaited them. They were all ready to follow their commander to the ends of the earth.

Dionysius in the meantime had arrived at the site of the secret rendezvous: an abandoned tufa quarry on the road to Catane. His friends, all members of the Company, joined him a few at a time; Philistus arrived last. When they had all gathered, Dionysius posted sentries all around and began to speak.

'The Assembly's decree was scandalous,' he began, 'and Hermocrates's exile is a monstrous injustice. No formal charges have been made against him; it's just slander and suspicion that are keeping him out. In reality, he is the best of us all, a brave man whose only offence is having served his homeland faithfully. At the price of harsh sacrifice, without ever asking for anything in exchange! But this is not the point. We know for certain that the Carthaginians are preparing a new campaign for next year, and they're determined to wipe us all out this time, even Syracuse.'

'How can you be certain?' asked one of the men.

'Let me explain that,' intervened Philistus. 'One month ago a Carthaginian legation went to Athens to ensure that the city government would be continuing their war against Sparta. Why do you suppose they did that? It's quite simple: if the Athenians keep the Spartans busy in the Aegean Sea, Sparta won't be able to come to our aid as she did seven years ago. Carthage will be free to attack; and you can be sure that she will.'

'Given the situation,' continued Dionysius, 'the only man capable of leading our army in such a conflict – which I believe is inevitable – is Hermocrates. You've all seen what happened at Selinus and Himera because of the lack of determination and of a unified command. The same thing will happen in Syracuse if we continue to waste time on questions of political theory. We're talking about our survival here. Are you with me?'

All of the men nodded their assent.

'Good. Then we'll bring him back to the city.'

'That's easily said,' objected Doricus, a youth of about twenty-five with hair as red as his father's, who came from Thrace, and eyes as black as his Italian mother's.

'And not too difficult to accomplish,' replied Dionysius.

'It's madness!' shot back Iolaus, one of his most trusted men and, like Doricus, a boyhood companion. 'As soon as the people get wind of it, they'll have our heads.'

'We'll catch them unawares,' continued Dionysius without missing a beat. 'Everything can be prepared from the inside. We'll take control of the western gate and we won't open it until our scouts report that Hermocrates is ready to move in. In a matter of a few hours, the city will be in our hands. The people will just have to accept an accomplished fact.

'If we don't act, we'll just have to put up with the same rigmarole all over again – discussions that go on for days and days in the Assembly before a decision is made. And executed, at that point, by an amateur, a salted fish merchant or a naval carpenter instead of a warrior, son and grandson of warriors. Remember this, my friends: until just a short time ago, the barbarians feared us – overestimating our power, perhaps, simply because they'd seen us defeat the Athenians. But Diocles's insane behaviour has now convinced them that we're no longer capable of defending our allies, and thus incapable of defending ourselves as well. They will attack, heed my words. And they will not stop until they've exterminated us. Only Hermocrates can save us. Believe me, we have no alternative.'

'I think you're right!' exclaimed Biton, the most quarrelsome and impatient of Dionysius's companions, a strong lad always eager to come to blows and, if necessary, to take up arms.

'Who's with me, then?'

They all raised their hands.

'Excellent,' concluded Dionysius. 'We all agree. All we have to do now is put the plan into effect. But first let us renew the oath that keeps us united; the gods will curse any of us who break it. Let us vow that if any one of us should betray another, we will hunt him down until we have found him and punished him.'

All those present swore allegiance to their oath. Being part of a Company meant having important advantages in social and political life, and in the army as well, but also involved unswerving commitment. Defection could mean death.

They departed a few at a time, just as they had arrived. One by one or in small groups, they took different routes of return so as not to engender suspicion.

Philistus had not spoken during their meeting, hanging back to listen and to watch. He approached Dionysius now. 'It's hard to believe that there's not one bad apple in the bunch.'

'No one has ever been disloyal to the Company,' replied Dionysius calmly.

'The stakes have never been so high. We're talking about the destiny of the city, and perhaps of all Sicily,' observed Philistus.

'In any case, it's a risk we have to run. We can't turn back now.'

Philistus fell silent for a spell, watching the last men mounting their horses and riding off down the dusty road. He asked: 'When are you going to let Hermocrates know?'

'Tonight one of my men will set off on horseback for Selinus.'

'Will he agree to it?'

'Without hesitation. There's nothing he wants more. Returning to Syracuse is his obsession, and it would be mine as well if I found myself in his situation.'

'Have you thought of how you'll coordinate your actions with his? Everything must happen at exactly the same moment.'

'We'll use dispatch riders. But in any case, we know exactly how long it takes an army to get from Selinus to Syracuse.'

'That may be, but mark my words: this will be the crux of the whole enterprise. Dedicate your utmost attention to this problem. The rest will fall into place. When will it happen?'

'In exactly fifteen days' time. We'll attack at dawn. By sunset it will be all over.'

Philistus drew close. 'Dionysius,' he said, 'you know that I'm a man of letters, not of arms. I'd be more of a hindrance to you than anything else in this. Tell me what I can do for you.'

'Nothing. Watch what happens and ponder, so that you can pass it on to those who will come after us. This is your task. What will remain of us – after we've crossed the threshold of Hades – will be not the truthful account of our deeds, but the image that history has shaped of us. Go now, before it becomes dark.'

Philistus nodded slightly, tossed his cape over his shoulders and walked over to his horse.

*

Hermocrates received Dionysius's message written in code on a *skytale* in the Spartan tradition. Intense agitation gripped him as soon as he had read it. The tone of the message made it clear that this was an opportunity that might never offer itself again; it was essential to act at once. Although the situation demanded attentive reflection, Hermocrates allowed himself to become overwhelmed by a fierce desire to see his city once again and to reclaim his rightful position. He would take revenge on those scoundrels who had taken advantage of his absence to revoke his most inviolable rights, defaming and disgracing him in front of the people.

He tallied up the number of men available immediately: just over a thousand warriors, ready to move at his orders. The others were off in various locations conducting raids on the Carthaginian garrisons, and it would take a day or two to bring them back to base.

'I can't wait for them,' he announced. 'They will have to set off as soon as they return and join up with me in Syracuse.'

'I think you're making a mistake, *hegemon*,' protested one of his officers named Cleantes. 'Why such haste? Wouldn't it be best to wait and move out with all the troops at once, in full force?'

'No. I'm told that this is the most opportune time. It's now that we must move.'

'As you wish,' replied Cleantes. 'You know you can count on me. But I can't believe that waiting a couple of days would change matters much.'

Hermocrates seemed to hesitate, doubt worming its way into his mind. He was troubled by the thought of jeopardizing the outcome of the entire venture because of a single ill-considered decision. Then he suddenly seemed to have found a solution.

'You may be right,' he said. 'This is what we'll do: I'll leave immediately. You'll follow me at a forced march with the second contingent. You won't need to leave more than one thousand men here at Selinus. The rest you'll take with you. Not just the heavy infantry; bring the peltasts as well, and the assault troops.'

'No cavalry?'

'We won't need them. We'll be fighting on the streets, down the alleyways . . .'

'I'm not sure how many I can round up,' admitted Cleantes. 'I'll do what I can.'

'You do that. I know I can rely on you. Wish me well, my friend. My future hinges on the success of this endeavour, as does yours. But so does the future of the city, and perhaps of all Sicily.'

'Good luck, *hegemon*,' said Cleantes. 'Let us hope that our allies in the city are just as sure about what they're doing.'

The sun had not yet risen when the bugler sounded the fall-in the next morning, and before long one thousand hoplites and a hundred light infantrymen had mustered at the centre of the agora.

Hermocrates was clad in full armour; he reviewed the troops in the dark, then made a short speech.

'Men! The task which awaits us this time is much more arduous and grievous than any we have undertaken thus far: we are returning to Syracuse. But only a part of our fellow citizens are with us. The others will fight us, to the death, perhaps, and we may have to kill them. I'm afraid we have no choice. Once we have returned to Syracuse and reclaimed power, we shall wage war against the barbarians and drive them out of Sicily, but not before we make them pay for the bloodbaths at Selinus and Himera. One day, our wounds will heal and our restored prosperity will help us forget the past.

'But now we must achieve the task before us. We will be racing against time, and I refuse to hear the words "I'm tired" from any of you! We'll be marching from the first light of dawn until dark, stopping only briefly at midday to eat. We must find ourselves at the western gate of Syracuse in seven days' time. You'll be marching light; the carts will be carrying your shields. The password is "Arethusa". May the gods assist us. I have nothing more to tell you.'

Hermocrates took his spear and marched away. The men, drawn up four-across in long columns, followed him. One of the officers struck up a marching song, but the commander set such a fast pace that they all became too winded to sing and the march continued in silence for the rest of the day.

8

DIONYSIUS PUT HIS men on the alert three days before Hermocrates's planned arrival; they were to be ready to intervene at his
signal. The plan was to occupy the western gate in the Achradina
district and hold it until Hermocrates and his men had entered. At
that point, they would split up into two units. The first, commanded by Dionysius, and composed of lightly armed skirmishers,
would clear the streets of the patrols. The second, led by Iolaus
and Biton, would keep a passage open for the heavy infantry led
by Hermocrates, who would occupy the agora.

They would then attack Ortygia and arrest the leaders of the
opposition party. The people would be called to Assembly by the
heralds and informed of the change in the political situation in
the city.

Dionysius had not reckoned, however, with Hermocrates's
haste to reach Syracuse as soon as possible. His march had been
so fast that he had achieved a sizeable advantage over the second
contingent, led by Cleantes, which had left more than a day later.
Although they soon managed to make up for this delay, they still
lagged far behind the first contingent, so that as Hermocrates
approached the city, Cleantes's troops were at a full two days'
distance. Cleantes had sent scouts ahead on horseback to discover
how far Hermocrates's advance guard had progressed and to alert
them to the distance that separated them, but the mission was
unsuccessful.

The first contact between Dionysius and his father-in-law was
in code:

We are ready to act on the established day and time. It is important that you enter with your full forces: the Syracusans must have the impression that the city is occupied and in our power. If a battle should ensue in the streets, the outcome could be uncertain.

Hermocrates was once again gripped by doubt. He who had never hesitated his whole life before the enemy was assailed by uncertainty at the very moment of conducting a military coup against his own city. He realized that if he waited too long, the presence of his troops would certainly be noticed and the alarm would spread throughout the city. Perhaps the entire army would come out against him and engage his one thousand men in pitched battle, dooming them from the start. He couldn't risk the wait: he sent a coded message back to his son-in-law saying that he would be at the western gate at the established time and date; that was, the next day at dawn.

But the leaders of the city government had been informed of suspicious activity west of the city and had sent out sentries to various points of the territory, along the shores of the Anapus and on the hills, to preclude any surprises.

Hermocrates succeeded nonetheless in eluding them by moving his troops in silence, under the cover of darkness; they took up position at a very short distance from the western wall. When given the go-ahead signal, they rushed in through the gate, finding Dionysius and the men of the Company drawn up as expected, fully armed and ready to fall in at Hermocrates's orders.

Father and son-in-law embraced. 'We've finally done it!' exclaimed Hermocrates. 'We'll attack the agora together, and from there we'll assault Ortygia. If we succeed in occupying the island, we'll have control of the dockyard and harbour as well. The rest will fall into place. Are your skirmishers ready?'

'Certainly,' replied Dionysius. 'Here they are.' He presented about fifty peltasts armed with bows, arrows and short swords and carrying small Thracian half-moon-shaped shields.

'You go ahead with them to clear the road for us. Get any patrols out of the way before they can give us trouble.'

Dionysius nodded and dashed forward with his men.

Hermocrates started his men off at a run, drawn up six-across as the width of the streets allowed.

As Dionysius advanced with his peltasts, the whole district seemed strangely quiet. There was not a living soul out on the streets. A stray dog might wake up suddenly as they passed and start barking, but no one seemed to respond to that growing chorus of alarms; doors and windows remained bolted shut. Dionysius kept on running as his heart grew heavier with anxiety; he was worried over the excessive ease of their advance and by the total absence of any guard patrols making their rounds. He was almost tempted to stop, to turn back and convince Hermocrates to desist, but then he thought he was fretting over nothing, that the calm was due to the early hour. They'd surely find most of the patrols between the dockyard and Ortygia.

The colonnade which marked the entrance to the agora loomed up before him all at once, just one hundred feet away. They had to cross the vast square designated for assemblies in order to make their way across the causeway that joined Ortygia to the mainland. The columns glowed whitely in the dim light of the coming dawn, shrouded in the mist that rose from the sea.

Dionysius motioned for his men to stop and flatten themselves against the walls of the houses at the sides of the street. He called Biton and Iolaus forward and sent them to reconnoitre the area. 'Stay close to the walls and in the shadows until you reach the colonnade; if you don't see anything suspicious, whistle and we'll follow. We'll garrison the entrance and the exit to the agora until all the heavy infantry has passed, then we'll rejoin the head of the formation and advance so we can open the road to the causeway and cross over to Ortygia. Understood?'

They nodded and set off without making the slightest noise. Dionysius waited, his heart pounding, until they had reached the colonnade. At the same time, he strained to hear the cadenced step of the hoplites advancing under Hermocrates's command. A few moments later, he heard Biton's whistle: all clear.

Dionysius ran forward with his men.

'There's no one anywhere,' said Iolaus.

'That's good, but keep your eyes open.'

Dionysius divided his men into two groups. 'You come with me,' he said to the first lot. 'We'll go to the Ortygia exit. The rest of you stay here with Biton and Iolaus and wait for Hermocrates to arrive with his men. When they've all moved through, join me at the head of the column and we'll advance together again.'

A group of about twenty men followed Dionysius to the eastern exit of the agora. There was no one on the other side, either, and Dionysius took position at the foot of the colonnade to defend the hoplites' passage. It wasn't long before the head of Hermocrates's column appeared. Most of their plan had already been accomplished: the causeway to Ortygia was just a few hundred feet away and the first rays of the morning would soon be striking the gilded acroteria of the Temple of Athena at the highest point of the island. The sun's salute to Syracuse.

Instead, all hell broke loose. Just as the last of Hermocrates's men were entering the agora, columns of armed warriors – who had remained hidden until that moment in the houses lining the square – rushed in from the side streets on the right and the left, from the east and west, blocking off all exits. Thousands of arrows rained down from the rooftops of the buildings all around, loosed by invisible archers who shot into the body of men, sure to make their mark.

Dionysius reacted instantly with the men of his Company; he tried to force the eastern side of the square and open a passage towards the dockyard, but their assailants had foreseen such a move and counter-attacked vigorously with a large contingent of select troops.

Fighting broke out in every corner of the great square and, with the light of dawn, the proportions of the disaster became horribly evident. Blood flowed copiously and the ground was strewn with dead and wounded men. The vice tightened as the defenders slaughtered the warriors besieged at the centre of the vast paved square, leaving them no way out.

Hermocrates tried to gather his best men around him and to

break out of the encirclement on the right side of the square; there seemed to be a spot there where the enemy ranks were thinning. It was a difficult task to maintain a cohesive line in such a restricted place, and to keep the pressure steady throughout.

Dionysius grasped Hermocrates's intentions and ran over to back him up. He and all his men lunged forward, gripping their spears and shouting loudly to muster their courage and spur on their fellow combatants. The enemy front wavered under the thrust of those desperate men and began to falter. Dionysius lashed out with his sword in close hand-to-hand combat, downing three adversaries one after another. Intuiting the chance of breaking out of the trap, his comrades began to push forth forcefully from behind their shields, providing the front-line fighters with a surge of power. They finally succeeded in overwhelming the enemy and Dionysius's men sought escape towards the western quarters of Achradina. But just at that instant one of the enemy officers realized what was happening and took aim with a javelin from a distance of about twenty feet; he let fly straight at Hermocrates, who stood enveloped in the light of the dawning sun, and struck him full in the chest.

His heart pierced, Hermocrates crashed to the ground and a cry of dismay arose from his men, who nonetheless continued to fight with unflagging fury, driven on by the sight of their fallen commander as they fought now to avenge him.

Dionysius had nearly fought his way out of the square when he turned back to see what was happening and a sword's blade sank into his right shoulder. He dropped the weapon he was carrying with a howl of pain and found the strength to fell the man who had wounded him with a great swing of his shield. Iolaus seized him before he could fall and dragged him off, leaving a stream of blood in their wake.

They stopped, panting, under the shadow of an archivolt which opened between two narrow side streets. From there they could hear the screams echoing between the city walls like the bellowing of cattle being slaughtered.

Iolaus propped him up and grabbed him under an arm, urging

him to walk. 'They'll be out here searching for survivors in no time! We have to get away while we can.'

Dionysius leaned against a wall and was suddenly overcome by a terrible thought. 'Oh gods, Arete!'

'What?'

'I have to reach my wife. She's at home alone and they all know by now that I've taken part in this assault. This ambush was the work of a traitor.'

'You need a doctor, now, or you'll never make it.'

'No, my wife first. Help me, please.'

'All right,' panted Iolaus. 'But I have to take care of this wound or you'll bleed to death.' He ripped a strip of fabric off his cloak, wrapped it tightly over the gash and secured it with one of the straps from his shield. Then they set off.

People had begun pouring into the city streets, running every which way, with absolutely no idea of what was happening. Government heralds appeared at the street corners, publicly proclaiming Hermocrates's and Dionysius's attempted coup a failure, and promising generous rewards for anyone who captured the survivors or reported their whereabouts.

'I told you,' hissed Iolaus.

'I know, I know, but you have to help me . . . I'm afraid . . .'

Iolaus looked over at him: his face was ashen, and he was icy cold. He groaned with every step he took and was sweating copiously. Iolaus made him stop again and again so he could catch his breath. At the bottom of the little hill that led up to his house, Dionysius stopped, leaning heavily against the shrine to Hecate that always stood at the meeting of three roads. When he pushed off, he left a wide swathe of blood on the wall.

They had to stop again, to avoid a group of Syracusan soldiers on patrol, searching for fugitives. Any who were found were immediately executed. Bands of ruffians were already roaming the city, hunting out the houses of the conspirators to plunder and devastate them.

The house with the trellis was close now and Dionysius was seized by unbearable anguish. Iolaus propped him against the enclosure wall. 'You wait here,' he said, 'I'll go ahead; there may be someone waiting inside to kill you.' He approached the gate of the garden at the back of the house, entered from the rear door and made his way towards the atrium, checking all around. As soon as his eyes had become accustomed to the dim light, his face twisted into a grimace of horror. He wheeled around to rush back outside, but he found Dionysius close behind him, pale as death, unsteady on his feet. 'There's no one left inside,' said Iolaus, trying to appear normal. 'Let's go now, we have to find you a doctor. You can't even stand up.' But his eyes were still full of the horror he had seen.

Dionysius understood and pushed aside his arm. 'Let me through.'

'Please . . .' begged his friend, no longer able to hold back his tears. 'Please, Dionysius, don't go in there.'

But Dionysius had pushed past the threshold, and was already in the house. Iolaus soon heard his voice, rent by horror, howling meaningless words. He could hear his sobs echoing from the bloodied, befouled walls. Iolaus came close but did not dare touch him or say a word. Dionysius was on his knees in front of the naked body of his wife and was weeping disconsolately.

Arete was nearly unrecognizable; she had been raped to death. She lay in a repugnant pool of semen, blood and spit. Her face was swollen, her lips cracked, her body full of cuts and bruises. They had even cut her hair off, like a prostitute's.

Dionysius took her into his arms and held her close, swaying back and forth as if to rock her gently to sleep. He abandoned himself to a mournful, heartbroken keening, like the whimpering of a wounded animal.

'Let's leave,' pleaded Iolaus. 'They'll be back looking for you, you can be sure of it. You have to save yourself, Dionysius. You have to save yourself to avenge this horror.'

Dionysius started at the sound of his friend's voice. 'You're right,' he said. 'She will be revenged. I will find them, one by one. I will hunt them down and kill them all. But I can't leave her here . . . I can't let her body suffer any more insults . . .'

'She suffers no longer, Dionysius, and if she could she would tell you to save yourself.'

He brushed her forehead with his fingertips. 'Help me to bring her downstairs, I beg of you. There's a hiding place in the cellar. I'll wait there with her and I'll keep her company – she always was afraid of the dark.'

Iolaus helped him, bearing almost all of the weight of the girl's lifeless body, because Dionysius looked as if he would pass out at any moment. They lifted a trapdoor, went down a few steps and found themselves underground.

Dionysius pointed at a passageway that led to a room dug into the tufa, hidden behind shelves which held wine amphoras. 'Now,' he said, 'go up to the attic. You'll find a chest with clean clothes. Take off your armour and change; wash your face. You'll manage to get by unobserved. Go to Philistus: he lives in Ortygia, in the house with the portico behind the Arethusa spring. Tell him I'm waiting for him here.'

Iolaus nodded. 'I know where his house is. Promise me you won't move or do anything rash. Keep as still as you can. I'm going to get you some water – you must be burning up with thirst.'

Dionysius said nothing. He was crouched near the wall, cradling Arete's body close as if he could warm her. Iolaus brought him water, changed and left.

He returned a couple of hours later, just fifty steps in front of Philistus and the doctor, so as not to attract attention. They found Dionysius unconscious, still embracing Arete. Philistus could not hold back his tears and stood there stock-still, in silence, overcome by emotion. The doctor came in, and they moved Dionysius to the bedroom and stretched him out on the bed. He was still breathing but his heartbeat was very weak; his body was cold and his lips livid. They stripped off his clothing and uncovered the gash that the sword had opened between his shoulder and pectoral muscle.

'It's a miracle it didn't shear through the tendons of his arm, or the big vein right here,' said the doctor, pointing his surgical instrument at a point under his collar bone. 'Hold him still.'

Philistus and Iolaus immobilized his arms while the doctor

washed out the wound with wine and vinegar. He then heated the iron until it was red hot, on the fire he'd built using the flame from his lantern. He cauterized the inner part of the wound which was still bleeding and started to stitch up the cut. Dionysius was so exhausted that he didn't move a whit. He only let out a long groan when the doctor scorched his flesh.

'He must rest now. I've done everything I can; the rest is in the hands of the gods. I only hope the wound does not become gangrenous.'

Philistus took him aside. 'You must speak with no one of what you've done here. If you keep quiet, you won't regret it; we'll find a way to recompense you well.'

The doctor nodded and reached out to take the money Philistus was holding out for him: five silver coins with the image of Arethusa circled by dolphins.

'What shall we do with the girl's body?' whispered Iolaus.

Philistus sighed. 'For the time being we'll bury her here underground, until it becomes possible to celebrate funeral rites for her and bury her in a tomb worthy of her rank and of Dionysius's love for her.'

They laid her in a grave dug in the tufa and Philistus tried to keep back his tears as he murmured: 'Welcome her, O Demeter and Persephone, into the Asphodel fields, let her drink the waters of Lethe so that she may forget the horrors of this ferocious world and may find peace, awaiting the day in which she will be rejoined with the only man she loved in her life.'

They went back up to Dionysius's room and waited until it became dark. Philistus had already organized everything. One of his servants drove up on a hay-laden cart pulled by a couple of mules; he entered from the garden, shielded by the enclosure wall. They laid Dionysius on the cart, covering him with a sheet and then with the hay.

The cart headed towards the western gate, guarded at that moment by two members of the Company, ready to kill the other two sentries who were on duty with them if they should become too diligent in checking the people and goods seeking passage.

It was not necessary. The cart was allowed to pass the gate untouched, and the driver directed it to the shores of the Anapus, where a boat was waiting for them. It travelled up-current, amidst dense cane thickets.

Late that night, in a city fallen silent after a day of bloodshed and wailing, a song was heard rising up near the house with the trellis, a hymn to love; an ancient wedding melody, sweet and heart-rending in that desolate and profaned place; the last homage of a fugitive near death, a serenade for his lost love.

*

None of those who participated in the unhappy endeavour were spared. All of the prisoners who belonged to the hated caste of the landowners and who had been exiled from Syracuse were executed. Those who had followed Hermocrates in the hopes of seeing the cities of Selinus and Himera liberated and rebuilt were not put to death immediately, but condemned to long years of prison.

Dionysius was sentenced to death in his absence, since no trace of him had ever been found. Philistus artfully spread the word that he had died of his wounds and that his body had been secretly cremated at night by his friends along the marshy shores of the Cyanes.

A new popular leader rose up in the Assembly: his name was Daphnaeus and he boasted of killing more than twenty enemies during the terrible morning of the battle in the agora. He proclaimed that their victory had forever sanctioned the triumph of democracy and that no one would ever again dare aspire to tyranny in the future.

Daphnaeus's boasting encouraged others to brag in the port taverns of how they had got their thrills between the thighs of that little whore, the daughter of the traitor Hermocrates. No one would have ever been so bold as to say such a thing about a woman who still had a husband or father or brother, but Arete's memory was undefended and so anyone could get away with saying anything about her. But Philistus had eyes and ears everywhere, and plenty of money to spend: he was a wealthy man, and the Company had put their treasury in his hands as well. On the basis of the information he was getting, he diligently made a list of first and last names, addresses, professions, friends and associates, along with anything else he was able to gather.

Despite the losses it had suffered, the Company was in fact still strong and numerous, and when the news came out in great secret that Dionysius was alive and hiding in an inaccessible spot in the mountains, many offered to put themselves at his service.

*

At the same time, Philistus sent a trusted messenger named Demetrius to Asia to inform Dionysius's younger brother Leptines, who lived in Ephesus, about what had happened.

A slave opened the door to his house, saying that his master was not in.

'Well, where is he?' demanded the envoy.

'I don't know; when he goes out at night, he never says where he's going.'

Demetrius sighed. 'I suppose that means I'll wait for him here until he gets back. It's a matter of the greatest urgency! You may as well bring me something to eat in the meantime, seeing as I haven't had supper.'

The slave was reluctant to let the stranger in, but he didn't have the courage to keep him out either. So he served him a plate of olives and a chunk of bread.

Demetrius began to eat, accompanying the food with a few sips of wine from his own flask. 'Does he usually get back late?' he asked.

'Usually not before morning,' admitted the slave.

But Leptines arrived shortly thereafter, panting, and bolted the door behind him. 'Who are you, friend?' he asked, without showing any surprise.

'My name is Demetrius and Philistus has sent me to tell you that . . .'

But as he was speaking, Leptines had already opened a chest

and was stuffing some clothes into a sack. 'You'll tell me about it on our way out of here. This city has become impossible! Have you got a boat?'

'Yes, the one that brought me here . . .'

'Good. Let's get moving then. Husbands around here can get very touchy when they find you in bed with their wives. Even violent sometimes!'

They rushed out as the slave was shouting: 'Master, what am I to do?'

'Nothing!' shouted back Leptines. 'If anyone shows up, tell them I've gone. Keep anything you want from the house, and may the gods assist you!'

They had just rounded the street corner when a group of men armed with clubs reached the building and burst inside.

The two fugitives ran at breakneck speed down the dark streets of the city until they reached Demetrius's boat, secured to the wharf with a couple of ropes.

'The gangplank!' ordered Demetrius, who had taken stock of the urgency of the situation.

The sailor on guard recognized him and lowered the gangplank to the ground so that they were able to scramble on board to safety.

Leptines drew a long breath, sat on a bench and, as if nothing had happened, turned to Demetrius. 'Well then? How are things going in Syracuse?'

Demetrius turned to him with a serious expression. 'Badly,' he replied. 'It couldn't be worse. Your brother needs your help.'

Leptines frowned. 'We won't be able to set sail for a couple of hours. Tell me everything.'

Demetrius's boat dropped anchor at the Laccius harbour ten days later, and Leptines hurried to Philistus's house.

'Where is Dionysius?' he asked even before he had entered.

Philistus gestured for him to lower his voice and accompanied him into his study. 'He's safe.'

'I asked you where he is,' insisted Leptines with a peremptory tone.

'I can't tell you,' replied Philistus. 'It's too dangerous. How long do you think your arrival in the city will remain a secret? If you wanted to find out where he was, who would you keep your eye on, knowing that his wife is dead?'

Leptines understood what Philistus was trying to tell him and gave up.

*

The night after the battle at the agora, Dionysius was handed over to friends from the Company who transported him by boat along the Anapus river for as long as possible, rowing against the current at first and then hitching it up to an ass, which ploddingly towed the boat along the shore. When the terrain along the river bed became too rough, his friends bought another ass from a farmer, fashioned a litter and laid the wounded man upon it, securing the frame to the two animals, one in front and the other behind. They continued slowly, avoiding violent jolts, all the way to the source of the river.

The place was enchanting: a spring of crystalline water in the middle of a meadow full of multihued oleander blossoms and intensely scented broom. It was surrounded by towering rock walls perforated by a great number of niches dug by the most ancient inhabitants of those lands to bury their dead close to the sky.

Someone had been told to expect their arrival. A rough-hewn frame was lowered to the ground with a creaky pulley by the light of the moon. His friends laid Dionysius gently upon it and tied him on to it with leather straps, then shouted up to have him hoisted. They watched as the fragile bed of intertwining sticks swayed in the void over their heads. It reached a dizzying height and was pulled into a recess in the rock, as dark and gloomy as the eye socket in a skull.

The men had managed to bring the task assigned them to completion with skill and shrewdness, and they headed back now to report to Philistus on the outcome. Dionysius was in good hands, in a shelter as hard to reach as an eagle's nest, in the middle of the mountains. The man whose care he had been entrusted to was a native Sicel from the interior, a medicine man venerated and respected by his people. Philistus trusted him more than he did the doctors of Syracuse; although they were expert surgeons, accustomed as they were to cleaning, cauterizing and stitching up the wounds of the warriors returning from the battlefield, they were not as good at curing the insidious infections that could burgeon from a wound.

Dionysius lay between life and death in that isolated place for days and days, often sunk in a deep slumber provoked by his severe loss of blood, helped along by the sleeping potions that the old Sicel mixed up for him with wild honey. When he finally regained consciousness, the first sensations that struck him were a circle of light crossed by clouds and by birds in flight, the twittering of skylarks, the fragrance of broom and the song of a woman that seemed to come from inside the solid rock that surrounded him.

Then she appeared to him: her skin was golden from the sun, her eyes and hair were pitch-black and she had the curious, fleeting glance of a wild creature.

9

THE STRANGE APPARITION vanished instantly. Perhaps she had been a figment of a dream. Or perhaps one of the many likenesses that Arete took on to visit him when his soul was stabbed by the thought of her.

He fell back with a groan on to his bed and probed his wound with his left hand. The scar was still sore to the touch, but almost dry. He touched his face as well and realized that his beard had grown long and thick. He was so weak that any movement made him break out in a sweat and strained the beating of his heart. He found a bowl of water and drank it down in big gulps, then dragged himself to the opening of his strange refuge and looked outside.

He found himself on the rim of a precipice. Down below, the sun flashed intermittently on a pool of pure water at the centre of an expanse of flowers. The long branches of a plane tree stretching over the spring swayed in the wind, intercepting the golden reflections of the sun. Dionysius felt dizzy, sucked in by that luminous abyss. He felt that he might at any moment plunge down like a lark inebriated by the sun, thus banishing the intolerable anguish that rose from his heart as he realized how bottomless his solitude had become.

He was yanked back by a hairy hand and a sharp voice calling him back to reality. 'If you want to die, you'll have to wait until after your friends have paid me. I promised I'd give you back in one piece.'

'Who are you?' asked Dionysius. 'What is this place?'

'It's no affair of yours who I am. This, my friend, is a cemetery.

Just the right place for someone given up as dead.' He spoke a rough but understandable Greek, with a heavy Sicilian accent.

'How long have I been here?'

'A month. And it will take another month before you're back on your feet.'

'I want to go down there by the water; I think it would do me good. I can imagine the scent of those flowers. And I need to bathe – the smell in this place is revolting.'

The old man set down a basket with some bread and cheese. 'Eat. You worry about getting your strength back and I'll let you go down there very soon. Use the water in that bag to wash for now,' he said, pointing at a goatskin hanging from a nail.

'Has no one come looking for me?'

'More then once. But you were in no condition to see or to hear. The man who had you brought here will be coming tomorrow.'

'Philistus?'

The old man nodded. He looked Dionysius over once and then left through a crevice at the end of the cave, closing a kind of wooden gate behind him.

Dionysius waited until he had gone, then plucked the cork out of the goatskin and poured the water over himself, savouring the pleasure of that rudimentary bath. He ate and then, exhausted again, stretched out and fell deeply asleep.

Philistus arrived the next day towards evening and was brought to Dionysius's refuge. They embraced each other warmly, but then fell silent; neither of the two wanted to let the lump in his throat betray his emotion.

It was Philistus who spoke first. 'Your brother's back, have you heard? We're busy preparing for your return and—'

'Who did it?' growled Dionysius.

'Listen . . . you must listen to me, understand? I've always given you the right advice, haven't I? Do not allow yourself to be driven by rage; you mustn't take what happened personally. What happened was political, can't you see that? Whoever unleashed those dogs wanted to ruin you, to annihilate you, even if you managed to survive the wounds on your body. They are only too aware of your courage, of your will power. They know how you, your ideas, hold the people in sway, especially the young. And they're afraid of you. They know that no one could stand up to you in the Assembly.'

'I want their names,' repeated Dionysius in a low voice.

'I've gathered information,' replied Philistus after a few moments' hesitation. 'But if I tell you, do you promise you won't act on your own without consulting me first?'

'I can promise,' replied Dionysius. 'But the fact is that I want them all dead. From the first to the last. That I refuse to discuss. If you want to help me, I'll be grateful. If you want to stay out of it, I'll do it myself. You . . . you weren't there when we found her . . . you can't imagine . . . you don't know what I feel every time I open my eyes and realize that it all really happened.' He broke off because his voice failed him, and his head dropped to his chest.

'Iolaus told me everything. I cared deeply for Arete myself, you know, I loved her like a sister and I'm tormented by the thought that I wasn't able to protect her. Everything fell apart at once, understand? There was no time to organize; the military succeeded in keeping their plan secret until the very end. Not a thing filtered through, can you believe me? I knew they were watching me and so I couldn't run certain risks. They're well aware that I'm your friend, so I have to prove that I've got the State's best interests at heart without letting personal matters interfere. Otherwise I never would have been able to continue helping you, nor could I help you now. Dionysius, believe me, the horror of what happened keeps me from sleeping, it gives me no peace nor respite . . .'

'I'm not blaming you. I'm grateful for what you've done for me. I owe you my life. But I must do what my honour demands and my religion orders. Arete's shade must be appeased. I am sure that she has not found peace . . . she's suffering . . . she's cold. She's always cold, and she's afraid of the dark . . .' He lifted his eyes. 'She calls me, you know? And she comes to visit me in my dreams. Yesterday she appeared to me in the guise of a wild woman. She was suspended in thin air, right there, in front of that opening. Only a spirit can float in the air . . . isn't that so?'

He was irrational; Philistus looked at him, trying to hide the compassion he felt, pretending not to see the tears streaming down his bristly cheeks.

Dionysius stared straight into his eyes: 'They must die. Die a slow and very painful death. Well then, are you with me?'

'I'm with you, of course I am,' replied Philistus. 'How could I not be? But I implore you, accept my advice. Listen to me: the Company is still strong and we have men in important positions both in the army and the city administration. Among the clergy as well. I told you, I've gathered information. I know who her executioners were, and I know who sent them. Money opens a lot of mouths. But there are other problems.

'It appears that the Carthaginians mean to attack next spring, and it's Acragas's turn to be worried: they're on the border now. I've received a message from Tellias; he says that he has learned that they will almost certainly attack in great numbers with a powerful fleet. He has already taken action, though. He has convinced eight hundred of the Campanian mercenaries garrisoned on Carthaginian territory to come over to Acragas. He's paid them in person, an enormous amount. As you know, money's no obstacle for him.

'What I'm concerned about is the position of Syracuse. If we don't strike the right policy in this war, if we let Acragas fall, it will be Gela next and then us, there's no doubt about it. So first of all and above all, Dionysius, we must prepare your return to the city.'

'I imagine there's a price on my head.'

'No. You're dead. People have testified to that before the authorities.'

'Well, dead men don't come back.'

'That's not always so. There's a law – although most of your fellow citizens ignore its existence – that says that when a man is given up as dead without a will in his name, his worldly goods go to his closest heirs, if he has any, otherwise they are confiscated by the State. That's why I had your brother Leptines return from Asia. If this supposedly "dead" man should, by chance, reappear, he can no longer claim rights to anything, not even his citizenship, unless . . .'

'Unless what?' asked Dionysius, his curiosity aroused by that sequence of improbable events, and by Philistus's formidable ability to come up with new strategies.

'Unless he's adopted by someone. In this case, he regains full access to his functions and rights, and what's more, he becomes untouchable. It's assumed that a man given up as dead by everyone, who then turns up alive, is manifesting the will of the gods, and no one will dare challenge that. His reappearance and adoption, in other words, are considered the same as a second birth.'

'Who would ever want to adopt someone like me?'

Philistus smiled. 'Do you remember Heloris, the horse breeder?'

'Yes. He helped me in the Council when I needed them to approve the departure of my contingent for Selinus.'

'That's right. It was no problem to convince him. He said he'd be happy and honoured to adopt you because he admires you greatly. So that much is done. This is my plan: you will remain here until you have completely recovered your strength. At that point, I'll arrange for you to return to the city in secret; you'll be able to obtain justice over those who have offended you. When you've got them all out of the way, I'll organize your comeback, which will take everyone by surprise.'

Dionysius fell silent, fascinated and still unbelieving at such skilful manoeuvring. He was above all comforted by this demonstration of such deep, faithful friendship. He hugged his friend without saying a word, but the force of those arms expressed what he felt in his heart and Philistus understood.

'Take care and don't do anything foolish,' he said. 'I'll be back as soon as I can.'

Dionysius nodded and watched as he walked past the gate.

Just before leaving, Philistus turned towards him again. 'Listen

... what you saw ... I don't think it was Arete, you know. There's this poor wretch who lives all alone here in this necropolis. She lost her parents when she was just a child and she's grown up wild in this cemetery. The people who live around here believe she's a spirit because she appears and disappears like a ghost and she climbs all over these cliffs like a spider. You know how superstitious the Sicels are ... Take care, my friend.'

*

Dionysius made his way down to the spring at the bottom of the chasm ten days later. It felt like being born again: plunging nude into that pure water, breathing in the fragrance of all those flowers, feeling the sun's caress on his shoulders, the wind in his hair. The spot was blindingly beautiful, completely isolated by the towering cliffs which surrounded it on almost all sides. And deserted as well; the local religion severely prohibited access to the valley of the Anapus except during the annual festivities at the end of the summer. A colossal plane tree stood on the shore, its branches stretching out to skim the surface of the water. Some of the boughs were so big they seemed trees themselves, and nurtured countless birds' nests scattered here and there among the leafy fronds. Their song mixed with the chirping of crickets, the only sounds to be heard echoing between the rocky walls covered with blonde broom. A garden as enchanting and secluded as Elysium!

Dionysius felt life flowing through his veins again and strength swelling his muscles. The spring must possess miraculous powers, he thought, that could restore his vigour. He stretched out on the clean, sandy shore to dry in the sun and abandoned himself to a wave of memories. He listened to a nightingale's warbling, and thought he recognized the melody of the last serenade sung for his lost bride – the last notes he had heard before pain made him lose consciousness, before he'd had to leave his city under cover, like a scoundrel.

If only Arete could join him for but an instant! If only he had the gift of song, like Orpheus, so he could move harsh Persephone to let his beloved return to the surface, emerging from the crystal lake into the light of the sun, just for an instant, oh gods, for even just an instant!

He was startled instead by a rustling of leaves and there was the creature, crouched in a fork of the branches at an incredible height. She was watching him, seemingly more curious than afraid. She was a frightful sight to see, her hair tangled and dirty and so long it covered her face and most of her body. Her skin had the dark cast of one who is constantly exposed to the sun and her feet were grey with dust and calluses.

Dionysius turned away and closed his eyes, seized by sudden weariness. When he opened them, the little valley was already in shadow and the long-haired creature was sitting on a lower branch, her feet dangling near the water. She must have been guarding him the whole time he slept, to judge from the number of plane leaves that she had plucked off to while away the time, floating now on the water like a fleet of tiny vessels pushed along by the evening breeze.

He got to his feet without covering himself, feeling as if he were in the presence of an animal rather than a human being. 'Who are you?' he asked. 'Have you got a name?'

The sound of his first word was enough to scare her off. She fled through the branches of the tree with great agility, then jumped to the ground and began to scale the rock wall. Her limbs stretched out over the cliff with incredible grace and dexterity, apparently without effort and certainly without fear. She would hang between two outcroppings and then, with a little swing, abandon one and grab the other, hoisting herself, with a single arm at times, up to the next hold without a worry for the abyss that yawned beneath her.

She vanished all at once, swallowed up into one of the many dark openings that studded the rock face, leaving her observer open-mouthed with wonder.

Dionysius gathered up the nearly dry tunic that he had attempted to wash in the spring, put it on and set off at a slow pace back up to his refuge. He found his usual dinner of bread, cheese and beans and, for the first time, a jug of wine. He drank it with pleasure, although it was quite tart, and he felt warmed by the potent dark red liquid. But now that he could get around and he felt his strength coming back, the place he found himself in seemed an unbearable prison. He could think of nothing but those who he wanted dead but who were still alive, and every moment of their illicit living seemed an intolerable offence. Dionysius longed to leave, but he had no idea how to escape the place and he realized that, if he were recognized, all the efforts of those who still cared about him would be thwarted.

He forced himself to kill time by exercising and swimming in the chilly waters of the spring below, until one day he saw the mysterious inhabitant of the valley again. She was sitting on a jutting rock, her feet swinging over the void at a great height. He was struck by the idea that he could do the same thing: climb up to the little cave that he had been living in for so long.

He began to scale the rock wall slowly, ignoring the pain in his right shoulder, scratching his feet and hands on the rough crags, under the curious gaze of the creature. When he had made his way about ten feet up, the girl took fright and disappeared, but Dionysius continued to climb the wall, biting his lips to suffocate the pain while the strain became almost unbearable. He did not even understand why he was doing it, but he continued to attack the bare rock, increasingly steep now, as if danger didn't exist, in a senseless game which put his very life at stake.

He finally found himself at a spot from which it was impossible to descend and impossible to go up. He turned around and saw the chasm; he felt the void crushing his lungs, fatigue assailing his muscles with painful cramps, and he knew that he would soon be dead, smashed to pieces on the bottom of that abyss. But it made no difference at all. He was no longer afraid of anything. And he made the move that only a man who cared nothing for his life could make: he let go, imagining that he could manage to seize a rocky outcropping about twenty feet below him. But as soon as he had slackened his grip, a hand closed around his wrist like a talon and, with incredible strength, began to hoist him up. The creature's legs were wrapped around the trunk of a wild fig tree growing out of the rock above him; hanging head down, she had grabbed him at the last moment, slipping out of some hidden crevice. She pulled him up to a point from which he could continue his ascent without great danger, then she let herself drop down, and completed the move that he would certainly have failed. In a few moments she had reached the bottom with the agile bearing of a wild feline, and disappeared into the shadows of the plane tree.

He didn't see her again for a very long time, but he was certain that she was watching him. Perhaps even as he slept.

One day, when Dionysius felt close to being completely healed, he witnessed an event that moved him deeply: the great native Feast of the Three Mothers. His guardian had made him promise not to descend to the valley for any reason in the world if his life meant anything to him. He was to remain hidden in his refuge for the entire duration of the ceremony. He watched it all from that privileged position in the highest part of the rock wall.

Dionysius saw a long line of men and women of all ages walking along the Anapus valley to the spring, preceded by those who must have been the high priests. They were venerable old men with white beards wearing full-length tunics of raw wool, who advanced leaning on carved staffs from which bronze bells hung, jingling with their every step. Behind them were the images of the Three Mothers: rough-hewn wooden statues whose shapes were difficult to make out, but which seemed to be seated women nursing two infants each at their enormous breasts. Each statue was borne by six men on their shoulders, and swayed back and forth with the uneven terrain. A group of players with reed pipes, drums and rattles filled the narrow valley with their jarring music. When the procession reached the spring, the statues were deposited on the ground in the shade of the plane tree. The priests drew water from the spring using wooden bowls and sprinkled it on the images of the Three Mothers, chanting a rhythmic, unvaried tune made up of long, low notes. Once the rite was over, one of the priests, who seemed to be presiding, made a gesture and a long line of very young girls came forward. Each girl approached the three statues and knelt before each one of them in turn, laying her forehead on the goddess's lap, perhaps to receive a fertility blessing.

The music became more intense and the tone of the singing higher and more acute when, all at once, the sound of a horn echoed hard and long in the valley and a number of youths who had remained hidden until then came forth. Each boy took a girl by the hand and led her to a spot in the middle of the thickets of oleanders, myrtle and broom. The music of drums, pipes and cymbals increased sharply in intensity until it became an uproar amplified and multiplied beyond measure by the surrounding walls.

Dionysius imagined that that barbaric clamour was meant to accompany the mating rites of those young men who had withdrawn with their chosen virgins, and certainly this was close to the truth. That primitive people, who lived contentedly on the meagre offerings of their mountains, thus celebrated that which all the peoples of the world celebrate in different yet similar ways, the most intense and mysterious, most frenetic and consuming moment of human existence: the love that joins a man and a woman and perpetuates life.

When night fell and the valley filled with campfires and with the monotonous chanting of the poor shepherds, Dionysius thought of Arete's description of the fires of Acragas and of the invisible singer who had struck up his wedding hymn amidst the radiant temples on the hill. He felt ever keener grief for his woman, violated and murdered, bitter regret for his lost love.

10

Philistus came to fetch him at the end of the month and accompanied him, disguised, to Acragas, leaving him in Tellias's care in the interim before his return. As he was about to leave, he left him a tablet. 'A gift,' he said.

'What is it?' asked Dionysius.

'The list,' replied Philistus. 'Complete. Every single one. It wasn't simple or easy, but there they are, all of them. Including the instigators.' He bid Dionysius farewell and left.

Tellias approached and placed a hand on his shoulder. 'A list of the living or the dead?' he asked.

'Dead men,' replied Dionysius, reading the list. 'Dead men who are still walking. But not for long.'

'Take care!' replied Tellias. 'Revenge can be a balm for an embittered soul, but it can also set off a chain of bloodshed without end.'

'I don't think so,' replied Dionysius. 'I can kill many of them; they only have me to kill. I have the advantage, no matter how you look at it.'

He returned to Syracuse at night, at the end of the following month. He met with Philistus at Biton's house. Dionysius embraced both of them, one after the other, without a word. It was always his way of reacting to powerful emotion.

'Finally!' exclaimed Biton. 'I thought you'd never come back. How are you?'

'Better,' replied Dionysius, 'now that I'm home.'

'There's a person here who can't wait to see you,' said Philistus. He opened the door to a room facing the atrium and

Leptines appeared. The two brothers stood without saying a word at first, then clasped each other close.

'You've been through hell and high water,' said Philistus, 'but it seems you have nothing to say to each other!'

Leptines pulled away from his brother and looked him over from head to toe. 'By the gods!' he said, 'I feared much worse! You look wonderful.'

'So do you,' replied Dionysius.

'I know how badly things have gone for you,' started up Leptines again. 'I'm sorry. I wish I could have . . .'

'Your presence wouldn't have changed things much, I'm afraid . . . I'm happy to see you.'

'As am I, by Heracles! Together again like when we were boys. Remember when we used to lie in wait to pelt the lads from Ortygia with stones?'

'I surely do,' replied Dionysius with a smile.

'Well, things are going to change now that I'm back . . . in fine style! I'm spoiling for a fight. Who shall we start with?'

Dionysius pulled him aside and whispered something in his ear.

'I know,' nodded Leptines. 'I'll wait.'

Dionysius left them and remained hidden for some time thereafter, alternating between the houses of Iolaus, Doricus and Biton so as not to put Leptines or Philistus in danger. He did not cut his hair or his beard and went out only at night, wrapped in a cloak which covered his sword and dagger. He studied the moves of his enemies, spying on their habits and routes. When he felt sure, he called on Leptines: 'I'm ready, but I need help. Are you up to it?'

'Are you joking? I can't wait, man.'

'Fine. You'll help me to catch them, but the rest I'll do myself, understood?'

'Of course I understand. Let's get moving, then.'

They went out that night and the nights after that, silent, unexpected, invisible, inexorable. And they captured them, one by one. It was easy, because none of them expected it and they had taken no precautions.

One was called Hipparcus.

The second Eudossus.

The third Augias.

They managed to take them alive and Dionysius dragged them, alone, as they had decided, to the cellar of the house with the trellis. He laid them out in the place where Arete was buried, bound their hands and feet and cut off their genitals. He left them to bleed to death slowly. Their cries rose distorted and suffocated from that place, like the howling of beasts or the groaning of ghosts in the deep of the night, but instead of attracting someone who could help them, they scared the locals to death and gave rise to terrifying rumours which spread through the entire city.

Another two of them were murdered on the street as they walked home from a party. They were called Clitus and Protogenes. Their swollen, fish-eaten corpses were found in an inlet of the Great Harbour. Their genitals were missing as well, but the cut was too clean to blame the fish.

At that point the others began to realize that someone was making his way down a list with his sword's edge: only one man would be so single-minded. They met to devise a plan of defence.

There were six of them left: Philippus, Anattorius, Schedius, Calistemus, Gorgias and Callicrates. All prided themselves at being good with their fists. Four were single and two married. They decided to live together for a while and to bring in abundant supplies of weapons and food. They resolved that one of them in turn would always guard the others while they slept, so there would be no possibility of catching them by surprise.

They stayed awake far into the night, fearful of the unconsciousness of sleep, too similar to death. They tried to keep up their spirits by eating and drinking; sometimes they would invite some girls to keep them company so they could fuck themselves into a state of exhaustion and forget about the threat of death hanging over their heads. But sooner or later their talk always turned to that subject, sometimes with a scoffing, cocky tone, sometimes in a whisper, muttering oaths under their breath.

'We won't be slaughtered like lambs!' boasted Anattorius. 'There are six of us and that bastard is all alone: what's there to be afraid of?'

'Alone?' retorted Schedius. 'Who says he's alone? How did one man alone manage to kill five of us, all quick with their swords and their knives? All big, burly men, used to fighting on the front line and holding a shield steady for hours.'

'It's stupid to waste time talking about it,' insisted Gorgias. 'All we have to do is hold out and watch each other's backs. He'll come out of hiding sooner or later and we'll get the bastard and make him pay for what he's done. Or else he'll realize that he hasn't got a chance against us and just give up. If he's smart, he'll lay low. This city is a more dangerous place for him than it is for us. I say that if we manage to keep out of his way for a month, he'll call it quits. It's just not worth it to him to risk his own neck.'

'You know,' added Callicrates, 'we may just be worrying ourselves over nothing. Maybe he doesn't know we were there; maybe he thinks he's already got his due . . .'

But they soon grew tired of the sound of their voices and silence got the better of them, one by one. Their memories of the rape mixed with the images of their friends' bodies, rot-green and swollen as toads in the still waters of the Great Harbour.

Once they even considered the opportunity of offering to pay the killer off, but no one was convinced.

'I don't think there's enough money in the whole city to calm that maniac down,' Schedius cut the others short. He was the one who knew Dionysius best. 'The only coins he'll accept are our balls, served up on a platter like boiled eggs. Anyone ready to make the sacrifice?'

They all burst into coarse, ominous laughter and no one brought up the subject again.

They continued as they had decided: every night, one of them in turn stood guard on the roof, crouching in the dark while the others slept, until the next man came to relieve him. Some time passed without anything happening and they began to think that their nightmare was really over and that the danger had been put to rest.

Instead, on a night with a full moon, Gorgias – who was standing sentry on the roof – was pierced by an arrow loosed with incredible precision from a neighbouring house. He died then and there. Just before the second guard shift, flames rose from every corner of the house and flared up high, driven by a land wind. The other five men were burnt alive, while the blaze menaced the nearby houses. It was only put out thanks to the hundreds of people who rushed to the scene and passed buckets of water and of sand that whole night and the next day.

The only two left on the list were the instigators, who no longer had any doubts about the nature of those deaths. It had become public knowledge that the night before the fire, three amphoras of pitch had disappeared from a warehouse at the port, near the dry dock, and that the unmistakeable stench of sulphur had been smelled just before the flames had blazed up. They had no illusions about the end that awaited them if they did not take immediate action. They were two important members of the democratic party called Euribiades and Pancrates, and they appealed to Daphnaeus – who had political control of the Assembly and was their party leader – for protection.

'If you want me to help you,' replied Daphnaeus, 'you have to tell me what you're afraid of and why. But I need to know every minute detail, or I won't lift a finger. I've heard strange stories about these deaths, stories that I would like not to believe, because if they turn out to be true, I'd have to intervene myself to punish the offenders. Have you got the gist of that?'

They had, and they realized that they could count only on themselves to save their skins. They decided together to leave the city and move to Catane, hoping that sooner or later the storm would abate and they would be able to negotiate a return or a ransom.

In an attempt to pass unobserved, they decided to waste no time in long preparations and they left at dawn the next day, accompanied only by a couple of slaves and a cart for their baggage. They set off walking down the road for Catane, throwing their lot in with a group of merchants. They were transporting livestock, a flock of sheep and about twenty slaves that they hoped to sell at the market along with the animals. They were happy to let the newcomers join them; the more numerous the group was, the less chance that they would be attacked by robbers or brigands.

All went well for three days, and the two fugitives began to relax and to cheer up. They even fraternized with the merchants: people from the west of the island, judging from their accent, a happy and friendly lot who didn't mind sharing their supplies and greatly enjoyed the excellent wine that their two wealthy travel companions were quick to offer when they set up camp after dark.

On the fourth day, the convoy stopped at a little city where a fair was being held, and they sold off part of their livestock. The next day, a few day workers directed to the plains of Catane to help with the harvesting asked to join them; they were admitted to the company for the remainder of the trip.

But that same evening, the reapers stripped away their cloaks, threw aside their sickles and pulled out their swords. They surrounded the group, ordering the merchants to clear out and the two Syracusans to drop their arms and put their hands behind their backs so they could be bound.

Euribiades and Pancrates imagined a robbery and tried to negotiate. 'We're willing to pay,' promised Euribiades. 'We've got money with us, and we can get more from Syracuse or Catane in short order.'

'We don't want your money,' said one of the reapers, a young man no older than twenty with hair as thick and curly as a sheep's but black as the wing of a crow.

That phrase frightened them to death. They knew just how dangerous a man uninterested in money could be.

'What do you want then?' demanded Pancrates with a quavering voice and a soul full of dark imaginings.

'Us?' replied the boy, smiling. 'We don't want anything with you. So long.' And he walked off, followed by his travel companions and the animals; they even took the men's slaves with them for good measure. The jingling of the sheep's bells faded off into the evening as they walked away, until the two Syracusans were all alone in the middle of the silent countryside.

'What idiots we've been!' swore Pancrates. 'I could have told you this would happen. Everything was going much too smoothly.'

'So now what do we do?' asked Euribiades.

'Let's try to get free,' suggested Pancrates, 'before someone else shows up. Come on now, move! Put your back to mine and try to loosen my knots, then I'll untie you.'

But Euribiades did not move. 'Forget it,' he said with a resigned tone. 'There's someone coming.'

There was a figure on horseback silhouetted on the top of the hill. The mysterious man touched his heels to his horse's flanks and began to descend towards them.

'It's all over,' said Pancrates. 'We'll come to the same end as the others, or worse.'

'I'm not so sure,' replied Euribiades. 'If he wanted to kill us he would have done so already. He's obviously been observing us from the start. I say he wants to negotiate.'

The man dismounted from his horse and turned towards them; they stared back in dismay. A black cape fell from his shoulders to his feet, and a hood covered his head. His face was hidden by a comical theatrical mask, but nobody felt like laughing. He stared back at them, unmoving, without saying a word, and his invisible gaze terrified them even more than looking him in the eye. He slowly pulled a sharp knife from his cloak and said: 'I could make you die the most atrocious of deaths, make you curse the bitches who brought you into this world. You know that.'

They realized now why the man was wearing the theatrical mask: not only to cover his face, but to distort his voice as well.

'We know that,' replied Euribiades for both of them. 'But you're certainly blaming us for something we haven't done.'

'I know exactly what you're guilty of, down to the last detail. As I'm talking to you, others are receiving their just punishment. Not because they participated in that abominable exploit, but only because they boasted of doing so. But they're stupid wretches who count for nothing. You have a political standing that can be exchanged with something I'm interested in.'

Euribiades realized it was best to drop the matter of blame so as not to further irritate the masked man; best to go straight on to negotiations. 'I don't know what you're referring to, but we're ready to listen to your proposal,' he replied. 'Speak.'

'Now you're talking,' said the stranger. 'These are my conditions: in one month's time, a person who was believed dead will return to the city and go before the Assembly, under the sponsorship of an adoptive father, to reclaim his rights as a citizen. You surely know of whom I speak.'

'We think so,' admitted Pancrates.

'Just so that there are no doubts about it, I'll tell you that his name is Dionysius, presumed dead after the massacre of Hermocrates and his men in the agora. You two have a determining vote in the Council. Can I assure him that your vote will be favourable?'

'Oh yes, yes, of course,' they promised in unison.

'I was sure we'd come to an agreement. But allow me to remind you that, should you go back on this pact of ours, your punishment would be much, much worse than what was dealt out to your henchmen.'

He approached with his knife and the two men trembled, fearing that he was about to give them a taste of their threatened punishment. Instead, the stranger cut the rope binding their wrists and ankles. Then he turned his back to them, mounted his horse and rode off at a gallop, quickly vanishing behind the hill.

*

One month later, the Assembly convened by Daphnaeus was discussing the Carthaginian preparations for war when Heloris stood and asked for the floor.

'You have permission to speak,' replied the president of the Assembly.

'My fellow citizens and authorities of Syracuse,' he began, 'some time ago, as I was travelling inland to buy some horses, I found an unconscious man at the side of the road. He was severely wounded and gave no signs of life. I nursed him back to health until he was fully cured and had regained all his strength. That man was Dionysius, the son-in-law of Hermocrates . . .' A buzz of disbelief and much cursing could be heard among those present. Heloris continued undaunted: 'We all know of his fame as a valiant combatant, one of the most courageous of the city.' More muttering spread through the crowd. But this time, much acclamation rose up as well. The members of the Company were well distributed throughout the hemicycle.

'I know why some of you protest,' continued Heloris. 'Dionysius set himself against his own city by participating in the ill-fated onslaught of Hermocrates, but I would ask you to try to understand him. Blood ties – the love he had for his bride and the admiration he had for that man who had served the city with great devotion for years – convinced him to take part in that foolhardy act. The punishment he received was harsh: his house was devastated, the bride whom he loved violated and killed. Don't you believe that he has paid a high enough price for his errors, errors which his young age and inexperience alone would suffice to excuse? He escaped death – not certainly by chance but because of the will of the gods – and he has admitted his blame to me. I trust him and I have adopted him as a son. I am here to ask you, citizens and authorities of Syracuse, to restore his right to vote in this Assembly and to allow him to reclaim his place among the ranks of warriors drawn up in battle. The threat of another war looms on the horizon and the city will need all of her sons, especially those most valiant.'

With these words Heloris concluded his speech, and a fist-fight broke out immediately between the supporters and the adversaries of the born-again Dionysius. All of the members of the Company had reported to the Assembly that day, and their massive presence intimidated the trouble-making factions at first, then shut them up completely. The only voices to be heard were now shouting out: 'It's only right! Dionysius is a hero!'

'He's a victim, he's not to blame!'

'We need his courage!'

'Restore his rights!'

The last word still belonged to the Council, who met in a closed session under the portico that faced the hemicycle.

'We cannot come to a decision under this sort of pressure!' began Daphnaeus.

'You're right,' replied a councillor. 'There's too much of an uproar, and it's obvious that Dionysius planted his supporters so that they would cow the other citizens and prevent them from expressing their true opinions.' The man who had spoken was called Demonattes; he was a relative of one of the men burnt alive in the house near the harbour.

'Well, I wouldn't say that exactly . . .' Euribiades put in weakly.

Demonattes spun around to face him as if he could not believe his ears. 'What do you mean, you wouldn't say so? Even a blind man could see what is happening in this Assembly. I'm shocked at your reaction: weren't you one of those who wanted Dionysius condemned to death at all costs if he was captured?'

Pancrates rallied to his friend. 'Things can change. Only stones don't change, by Heracles! There's been a development in the course of events that—'

'Development? Ten men were carved to pieces or burnt alive by a cruel murderer, and if you can't guess just who that was, I suppose I'll have to spell it out for you. What's more, if the two of you insist on this ridiculous posturing, I'll demand that an official investigation be opened on your account. Such sudden changes in mood can look very suspicious.'

The situation was worsening, and Pancrates tried to assume a more accommodating, wait-and-see attitude that could be shared by his fellow councilmen. He suggested that the order of the day which could restore Dionysius's rights might be postponed. But Euribiades nudged him hard with his elbow, motioning with his eyes at something at the top of the hemicycle.

Pancrates noticed his panicked expression and shifted his gaze to the colonnade that closed off the Assembly auditorium. He couldn't help but startle when he saw the comic theatrical mask hanging from one of the columns; the same one, it seemed, worn by the mysterious figure in the countryside south of Catane. The mask's grotesque leer reminded them quite effectively of their pact – unwritten but extremely binding nonetheless. Pancrates sighed and didn't speak for a few moments, after exchanging an eloquent look with Euribiades. As soon as Demonattes started up his fiery oration again, he whispered something into his friend's ear.

Euribiades asked for the floor then and said: 'It is useless to put off dealing with our problems; certain matters are best faced at once. In order to avoid a repeat of the intimidatory situation which we've seen today in the Assembly, I would ask the Council members to vote now, in a secret ballot.'

'I approve,' said Pancrates. 'It's the best way.'

There was no reason to oppose such a common procedure, and no one protested. Dionysius's restoration was approved by a single vote and Demonattes indignantly abandoned the Council.

Dionysius received the news from Heloris himself, but his adoptive father warned him not to attend meetings for a while, to avoid provoking quarrels and controversies that his adversaries could fault him with. He didn't show his face until the Company had ensured the goodwill of a wide majority of the Assembly, winning the contentious factions over by fair means or foul.

He made his entry with his cheeks perfectly shaved, his hair gathered at the nape of his neck, dressed in a beautiful light-blue chlamys. He sat in the midst of his friends, protected and guarded on every side. Pancrates and Euribiades shot him captivating smiles, as if to demonstrate that the mostly favourable atmosphere was due to their intervention. Dionysius smiled back and they were convinced that the score was settled.

They were wrong.

One evening, just after dusk, Pancrates was captured as he was returning home from a dinner with friends. He was bound and gagged, bundled up into a cloak and brought to the cellar of the house with the trellis. Two days later, Euribiades was captured in his own home in the middle of the night. He had heard his dog barking and had got up with a lantern to see what was happening. A yelp, and then silence. When he saw his slaves gagged and tied to the gate he realized that something was wrong, but it was too late. Four armed men jumped on him, knocked him out with clubs and carried him off in a sack.

He came to his senses in the house with the trellis, underground. Next to him was Pancrates, white as a sheet, who stared at him in terror. Dionysius stood before them, sword in hand. 'But . . . we had an agreement . . .' he stammered.

'I don't remember making any agreement,' replied Dionysius.

'The man with the comic mask . . . was you . . . or one of your friends. He promised to spare our lives in exchange for our votes in favour of restoring your rights in the Assembly.'

'I've never worn a mask in all my life. I always show my face to my enemies.'

'But we helped you!' protested Pancrates, while his companion sobbed softly.

'That's true, and for this you will be granted a quick death. Don't find fault with me: if I obeyed my heart, I would slowly cut you up into little pieces and feed you to my dogs. You can't imagine the sight I was greeted with when I crossed the threshold of this house after the debacle in the agora. You can't imagine what I felt when I saw my wife's naked, broken body. Those who tortured and raped her at least took responsibility for their actions. You didn't even have the courage to do that.'

'I beg of you,' insisted Euribiades, 'you're making a mistake! We had nothing to do with that, we have no blame in what happened. We are sorry, and we can understand your anger, but we did nothing wrong, believe me. In the name of the gods, do not stain yourself with the blood of two innocent men!'

Dionysius came closer. 'I may be making a mistake, and in that case I will have to face the judgement of the gods. But Arete's shade must be appeased. Farewell.'

He said no more and ran them through from front to back, one after another, with clean blows to the bases of their throats.

Their bodies were never found.

Philistus met Dionysius two days later in an olive grove near Epipolae. 'You told me you would spare them if you were readmitted to the city,' he said reproachfully.

'I lied,' said Dionysius. And he walked away.

11

OVER THAT SUMMER, the attention of the authorities and of the common people of Syracuse was distracted by menacing news brought by informers from both Carthage and Greece. Settling up local affairs now seemed a trifling concern. The word was that the Carthaginians had sent an embassy to Athens to convince the city government to continue their war against the Spartans, even though the foremost Athenian general, Alcibiades, had fled to Asia. This would prevent Sparta from coming to the aid of Syracuse in Sicily when Carthage decided to attack. They also learned that the Athenians had sent a delegation to meet with the Carthaginian generals in Sicily. Athens hated the Syracusans with such a passion that she would have made a pact with anyone if it could wreak harm to the city that had routed and defeated her men seven years before.

The government of Syracuse protested with an official note against the preparations for war, but they did not even obtain a response. Daphnaeus decided then to send a fleet of forty ships into the waters of western Sicily, and to repair the port of Selinus as well as possible in order to prevent a Carthaginian disembarkation. In their first engagement, the Syracusans sank fifteen of the enemy ships but as soon as Hannibal sent his entire fleet of eighty massive battleships out to sea, Daphnaeus ordered his vessels to retreat so they would not be totally wiped out. He immediately sent off envoys to request help from the Italian Greeks and from the Spartans as well. Sparta agreed to send one of their generals, Dexippus, with one thousand five hundred mercenaries. The Spartan landed at Gela and made his way to Acragas, where he also took command of the eight hundred Campanian mercenaries whom Tellias had convinced to abandon the Carthaginians with his generous recruiting offer.

Hannibal landed his troops in the immediate vicinity of Acragas in the early spring. He was getting on in age now, and was flanked by his cousin Himilco, a younger and more energetic man. He positioned a division east of the city to preclude raids from that direction, and raised a fortified camp to the west. He immediately began to demolish the monumental tombs of the necropolis to procure materials for an assault ramp which would give his troops access to the city.

Inside the city, no one seemed to take the threat of an army seriously, albeit one that had already annihilated Selinus and Himera. Supplies were abundant and their sturdy walls were built on a rocky base which was considerably higher than the surrounding plain. They considered their city impregnable. They were also confident in the knowledge that Daphnaeus would soon be arriving from Syracuse at the head of the confederate army. The climate was so relaxed that the commanders had to issue an order that sentinels posted on the city walls could use no more than one mattress and two pillows apiece. Every now and then, the cavalry would even make a few sorties, attacking isolated units that had gone out to collect forage for their animals and supplies for their men.

The heat soon became torrid and the stink of the waste and excrement of sixty thousand men and five thousand horses crowded into those damp, poorly aired lowlands drifted all the way up to the top of the walls.

Every morning, Tellias would go up to the battlements to observe the plains, taking advantage of the hour when the land wind would usually carry off that revolting stench. The city was still asleep and the last sentry had just gone off duty to allow the day shift to take over. The rising sun illuminated the great sanctuary of Athena on the acropolis, and then, little by little, lit up the houses, the gardens, the colonnaded porticoes and last of all the immense bulk of the Temple of Zeus still under construction. Work had not been interrupted, and the sculptors were busy carving the huge pediment that represented the fall of Troy: the entangled limbs of the heroes were taking on clearer definition and shape with each passing day. Only the figures of the gods had been completed; tall under the slopes of the tympanum, they regarded passers-by with their stony glares, awaiting the wash of bright colours that the painters had just begun to apply to their faces, limbs, hair and garments. The giants of the colonnade seemed to flex their muscles in the titanic effort of holding up the storied architrave; the gilding on the acroteria glittered in the morning rays, and flocks of pink ibis rose from the mouth of the Acragas, gliding over the almond and olive trees in the valley.

The spectacle was so enchanting, the harmonious work of man and nature so sublime that the vision of human stupidity – jeopardizing such beauty with the threat of war! – filled Tellias with a sense of deep dismay, a bitter forewarning of the imminent end. He could not shake the thought of Arete from his mind: he remembered how much she had loved Acragas, how fascinating she had found the extravagance of a city always restless and hungry for life. He remembered how keenly she desired to become the bride of the man she had chosen as her companion. He grieved deeply at the thought of her cruel end, and could take no consolation in the vengeance that Dionysius had inflicted with equal cruelty.

His only hope was that Acragas would survive! At times he recited Pindar's verses softly to himself like a prayer. Acragas . . . high and luminous on her rock, the distant sparkle of the sea, the forests of pine and oak, the olive trees planted by her founding fathers, the sacred fire of the acropolis which had never been extinguished since the first time it was lit . . . could all of this be suddenly wiped out as though it had never existed? Was that possible? Could the fate of Selinus and Himera be perpetuated and infinitely repeated?

One day, as he was immersed in contemplation, Tellias was startled by the voices of the generals who commanded the army. They were ridiculing the enemy, who seemed so distant and impotent down there. The Carthaginian ships – so tiny on the horizon – seemed as inoffensive as the boats which the children toyed with in the big pond at the bottom of the valley. They were so sure of winning! They must have their reasons, thought Tellias. One of them scoffed: 'Look at them, camped out in their own shit! They must think their stink will make us surrender!'

When plague broke out in the Carthaginian camp, mowing down thousands of men and dispiriting the enemy troops, it seemed that Acragas's most optimistic predictions had come true. The smoke of the pyres and the insufferable odour of burning flesh befouled the air all throughout the surrounding territory. Hannibal himself fell ill and died; when the news became known in the city, the people exulted, imagining that the Carthaginians would raise the siege and go home.

Tellias took such heart that he managed to think up a clever strategy for scaring them off. He recruited a number of tragic theatre actors and paid them to wander at night, like ghosts, among the ruins of the tombs demolished by the Carthaginians, wailing and groaning and letting out horrible curses in the Punic language. Spectral lights appeared in the cemeteries on moonless nights, and other terrifying apparitions would assail groups of Carthaginian auxiliaries intent on searching for forage or food along dark country roads. Their superstitious terror sowed panic among the besieging troops, to such an extent that no one would leave camp at night any more.

But the surviving commander, Himilco, was no fool. He summoned diviners and ordered them to suggest an immediate remedy to placate the offended spirits of the dead chased from their tombs. Divinatory rites were performed, and they ruled that nothing but a human sacrifice would do.

A poor native boy, taken as a slave during the previous campaign, had his throat slit on the altar and his body cast into the sea. Himilco then proclaimed that the spirits had been satisfied and that things would soon start to change for the better. A couple of torrential rainstorms washed away the filth that had been surrounding the camp, and the situation did improve, confirming the diviners' prophesies and the commander's promises. The construction of the ramp was resumed with great zeal.

Tellias watched, worried by their constant progress.

Meanwhile, in Syracuse Dionysius had regained a position of considerable prestige. When the confederate army – a force of twenty thousand Syracusans, ten thousand mercenaries and twenty thousand Italians from allied cities – was ready to march, he was conferred the rank of adjutant to the board of generals.

The night they were to leave, he had Arete's body exhumed from the cellar where she had lain and buried her in a proper tomb that he had had built outside the western gate along the road to Camarina. Her body was found incredibly intact and Dionysius took this as a sign from the gods, rather than a consequence of the salinity of the ground, as Philistus maintained. It was his vengeance, Dionysius felt, that had engendered this miraculous event.

The funeral took place quietly, after sunset, and when the massive slab of limestone was lowered on to the sepulchre, Dionysius asked to be left alone. He talked to her, at length, in the hope that she would answer him. In the end he fell asleep at the foot of her tomb, overwhelmed by weariness, and he dreamt of plunging headlong from the cliff into the crystal pool, falling breathlessly in a sort of infinite, agonizing abandon.

He was awakened by Leptines, who had become his bodyguard and followed him everywhere, never too close and never too far. 'Let's go,' he said. 'Let's go home.'

The confederate army set off the next day before dawn: Syracusans in front, the mercenaries in the middle and the Italians last. The cavalry brought up the sides. At their head was Daphnaeus with the commanding generals and Dionysius himself. Leptines rode at a short distance behind them, with his group of scouts. The cavalry proper was made up only of aristocrats known as Knights, who tolerated no one else in their presence.

They covered the entire distance from Syracuse to Acragas in seven days, receiving supplies from the fleet, which sailed under convoy. Whenever necessary, they sent a number of dinghies ashore with provisions; they would shuttle back and forth for hours between the ships and the mainland.

They came within view of the city on the evening of the seventh day, and set up camp near the eastern detachment of the Carthaginian army. Dionysius deftly spurred on his horse, followed by Leptines, Biton, Doricus and some other friends from the Company, on a reconnaissance round; they estimated the enemy strength at about thirty-five thousand men. They could immediately see that the city was not inaccessible at all; the enemy strategy was becoming clear. The eastern detachment was there to prevent reinforcements from Syracuse from getting in, as most of the army prepared for the definitive assault from the nearly completed ramp, using siege engines and rams.

Before night fell they circled the northern part of the walls, skirting the western necropolis from which they could see the ramp which had already reached the height of the natural rock platform that the city was built on. To defend themselves from the archers on the battlements, the Carthaginians had fashioned a kind of moving roof on wheels, covered with untanned, fire-proofed skins which protected the men who were working on the ramp pavement that would allow the machines to advance.

When Dionysius got back to camp, he was informed that a meeting of the general staff had already begun, and he hurried to join them.

'First of all,' Daphnaeus was saying, 'we must attack the eastern division of Himilco's army. They're in an open field, and the terrain is mostly flat. We'll attack at dawn, when it's still cool. In a closed formation, eight rows deep: we'll be at the centre with our Sicilian allies. The Italians will be on the right, the mercenaries on the left. The cavalry on both sides.'

'What if the bulk of Himilco's army attacks us while we're in the middle of combat?' asked Dionysius. 'I propose that we station a few cavalry detachments between us and the fortified Carthaginian camp at the west, so they can warn us if they make any moves.'

The commander of the cavalry, an aristocrat of ancient lineage called Cratippus, gave Dionysius a disdainful look as though he had offended him. 'I wouldn't say you have any authority at all in establishing where and how the cavalry will be drawn up,' he said in a scornful tone.

'Do as you like,' shot back Dionysius, 'but I'm convinced that rejecting a sensible proposal merely on a question of principle is the worst thing you can do. If it were up to me, I'd already have had you arrested with the most serious charge in time of war: stupidity.'

Speechless, Cratippus drew his sword to wipe out the offence with blood, but Daphnaeus pounded his fist on the table to put an end to the dispute. Philistus, who had been admitted to the Council as an adviser, couldn't hold back a mischievous smile.

'We'll post dispatch riders,' said Daphnaeus. 'We have to know what's happening beyond our line of battle.'

'May I speak?' asked Dionysius.

'As long as you don't offend anyone else,' retorted Daphnaeus.

'Are we coordinating our efforts with the Acragantines inside the city?'

'No,' replied Daphnaeus. 'Why?'

'Why?' shouted Dionysius. 'It's sheer madness not to do so! How are they to know what they should do, or shouldn't do for that matter? And how can we take advantage of the invaluable support of the thousands of warriors who are waiting armed and ready inside the walls of Acragas?'

'It won't be necessary to tell them anything,' Daphnaeus cut him short. 'We don't need the Acragantines. What's more, I don't trust their Campanian mercenaries: they were once in the service of the Carthaginians and now they're fighting against them; they may very well cross back over in the middle of the battle. Tomorrow we will attack and we will overwhelm those barbarians. Then, as soon as we have the opportunity, we'll attack the fortified camp on the west and chase them all back into the sea! I've nothing more to say. You can go. There will be no bugle call; the wake-up signal will pass from man to man. The password is "*Nike*". Good luck.'

Dionysius retired to his tent, changed into a dark cloak and left camp on the western side together with Leptines, with the excuse of making the rounds of the guards. But as soon as he was outside the others' field of vision, he and his brother began running through the thick holm-oak forest which led up to the base of the escarpment that Acragas's walls were built on. When he was close enough, he ordered Leptines to stay behind to cover his return. He then called up to the sentry who was marching back and forth, patrolling the walkway. 'Hey!' he yelled. 'Hey, you!'

'Who goes there?' replied the sentry.

'I'm a soldier from Syracuse. I'm alone. Let me in, I have to talk to one of your chiefs.'

'Wait there,' said the man, and went to call the officer on duty.

'What is it you want?' demanded the officer, leaning slightly over the parapet.

'Let me in, fast,' he insisted. 'I've come from Syracuse and I have to talk to one of your commanders.'

'What's your name?'

'Dionysius.'

'Is there anyone in the city who knows you?'

'Yes. A very reputable man named Tellias.'

'Walk to your right, down to that bush over there,' said the officer. 'There's a postern behind it; I'll send someone to open it. My men have got you in their sights: any false move and you're dead.'

Dionysius did as he was told and soon found himself inside the city, in the presence of a group of high-ranking officers.

'Who sent you?' demanded one of the generals, a man of about forty with a neatly trimmed beard, dressed in what looked more like parade armour than battle gear.

'No one. I've come of my own initiative.'

'What?' exclaimed the officer, then turned to his fellows. 'I don't like this. He could very well be a spy. I say we lock him up until we find out more about him.'

'I'll vouch for that boy!' rang out a voice at their shoulders. It was Tellias who advanced, panting, towards the base of the walls, the front hem of his garment balled up in his hand so he wouldn't trip on it. His bulk made the climb slow going. The four generals turned to face him. 'How can it be . . .' gasped Tellias, wiping his brow, 'that you don't recognize him? It's Dionysius, the hero who brought the refugees of Selinus all the way here, and who fought like a lion under the walls of Himera. Talk, boy, our valiant commanders are all ears.'

No one breathed a word: the prestige and authority of the man who had enrolled nearly a thousand mercenaries at his own expense sufficed to command their full attention.

Dionysius began to speak: 'Are you sure there are no spies among you?' he asked.

'How dare you . . .' retorted the officer who had spoken first.

'The boy's right!' protested Tellias. 'Let's continue this meeting in the Temple of Athena, where no one can hear us. Many cities have fallen due to treason! There's no need to be shocked.'

Inside, the temple lamps had already been lit for the night and the little group gathered in a quiet corner of the cella, behind the statue of the goddess.

'In reality,' Dionysius started up again, 'I guess you could call me a spy of sorts.' The group stared at him incredulously, but Tellias motioned for him to go on. 'That's right, a friendly spy. My commanders have not yet arranged to send you a delegation to coordinate our actions, so I thought I'd come and let you know how things are going. Our army is nearly fifty thousand men strong, all well trained and armed. You'll be able to see our fleet tomorrow from the bastions: about thirty triremes and ten transport vessels.

'Tomorrow, before dawn, Daphnaeus plans to attack the Carthaginian division out in front here to the east and wipe them out, so we can then concentrate our joined forces around the fortified camp. I suppose that's when he'll ask for your help.'

'Your behaviour merits the harshest of punishments!' exclaimed another officer, older than the first, tall and wiry, wearing black leather armour decorated with silver studs. Dionysius had never seen such elegant generals in his whole life. 'You've taken a dangerous initiative without consulting your superiors. You've risked being captured by the enemy and revealing important military secrets, you've—'

'I've done what was right to save this city,' Dionysius interrupted him with a peremptory gesture of his hand, 'risking my own skin and no one else's. Because I've already seen two cities fall, and I don't want Acragas to suffer the same fate. Do as you like, I've warned you. If I had command of the Acragantine army, I'd order a raid: you could take the troops camped out in front of the city from behind as we are attacking them from the front; between us we'd annihilate them. It would be sufficient to leave one unit to garrison the walls, because after we've finished off the eastern camp, our joint forces will take on the fortified camp west of the city as well. If the Carthaginians stage an attack to take advantage of the reduced number of defenders remaining in the city, we'll come up behind them and crush them against the base of the walls.

'That's what I'd do. But the responsibility is yours. I just wanted you to know. If you have nothing else to ask me or no messages to give me, I'll be going back to camp before they realize I'm gone and put me in shackles. I don't want to miss the action tomorrow.'

'I say we arrest him!' said a third officer, certainly an old-fashioned aristocrat from the way he wore his long hair styled into a bun at the top of his head. 'We'll hand him over to his commander once the war is over and we'll see if he still feels like showing off.'

Dionysius drew up close and glared at him. 'You just try,' he said.

Tellias stepped in again to relieve the tension. '*Hegemones*, please, there's no need for such serious measures. You've received the informal visit of an allied officer, that's all. What's so strange about that?'

'Attack from behind as soon as we've engaged the enemy,'

said Dionysius then, backing off and staring each one of the generals in turn straight in the eye. 'Attack, without waiting a single moment. Farewell.'

He turned to go, but then spun around and stopped in front of Tellias. He gave him a long look, and his old friend understood that there were many things that he wanted to say and that he couldn't say a single one.

Tellias slapped him on the back. 'Go now. We'll have plenty of time to talk once all this is over.'

Dionysius walked off without a word, as he did when his heart was burdened. Tellias quietly listened to the sound of his footsteps echoing off the walls of the great sanctuary.

'How did it go?' asked Leptines when he appeared before him like a ghost.

'Badly,' replied Dionysius.

12

HIMILCO HAD BEEN promptly informed of the intentions and of the strength of the confederate army, and he immediately sent out reinforcements. Iberian and Campanian mercenaries went to take position during the night, marching in silence through the woods that stretched between the city and the sea.

Daphnaeus had meanwhile drawn up his army on the Himera river before the break of dawn. He ordered the men to cross the river and to approach the enemy camp.

The column advanced, then fanned out wide, lining up in eight rows for a frontal attack. Daphnaeus himself, on the left, gave the password, which flew through the ranks until it reached the far right end of the formation. As the word ran its course down the lines, each man would raise his shield and lower his spear, so that a wave of bronze and iron surged across the length of the impressive array.

A long, tension-laden silence followed as they waited for the thin red line edging the eastern horizon to widen and shed its light on the earth, making the ground visible. Daphnaeus had told his men that the attack signal would be given when they could see their shadows, and so each man stared hard at the ground before him, waiting with increasing dread for his shape to take form.

All at once their shadows leapt out, long and distinct, and at that same instant the bugles blared and the officers launched the war cry that was repeated in a roar from the ranks. The mighty phalanx charged.

The prolonged wailing of war horns responded from the

opposite front, and the Carthaginian army stormed forward as well. They were led by the Iberian and Campanian mercenaries, veterans of countless battles fought under any number of standards. The Iberians wore metallic plates over their white tunics and red-combed leather helmets on their heads. The Campanians donned thick leather cuirasses and helmets topped by spectacular three-feathered crests, and carried large painted shields. Shouting as they advanced, they shot stones from their deadly slings and let loose wave after wave of arrows. The phalanx would raise their shields to ward off each new attack of hail that rained down on the heavy bronze, and then push on, seeking impact.

The two armies crashed into each other with a fearsome din at half a stadium from the enemy camp. The sheer mass of metallic shields and spears in the hands of the Greeks mowed down the Libyans, Iberians and Campanians like an avalanche. The mercenaries had superior individual combat skills and greater experience, but were less resistant in a frontal collision with such a heavy, compact formation. The neck-and-neck contest went on at length as the battle became fiercer and more bloody, and then the Carthaginian line began to lose ground under the untiring drive of its adversaries. The ground was soon covered with the dead and wounded. The latter were finished off one by one by a spear thrust, as the men in the last rows advanced behind their comrades.

In the meantime, a huge crowd of warriors had gathered on the bastions of Acragas. They urged their allies on with great shouts and yells, as if those soldiers, immersed in the fury and uproar of battle, could hear them. But their yelling certainly reached the ears of the enemy at the fortified camp, stirring up discouragement and fear.

At a certain moment, when it had become clear that Himilco's troops were falling back, the Acragantine warriors began to assemble around their commanders, demanding that the gates be opened so they could jump into the fray and wipe out their enemies once and for all.

'What are we waiting for?' they shouted. 'Let's move, let's get this over with! Now's the time!'

'Let's kill them all!'

'We'll avenge Selinus and Himera!'

The general called Cratippus tried to calm them down. 'Silence!' he exclaimed. 'Be still and listen to me!'

The tumult seemed to die down, but the sound of the battle which rose all the way up to the bastions was driving the men into an uncontrollable frenzy; their excitement was plain in their faces, in their eyes, in their twitching limbs. They all wanted a chance to take part in these savage festivities, this killing party, before it was all over.

'Heed my words!' repeated Cratippus. 'If we go out now, we'll leave the city undefended and commit the same error that condemned Himera. Himilco could attack from the fortified camp while we are outside the walls and take Acragas in the first onslaught. Don't you realize that?'

'Shut up and let us get out on the battlefield!' shouted one of the men.

'What kind of commanders are you?' grumbled another. 'You won't even lead your men into combat!'

As they spoke, news reached them that a sally was being prepared in the city. Thousands and thousands of armoured warriors carrying their shields and spears had gathered in a rowdy crowd, cursing and shouting, eager to drive the barbarians out of Acragantine territory. The warriors up on the bastions, who could see what was happening below, started yelling even more loudly, as if they were at the stadium or the hippodrome, and the din rose to the skies.

Fearing that he was about to lose control of the situation, Cratippus called over one of his adjutants, a young man of just over thirty named Argeus, and whispered into his ear: 'Go straight to the headquarters of the Campanian mercenaries and order them to bar all the gates and establish garrisons. We cannot allow our men to rush out in disarray, leaving the city undefended. Move fast!'

Argeus ran off, pushing his way through the crowd that rained insults on him and those of his ilk: 'Fucking cowards! You spineless dastards!'

It took some time for the order to be put into effect, and just as the first soldiers reached the swelling mob, announcing that the gates had been bolted and put under guard, voices sounded from the wall: 'Look! Get over here, come and see this!'

At his words, there was a general rush up the access stairs to the sentry walkway. They leaned eagerly over the parapets: the Punic army was routed! The troops were running at full tilt towards the fortified camp. A cry of wild exultation broke out, but the clamour of their cheers soon mixed with disappointed cursing when it became clear that Daphnaeus was holding his men back, preventing them from chasing the enemy. He must have been afraid of falling into an ambush, wary of Diocles's experience at Himera. If the men at the walls had been any closer, they would have heard Dionysius himself, drawn up on the right flank, still covered with blood from the slaughter, wildly yelling the same words they were yelling, exhorting the troops to push on and exterminate the enemy, down to the last man.

Nothing of the sort happened. The confederate army came to a crashing halt, obeying the bugle signals, and thus the bulk of the Carthaginian army, unharmed, found shelter inside the fortified camp.

At that sight, the Acragantines had to resign themselves to what had happened. The confederate army was two stadia away now; attacking without their allies made no sense. They bitterly acknowledged that the opportunity to eliminate the threat that loomed over them had been lost.

But disappointment soon led to frustration and then to anger. The warriors crowded menacingly around their commanders and started shouting: 'You sold us out!'

'How much did the barbarians pay you?'

'Traitors!'

'Scheming bastards!'

Tellias did all he could to placate their anger. 'Calm down!

You can't accuse them of such things without any foundation!'
But his weak, clucking voice could not be heard over the growing
uproar.

Stones began to fly and many hit their mark. Struck in the
head, Cratippus fell to the ground, and after him the three fellow
generals who had supreme command over the large army units.
Only Argeus, the young officer who had gone to take orders to
the mercenaries at the gates, was spared. When he arrived, the
four commanders were already dead, half buried under a heap of
rocks. The men who had stoned them stood now in a circle
around the corpses, in silence; they didn't even notice him when
he appeared among them and walked pale and speechless towards
the lifeless bodies.

They were all overcome with bitterness and disgust for what
they had done. They were only too aware that justice had not
been served by summary execution. What they had punished
with such extreme fury was perhaps mere indecision or simple
stupidity.

*

The encounter had been devastating for the Carthaginians: nearly
six thousand men had been left on the field. Fewer than three
hundred of the confederate combatants had fallen, but their
frustration over the way victory had slipped from their hands was
immense.

Dionysius rushed over to Daphnaeus and shouted: 'Why didn't
you let us go on? Why did you stop us? You know what this is,
don't you? This is cowardice, this is—'

'One more word and I'll have you executed. Immediately!'

Dionysius bit his lip and returned to the ranks, smouldering
with repressed rage.

Daphnaeus had no intention yet of attacking the fortified
camp, defended by a deep trench, a mound and a palisade, and he
led his men to the eastern camp that the enemy had abandoned
in their flight. That same night a delegation from Acragas arrived
to report on what had happened in the city and on how the

commanders had been punished. Daphnaeus shuddered and was at a complete loss for words.

Dionysius stepped forward. 'If you had only listened to me, this never would have happened. Himilco would have taken to his heels without a chance in the world of saving his skin.'

'No one can tell what would have happened,' replied Daphnaeus. 'Keeping a cool head is the greatest virtue in war. Now they're on the defensive, cooped up in their camp, while we control all the roads of access and exit; we can cut off their supply lines and starve them out if we want. As soon as their mercenaries find themselves with no food and no pay, they'll rise up against Himilco, and it will be all over.'

Events seemed to prove Daphnaeus right for some time. It was already late in the season, and they were told – although no one would later remember who had said so – that the Carthaginian ships in Panormus had already been docked or pulled aground for maintenance, and that they would not be put back out to sea until the following spring. The Syracusan fleet, on the contrary, was still perfectly efficient and continued to provision the army.

Whenever Himilco sent out a unit in search of supplies or forage, the Syracusan cavalry would set off in pursuit and promptly wipe the men out. Surrender was expected from one day to the next, especially since bad weather was already setting in.

Precisely because a worsening of the weather was predicted, Syracuse decided to send a large consignment of grain and other foodstuffs by sea to provision Acragas before conditions made navigation impossible. But when the Syracusan convoy came into view of the city, they were shocked to find the entire Carthaginian fleet of nearly fifty ships in full battle order.

The fate of the battle was sealed from the start: the heavily laden Syracusan ships were too slow, while the Carthaginian vessels, already dismasted, more numerous and with the wind in their favour, launched the assault with infinitely superior speed and manoeuvring capability.

The few Syracusan ships capable of counter-attacking were

almost immediately disabled and sunk, while the others were driven ashore along the stretch of coast that flanked the Carthaginian camp. Himilco's mercenaries, who were reduced to serious straits and had been threatening desertion, rushed to plunder the ships and slaughter their crews, carrying all the grain meant for Acragas off to their own camp.

The events reversed the fate of the war, which had until then seemed decided. The Acragantines, who had never exercised restraint or rationed their provisions, realized all at once that their stores were extremely low.

The Spartan commander Dexippus, one of the few generals to have escaped death, assembled his officers and held council. 'How many days can we hold out with what we have?'

'Three or four days at most,' they answered.

'Then we must evacuate the city. Tomorrow.'

Utter silence met his words. No one dared reply, but each one of them was searching desperately within himself for a solution.

'We must inform the Council,' said one of his officers, 'so they can notify the population.'

'Just one moment,' intervened one of the commanders who had not spoken until then, a man from Gela called Euritous. 'Are you saying that we have to empty a city of two hundred thousand people and leave . . . just like that?' He clapped one hand hard against the other.

'Just like that,' repeated Dexippus, unperturbed. 'Do you have any other proposals?'

'Fighting. We could fight them. Open a corridor leading inland and get provisions from the countryside.'

'Combat on the open field alongside the Syracusans,' shouted another, a young Acragantine battalion commander. 'We can still beat them!'

There was no need to advise the Council. Guided by Tellias, the elders were at that moment arriving from the nearby *bouleuterion* to meet with the military chiefs and review the situation.

'Can I have understood correctly?' blurted out Tellias immediately. 'Is there someone here who wants to evacuate the city?'

'You've understood full well,' retorted Dexippus. 'We have no choice. There's no way we can resist without food and provisions.'

'You are crazy or a coward or both things together!' screamed Tellias in his shrill voice. 'We'll throw open the gates, we'll send out our boys armed to the teeth and they'll break those scabby bastards' arses! Then we'll take back our grain and all the rest and make them sorry they ever thought of showing up here!'

'If it were that simple,' replied Dexippus, 'I would do the same myself. I'm afraid it's not. They won't be lured into a battle on the open field. Why should they? They've got everything they need inside their fortified camp. They'll wait until we're half starved, then they'll attack and finish us off. It's much better to get out now while we're still in time.'

Tellias shook his head. 'This just isn't possible,' he muttered. 'I can't believe this is happening. There must be another way! There must be another solution!'

He hadn't finished speaking when a sentry who had been on duty up on the walls arrived. 'Our Campanian mercenaries are deserting! They're leaving from the southern gate and are headed towards the Carthaginian camp. When they found out there was nothing more to eat, they abandoned the stretch of walls they were guarding!'

'See?' said Dexippus. 'If I had any doubts at all, they're gone now. More than an entire stadium of the city's walls are now unguarded. Do you know what that means?'

'But the Syracusans and our Italian allies are still out there, by Heracles!' broke in Tellias, anguished. 'We can win even now with their help! Listen to me. We'll contact Daphnaeus and the allies and decide together what must be done. We can't rush into this . . . There's still time . . .' But his voice was suddenly tired and spent as he spoke these words.

'As you wish,' said Dexippus. 'But we must act immediately.' He called a sentry. 'Take a horse, go out of the eastern gate and report to Daphnaeus. Tell him we have no food left and that we are planning to evacuate the city unless he has another feasible solution. Understand?'

'Yes,' nodded the sentry, and turned to do as he had been told.

'Wait,' said Tellias. 'Tell him that we're ready to meet him now, wherever he wants. And ask for an officer called Dionysius; he's the field adjutant of the board of generals. Request his presence, if there is to be a meeting.'

'I'll do so,' replied the sentry, and left. He was seen shortly thereafter riding at full tilt towards the Syracusan camp.

A cold, bone-chilling wind rose up, and a fine drizzle began to fall from the grey sky. The assembled men took shelter under the portico and waited at length, in silence, for the messenger to return with the sentence that would decide the fate of Acragas. But in the meantime, news filtered out that the city was to be evacuated and spread like fire from one house to the next, through every quarter. Despair did not spare a single home, not even the luxurious dwellings of the rich. Anguish gripped them all at the thought of leaving the place they were born in, and their anguish was joined by uncertainty and incredulity. Their authorities had not come to this decision after long agonizing, but suddenly, with no forewarning! It was true that the war had been going on for months, but it hadn't really touched anybody; there had been no victims in the city, no damage to their property.

Daphnaeus's answer arrived as evening was falling: he would meet the authorities and the military commanders of Acragas at the eastern necropolis, where it was flanked by the road that went inland towards Kamikos. The sentry mentioned that he found him to be discouraged and in a terrible humour. 'Don't expect miracles,' he said after he'd reported on the outcome of his mission. 'The morale in the Syracusan camp didn't seem any better than here in the city.'

'Wait before you say that,' interrupted Tellias. 'Let's wait to hear what Daphnaeus has to propose. Such an extreme decision can only be taken when there's absolutely no other way out.'

They set off immediately for the appointed place on horseback, leaving from a postern on the eastern side of the city. Tellias rode a mule, a meek animal who was used to his master's outbursts of temper.

Daphnaeus was already there, flanked by two of his most highly ranked officers and by Dionysius. They were armed from head to toe and had been escorted by no less than fifty cavalrymen and about thirty lightly armed skirmishers.

Tellias noticed that, as far as he could tell from the coats of arms on their shields, they all appeared to be from Syracuse, Gela and Camarina; it seemed strange that only the Sicilian Greeks should have come.

He spoke up first, made confident by Dionysius's presence. 'Some of our military commanders, in particular Dexippus, here on my right, feel that we should evacuate the city tomorrow, because the remaining provisions will last us only a few days—'

'What's more,' interrupted Dexippus, 'our Campanian mercenaries have deserted to the enemy, leaving a segment of nearly one stadium of our walls undefended.'

'Too big,' thought Dionysius, and he seemed to remember once pronouncing or thinking those same words, in a dream perhaps.

'I saw them go,' said Daphnaeus.

'It's true,' Tellias insisted stubbornly, 'but we still have thousands of well-armed soldiers inside the city, and you have a powerful army out here. We can fight together and defeat them, can't we?'

Daphnaeus did not answer at once, and those long moments of silence weighed like a stone in the heart of each man present. Dionysius gazed into his friend's eyes with an expression of intense discouragement. Daphnaeus finally spoke: 'Not any more, I'm afraid. The Greeks of Italy are leaving us. Tomorrow.'

'What?' exclaimed Tellias. 'You can't be serious!'

'I am, unfortunately. They're leaving, I tell you.'

'But why?'

'That was the agreement: they would stay on until the winter solstice. They have to prepare their fields for sowing, and they don't want to risk letting the bad weather get between them and their homes. In truth, the solstice is seven days off, but I don't think that changes matters much.'

'I just can't believe it,' said Tellias, shaking his head in consternation. 'I can't believe it . . .'

'As you see,' stepped in Dexippus, who seemed to have been just waiting for the chance, 'I was right. It's best that we evacuate the city. We'll use our troops to escort the refugees.'

'You can take them to Leontini,' suggested Daphnaeus. 'The city is still under construction. We'll have them add new—'

'This can't be true . . . this can't be happening. There must be another way,' protested Tellias. 'You're a warrior, for the sake of Heracles! You must tell me why you don't want to fight: why are you carrying those arms? What's that sword of yours good for?' His distress was growing, and his shrill voice sounded like the shriek of a wounded bird.

'You have to resign yourself to the facts,' replied Daphnaeus. 'We can't risk it. If I gamble everything I have in a pitched battle – where we will be greatly outnumbered – and I lose, that will leave Syracuse undefended. And if Syracuse falls, that's the end. I just can't risk it; you must understand.'

'That's the true reason then: you're afraid of losing! But don't you understand that by defending Acragas you're defending Syracuse? Can't you understand that? You're committing the same error that Diocles made at Himera. Terrible . . . terrible and stupid.'

Daphnaeus lowered his head without saying a word, as the rain began to fall more heavily, wetting their helmets, their breastplates and their shields, making them gleam in the flashes of distant lightning.

Tellias, his face dripping with rain and with tears, drew himself up with great dignity and said to Dionysius: 'Do you think he's right? Tell me, are you with him?'

Dionysius shook his head in silence, then raised his eyes and looked straight at Daphnaeus and then at Dexippus with an expression of burning disdain.

'They worked all this out between them, didn't they,' continued Tellias relentlessly. 'It was all decided. Maybe they even let themselves be bribed. Yes, that's certainly it. Otherwise why would they have told us that the Carthaginian fleet had been laid up, just as they were getting ready, in actuality, to assault the ships of Syracuse. Why else?'

'You're mad,' said Daphnaeus. 'You have no idea what you're saying. I won't kill you because you're an old man and you're raving mad. But I won't listen to you for another moment.' He turned to the Acragantine councillors, who were dumbstruck and appalled. 'Follow Dexippus,' he said to them. 'Do what he says and at least you'll save your lives. Farewell.'

He mounted his horse and vanished into the dark, his escort trailing off after him.

Tellias fell to his knees sobbing, indifferent to the falling rain.

Dionysius helped him up and clasped him to his chest. 'Go back to the city,' he said, trying to console him, 'go home and take care of your wife. Get ready to leave. I'll welcome you to my own house, I'll love you as if you were my parents. Please, take heart, Tellias, do it for me . . .'

A flash of lightning lit up the desolate landscape of the necropolis, followed by a roll of thunder. Tellias wiped his face. 'I'll never leave my city, boy,' he said. 'Can you understand that? Never!' And he rode off on his mule.

The next day, the authorities gave the order to evacuate and the entire city was filled with weeping and despair. The Council house was surrounded by an enraged crowd, but there was no one there to listen to them, nor to take any measures other than those which had already been announced. Panic spread like wildfire. The population started pouring out through the eastern gate as if the enemy were already inside the walls, and it took all the determination the soldiers could muster to restrain them and direct them as best they could along the road for Gela.

In the chaos of wails and screams, in the vortex of terror that swept through the city, the weak, the elderly and the sick were left behind; they would never have survived the hardships of a march hundreds of stadia long. Some took their own lives, others awaited their destiny, feeling that death was preferable to the loss of their homeland, of the places dearest to them, of the most beautiful city in the world.

Tellias and his wife, who refused to leave him on his own, were among them. In vain Dionysius scanned the lines of refugees anxiously; unanswered he shouted out their names, riding back and forth, up and down that straggling column, asking all those he met if anyone had seen them. He could not know that at that very instant, they were up at the highest point of the city, on the glorious Athenaean rock, tearlessly watching the long dark serpent as it wound through the plains: the hosts of refugees abandoning Acragas like a stream of blood flowing copiously from a body wounded to death.

Then the streets exploded with the howls of the rampant barbarians who sacked, destroyed, butchered everything in their way. They set fire to the grandiose Temple of Zeus down in the valley, still surrounded by wooden scaffolding, and the marvellous sculptures of the fall of Troy carved into the stone of the pediment came to life with tragic realism in the glow of the flames.

Tellias then took his wife by the hand and together they walked towards the temple of the city's protector, whose divine mass dominated the acropolis. They strolled tranquilly, as though they wanted to enjoy a last walk along the city's most sacred road. They stopped under the colonnade, and turned around to see the screaming horde flooding towards the ramp that led to the landing and the podium. Then they entered the temple and closed the door behind them. Tellias held his lifelong companion in a last embrace. They silently exchanged knowing glances, then Tellias took a torch and set the sanctuary aflame.

He burned with his bride, with his gods and with his memories.

13

ALL OF THE roads and paths that led to Gela were fraught with an enormous throng of desperate and terrified refugees. They were women, children, the elderly. All of the able-bodied men were armed and escorting the column. The old and the infirm had been abandoned because they would never have been able to withstand the long and difficult exodus. Many of the young women, even those from the richest and most noble families, journeyed on foot, carrying their younger brothers and sisters in their arms, showing great strength of character and courage as their delicate feet, used to wearing elegant sandals, became covered with blisters and wounds. They bit their lower lips like warriors in battle and swallowed their tears so as not to foster the fears of the little ones while their parents stumbled on, oppressed by the infinite grief of forsaking their homeland, the houses they had always lived in and the tombs of their ancestors. The refugees were like trees uprooted by the winds of a storm and dragged towards an unknown and inhospitable destination. Their pain was compounded by bewilderment, because many of them did not understand the reason for such a sudden and frightening calamity. The fragments of information that reached them as they trudged along were often absurd and conflicting.

They had no shelter from the harsh winter weather, nor against the hardships of such an arduous trek; few had taken food with them, and even fewer had water. They pushed on down the muddy road, but every now and then they would turn around as if insistent voices were calling them back – the regrets and the memories of the lives that they were leaving behind them.

Among the many torments that afflicted them, besides hunger and fatigue, were the cold wind, the drizzling rain, the leaden, hostile sky.

Their only consolation was the presence of their loved ones; although the men had formed ranks, they tried to march as close as they could to their families so the sight of them would give them the strength to continue.

Dionysius had ridden down the length of the long column time and time again searching for Tellias and his wife, and had asked anyone he knew or thought he recognized about them, with no success until a man finally gave him the news that he was afraid of hearing: 'Tellias stayed behind. I saw him together with his wife. As all of us were fleeing towards the eastern gate, he was walking up towards the acropolis, holding her hand. Headstrong old man! He always had to do things his way.'

Upon hearing these words, Dionysius spurred on his horse, caught up with Daphnaeus at the head of the column, and asked for leave to turn back.

'You're mad! What for?' replied Daphnaeus.

'Some friends of mine remained behind. I want to try to help them.'

'There's no one left to help, I'm afraid. You know the barbarians will have cleaned out the city. The able men they take as slaves to sell them off, the others they kill. Who were your friends?'

Dionysius shook his head. 'It doesn't matter,' he said. 'It doesn't matter.' He turned back down the column. He was struck by the sight of a shivering, mud-splattered young woman who was holding a little boy and girl by the hand, perhaps her younger siblings. She reminded him somehow of Arete and of the similar situation in which he had met her; he suddenly felt that the gods had given him another chance to help her, to soothe the pain that must still afflict her in Hades.

He approached the young woman, got off his horse and handed her his cloak. 'Take this,' he said, 'I don't need it.'

The girl replied with a wan smile, and continued walking under the rain.

★

The Carthaginian army was installed in Acragas after having amassed the huge amount of booty taken from a city which in the two hundred years since its founding had never been defeated or sacked. They had been careful not to damage the houses so they could occupy them for the rest of the winter. In doing so they showed their manifest intention of continuing their campaign of conquest. They would not stop as long as a single Greek city remained in Sicily.

The new frontier was Gela, the city where Aeschylus, the great tragedian, had died. The epigraph on his tomb in the necropolis said not a word about his glory as a poet, but commemorated him as a warrior, fighting at Marathon against the Persians, words that sounded now like a warning of imminent grief. The Acragantine refugees were settled in Leontini, where they would stay until the situation allowed their return.

Daphnaeus held council in Gela with his officers, including Spartan commander Dexippus, and the Geloan generals. 'What do you think should be done?' he asked the Geloans. 'What are your intentions?'

'We want to stay,' replied their chief commander, a man of about fifty named Nicandrus. He was an aristocrat, old-fashioned and inflexible, and he seemed absolutely determined, even though every feature of his face and every wrinkle of his brow betrayed his distress.

'If this is your decision,' replied Daphnaeus, 'we shall help you. We will do everything in our power to drive away the barbarians and prevent another catastrophe. What happened at Acragas will not repeat itself. Events somehow took an unforeseeable turn there, I suspect as the result of betrayal. We were taken by surprise when we were already sure of victory.'

'Never say the word victory until the enemy is annihilated,' retorted Nicandrus dryly. 'I thank you, nonetheless, in the name of my city for your willingness to draw up at our side.'

'Dexippus will remain here,' said Daphnaeus, 'together with his mercenaries, until operations resume.'

'Dexippus is an idiot,' thought Dionysius, 'if not a traitor.' But he didn't say a word. He stood at the back of the Council room, leaning against the door jamb, with his arms folded like a caryatid's; his face showed no emotion, as if it were made of marble. He thought of Tellias and his wife, who he had loved deeply and would never see again, and of the suffering they must have borne before dying. He thought of Acragas, lost and violated, of the girl he had given his cloak to; perhaps by now she'd fallen exhausted into the mud, leaving the two little ones to weep under the lashing rain. He too wanted to weep, to yell, to curse.

He left instead, after fulfilling all his duties, along a dark road that led to the western gate. Absorbed in thought, he was sure deep down that Gela would fall, as Selinus, Himera and Acragas had fallen, because of the incompetence of the commanders, the cowardice of Daphnaeus, the stupidity of Dexippus.

The Geloan authorities had arranged for the command to be hosted in the prytaneum, but Dionysius had preferred to rent an anonymous little house for himself near the walls. He had no esteem for the other officers, and no desire to stay with them. He entered the house and went up to the terrace to contemplate the view of the city and the sea.

He knew what needed to be done! A commander had to observe, analyse, study every detail of the territory, all the roads of access and escape, the weak spots in the walls, the fastest ways to get provisions, the play of currents in the sea, the winds in the sky, the passageways both inside the city and along the coast. And then come to a decision, grit his teeth and get on with it, at any cost, without listening to anyone. Overwhelm, wipe out, annihilate. That's what it meant to command an army and lead it to victory! What did those faint-hearted windbags know about it? All they were capable of doing was filling their mouths with high-sounding promises they'd never be able to keep.

The sun emerged from behind the thick bank of clouds for a few moments, shedding its last red and purple light before vanishing behind the horizon. The sea turned to liquid lead, swollen by the powerful push of the south-west wind. The billows, edged with grey foam, surged, roaring, all the way to the hill of Gela. Lamps were lit in the houses, smoke curled out of the chimneys and the moon was a pale ghost behind a frayed curtain of clouds. Dionysius sighed.

He was startled by the sudden noise of someone knocking insistently at the door downstairs. His thoughts interrupted, Dionysius went down to the ground floor and said: 'Who's there?'

'It's me, open up,' replied Philistus's voice.

'Look at you!' said Dionysius, opening the door. 'You're soaked, give me your cloak.'

Philistus came in, pale, his teeth chattering with the cold.

'Wait, let me start the fire,' Dionysius said, lighting a torch from the lamp burning in front of an image painted on the wall. He set aflame a little pile of runners on the hearthstone at the centre of the bare room. The crackling of the pine branches filled the room as they burned, diffusing a cosy warmth. 'I don't have much to eat,' he said. 'A chunk of bread, I think, and a little cheese. And there's only water to drink.'

'I'm not here to eat or to drink,' replied Philistus. 'I bring you the greetings of your brother Leptines, your adoptive father Heloris and the chiefs of the Company. The news of the defeat of Acragas has already reached Syracuse and the city is in an uproar. What have they decided, here in Gela?'

'To resist,' replied Dionysius, setting the bread and cheese to warm on the hearthstone and adding a little wood to the pile.

Philistus shrugged. 'Like Acragas, like Himera, like Selinus.'

'Yes.'

'We can't wait and watch another disaster without doing anything.'

'There's only one way to prevent it,' said Dionysius, staring into his friend's eyes in the glow of the flames.

'I feel the same way. Are you ready?'

'I am,' replied Dionysius.

'So are we.'

'Proceed. I'll reach you in Syracuse.'

'When?'

'With the army, when we return.'

'Too late. We'll act at the next Assembly; everything is ready. In seven days' time.'

'I can't just go off. Daphnaeus is just waiting for the chance to accuse me of desertion. He'd love to see me with my hands tied behind my back in front of a squad of archers.'

'I'll take care of that. Tomorrow at dawn you'll receive an order from the Council that demands your immediate return for reasons of State. False, obviously. You try to object, as if you were displeased with the order. Not too strenuously, of course.'

'I understand.'

'Fine. I'll be waiting for you in Camarina, at the house of Proxenus, the shield-maker. We'll continue the journey together.'

Dionysius nodded in silence. His gaze was fixed on the flames in the hearth. 'Have you heard about Tellias?' he asked suddenly.

'What?'

'He remained at Acragas, with his wife.'

'I wouldn't have imagined otherwise. You know that Tellias would never have left his city. He could never have accepted the humiliation of defeat and deportation.'

'I've lost them. They were very dear to me.'

'I know. They loved you as well, like the son they'd always dreamed of and never had.'

'A lot of people are going to pay for this. Both Greeks and barbarians.'

Philistus did not answer. He picked up the cloak that had been drying near the fire.

'It's still wet,' protested Dionysius.

'It doesn't matter. I don't have time to wait for it to dry. I must go back.'

'It's dark out. Sleep here and leave first thing in the morning.'

'It's always dark, lately. What difference does it make?' He threw the cloak over his shoulders and went out.

Dionysius stood at the threshold, watching the hooded figure as he walked away and listening to the thunder rumbling in the distance on the crests of the Hyblaean Mountains.

The next day he was summoned by Daphnaeus shortly after dawn.

'You must leave immediately for Syracuse,' he told him. 'You must report to the Council within three days at the most. You'll be able to change horses at our garrisons along the way.'

'Why must I leave? I'm much more useful here.'

'You must leave because I've ordered you to do so. We'll do fine here without you.'

Dionysius feigned disappointment. Before departing, he took a glance at the missive on Daphnaeus's table, the fragments of the wax seal still scattered around it. He then cast a last look into his commander's eyes; his expression was difficult for Daphnaeus to decipher but promised no good.

Dionysius tore through the countryside on his horse and arrived at Camarina before evening. He found Philistus already at Proxenus's house, where they would be spending the night.

The news of the fall of Acragas had spread panic through the city; some were already preparing to leave for destinations inland, particularly those who had estates and farms, but both the government of the city and the Assembly of Warriors had decided to send reinforcements to Gela, if she were attacked, and to defend her at any cost.

'They've finally understood that no city can suffice unto herself,' concluded Philistus.

'No, I think they've always known that,' objected Dionysius. 'And the army at Acragas was twice as strong as the force that the Athenians attacked us with during the war. What's been missing is a hand capable of guiding them.'

'That's true,' commented Proxenus. 'Look what's happening now in Athens. I was there three months ago selling weapons.

They've never recovered from the setback they suffered here in Sicily, and now they've driven off the only man who could still win a naval battle: Alcibiades, Pericles's nephew. They said he'd gone off whoring while his fleet engaged Lysander in battle; it may very well be true, but now who are they going to get to command them? Conon, can you imagine? The poor idiot has never won a battle in his life. In fact, the first thing he did was to get himself stuck in the port of Mitilene—'

'Did you go to the theatre in Athens?' interrupted Philistus, changing the subject.

'Yes, but there's very little left to see any more. Tragic theatre died with Euripides and Sophocles. But comedy, now that's another matter. I went to a comedy by Aristophanes and let me tell you, I nearly died laughing. There's never been anyone like him – he insults politicians, lawyers, philosophers, even the people in the audience, calls them assholes, and yet everyone in the theatre is rocking with laughter.'

'If the Spartans won,' broke in Dionysius, bringing the conversation back to their prior topic, 'they'd be free to send the army and fleet to Sicily to help us.'

'Don't count on it,' replied Proxenus. 'They've had enough of all these wars themselves. Hostilities have been going on for almost thirty years. No matter how things end up, there will be no winners or losers. They're all grieving over their best young men lost on the battlefield, their scorched fields, their destroyed crops. Tens of cities have been razed, entire populations sold into slavery. Without even considering trade, which has practically disappeared; prices are sky high. When you can find something to buy, that is. Even the essentials are hard to come by.'

'It's different here,' insisted Dionysius. 'It's our very existence that's at risk. But it doesn't matter, we'll handle this on our own if we have to.' He paused. 'On our own,' he growled.

*

A few days later, Philistus and Dionysius arrived in Syracuse, in time to participate in the plenary Assembly. Dionysius had registered to speak and was number twelve on the list. Leptines was at his side, and every now and then he would exchange glances and imperceptible signals with other friends from the Company scattered throughout the Assembly. When the moment came, the registrar raised a placard with the letter 'M' which meant that the twelfth person was authorized to speak. Dionysius took the floor.

Heedless of the winter's chill, he was wearing only his short military tunic as he took his place at the podium; he wore the recent wounds he had suffered on the battlefield to his arms, his thighs, his shoulders, as decorations. He was greeted by a roar of approval and applause. He raised his muscular arms to thank the Assembly and to ask for silence, and then began to speak.

'Citizens and authorities of Syracuse! I have come to denounce a new catastrophe. I know that you've already learned of the fall of Acragas and of the end of this glorious city, which has always been our ally and our sister. But believe me, no one better than I can describe the true extent of this disaster, the worst that we have experienced in all these years. This tragedy was entirely attributable to the injudicious behaviour of the officers who commanded our troops . . .'

The registrar rose and called the Assembly to order. 'Beware of how you speak!' he warned Dionysius. 'You will not be allowed to offend men who still enjoy the trust of the city as the high commanders of our army.'

'Then I will be more precise,' continued Dionysius and, raising his voice, thundered: 'I accuse, before all of you gathered here today, commander Daphnaeus and his entire staff of generals of high treason and collusion with the enemy!'

The registrar interrupted him again. 'An accusation of such magnitude, formulated using such inflammatory language, is an offence. You are hereby fined ten minae. Guards!'

The two mercenaries on duty went to Dionysius to exact the sum that he most certainly did not possess; if he were unable to pay, they would arrest him.

Philistus stood immediately, raised his arm and shouted: 'I'll pay! Continue.' He sent his servant to pay the ten minae under the registrar's astonished eyes.

'I accuse them of treason,' continued Dionysius, 'because although definitive victory over the enemy was close at hand, they stopped us as we charged forward and enjoined us to fall back. They betrayed with intent to deceive, taking advantage of our sense of discipline and our obedience to our homeland and our commanders, in order to open an escape route for the barbarians!'

Shouts, applause and cries of indignation burst out all over the Assembly, where numerous groups of Company members made public display of their enthusiasm or disapproval, communicating their feelings energetically to those alongside them.

In the meantime, the registrar, speechless at Dionysius's unstoppable oration and at the unprecedented break with procedure, anxiously watched the sand shift through the hourglass, waiting for the moment at which regulations allowed him to impose an even greater fine. 'Twenty minae!' he shouted, as soon as he saw the top bowl empty, without even taking notice of what Dionysius was saying.

'Paid,' shouted Philistus, raising his arm.

Another roar exploded, as though people were at the stadium urging on their favourite champion, and Dionysius continued with his unrestrained harangue. He vividly evoked the significant moments of the battle, the senseless decisions, the dramatic meeting with the city's representatives, the absurd order to evacuate. He also told of how they had been deceived into believing that the Punic ships had already been pulled aground in Panormus, while in truth they were waiting to swoop down unawares on the Syracusan fleet. He attributed this false account without a qualm to Daphnaeus and his cohorts, convinced as he was deep down that it was the truth; the fact that it was not provable at the moment was a matter of little or no importance.

The increasingly querulous voice of the registrar continued to announce higher and higher fines, all of which were promptly covered by Philistus's apparently bottomless fortune, so that the spectators were not certain at times whether they were at the height of the most dramatic of assemblies, or at an auction where the commodity for sale was nothing less than the truth.

The registrar gave up in the end and let Dionysius's sweeping eloquence flow without restraint. His words inflamed the crowd, the scenes he recalled moved them to tears, made them tremble with indignation and shout out their rage, their disappointment, their shock.

When he realized that he had the Assembly just where he wanted them, he concluded his speech, certain that nothing would be denied him.

'Citizens!' he roared. 'The barbarians will uproot our city, glorious victor of Athens, as well. You will see your wives raped, your children enslaved! They will string you up on their swords and torture you to death. I've seen them, I've fought them, I've killed hundreds of them to save our brothers in Selinus, in Himera and in Acragas, but the love or the valour of one man alone cannot suffice to deliver our threatened homeland. You who risk your lives on the line of combat, you who carry a shield and wield a spear, you must elect your generals not on the basis of their wealth and social standing, but on the basis of your own personal esteem! You must condemn these faithless officers who have betrayed you and sold themselves to the enemy, sentence them to perpetual exile, or even to death, if they dare to enter the city again without your permission. And then you must put those you do esteem in their places: those who you have always seen battling with honour and with passion, those who have never tossed aside their shields and taken to their heels. They must be the men who will lead you in battle and guide our allies. Let us put an end once and for all to this shameful sequence of defeats and massacres! How can barbarian mercenaries get the better of disciplined, courageous citizens, if not aided by betrayal? Let me say more: those who govern us are incapable and undeserving of the offices they hold. We must drive them out once and for all and elect men who are worthy of our trust!'

Such a huge clamour arose in the Assembly that even Dionysius and Philistus had difficulty in quelling the uproar. Heloris proposed immediately that the traitorous generals be sentenced by default that very day. When his proposal was approved by an enormous majority, he presented a list of candidates to cover the positions of command in the main battalions of the army. They were mostly unfamiliar names, except for Dionysius, who won nearly unanimous approval.

When he left the Assembly at noon amidst ovations, Dionysius was the most powerful man in Syracuse; his fellow officers were less than his shadow and they owed him everything, including their election.

Three days later, Daphnaeus and his generals received a copy of the proceedings of the session which sentenced them to exile. Dionysius was officially named the supreme commander of the armed forces, and he presented himself to the troops wearing a suit of shining armour decorated in silver and copper, holding his spear in his right hand and a shield with the image of a bloody-fanged gorgon in his left. The shouts and cheers of his warriors rose all the way up to the Temple of Athena on the acropolis, their echo booming against the great doors of bronze.

14

THE EXILED SYRACUSAN generals settled in Henna, awaiting better times. They must certainly have realized what hundreds, or even thousands, of citizens had felt when political defeat drove them from their cities. Daphnaeus was said to be planning his return, but he was found dead in his house at the end of the winter. His death was rumoured to be a summary execution ordered by Dionysius and carried out by some member of the Company.

Dionysius in the meantime was preparing to consolidate his power in the city and to wage the war his way. He wanted no limitations, would accept no conditions.

'That won't be easy, in a democracy,' observed Philistus as they met one day in his study.

'I want to win, and to win I need full command.'

'Diocles had full command at Himera, as did Daphnaeus at Acragas, and both lost.'

'They lost because they were incompetent. If they had been given greater powers, it would have been worse. That won't happen to me: I know what needs to be done, I swear it. Everything is very clear in my mind. Remember that night in Gela?'

'That night it was storming . . .'

'After you left, I tried to get some rest. I was dead tired, but I couldn't fall asleep and so I decided to take a look around. I covered the entire sentry walkway up on the walls, both on the side facing the sea and on the side facing inland. I've been back, several times, in secret. Himilco will strike Gela soon, when the weather begins to turn warm, and I'll be ready. I'll rip him to pieces.'

'Careful.'

'I know what I'm saying. You'll leave as soon as it's possible to set out by sea and you'll go to our allies in Locri, Croton and Rhegium and convince them to send all the troops they have available. Convince them that if they let us fall, it will be their turn next. If necessary, you can make up some false document in Punic detailing a plan of invasion of the Greek colonies in Italy, tell them that we got it from a spy and ... you know, you're good at these things. You know what I mean.'

'I do.'

'Will you do it?'

Philistus smiled. 'Have I ever disappointed you?'

'Good. Now I have to get rid of the other officers, at least the ones who are getting in my way.'

'You can't do that!'

'Of course I can.'

'You know what that means, don't you?'

'No, no, it's not what you're thinking. I just want to discredit them for the time being. We'll start the rumour that they're in league with the Carthaginians, that they're taking money from Himilco.'

'Don't count on me. They want nothing to do with him and you know it. What you propose is detestable.'

'It's necessary to save the city.'

'And the security of the city coincides with your rise to power.'

'With my leadership. I must lead the people into battle, because only I can deliver the city from annihilation, protect her temples from profanation, save her people from slavery.'

Philistus fell silent, not knowing what to say. He was pacing back and forth in his study and he felt Dionysius's gaze resting heavily upon him.

'You know,' he said, stopping right in the centre of the room, 'you should have been born at the time of Homer. That was your era. You should have been born a king, like Achilles, Diomedes, Agamemnon ... But those times are over, Dionysius. For ever, and they'll never come back. We live in big cities where all the social classes want to be represented, and where leaders are elected and dismissed on the basis of their merits and demerits.'

'On the basis of their scheming!' exclaimed Dionysius.

'Scheming? And just what are you doing? Are you any better?'

Dionysius loomed up close in silence, with a look so fierce that Philistus feared he was about to attack him. Instead he lowered his head and his voice: 'I need your advice, I need your friendship. Don't leave me alone. I don't know how to make you think I'm any better. I can only ask if you believe in me or if you don't, if you're my friend or if you aren't. If you're with me or against me, Philistus.'

'You have Leptines. He's your brother.'

'Leptines is a good lad and he's faithful to me, but I need your intelligence, your experience and, most of all, your friendship. What's your answer?'

'You're asking me to blindly accept your decisions, and your vision of the world.'

'That's what I'm asking. In the name of everything that binds us, of everything we've gone through together.'

Philistus sighed. 'You know I'd do anything for you. But I have certain moral convictions that are difficult to give up. More than difficult . . . painful.'

'I know. And as strange as it seems, I understand you. In any case, the problem is troublesome but simple: you must simply look inside yourself and see whether the love you have for me is stronger than your principles. That's all. But I need your answer. Now.'

Philistus fell silent and walked over to the window to watch the seagulls flying amidst the masts and sails of the Great Harbour, over the red roofs of Ortygia and the Temple of Athena. When he turned, his eyes were shiny and he seemed to have lost his usual assurance, his proverbial control over his emotions. 'I'm with you,' he said with a sigh. 'I'm ready to follow you.'

'All the way to Hades?'

'All the way to Hades.'

Dionysius embraced him, then looked him straight in the eye. 'I knew you wouldn't abandon me.'

'I was about to do just that.'

'You're still in time. No one's stopping you.'

Philistus said nothing.

Dionysius handed him a little slip of paper with a list of names. 'These are the officers we need out of our way. The others owe us their election, so they'll do as I say, at least for a while.'

Philistus nodded and took the sheet as Dionysius turned to go. 'Wait,' he said.

Dionysius, already at the threshold, stopped.

'You weren't like this. You were never like this; why such ruthlessness now?'

A despairing light flashed in Dionysius's eyes, so sudden and brief it was nearly imperceptible. 'You know very well why,' he said. And left.

Philistus returned with slow steps to watch the seagulls wheeling outside. But only the swallows circling close under the roof saw his tears.

Seven days later, the narrow streets of Ortygia echoed in the deep of night with the pounding footsteps of Dionysius's mercenaries: six of the ten officers who formed the War Council were arrested as they slept and taken to prison, accused of collusion with the enemy. The remaining four were quick to confirm their complete, unquestioned loyalty to their chief. The imprisoned officers were replaced by friends of Dionysius, including his adoptive father Heloris, his brother Leptines and his friends Biton, Iolaus and Doricus, members of the Company all.

Springtime came late that year and a series of storms made navigation impossible for long months. When Himilco left Acragas, it was nearly summer; he had burned down the temples, profaned the sanctuaries and disfigured the artwork that adorned them. The statues of the gods and heroes, many of which were true masterpieces, were hammered to pieces. The bronze, the silver, the gold and the ivory were plundered and sent to Carthage.

Among them was the famous bronze bull that the tyrant Phalaris was rumoured to have used to torture and kill his political adversaries. The Carthaginians sent it to Tyre, their metropolis, as a token of their homage and respect.

Then the army moved towards Gela overland, as the fleet followed by sea, carrying the disassembled pieces of the war machines.

Gela's citizens decided at first to evacuate their women and children to Syracuse, but they refused to obey. As the women of Selinus and Himera had before them, they took refuge in the temples and hung on to the altars, vowing not to abandon their city and their homes for any reason. There was no convincing them, but the reoccurrence of the same gestures in the same situations was an ominous reminder of what had already come to pass.

At first Himilco had planned to locate a detachment east of the city on the Gela river, as he had at Acragas, but he then changed his mind and concentrated his forces in a fortified camp west of Gela. He assembled the assault towers and began to batter the walls with the rams.

The walls of Gela were similar to the walls of Selinus, built when machines of that sort were not even imaginable, and they began to crumble and give way at the first blows of the huge, powerful rams. But by night, while the combat-weary warriors slept to recover their strength, the women, old men, slaves and children worked like ants to repair the damage, to close the breaches, to reinforce the weakest stretches. In this way over a month passed without either of the adversaries prevailing.

Vexed by the obstinate resistance of the Geloans, the Carthaginians turned to one of the city's most sacred symbols: a gigantic statue of Apollo which stood outside the walls, not far from their camp. It was twenty-two feet tall, and had stood there on the beach from time immemorial, marking the spot where the city's founders had landed. The monument commemorated Apollo, Leader of Men who had guided the voyagers by sea to the foot of the hill where they had established their community.

The Carthaginians used their war machines and the winches from their ships to wrench it from its pedestal and tip it over. They then slid it down tallow-greased wooden ramps, loaded it on to a ship and had it towed all the way to Carthage.

Watching that sacred image being taken from Gela was a terrible blow for all her people, as if the whole history of the city had abruptly been wiped out. But their rage sustained the combatants and imbued them with new energy.

Time passed, and the Geloan generals sent continuous, desperate requests for assistance to Syracuse, where Dionysius had still not resolved all his problems with the Assembly. In a tempestuous meeting, he proposed the recall of the political exiles who had participated in Hermocrates's attempted coup, arousing indignant protests from many of those present.

'With what courage can we ask our allies,' proclaimed Dionysius in an ardent speech, 'to risk their lives to support us when we are preventing hundreds of Syracusans from fighting for their own city? I'm not here to discuss the gravity of their offences, and you all know that I have never had any sympathy for aristocrats and landowners: I am one of you, one of the people! But one thing is certain: they've often been asked by the barbarians to fight in their ranks, lured by promises to restore their lost pride and confiscated property, but they have always refused! Now our city needs all of her sons. Now that we are facing mortal danger, we cannot be divided by internal disputes. I'm asking you now to call them back and allow them to atone for any misdeeds they may have committed.'

Once again, Dionysius's sweeping eloquence had the desired effect, and his order of the day was approved. He also succeeded in having himself named autocrator, or sole commander, a position which gave him nearly absolute power.

The Italian allies finally arrived, accompanied by Philistus. Dionysius felt greatly encouraged, and certain now that he could win, despite the news arriving from Gela which described the city as being on her last legs, incapable of resisting much longer. But Dionysius was not thinking of the military campaign alone.

Convinced as he was that his power must be consolidated at any cost, he delayed taking action until his friends were successfully installed in the key roles of the State and in all the centres of power.

Still not content, before leaving he persuaded the Assembly to double the salaries of his mercenaries, producing evidence that Himilco had infiltrated paid assassins into the city with the aim of having him murdered. By the time he was finally ready to move, it was the end of the summer.

*

His army boasted nearly thirty thousand Sicilian Greeks, of whom twenty thousand were Syracusans. They were joined by fifteen thousand Italian Greeks and five thousand mercenaries. The cavalry, composed almost completely of aristocrats, counted a couple of thousand equipped with the finest gear money could buy.

When the confederate army came within sight of Gela, the cheering from the walls was so loud that it reached the Carthaginians' fortified camp. Dionysius entered the city on horseback, his armour blazing and his crested helmet low over his forehead, as the crowd screamed with joy, parting to let him pass. Behind him were his select troops, marching with a cadenced step, covered with bronze and iron, carrying big shields decorated with fantastic monsters: gorgons, dragons, hydras and sea serpents. A triskelion, the symbol of Sicily, stood out on Dionysius's shield of shining silver.

And yet, even amidst all the applause and acclamation, many in the crowd could not help but think of the enemy army camped outside, towards the west: unceasingly victorious, inexorable, implacable. They had uprooted and destroyed one community after another, and neither men nor gods had ever been able to stop them.

Dionysius held council that same evening alongside the Geloan generals, some of whom were haughty, presumptuous noblemen, and he immediately met with difficulty. After their initial euphoria, they remembered that they had already seen that arrogant young man the previous winter, and they couldn't believe that he held the supreme command of such an army. They felt, on the contrary, that the direction of the war should be shared equally, and decisions made collectively.

Leptines took care of the matter personally, doing away with four out of seven, the most stubborn, in less than eight days. He spread the word that they had deserted and gone over to the enemy. Their property and goods were confiscated and Dionysius used the money to pay Dexippus's mercenaries, who were considerably in arrears of their salaries. He detested the man and considered him incompetent, but at the moment he had no choice; he needed all the help he could get.

Dionysius called a War Council seven days later. Leptines, Heloris, Iolaus, Biton and Doricus were present, along with the three Geloan officers and two Italians, the cavalry commander, Dexippus and even Philistus, admitted as councillor to the commander-in-chief. They met on the highest tower of the walls, from which they could view the entire city, the inland region, the coastline and the Carthaginian camp.

'My plan is perfect,' Dionysius started. 'I've been studying it for months. It's all engraved in my mind: every move, every phase, every detail of the action.

'Now we're on difficult ground here, because the city is stretched out on this hill parallel to the sea; Himilco was very astute to set up camp so close. It doesn't leave us much space to manoeuvre. If I had commanded the army here in Gela, I would have made sure to occupy that land a long time ago, but what's done is done, and there's no sense laying blame now.

'You'll notice that the Carthaginian camp is unfortified on the seaward flank: they're obviously not expecting a threat to come from there, and it is from there that destiny will strike. We'll make the first move. Heloris will lead the Sicilians, flanked by the cavalry; they'll approach from the north shortly after dawn and will immediately draw up in fighting order. Himilco will imagine that we are seeking a decisive frontal battle as Daphnaeus did at

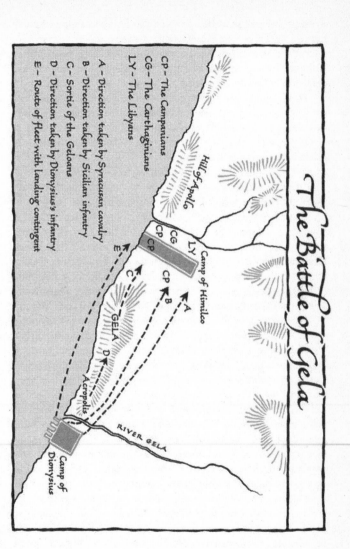

The Battle of Gela

Hill of Apollo

Camp of Himilco

CP CG LY

CP

CP B

A

C

E

GELA

D

Acropolis

RIVER GELA

Camp of Dionysius

CP – The Campanians
CG – The Carthaginians
LY – The Libyans

A – Direction taken by Syracusan cavalry
B – Direction taken by Sicilian infantry
C – Sortie of the Geloans
D – Direction taken by Dionysius's infantry
E – Route of fleet with landing contingent

Acragas, and will send ahead the Libyan heavy infantry, who will have to fight with the morning sun in their eyes. But at the very same time, the Italians will be attacking from along the sea; they will assault the entrenched camp at the one point in which it isn't defended . . .'

'How's that?' asked one of the Geloan generals. 'There's not enough space to put through a contingent that would be numerous enough to storm the camp. They would have to advance in single file, and when the first are ready to launch the attack, the others will be too far behind.'

Dionysius smiled. 'They'll be landing from the sea, all at once. The fleet, concealed behind the hill, will advance until it's very close to the shore and will disembark five battalions. They'll wait on that wide clearing you see down there, hidden from the enemy's sight, until they receive the signal that I myself will give from the western gate: a red cloth, raised and lowered three times. In the meantime, I will have crossed the city from east to west at the head of my select troops and the mercenaries. At this point Heloris, leading the bulk of our troops, will send ahead the cavalry in a converging manoeuvre. Doricus and Iolaus will back him up.

'Himilco will be forced to split up his forces to face the double threat: Heloris from the north and the Italians from the south. That will be my moment. I will be at the western gate, ready to launch the attack. I'll plough into the enemy lines with my assault troops and skirmishers, and the Geloan heavy infantry will come up from behind to support our assault.

'Heloris's cavalry will be circling around the Carthaginian contingent out on the field, while his heavy infantry, led by Biton and Iolaus, are engaging them frontally. In less than an hour, the joint manoeuvres of my troops and of the Italian allies will have won the upper hand over the camp's defenders. Himilco will be crushed between my contingent – united with the Geloans and the Italians – and Heloris's forces. There will be no way out.

'Spare those who surrender en masse; we can sell them to pay off some of the war expenses. The Carthaginian officers will be executed immediately, without torture. We'll take in the mercenaries if they decide to desert. I want Himilco alive, if possible. If there's someone here who feels differently, please speak up. Good advice is always welcome.'

No one spoke. The audacity of the plan had taken them all by surprise and no one seemed to have any objections. It was all so clear, the movements on the ground so evident, the various divisions so perfectly coordinated.

'I have a question,' said Dexippus all at once.

'Speak,' replied Dionysius.

'Why are you starting off from the eastern side of Gela with your contingent? You'll be forced to cross the entire city to reach the western gate from where you plan to attack.'

'If I moved from any other direction, I'd be seen. Mine will be the final hammer blow. I'll come out of the Acragantine Gate like an actor emerging from behind the stage and then the show will begin! What do you say?'

Several interminable moments of silence followed instead of the acclamation which Dionysius had expected, but then a Locrian officer named Cleonimus said: 'Brilliant. Worthy of a great strategist. Who did you learn from, *hegemon*?'

'From a master. My wife's father, Hermocrates. And from the mistakes of others.'

'In any case,' replied Cleonimus, 'we'll still need luck. Let's not forget that at Acragas we'd already won.'

*

Philistus went to visit him late that night. 'Worried?' he asked.

'No. We'll triumph.'

'I hope so.'

'And yet . . .'

'And yet you don't feel right and you can't get to sleep. Do you know why? Because it's your turn now. The other commanders always had some excuse: limited powers, quarrelsome staff officers, internal dissent . . . You have full powers and the greatest army ever assembled in Sicily in at least fifty years. If you do lose, it will be your fault alone, and this is what frightens you.'

'I won't lose.'

'That's what we all hope. Your plan is very interesting.'

'Interesting? It's a masterpiece of strategic art.'

'Yes, but it has a defect.'

'What?'

'It's like a table game. On the battlefield things will be different; the unexpected always comes up. Linking the forces, enemy response, timing . . . Timing, above all. How will you manage to coordinate the manoeuvres of a military initiative on the battle-field, a contingent to be disembarked, a citizens' army making a sortie and a battalion of assault troops which has to cross the entire city?'

Dionysius smirked. 'Another armchair strategist! I didn't know you were such an expert on the ways of war! It will work, I'm telling you. I've already arranged for all the signalling points and for dispatch riders as well. It has to work.'

*

Dionysius raised his eyes to the mask of Gorgon displayed on the eastern tympanum of the Temple of Athena Lindos and leaned over the battlements to scan the countryside to the north of the city: Heloris's army was advancing with the Sicilian contingent, twenty battalions spread out over a wide front in two long lines. He could even make out the commander, riding ahead of all the rest.

He waved a red cloth from the roof of the Athenaion and waited for a like signal from the head of the advancing army confirming that the order had been received. He crossed to the opposite side of the walls, towards the south, where the fleet was rocking at anchor in front of the mouth of the Gela river. He signalled three times using a polished shield that reflected the light of the newly risen sun. The flagship responded immediately, hoisting a red flag on to the stern staff. He soon could see the oars dipping into the water, and the large battle vessel began moving slowly westward, hugging the coast, followed by the other ships four-across.

Dionysius pounded his fist on the parapet and shouted to his officers: 'Perfect! Everything's going according to plan! It's our turn to move now: we'll cross the city in the same amount of time that it will take the fleet to cover the stretch of coast between the mouth of the river and the Carthaginian camp. The coordination of all the subsequent operations depends on us. All right men, let's go!'

They marched along the southern side of the temple, down towards the centre of the city, setting off through the maze of alleyways that crossed the city in a more or less parallel design. But they soon met with trouble.

Dionysius had ordered the townspeople to remain in their homes until his contingent had passed, but instead his column found itself at the head of a street packed with people making their way with carts and assorted goods towards the eastern gate, that is, heading in the opposite direction to which the troops were marching. Clearly a good number of citizens did not believe that the confederate army would manage to win. The rumour had in fact spread that the high command was held by a twenty-four-year-old youth who had never had experience commanding a battalion, much less a division.

Dionysius was seized by a dizzying sense of anguish: the risk that Philistus had warned him about. *Tyche*. Fickle, evil fortune, already acting to interfere with the perfect mechanism he had conceived. He immediately had the heralds shout out orders to clear the road and let the column through, but many did not hear and those that did hear could not turn around, since they were being pushed from behind by those who had heard nothing. The troops could certainly not clear the way using their weapons; the crowd was defenceless, the city Syracuse's sister and friend . . .

Heloris meanwhile continued to advance, but the recently ploughed fields, the burnt stumps of the olive trees and rubble of various nature obstructed their march and delayed the army's progress. Much of the element of surprise was thwarted; when the Sicilians were finally ready to draw up in battle array, they had already been spotted, and Himilco's army charged into combat with great impetus.

On the opposite side of the camp, the Italians had landed and were regrouping according to their cities of origin. They took position behind the cliffs of the southern promontory so as not to be seen, but a dispatch rider soon galloped up and reported that the Carthaginian camp was unprotected on that side, since the heavy infantry were all out fighting Heloris's army corps. He urged them to attack immediately, before their presence was noted.

'No,' replied Cleonimus, the Locrian commander, 'we've agreed to wait for Dionysius's signal from the western gate! Let no one move without a direct order from me!'

The troops were held in check, but their commanders realized that the men were already pervaded by the excitement of the attack, by what the veterans call *orgasmòs*: that frenetic congestion of mind and muscle that precedes a battle, compressing all the combatant's energy into his body as he readies to enter the fray, a tension that cannot be sustained at length without gravely damaging both physical strength and morale.

'By all the gods! We have to do something here!' exclaimed a battalion commander by name of Carilaus.

'No,' replied the Locrian officer obstinately. 'I promised I would wait for the signal.'

Carilaus turned and gave an odd look to a comrade, who shouted at once: 'The signal! I see the signal! Look!'

'I see nothing,' replied the Locrian commander.

'I'm telling you I saw it, up there. There, look! Those are Dionysius's troops!'

They could indeed see a heavy infantry contingent exiting the gate and drawing up at the top of the hill.

It was not Dionysius. They were Geloan warriors who, nervous at not seeing their commander arrive, had taken position overlooking the camp so they would be ready to intervene if necessary.

Finally convinced, the Locrian commander imagined that

Carilaus's comrade must have actually spotted the signal; even if that were not the case, they couldn't wait much longer. He gave the order to attack. The Italian allies bellowed their war cry and, shields held high, came out of hiding and rushed towards the camp. They covered the brief distance in no time and fiercely engaged the Carthaginians who were thronging towards the threatened sector to keep them out.

At first they managed to force the defenders back and to break into the camp but, once inside, they soon found themselves greatly outnumbered by the well-equipped contingent of Iberian and Campanian infantry left by Himilco to defend the camp.

Surrounded on all sides, the Italians fought it out hand to hand until they were driven back and pushed out towards the coast. The Geloans charged down the hill then to come to the assistance of their routed allies, who were already at the water-line at this point and seemed to be in serious difficulty. Fortunately, someone on the ships ordered the archers to let loose, and swarms of arrows struck the Iberian and Campanian pursuers, decimating them. The defenders finally retired back into the encampment.

Their attempt having failed, the Italian Greeks scrambled on to their ships and set sail, while the Geloans, who were loath to abandon the defence of their walls, disengaged with the enemy and poured back into their city.

When Dionysius finally emerged from the western gate, he saw Heloris retreating towards the north; now that Himilco had staved off the other attacks, he was fighting the Sicilian contingent in full force, with greatly superior numbers. Dionysius managed to pull back into the city just in time to avoid a catastrophe. The Italian allies had lost six hundred men and Heloris more than one thousand, although they had also inflicted heavy losses on the enemy.

Dionysius's careful, long-studied plans had failed. No one believed any more that he was capable of leading a second operation against the Carthaginians. The city was doomed.

15

DIONYSIUS CALLED A Council of War that same night, in a climate poisoned by protests, recriminations and accusations. He himself was overwhelmed at such a crushing and totally unexpected defeat, but he realized that he had everything at stake here and that he must not defend himself, but attack. He began immediately to speak in a very loud voice to be heard over the grumbling of the officers present. They fell silent.

'Friends!' he began. 'The plan which I proposed to you and which you approved on the eve of this unfortunate battle was a perfect one. What occurred cannot be explained except by treason!'

Prolonged muttering from the generals met his words, joined by sneers from the commanders of the Syracusan cavalry, all aristocrats.

'I'm not accusing any of you present here,' he continued, 'but how can you explain what happened this morning? How else can you explain those throngs of people along the only road that we could traverse in time to reach the western gate? My brother Leptines covered the route at least five times with a squad of armed men to calculate how long it would take to get to the appointed rallying point. And yet, my fellow commanders, this morning it took us five times longer than it had taken him! I measured it myself, by the length of the shadow of my spear!'

'It's true!' confirmed Leptines. 'I myself issued the order to keep the road clear!'

'What were all those panic-stricken people doing there at that time, in that place? Who told them to get ready to flee from the

Camarina gate?' The protests ceased. 'Who gave the order to attack the camp? Certainly not I, because when I arrived, our Italian allies were already withdrawing.'

Cleonimus instinctively glanced over at the officer who had claimed to have seen the signal from the western gate, but the man avoided his eyes. He had noticed him shortly beforehand exchanging words with one of the Syracusan cavalry commanders, and that had seemed strange to him. But he called out loudly: 'It was I who gave the order! One of my men said they'd spotted the signal and immediately thereafter we saw armed men exiting the gate. It was the Geloan infantry, but at such a distance, how could we tell?'

'I'm not accusing you, Cleonimus,' replied Dionysius. 'But have the man who claimed to have seen the signal investigated; you may be surprised by what you find.'

'It's useless to return one accusation with another!' began an officer of the Syracusan cavalry, a certain Elorus, a member of one of the oldest families of the city, a direct descendent of the founder himself, or so he claimed. 'What's done is done. We've been defeated, and—'

'That's not true!' exclaimed Dionysius. 'We had our losses, you all know that, but the losses we inflicted were much worse. In all fairness, if you look at the battle from this point of view, we are the victors. But that's not what I'm here to talk about. I'm ready to attack again as soon as tomorrow. This time, men, we'll strike with two corps: assault troops from the sea, and the bulk of our ground forces from land. We'll crush those bastards and then we'll see whose cock is harder!'

His ploy did not work. No one responded to his impromptu call to arms.

'It's not the right place,' said Cleonimus. 'We saw that today. We Italians have already held a council. This whole campaign has got off to too late a start. If the weather worsens, we won't be able to cross the Straits. Our cities will be undefended. We have our own barbarians to watch out for, as you all know.'

'I agree with him,' nodded Elorus, the Syracusan cavalry

commander. 'Many of our horses went lame in the middle of those blasted olive stumps and we had to bring them down. The terrain is no good for cavalry.'

Dionysius felt the ground suddenly collapsing beneath his feet. He turned to his adoptive father, Heloris. 'And you? Do you feel the same way?'

'It's not a question of courage here, boy; we have to consider all the elements at hand, the risks we're facing and the situation we find ourselves in. Let's say that bastard down there,' he said, pointing his thumb towards the sea, 'decides to close himself in and refuse to do battle. Why should he? But we have fifty thousand men here, and the population of this city to feed: if the weather changes, we're headed for disaster.'

'That's certain,' nodded Carilaus.

'If you want to attack, I'm with you,' protested Leptines.

'So am I, by Zeus!' exclaimed Doricus.

'As are we,' seconded Biton and Iolaus, the Syracusan infantry battalion commanders.

But Dionysius had to admit to himself that there was no morale or fighting spirit left among the men. The problem was that they no longer believed in him. They didn't feel that he could lead them to victory.

They had fought and he hadn't; they had faced the enemy, not him. They had risked their lives with their swords in hand and he had not. And when they had needed leadership and support, he wasn't around. He had never felt more alone and distressed.

Leptines must have realized his state of mind, given away by the sweat suddenly beading his forehead and his upper lip, because he drew close to his brother and murmured in the abstruse slang of the district they had grown up in: 'Careful, don't let them see your uncertainty or they'll tear you apart.'

Dionysius noticed the dismayed expression of Philistus, who stood aside by the doorway. He knew he had no choice, and the realization of what he had to do made him burn with shame, rage and frustration. He was about to perpetrate the same disgrace as

Diocles and Daphnaeus had. He was about to flood the city streets with desperate refugees, with women and children in tears. He was about to abandon the temples and the houses of a centuries-old city, founded in fulfilment of a sacred oracle, to violence and plunder. He knew that the only honourable gesture would be for him to find some excuse to leave the meeting and take his life with his own sword. An honourable solution, beyond reproach.

But Leptines sunk dagger-sharp fingers into his arm and hissed: 'React, for the sake of the gods!'

Dionysius started and spoke. His features were contorted but his voice was firm and hard. He said: 'Listen to me. A commander must foresee everything. Even treason, which is part of war. This is where I made my mistake, because I love my city – and all the Hellenic cities in Sicily and Italy – so much that I could never imagine betraying them, for any reason or any price. And so now I must make an unavoidable decision, the most bitter of my life. I will empty this city of her inhabitants and take them away, to safety.

'Yes, I'm speaking to you, valiant Geloan generals: you will see your people teeming down the road to exile this very night.

'I'm speaking to you as well, you valiant commanders who have come from Italy to help us, to offer the lives of the best of your youth, and I'm speaking to you, Syracusan friends. I swear to you now, upon all the gods and all the demons, that the barbarian will not triumph! I swear that I will drive him out of our cities; I will win them back one after another. I swear that I will bring you back to your homes and that the mere name of the Greeks of Sicily and Italy will strike such terror into the barbarians that they will never even dream of opposing us again.'

A deep silence fell on the hall. The Geloan officers seemed struck by lightning; they could not say a word. A low buzz arose from the Italians, but no one could certainly reproach them; they had shown exceptional bravery in their assault on the Carthaginian camp, paying a terrible cost in human lives. The Syracusans felt most directly responsible for the announced decision; they also knew that they would be the imminent target of the next Carthaginian move. They looked like people living in a nightmare they cannot awaken from.

Dionysius spoke again. 'Let us do the last thing that must be done, and let us do it immediately. Two thousand light infantrymen will remain on the walls all night to keep watch fires burning, so that the Carthaginians will assume that we're still here. The Geloan commanders will issue the order to evacuate quarter by quarter, so that the entire city will not fall into a panic. The people will be escorted by soldiers from their own district, who will inspire trust and tranquillity in their family members, friends and neighbours. Within one hour's time at the latest, the first columns will set off for Camarina from the eastern gate, in the dark and in complete silence.

'An embassy will leave immediately for the Carthaginian camp to negotiate a truce and the recovery of our dead. This will also gain time for us.

'Before dawn, the troops remaining on the walls will add extra wood to the fires, then disengage as quickly as possible before day has broken.

'I thank our allies for the help they have given us, and in wishing them farewell, I want to assure them that we shall see each other soon again, and that when we do, no one and nothing will stop us. I have nothing else to say. Go now, and may the gods protect you.'

He embraced the Italian Greek generals one by one, and the Geloan commanders as well. The latter received his embrace coldly at first, but then responded with more warmth as they saw Dionysius's eyes filled with consternation.

Dionysius went to his lodgings and began to pack his bags and prepare for the journey. Philistus entered.

'Have you come to remind me of your inauspicious predictions?' Dionysius asked him.

'I'm here to remind you that power alone is not enough to win certain challenges. I've come to remind you that you've just ordered an evacuation and that you're leaving the bodies of your fallen warriors unburied on the field of battle. I'm right, aren't I? The story of negotiating a truce is a farce, isn't it? You'll leave here with the first group out and you'll abandon them unburied, as Diocles did in Himera, as Daphnaeus did in Acragas!'

'I know!' shouted Dionysius. 'I know what happened in the past! Spare me your preaching!'

'You asked me to pledge my friendship and my blind faith. I have the right to know who I've placed my trust in!'

Dionysius turned towards the wall, hid his face in his arm and took a deep gasping breath. He said: 'What do you want to know?'

'If you were sincere when you said those words to the Council.'

'What words?'

'All that fine talk about the Greeks of Sicily and Italy, about reconquest, about young men fallen in battle . . . I want to know if those words were sincere and came from your heart, or whether it was just a hypocritical performance to avoid getting stoned like the Acragantine generals.'

'That's all you want to know?'

'I think so.'

'But I can't prove the truth of what I say.'

'No. I think not.'

'Then you may as well believe whatever you want to believe. And now let's get moving, we have a long night ahead of us.'

He girded his sword, slung his shield over his shoulder, grabbed a spear and left the room.

Philistus wanted to stop him and make him speak, but his voice wouldn't come out. He remained alone in the empty room, listening to the suffocated weeping of the women of Gela which filled the darkness.

*

Camarina had sturdy walls and was protected on the west by a marsh that would make it impossible to use the siege works on that side at least. The city would have been defendable if Himilco had remained in Gela. That was not to be so. As soon as he realized that the city had been deserted, the Carthaginian commander gave his mercenaries leave to sack it and to massacre the old and the infirm who had been left behind, and then he resumed his march. He was not worried about bad weather, he had no thought for the raging sea that might have damaged his fleet. He was convinced that nothing could stop him any more, and that the other Greek cities of Sicily would fall one after another like in some dreadful table game.

Every day, the dispatch riders who kept up the rear guard of the column reached Dionysius by sunset to report on exactly how close the pursuers were getting.

They weren't stopping. They wouldn't stop at anything.

The Italian Greeks had already separated from the rest of the confederate army, marching along the most direct route to the Straits, making any attempt at resistance unimaginable.

And so Camarina was abandoned as well.

Despite the considerable and evident low morale of the troops, Dionysius's orders were respected and he was still obeyed as the high commander of the Syracusan army.

The day after the evacuation of Camarina, Elorus, the commander of the Syracusan cavalry, claimed that suspicious movements had been reported at a point on the road still beyond them, at a distance of about fifty stadia. He requested permission to ride forward and open the passage, if necessary.

Dionysius consented and the officer galloped off with his men, about one thousand in all.

Leptines approached his brother. 'Where are they going?' he asked.

'Suspicious activity has been sighted at about fifty stadia from here. I'm afraid the Carthaginian light cavalry may have succeeded in passing ahead of us. They're going to secure the passage for us.'

'Secure a passage? Sounds to me like they're laying a trap for you. I don't like them. The Knights are all arrogant, insolent aristocrats who despise us because we don't belong to their caste and our accent is from the wrong side of town. You can be sure they're enjoying your humiliation. They couldn't care less about the troubles of these poor unfortunates,' he continued, pointing at the long line of refugees straggling along the path. 'All they care about is getting you defeated. Remember that.'

Dionysius said nothing. Naivety was the accusation that stung most. He would rather be considered a delinquent than a dupe. 'Where's Philistus?' he muttered.

'I don't know. The last time I saw him he was at the rear of the column, helping an old woman who couldn't walk.'

'I can't really believe that about the Knights. After all, I . . .'

'You married the daughter of Hermocrates? Forget it. Most of those assholes got drunk and made merry the night that you were wounded and she was . . .'

'Shut up!' shouted Dionysius with such vehemence that many of the refugees passing by turned towards him with an expression of fear.

'As you wish,' replied Leptines. 'But that's the way things are, even if you're hurt by it.'

'How can you be sure?' asked Dionysius after a while.

'There are some things I just know. Philistus does as well. Ask him.'

'He told me that everyone involved in the crime had been . . . taken care of.'

'Oh right, sure, those poor sons of bitches that we castrated, murdered and roasted. But the gentlemen, the noblemen, the descendants of the heroes and the gods, well that's a different matter. They don't get their hands dirty. They don't even have to bother to give certain orders; all they have to do is let someone know what would please them. And usually it doesn't even take that. All they have to do is look askance at somebody, or drop a name.'

'Get on your horse,' ordered Dionysius. 'Take a hundred of our fastest horsemen with you and follow them. Don't let yourself be seen. Then come back and tell me what you find. Go!'

Leptines didn't wait to be asked twice. He shouted out

something in slang and a group of skirmishers on horseback broke away from the column and caught up with him. At his signal, they launched into a gallop, as swift as the wind.

He was back a couple of hours later, his horse shining with sweat and nearly done in by exertion. In the meantime, Dionysius had asked for Philistus to come forward; his friend hadn't spoken to him since the night of the evacuation.

'Well?' demanded Dionysius.

'There's nothing up ahead. No Carthaginians, no trace of anyone else,' replied Leptines.

'What about our cavalrymen?'

'Vanished. Into thin air. Their tracks lead to Syracuse, though.'

Philistus approached, eyes blazing, and turned to Leptines. 'What in the name of Hades are you saying?'

'Nothing but the truth. I've loosed a dozen of the lads after them with orders to follow them and relay news back. If we get moving, we'll have fresh news every twenty stadia.'

'They're headed for Syracuse to rouse the people against me,' snarled Dionysius. 'I'm sure of it.'

'There's no doubt,' agreed Philistus. 'We have to move immediately, or it will be all over. You must go on at a forced march with all the available troops.'

Dionysius looked at the long line of refugees shuffling down the road and he felt his heart pounding as it had when he went into battle for the first time at eighteen. 'I just need a few men,' he said. 'The remaining cavalry and the skirmishers. Leptines, you'll take my place here . . .'

'Like hell I will. I'm coming to Syracuse with you.'

'It's the high commander speaking,' retorted Dionysius harshly. 'You'll do as I order.'

Philistus broke in. 'You'll need him, Dionysius. This is an extremely dangerous situation. Let Iolaus take command here. He's always been loyal to you and he already commands the fourth battalion of the phalanx.'

'All right. As you say. But let's get going, by all the gods!'

Iolaus was summoned urgently to take charge. Before mounting his horse, Dionysius embraced him and while his mouth was very close to his ear, he whispered: 'They mustn't suffer any more than they already have. Defend them with your life, if you have to.' He pulled away and, looking him straight in the eye, said loudly: 'Tell them that next year I'll be bringing them home.'

'I will, *hegemon*. See you at Syracuse.'

Dionysius mounted, waved briefly at Philistus and set off posthaste with his Campanian mercenary guard, Leptines and his skirmishers. A heavy infantry battalion followed them by forced marches.

Twenty stadia on they found the first relay team, consisting of three men on horseback who leapt to the ground, covered with sweat and dust. The weather was still very hot.

'*Hegemon*,' they greeted him. 'We are absolutely sure that the Knights are headed for Syracuse.'

'All right. Go join up with the rest of the troops, get something to eat and drink and take a rest.'

'If you'll permit it, we'd rather come with you. We are not weary, and we can be of use to you.'

'Then get yourselves some fresh horses and fall in.'

They made swift progress until they met up with the last team, at just fifteen stadia from Syracuse.

'The gate is barred,' reported the head of the squad, 'and we have no idea of what is going on in the city.'

'Is there an armed garrison at the gate?'

'No, I would say not.'

'Then they don't know we're here. Let's get moving.'

One of the horsemen stopped him. '*Hegemon* . . .'

'In the name of the gods!' burst out Dionysius. 'Tell me everything you have to say and let's get moving, once and for all!'

'They've done something to hurt you.'

Dionysius tried to imagine what they could have done at such a distance to hurt him, and couldn't think of a thing.

'They've opened your wife's tomb, *hegemon* . . .' blurted out the soldier.

'No!' roared Dionysius.

'And they've desecrated her body . . . the dogs have . . .'

Dionysius bellowed even louder, seized by such fury that the soldier was struck dumb. Stock-still he watched Dionysius spring on to his horse and lunge forward, sword in hand, as if his enemies were right in front of him.

'Follow him!' shouted Leptines. 'He's out of his mind!'

But Dionysius was perfectly lucid in his rage. He rode straight to the dockyards at the Great Harbour and ordered pitch to be brought to the gate. He burned down the doors to let his bodyguards and skirmishers through.

The Knights were holding council in the agora; they were planning to summon an Assembly the next day and declare the end of the reign of the 'tyrant', for it was such that they had already decided to call their political adversary.

They were completely taken by surprise. Dionysius, mindful of how he himself had been surrounded in that square along with Hermocrates and his men, had his troops enter from the side streets and alleys all around, blocking off any possible exit. He gave the order to attack and threw himself forward, his sword held high and his shield on his arm, plunging into the butchery with delirious abandon.

No one got away. No one was spared, not even those who threw themselves at his feet begging.

Late that night, assisted only by his brother Leptines, Dionysius burnt Arete's despoiled remains on an improvised pyre. He gathered up her ashes and buried them in a secret place that no one knew of but him. And on that same night he buried – in a place even more secret and hidden in his heart – all mercy, every trace of humanity.

16

THE MEETING OF Dionysius's most trusted friends was held at
Philistus's house in Ortygia. Besides the two of them, Iolaus,
Doricus and Biton were present; they were soon joined by Heloris,
overheated and out of breath. His brother was the last to arrive;
Dionysius nodded and Leptines told the others what he had
learned: 'They've sacked Camarina but they're not stopping there.
It's here they're headed.'

'Are you certain?' asked Dionysius, seemingly not too upset.

'I would say so. The road they've taken leads this way, and I
don't think they're coming on a courtesy visit.'

'Fine. They may succeed in getting here, but this is where
they'll get nailed. Our walls have driven back even the Athenians.
Our fleet is intact and so is our army. Why should they attempt
an endeavour that is destined to fail from the start?'

'Because they are convinced that they will not fail,' broke in
Philistus. 'They've succeeded five times, why not the sixth? Their
mercenaries are first-rate troops, and if they die, no one complains
about it: no public funerals, no speeches, no epigraphs. They toss
them into a ditch with a shovelful of dirt, and that's that. One less
salary to pay. We have to answer for every man we lose, answer
to his city and his family.'

'That's only right,' said Doricus. 'We are Greeks, after all.'

'Each one of us has a family,' added Biton.

'True,' admitted Dionysius. 'But then how did Theron of
Acragas and Gelon of Syracuse manage seventy years ago to wipe
out the Carthaginian army at Himera? I'll tell you how. Because
they had a vast territory from which they could draw all kinds of

material and human resources. The Greek cities are just clusters of houses stuck on the cliffs along the coast. The Carthaginians can pick us off one by one. In theory, our troops are superior in terms of weaponry and combat technique, but there is no true chain of command in our armies; someone decides to leave and off he goes. And no one can stop him. Fifteen, twenty thousand men go off at once and all of a sudden you are seriously deficient in numbers. Why? Because they have to go home and sow their fields. Their fields. Do you hear what I'm saying? By Heracles, war is a serious business! It must be fought by professionals.'

'I don't agree,' objected Iolaus. 'Mercenaries sell themselves to the highest bidder and think nothing of leaving you in the lurch at any time, for any reason. Remember Acragas? It was the desertion of the Campanian mercenaries that left the city defenceless.'

'That's not exactly true,' shot back Dionysius. 'Mercenaries stick with the winner; not with the loser or whoever looks like the loser. They stick with whoever pays them well, gives them the chance to plunder, knows how to lead them and won't squander their lives. They care about their skin just like we do, and they know how much it's worth.'

'You want a mercenary army?' asked Heloris with a note of wonder.

'At least the core, yes. Men who are nothing but soldiers; who spend all their time training, wielding weapons, fencing. Men who haven't got fields to cultivate or shops to manage, whose only source of income is their sword and their spear. It would be best if they were Greeks. It doesn't matter from where, but Greeks.'

Leptines got to his feet. 'I can't believe my ears. Those bastards are practically at our walls, and here we are talking about what we don't have and should have. Does anyone have any idea of how we're going to get out of this one?'

'Don't worry,' replied Dionysius. 'They're in for a sound thrashing at our walls. And if they try to come by sea, we'll send our whole fleet out to sink them. But I don't think that will be necessary. They'll see just how tough we can get and they'll be begging to negotiate. You'll see. What we have to do now is guard the walls day and night, reinforce the gates and station the fleet at the harbour outlets so that they can't lock us in. Then we'll sit and wait.'

'Wait?' asked Leptines, astonished.

'Wait,' repeated Dionysius.

Each of them left to carry out orders. Philistus sat down at his desk. He had long thought that the events he was witnessing deserved to be written down, and he was sure that what was about to happen would make history. It was going to be the fiercest fight ever fought between Greeks and barbarians, no less important than the Persian Wars narrated by Herodotus in his *History*. He was also convinced that he knew what his friend was planning: Dionysius would build a territorial Syracusan empire without giving a thought to anyone, Greeks or barbarians. He would create a new army, completely faithful to him, and use it in a duel to the death from which the Carthaginian enemy could expect no quarter.

Philistus took a fresh roll of papyrus from the drawer, laid it out and weighed down its sides on the table. He began to write a new chapter. Philistus did not usually dictate, as all those who intended to compose a literary work of any sort were wont to do; he preferred to write in person, like a humble scribe, because he liked to hear the slight sound the quill made as it glided across the papyrus lubricated by the ink, and to see the words being born and chasing one another on the white scroll. In doing so, he savoured a sense of power greater than any in the entire world: that of setting down human events for the years and perhaps the centuries to come. The power of representing men, their vices and their virtues, on the basis of his own irrevocable judgement. He was at that moment the *histor*: he who narrates because he knows; he who knows because he has seen and heard. But the terms of his judgement obeyed only the categories of his mind, and naught else.

And he was writing about Dionysius.

He had witnessed the destruction of splendid cities, the massacre of thousands of men, women and children, the deportation of entire peoples and, worst of all, the rape and murder of his beloved wife when she was still very young, killed by his own fellow citizens in a time of internal disorder. As most often occurs under such circumstances, two very strong concepts were branded into his mind: the first was that democracy is inefficient when it becomes necessary to make immediate decisions and conduct operations that involve radical choices; furthermore, a democracy is incapable of containing the excesses of either the lawless individual or the mob. The second was that any live Carthaginian in the land of Sicily was to be considered a threat for the existence of the Sicilian Greeks and therefore was better off dead. As far as the future of the Greeks was concerned, Dionysius was influenced by the disheartening example of the metropolises. Eighty years earlier, all of the main cities of Greece had allied and succeeded in defeating the empire of the Great King of the Persians, the largest that had ever existed on this earth, and yet now an endless struggle was going on among those very cities as they set themselves up for nothing but ruin. He was thus firmly committed to preventing this from happening in the West, and was sure that the only way of doing so was through the conquest and unification of the Greeks of Sicily and Italy in a single state. Autocracy, in his frame of mind, was the only way to achieve this. He was aware, I believe, of how much solitude a man who would govern on his own must face, how much danger and deceit. But – at least at first – he was able to count on the friends he had known since childhood and on his brother Leptines. They had lost their parents when Dionysius was but a boy.

Doricus was the son of a grain merchant and his mother was Italian, from Medma. He was the same age as Dionysius, and showed great daring. He had participated in the Olympic games as a boxer when he was an adolescent and had won in his category. He had taken part in all the military campaigns, receiving many wounds, whose scars he was wont to show with great pride.

Iolaus, just a bit older than they were, was attentive and reflective, virtues that he had developed by dedicating himself to his studies with a number of teachers. He was said to have attended Pitagoric schools in Italy, at Sybaris and Croton, where he had learned much about the secrets of the human body as well as the spirit.

Biton had survived a twin brother whose name was Cleobis, a mythological name like his own, recalling the heroes who had dragged their mother's chariot to the Temple of Hera, winning immortality. He was very strong, but quite calm-natured. Having lost his identical brother, he identified him with Dionysius and was completely devoted to him.

Besides being a brother, Leptines was a friend, the most one could hope for from life, but his impulsive temperament, his fondness for wine and for women and his sudden rages made him unreliable in war, where the valour and bravery that he possessed in great quantity were not always enough to ensure the favourable outcome of the operations.

In any case, this was the risk Dionysius took: founding his government on irreplaceable personal and family relationships. If they should fail him due to the whims of fortune or fall in battle or to disease, the solitude of the autocrat was destined to become greater and greater, and his soul ever more arid and similar to a desert . . .

*

Himilco arrived at Syracuse in early autumn and set up camp in the swampy plains near the mouth of the Cyanes river, the only place which could accommodate so many thousands of men. He soon sent a herald to Syracuse proposing an armistice. It was thus evident that deploying the Carthaginian army outside the city was more a manifestation of power than an actual threat. They were meant to strike fear rather than produce a true attack.

Dionysius received Himilco's ambassador in Ortygia, in the mercenaries' barracks. He had abandoned the house with the trellis in Achradina long before, and the grapevines had overrun the place, creeping even along the ground. They bore no fruit because there was no one left to prune them.

He met with the messenger in the fencing chamber, a large, bare room, hung on all four walls with spears and swords. He received him seated on a solitary stool, barefoot but wearing a breastplate and greaves and carrying a sword. The Corinthian helmet on a hanger next to him seemed a cold, impassive mask of war. 'What does your master want from me?' he asked the ambassador, an African Greek from Cyrene, a short man with kinky hair who sold precious purple-dyed cloth for a living.

'Noble Himilco,' he began, 'wants to show his generosity. He intends to spare your city, although he could conquer it swiftly, as he has all the others . . .'

Dionysius said not a word, but stared at the man with a gaze as penetrating as the tip of his spear.

'He is willing to allow the Sicilian Greeks to return to their cities, and to dedicate themselves to commerce and other activities. They must not rebuild the walls, however, and must pay taxes to Carthage.'

'Fucking bastard,' Dionysius thought. 'You want to repopulate the cities because you need their money and their taxes.' But he spoke with a detached tone, feigning indifference. 'Are there other conditions?'

'No,' replied the ambassador. 'Nothing else. But noble Himilco will also allow you to ransom the prisoners of war he has captured during the past campaigns.'

'I see,' said Dionysius.

The ambassador seemed uncomfortable as he waited for an answer that was not forthcoming. Dionysius glared at him in silence, his stare so icy that the poor man's blood ran cold. He felt that he should ask for a reply but he did not dare. He had the impression that if he broke the silence, the whole world would collapse. He finally gathered up his courage and said: 'What . . . what must I tell noble Himilco?'

Dionysius regarded him with the expression of a man who has suddenly awakened from a dream, and said: 'Don't you feel that I should have some time to think about it? It isn't an easy decision, after all.'

'Oh yes, of course,' mumbled the ambassador. 'Of course.'

Nearly an hour of total silence ensued, in which Dionysius did not reveal a single thought or move as much as a muscle on his face, as if he were a statue, while the ambassador nervously wiped his brow, shifting from one leg to the other, since there was no place for him to sit down.

Dionysius finally let out a soft sigh and curled his index finger to invite the ambassador closer. He complied with light, cautious steps, and Dionysius said: 'You can tell noble Himilco that I said . . .'

'Yes, *hegemon* . . .'

'If I could express myself as my soul suggests, I would tell him . . .'

'Yes?' prompted the ambassador encouragingly.

'To go get fucked up the arse.'

The ambassador rolled his eyes. 'To go . . .?'

'Get fucked up the arse,' repeated Dionysius. 'However,' he continued, 'my government responsibilities impose more conciliatory words. You will therefore tell him that for the moment I am willing to sign a peace treaty at his conditions and to ransom all possible prisoners, as soon as he has raised his siege and put an end to hostilities.'

The ambassador nodded, relieved to have finally obtained an answer, then backed up one step at a time all the way to the door and slipped out.

Himilco, who had expected an unconditional acceptance of his terms, decided to begin a military offensive without further delay. He was initially in doubt as to how to conduct the operations. The terrain was unfavourable, the massive walls intimidating and it was physically impossible to blockade the ports, both garrisoned by the toughest and most well-trained units of the Syracusan navy. A few aborted attempts to batter the walls with their siege engines led to naught, and the suffocating heat of the summer, which was obstinately persisting into the autumn, raised an unbearable humidity from the marshes which weakened and disheartened the men. The stench of the excrement of so many thousands of men saturated the swampy valley, making the air unbreathable, and before long plague broke out. Hundreds of bodies were laid on the pyre day after day as discontent grew among the troops, fomenting rebellion against the commander and his officers. Himilco kept hoping that something would occur – as it had at Acragas – to turn around the situation. He was convinced that the Syracusans might be tempted to attack frontally by land or sea, but the days passed and nothing happened.

Dionysius remained within his formidable circle of walls. Supplies continued to come in from the Laccius port at the north, so the people did not go hungry.

In the end, Himilco counted the dead and the survivors, and realized that his force was insufficient for an assault; he thus decided to raise the siege. He sent the Campanian mercenaries to the western part of the island to occupy the cities there, embarked the Africans and set sail for Carthage.

Dionysius had also had news that in Thrace, the Spartan fleet commanded by Lysander had surprised the Athenian fleet practically unmanned in the shallows, and had neatly wiped them out in a place called 'the rivers of the goat', a name nearly as absurd as the event itself. Conon, the Athenian admiral, had managed to get away with eight ships and had fled to Piraeus. But Athens was now blocked by land and by sea, and her situation seemed hopeless.

'What do you think?' asked Philistus.

'Things don't change much for us,' replied Dionysius. 'In theory, the Spartans should be freer to help us, but in reality, I'd rather they stayed away. We must settle our own affairs whenever we can.'

'No, you don't understand. I meant to say what do you think will happen to Athens?'

'You want to know what I'd do if I were Lysander?'

'Yes, if you'd like to tell me.'

'The Athenians are the best. They've taught the world to

think, and for that reason alone they deserve to survive, no matter what offences they've committed over thirty years of war.'

'It's just the excellence of the mind that counts, then? Don't actions mean anything?'

'Is it a philosophical discussion you're looking for? We've already spoken about these problems. Your question would have meaning if there were some supreme judge who absolves and condemns, some force who protects the innocent and punishes the evil. But there is no such judge, and no force except for blind, casual violence; like a hurricane or storm, it strikes at random, bringing death and destruction where it hits.'

'But the judge you're talking about does exist.'

'Oh, really? And who would that be?'

'History. History is the judge. It commemorates those who have done well by humankind, and condemns those who have oppressed or caused suffering without a reason.'

'Ah, history . . .' replied Dionysius. 'Now I understand. So you're saying that a man should regulate his actions in accordance with what history will have to say about him when he's nothing but ashes and he doesn't give a whit about anything any more? And who writes history, anyway? Certainly no one who is any better than I am . . .

'I'm the one making history, my friend. Understand? I know for certain that I can bend events to my will, even though everything seems to demonstrate the opposite. Remember, in any case, that you haven't seen anything yet. Nothing, understand? The best has yet to begin.'

'You're fooling yourself,' protested Philistus. 'History is the story of humanity, filtered by the intelligence of people who have the gift of understanding. And history goes where it wants, Dionysius, like an enormous river that sometimes flows with unstoppable strength, overwhelming everything in its path, and that sometimes advances slowly in lazy spirals waiting to be subdued and controlled by the most mediocre of men. History is a mystery, a mix of passion, horror, hope, enthusiasm, misery. It is both fate and chance, as it is also the product of the iron will of men like you, certainly. History is our desire to overcome our own unhappy existence; it is the only monument that will survive us. Even when our temples and our walls have crumbled into ruins, when our gods and our heroes are mere shadows, time-faded images, mutilated and corroded statues, history will remember what we've done. The record which survives us is the only immortality that we are granted.'

'Fine,' replied Dionysius. 'Then take note, Philistus, because I know that you've been writing, for some time now. I've already made my choice. I'm ready to condemn my name for centuries to come and be remembered as a monster capable of any sort of foul deed, but also as a real man. A man capable of bending events to my own will. Only this type of man resembles the gods. Only if you are truly great will people forgive you for having limited their freedom; otherwise, they'll tear you to pieces and trample you as soon as you've shown the slightest sign of weakness.'

Philistus held his tongue. He was struck by those presumptuous, arrogant words, but also by the nearly blind faith in his destiny that Dionysius managed to project with his voice and with the feverish intensity of his gaze. 'What are your intentions, then?' he asked him after a little while.

'I must enrol more mercenaries and build a fortress in Ortygia; it will be my residence, and will incorporate the dockyard so that I can never be blocked off from the sea. I will then raise a wall across the isthmus which will cut off the rest of the city on the mainland, so my enemies cannot reach me from any direction, neither from without nor from within. The enemies on the inside can be the worst, you know, and the most cruel: the ferocity of brothers knows no bounds.'

Philistus looked at him in amazement. 'That's an enormous project. Where will you find the money?'

'Don't worry, I won't be asking you for it.'

Offended, Philistus protested: 'I don't believe I've ever—'

'No, I didn't mean that. You've already done too much for me. I don't want to drag you down in my fall, if that is what happens. I want you to have a good life, as good as possible. In any case my friend, not even your wealth – not that I know how much you have – could suffice to cover a similar expense.'

'What will you do, then?'

'I don't know,' admitted Dionysius. 'But I'll find a solution. There's always a solution if you have the courage to think on a vast scale. Right now I need some fresh air. Sea air. Will you keep me company?'

'With great pleasure,' replied Philistus.

'Then put up your hood; it's best not to stir up idle curiosity in the city.'

They left the barracks from a secret door, shoulders and heads covered by their hooded cloaks, and began to walk down the darkening streets of Ortygia.

Dionysius headed towards the dockyard, where the huge combat vessels of his fleet had been pulled aground for autumn maintenance. From there they took the road that led north, towards the trade wharves.

'Look at that, how strange!' said Philistus at a certain point. 'There, down by the second wharf.'

A ship had managed to dock in the waning light of dusk and was putting a load of slaves ashore. They drew closer and Dionysius saw what Philistus had been referring to: one of the slaves had very blonde, almost white, hair. He was completely naked except for a small tattoo on his chest, and his skin was badly reddened and burned by the sun. The only thing he wore was a stiff neckband shaped like a rope with two small wooden snakes' heads dangling from either end.

Dionysius observed him for a few moments, then said to Philistus: 'Find out how much he costs.'

Philistus approached the merchant. 'My friend wants to know how much the Celt with the burnt skin costs.'

'Tell him to come by the market square tomorrow morning and get in line with everyone else to make his offer,' replied the merchant without even turning around.

Dionysius whispered something in his friend's ear, nodded in agreement with his answer and walked off. Philistus approached the merchant again. 'My friend is very interested in your slave and he's willing to pay a fine price.'

'I'll bet he is. You know how many old queers will be lined up tomorrow morning at the market to fight over the prick of that blonde northern Apollo? You don't think your friend is the prettiest of them all, do you? I've already told you: if he wants to buy that magnificent specimen, tell him to get his silver staters ready so he can outbid the other customers.'

Philistus lowered his hood and bared his face. 'My friend's name is Dionysius,' he said. 'Ever hear of him?'

The merchant suddenly changed expression and attitude. 'You mean *that* Dionysius?' he asked, widening his bulging white eyes.

'That's right,' replied Philistus, regarding him with a very significant look. 'And if you want my advice, I'd offer him a very good price at this point, if I were you.'

'So what's a good price, in your opinion?'

'Five minae seems honest.'

'Five minae? He's worth at least three times that much!'

'True. That's what I was planning to offer you, but you missed your chance. Now you'll have to be content with that, unless you're stupid enough to risk playing a dangerous loser's game.'

'How can I be sure you're not tricking me?'

'You can't, actually. You can decide to trust me, or not to trust me. If you're lucky, tomorrow you'll get double the amount at the market. If you're not, you won't earn a thing tomorrow. What do you choose?'

'All right, blast you,' replied the merchant in a huff.

Philistus handed over the agreed sum and gave instructions for delivery. He caught up with Dionysius at the sea gate.

'How did it go?' he asked.

'Five minae. In cash.'

'Good price.'

'Indeed.'

'I'll pay you back tomorrow.'

'Why are you interested in that slave?'

'Did you notice that collar he's wearing on his neck?'

'Yes, but . . .'

'And that tattoo on his chest?'

'It looks like . . .'

'That man belongs to a dreaded brotherhood of war. The most fearsome combatants alive. They're groups of nomads who behave like packs of wolves in search of prey, but sometimes they'll enlist as mercenaries. They are so strong that they go into battle naked, protected only by their shield and sword. They have no fear of death, and their only desire in life is to prove their courage at any opportunity. I can't figure out how they captured him alive. Do you know if he speaks Greek?'

'No.'

'Try to find out. Ask him where he comes from, and how he was taken prisoner. Find out everything you can about him. If he doesn't speak Greek, have one of our mercenaries help you.'

'You still haven't told me what you mean to do with him.'

'He'll be my bodyguard,' replied Dionysius.

17

FREED FROM HIS chains, the Celt haltingly entered the vast fencing room which was dimly lit by a couple of lamps hanging on the wall. In front of him was a man sitting immobile on a stool, his back turned to him. The warrior approached without making the slightest sound, his feet bare on the stone floor. He stopped at a short distance from the seated man, who seemed like a statue.

He held his breath and spotted, at that very moment, a half-closed door at the end of the room: a way out. Light as a shadow, he moved towards a long rack hung with dozens of spears and polished swords and grabbed one, lightning quick, twirling around, ready to strike, but his blue eyes darkened when he saw that the stool was empty. A flash of intuition made him spin around just in time to face the silent menace who loomed before him now. A sword sliced through the air and he barely managed to fend off the blow. The two irons met, spraying sparks, and the sudden clangour tore through the silence of the great empty room, resounded against the bare walls and ceiling, blow upon blow, echo upon echo, the din becoming deafening.

The Celt was incredibly agile. His naked, glossy body darted like that of an animal, with an energy that seemed to grow rather than diminish with each clash.

His adversary entered all at once into the halo cast by the lamps and stopped again, stock-still. He was barefoot and naked as well, but his head was completely covered by a Corinthian helmet; only his eyes gleamed from the darkness of the sallet. He was not panting: his chest was perfectly still, his burnished body seemed made of bronze. He raised his sword into a horizontal position and pointed the tip at the Celt's chest, advancing slowly. The Celt drew himself up, bending his knees, concentrating all his forces into the imminence of his spring, and stared at the point of the sword, preparing the blow that would give him his victory. He swooped a cleaving blow down on the outstretched sword to knock it out of his opponent's hand, but the iron was pulled back so swiftly that his stroke fell short. As he was thrown off balance, his faceless adversary dealt him a kick behind the knees, then kicked him again in the back, sending him reeling to the ground. A moment later, the Celt felt the tip of the sword chill his back between his shoulder blades.

'Death is cold,' rang out a voice distorted by the helmet. 'Is it not?'

The tip was raised and the blonde warrior took advantage of the moment to grab his own sword and twist around upon himself like a snake, but he immediately found his enemy's blade at his throat. It pressed down, cut his skin.

He was still armed, but if he had attempted even the slightest move, the sharp tip would have broken through the fragile threshold of life at once, cutting off his breath and the flow of his blood. He dropped back on to the floor, panting, and let his sword fall.

'Get up,' he heard, and then the voice had a face. The helmet was raised and rested at the top of the head, revealing dark, penetrating eyes, fleshy lips, a face shadowed by the faintest hint of a very dark beard.

'I know you understand Greek,' said the voice. 'What's your name?'

'Aksal.'

'What tribe are you from, the Insubres or the Cenomanians?'

'Boi.'

'Get to your feet.'

He got up and stood nearly a whole head taller.

'The Boi are in Gaul. What are you doing in Italy?'

'Many our people pass Liguria.'

'From where?'

'Mountains.'

'Who took you prisoner?'

'Etruscans. Ambush. Then sell me.'

'Why did you try to kill me?'

'For Aksal free.'

'You have only one way of being free: serving me. I am Dionysius, the chief of this very powerful tribe called Syracuse.' He pointed his finger at the neckband and tattoo: 'I know what that means.' The warrior pulled back as through the tip of the sword had stung him again.

Dionysius continued: 'I am also the chief of a "company" like yours, warriors who have sworn to help each other as brothers, and to be second to none in courage and use of our weapons. We are the best, and that is why I defeated you. But I've also spared your life. Now decide: do you want to be my shadow or do you want to return to your master?'

'Be shadow,' said the Celt without hesitation.

'Good. Go to that door: you'll be given clothes, weapons and a place to live. Someone will teach you to talk as well . . . with time. And cut off your moustache. You look like a barbarian.'

Aksal headed for the door with long, silent steps and disappeared on the other side.

Dionysius covered himself with a chlamys and went the other way, towards his own quarters. He lay down on his iron-hard horsehair mattress and fell into a deep sleep.

Leptines woke him up in the middle of the night.

'What's wrong?' asked Dionysius, sitting up on his bed, alarmed.

'Nothing. Everything's fine.'

'What are you doing here at this hour?'

'I've come from a meeting of the Company. We were all in Doricus's house. When I left, an old man who seemed a beggar came up to me and said: "I want nothing from you. Give this to your brother and tell him to read it with a number seven."' Leptines handed him a long strip of leather.

Dionysius got up, went into the corridor and examined it by

lamplight. There were letters, words, but they were cut short and illegible. 'A *skytale*,' he said. 'What did the old man look like?'

'Rather stout, and nearly bald. Just a crown of hair around his temples and the nape of his neck. I think he had black eyes, but it was dark . . . everything looks dark at night.'

'Are you sure he didn't say anything else?'

'Nothing else.'

'Didn't he have an accent? What I mean is, did he speak like us? Or like a Selinuntian? Or an Acragantine? Or a Geloan? Did he speak like a foreigner?'

'He just muttered those few words in a low voice, he gave me that thing and then he vanished. The only thing I can say is that he was Greek, not barbarian.'

Dionysius meditated in silence for a few moments, then said. 'Wait for me here, don't move. I'll be back.'

He returned to his bedroom, opened a safe hidden under the floor and extracted a bronze bar from about ten of them lined up inside. He wrapped the strip of leather around it, then went back out into the corridor to read the message in the light.

'What does it say?' asked Leptines.

'Nothing you'd be interested in,' replied Dionysius. 'Thank you. Now go to rest. Tomorrow come here to the barracks and take charge of training the new recruit, the Celt I bought at the port. No spears, just short arms. Try him with a bow – I think you'll find he's an expert. And ask Philistus to arrange for someone to teach him Greek: he speaks like a brute. You move in here and take my place. I'll be going away for a while.'

'Away? Where?'

'I can't tell you, but you stay on your toes. Keep your eyes open. No one must know I'm not here: it would be fatal. For all of us.'

'But when will you be back?' insisted Leptines.

'As soon as I can,' replied Dionysius, and disappeared into his room.

*

Dawn surprised him as he was riding inland, making his way up the Anapus valley. The vegetation was very dry due to a long drought, and the earth all around the river bed was parched and cracked. The flocks grazed on stubble when they could find it, or wandered aimlessly, heads hanging, in the dense, dim atmosphere. The valley soon dipped between high banks as the river turned into a narrow torrent. He continued until, towards evening, he reached the sparkling waters of the source. Dionysius's senses were plunged instantly back to that brief season spent there between life and death. Much closer to death than life, actually, yet magical in its own way, delirious.

He felt an aching energy as lost or buried feelings were awakened. He could feel the vital flow that issued from the spring, smell the scent of withered mint along the shores, hear the screeching of the birds of prey who swooped down from their shelters on the high rocky walls. And then he perceived a feral look, piercing him between his shoulders and neck.

A voice suddenly beckoned. 'Come closer.'

'Who are you?' asked Dionysius, putting his hand to his sword.

'Throw that away, you won't need it here. Come this way.'

He turned and saw a shadow slipping behind a wild olive tree. He followed. The shadow stopped and merged into the shaded hollows along the wall. 'Do you have a name?' asked Dionysius.

'No. I have a message.'

'What is it?'

'Someone has left a treasure for you.'

'Who?'

'If you don't know, I certainly can't tell you.'

'Tell me where it is, then.'

'At Acragas, in the pond. Go as far as the fourth column of the portico. You'll need pack horses. Three at least, perhaps four.'

'Who sent you?'

'Someone who doesn't exist any more,' he said, vanishing as if swallowed up by the rock.

Dionysius returned to the shores of the spring, seeking contact with that nearly miraculous vital fluid. He was about to submerge himself in the cold waters when he saw something moving under the surface . . . could it be the nymph of the spring?

She emerged suddenly, her shining hair falling on to her shoulders, drops of water streaking her dark face like tears, her eyes black under long lashes, her lips the colour of pomegranate. How could it be? Could she be that wild creature that had visited his dreams?

He drew closer as she continued to emerge from the water, her shoulders and then her breasts, as full and firm as the muscles of a warrior, her flat, taut stomach and then her pubis and her thighs, straight and gleaming like bronze. He was so close now that he could smell the scent of her skin. A sharp but pleasant smell, like that of new wine.

He thought of Homer's verses:

> Who are you, lady? A mortal woman
> or one of the goddesses who inhabit vast Olympus?

He let his sword drop as Menelaus had before Helen's nude breasts, like Odysseus in front of Circe; he then bent and picked a little wild lily, the last one of that long, scorching season, and offered it to her. She stiffened for a moment, backing up in the water, then took the flower and put it into her mouth, chewing it slowly. Dionysius let his chlamys drop to the ground and entered the spring. They came together effortlessly in the pure water, and she wrapped herself around him, biting and scratching him, yelping like an animal and crying out in her ecstasy, a husky, gasping cry which ended in a sigh of abandon. They stretched out alongside each other on the sandy shore, letting the warm breeze dry their bodies.

Some time passed, and again he heard the voice saying: 'Take her with you.'

Dionysius startled, as though he had forgotten the reason why he found himself in that place. 'How can I? She has never left here, she won't be able to get around in the world outside this valley.'

'Take her with you,' the voice repeated. 'She will follow you.'

'Why should I?'

'Because she can stay under water longer than any other being. Perhaps she is a nymph: you have won her over and she will protect you, as Athena protected Odysseus. I have told you all that I must say. Farewell.'

Dionysius ran over to the rocky wall, to where the voice was coming from, but found nothing there.

He had spoken with an echo.

★

He cut a circular hole in the middle of his cloak with his sword. He pulled it over her head and fastened it at the sides with a branch of twisted willow; docile, she put up no resistance. It was as if she had long awaited him, as if she would do anything to stay with him. The valley was still dark, but the sun was beginning to gild the edge of the cliffs far above. A suffocated neighing echoed at a short distance and Dionysius saw three horses tied to a tamarisk. He looked at the girl and said: 'If you want to come with me, you must get on a horse. Like this.'

He jumped on to his steed and took the first of the three horses by its halter as the others tramped behind. The girl followed on foot for a while, then seemed to stop and regard the rough gown she was wearing with a strange expression.

Dionysius stopped as well, and turned to say farewell with a last look, thinking that she would not dare go beyond the edge of the great rock basin. But she took off at a run and with a bound leapt on to the lead horse with extraordinary agility and marvellous ease. The animal did not shy, as if the creature were weightless and scentless, and continued tranquilly on his way, guided by those small, bare, rock-toughened feet.

That same day, at dusk, he used his sword to cut her hair neck-length, and once again her expression changed. She became a dark ephebus for a moment and then, for just an instant, for a single, brief, fleeting instant, she was Arete. She looked at him with Arete's eyes.

They started up again before dawn and ventured through deserted, solitary lands to which the war had dealt a death blow. They journeyed in silence the whole time. Her mute presence somehow accentuated his solitude and, at the same time, the desolate territory they were crossing seemed to emphasize and infinitely magnify the presence of that creature, making her seem divine.

They rode for eight days through the mountains, sleeping just a few hours a night, until one morning Acragas appeared to them, high on her hill in a spectral dawn.

The city was deserted and the wild animals – stray dogs, foxes, crows – had settled in. The signs of destruction were everywhere to be seen, as were the miserable remains of those who had been left behind and killed.

He did not dare go up to the acropolis, but he did pass in front of Tellias's house and went in. He was greeted by chipped walls, blackened ceilings and burnt furniture. Precious vases lay in shards on the floors. He leaned his head against the wall as tears rose to his eyes. The girl came close and put her hand on the nape of his neck. She could instinctively feel the pain that grieved him and tried to take part of it away into herself.

Dionysius turned and looked into her eyes. 'Come,' he said, 'let's go to the pond.'

The water was tepid, nearly warm, but there were no fish. The occupying forces must have taken them for food last winter. He dived in, but it took him several tries before he reached the bottom. He finally saw a couple of crates tied with hemp rope but he found it completely impossible to move them. He decided to cut the ropes and looked inside: there were hundreds of silver and gold coins. Tellias's treasure!

His lungs felt like they would explode, and he pushed on his legs to return to the surface but something held him back: the rope he had cut had twisted around his foot and was keeping him anchored to the bottom.

Was he dying? Was it all over? Bubbles surged up around his

body, the images of his life faded in a sickly green light, the groans of the dying flitted under his skin, fire blazed in his lungs, the eyes of weeping girls watched him from other worlds . . .

Then he felt a wrenching tug. His body emerged swiftly and an extraordinary force dragged him to the shore. The wild girl had climbed on to his chest and her knees pushed the vomit out of his stomach, the water – and the fire – out of his lungs. He coughed, spat, twisted and finally drew a breath.

He looked around and saw no one. But then he heard the water gurgling again and saw the girl tossing two big handfuls of gold and silver coins on to the shore before dipping again into the water.

She continued in and out untiringly, without ever stopping a moment to rest, the whole day, as Dionysius filled the packs to load on to the horses' backs.

By evening, nearly all the treasure had been taken from the water: an enormous wealth of coins.

'We can go now,' he said. He was going towards the horses to load the last sack when he suddenly heard a noise and stopped. The intense excitement of such an incredible day, their roaming through the ghostly city and the sight of so much money had plunged him into a kind of oneiric state, but that sound brought him straight back to reality. He felt a shiver run up his spine. He had been mad to think he could act alone in that way and that place.

'Who goes there?' he shouted.

He got no answer, but saw shadows slipping from one house to the next, brushing past the walls.

'Get on your horse, quickly!' he told the girl, and his gestures made it clear what those words meant. But she would not move. She seemed to be sniffing the air and was baring her teeth like an animal, recoiling. Dionysius grabbed hold of the horses' halters and began to drag them towards the eastern wall.

But more sounds were coming from there, voices calling to each other, and shadows advanced towards them. They were trapped.

A couple of individuals came forward, gripping clubs in their hands. They were covered with rags and had long hair and beards: brigands? deserters? . . . survivors? They seemed more like beasts than men. Dionysius stopped and drew his sword. The girl snatched up two stones and let fly with deadly precision. Both men were struck right on the forehead and they collapsed to the ground without a whimper. But more cries broke out and a mob of about fifty more charged forward, brandishing clubs and knives.

'Quick, this way,' shouted Dionysius, grabbing the girl by her hand and leaving the horses behind. But their pursuers were evidently seeking revenge for their companions and continued to chase them, waving their weapons.

Dionysius ducked behind the corner of a house only to run straight into a man coming from the opposite direction. He was about to strike him down with his sword when a voice in Greek shouted 'Stop, blast you! Would you cut my throat?'

'Leptines?'

'Who else!' He turned around. 'Go to it men, mow down those mangy dogs.'

Sixty mercenaries and Aksal himself lunged forward, slaughtering the first ones to get in their way, then used bow and arrow to cut down the rest of them in their panicked flight. Not one of them got away.

'I gave you precise orders,' said Dionysius when it was all over.

'By Heracles! I've just saved your life! Some nerve you have . . .' retorted Leptines.

'I gave you precise orders!' roared Dionysius.

Leptines lowered his head and bit his lip.

'I would have managed fine without you,' he continued. 'They were nothing but a bunch of lousy swine, but your disobedience could have had disastrous consequences. Don't you understand that?'

'I left Doricus in Syracuse: he's an excellent officer and he's always been a member of the Company. Nothing will happen there. I thought that it was too risky for you to go off on your own, so I followed your tracks. Next time I'll let you croak.'

'Next time you'll do as I say, or I'll forget that you are my brother and I'll have you executed for insubordination. Is that clear?'

Aksal arrived with a head in each hand. 'Aksal you shadow, see?' And he stuck them in front of his nose.

Dionysius grimaced. 'Yes, yes, all right. Take those horses and let's get out of here fast.'

'Who's that?' asked Leptines, nodding towards the girl.

Dionysius turned but she bolted away, vanishing into the deserted city now plunged in darkness. 'Wait!' he shouted, 'Wait!' running after her, but he immediately realized it was useless. He would never find her.

'Well, who was she?' asked Leptines again.

'I don't know,' replied Dionysius curtly.

They made their way through the eastern quarters all the way to the Gela gate. They emerged into the eastern necropolis as the moon rose behind them, shedding its wan light over the temples on the hill. Dionysius looked over at his brother who was trudging along silently, keeping step with the shaft of his spear.

It seemed strange to him that Leptines would have taken such initiative on his own.

'Tell me the truth. Who suggested that you follow me? Philistus?'

Leptines stopped and turned towards him. 'No. Philistus had nothing to do with it.'

'Who, then?'

'That fellow. The stocky bald-headed fellow, the one who brought me the message. He just suddenly showed up in the atrium of the barracks and he said: "Your brother is in danger. You must go to him immediately, on the road to Acragas." Then he vanished before I could say a word. What could I do?'

Dionysius did not answer. He resumed the march in silence and no one saw his eyes glittering in the darkness, nor heard the words that rose from his throat with the emotion of a sudden revelation: 'Tellias . . . my friend.'

18

As soon as he had returned to Syracuse, Dionysius commenced a couple of ambitious construction projects: a fortified residence connected to the dockyards in the heart of the old city, and a wall that blocked off the isthmus of Ortygia. He also had thirty battleships built. He took these initiatives without convening the Assembly, and it was thus clear to all that he would tolerate no checks on his power. His attitude provoked violent reactions from the opposition, especially from the families of the Knights who had taken exile at Aetna. They openly denounced the tyranny that had been established in the city, and incited the people to rebel.

Dionysius's reaction was unforgiving and harsh. He unleashed his mercenaries, who conducted massive house-to-house searches, arrested all his opponents and brought them to the fortress in Ortygia. There, after a summary trial, they were condemned to exile. Their goods and property were seized and distributed to the mercenaries, who were gratified by this new, prestigious style of living and thus twice bound to their lord and benefactor.

He didn't see the girl from the source of the Anapus in all this time, nor did he ever go back there, occupied as he was by so many plans and worries, but sometimes, at night, when he was resting in his huge bare bedroom in his fortress inhabited only by mercenaries, he thought of her and of how they had made love in the waters of the spring. How she had appeared miraculously, looking so different from how he had remembered her, and how she had followed him to the walls of Acragas on his quest. He thought of the voice that had spoken to him from the rocks, softly, almost as if not to be heard by anyone but him.

As winter turned to spring, ships started to arrive in the harbour and, with the ships, news. Athens had fallen, yielding to the hunger and hardship of so long a siege by both land and sea. The powerful metropolis had been brought to her knees, and had no choice but to surrender unconditionally. It was rumoured that Sparta's allies – the Thebans and Corinthians in particular – had insisted that the city be razed to the ground, but Lysander had refused: destroying Athens would be like depriving Greece of one of her two eyes. The conditions that she was forced to agree to were punishing: destruction of the Long Wall, the mighty fortification that connected the city to the port at Piraeus, surrender of the entire war fleet except for eight ships and, most humiliating of all, a Spartan garrison on the Acropolis.

Dionysius believed that the beginning of her relentless decline had started under the walls of Syracuse, where the best young men of Athens had been mown down. He realized that the time had come to commence with his plan, and he convoked the Council: Heloris, Philistus, Leptines, Doricus, Iolaus, Biton and three more friends from the Company. 'The war in Greece is over,' he said. 'Athens has lost. Thousands of men who have done nothing but fight for years and years, and who are incapable of doing anything else, are now at the disposal of the highest bidder. You, Leptines, will leave for Sparta to enrol all those you can. You'll try to meet with Lysander, and establish an agreement with him if you can. They tell me he's a practical man who knows how to deal with a situation.'

'What about Corinth?' asked Leptines. 'Corinth is our metropolis and has always shown interest in our internal affairs, either to help us or to put pressure on us.'

'Bring some offerings for the Temple of Poseidon on the isthmus. A formal act of homage is more than sufficient. We are stronger than Corinth: we don't need them. Sparta's in command now; Sparta is the true power that won the war. And Lysander is the most powerful man in Sparta, even more powerful than the kings. But there are things that must be settled here first. You, Doricus, will depart with the army and take charge of the complete subjugation of the Sicels. Our first objective is Herbessos. Once that city falls, the others will follow. You'll leave at once and take the Syracusan troops with you. I'll follow up with the mercenaries.'

'What about the Carthaginians?' asked Philistus. 'All this activity is bound to make them nervous . . .'

'They won't move,' replied Dionysius. 'I've learned that the plague is still raging, the city is weakened and Himilco no longer enjoys such consideration. They won't move. Not yet, anyway.'

*

Doricus set off with his army three days later. His objective was the Siculian city of Herbessos, in the interior. Before reaching the city, he sent a delegation forward to proclaim that since the Sicels had always been subjects of Syracuse in the past, their land was to be considered Syracusan territory. The city's inhabitants replied that they would never comply with a similar demand, and talk went back and forth for several days without great progress. Doricus temporized as he awaited the imminent arrival of Dionysius and his mercenaries to deliver the decisive attack.

One night, as he was inspecting the guard posts along the perimeter of their camp, Doricus was surrounded by a group of armed men hidden behind a hedge, and killed along with his escort. The officers of the general staff who were faithful to Dionysius were promptly murdered as well. The remaining Syracusan officers assembled the army and had the heralds proclaim the tyranny abolished and the exiled Knights recalled. They promised the assembled troops that all the barbarians in Dionysius's service would be cleared from the city, and that the tyrant himself would be captured and brought to justice. He would be sentenced to the punishment he deserved.

The army, presented with an accomplished fact, approved the order of the day and marched back in the direction of Syracuse, soon reinforced by numerous cavalry contingents; the Knights had obviously been forewarned of what was to occur.

Philistus was the first to be informed of the mutiny and he

immediately realized that they were not dealing with a spontaneous or improvised event: the prompt arrival of the banished Knights from Aetna, the ready proclamation of the officers and the attack directed at Ortygia were all part of a well designed plot, and perhaps the worst was yet to come. He sent a fast rider to notify Dionysius at once and began preparing the complex plan for defending Ortygia to the bitter end. In the meantime, he activated all his contacts in order to have a complete rendering of the situation; within three days he had all the information he needed.

All bad.

The Knights, from their refuge at Aetna, had contacted Rhegium and Messana, who had agreed to send out a fleet to blockade both of the city's ports. But they had even gone further: a delegation had arrived as far as Corinth, the metropolis of Syracuse, and had convinced the government to send a strongman with the task of restoring legality to her daughter city. The force that would accompany him was not impressive from a military perspective, but from the ideological point of view, this was a death blow. Since the metropolises never limited the independence and political choices of their colonies, direct intervention in the guise of an envoy who was to settle internal questions was seen as an outright condemnation. The man chosen by Corinth was one Nicoteles, a tough, war-hardened general with unashamed sympathy for the oligarchs. He had only one weak point, it was said: he drank straight wine, a dangerous habit for a Greek, and especially for a soldier; the Greeks were accustomed to diluting their wine with three or five parts water.

Dionysius had returned with his mercenaries at a forced march and closed himself up into his fortress. He blockaded the isthmus and had a chain drawn across the outlet of the Laccius harbour at night. Aksal followed him everywhere and even slept stretched out at the threshold of his master's bedroom, on the ground. The murder of Doricus, who had been a dear friend since childhood, had broken Dionysius's morale and invaded his spirit with dark pessimism.

The attacks on the isthmus walls began very soon and went on for days and days, relentlessly, severely trying the defences and the mercenaries' resistance.

Dionysius held council with his most trusted friends: Philistus, Leptines, Iolaus, Biton, Heloris and two or three other members of the Company. The atmosphere was oppressive.

'The situation is clear to us all,' began Philistus. 'I don't think we can get out of this one.'

In fact, there was no solution apparent to any of them. The only proposals being advanced concerned where they could flee to and how they could find refuge.

Heloris, seeing that Dionysius sat still on his stool without saying a word, had the impression that he was resigned to the inevitable. He wanted to somehow lighten the atmosphere, but the line he came out with was destined to poison their relationship from that day on. 'Remember,' he said, 'that the only way to get a tyrant to abandon his place is to pull him out by the feet.'

Philistus lowered his eyes, Leptines grimaced. Neither the word 'tyrant' nor the image of himself being dragged dead through the fortress like a slaughtered animal must have pleased Dionysius much. They saw him pale with rage and they feared, from the look in his eye, that he would lay hand to his sword. But nothing happened. He spoke as if nothing had been said, with a firm, steady voice.

'The time has come for you, Leptines, to depart immediately, before the Rhegines and Messanians arrive and blockade the ports. Go to Sparta, to Lysander, and strike a deal. The Corinthians are his allies but they've never given him anything but headaches. What's more, they are much wealthier and more powerful than the Spartans; we can use the jealousy and mistrust this situation engenders to our advantage. The war is over and they have thousands of men who know how to do a single thing: combat. That in itself could be destabilizing and cause problems for Sparta. So we can help them out here, at least in part: engage as many of them as you can and come back as quickly as possible. Is that clear?'

'I think so,' replied Leptines.

'I want no uncertainty. I must be absolutely sure that you will do as I have asked. Well then?'

'Of course. Consider those men already here.'

'I won't be giving you any letters, that would be too dangerous. You will speak directly in my name. You are my brother: it's as if I myself were speaking.'

'Yes, I understand,' confirmed Leptines again.

'Fine,' concluded Dionysius. 'Philistus . . .'

'Speak.'

'The mission I shall entrust you with is no less sensitive. You will leave on a merchant ship as soon as you can and sail west. You will go ashore at a sheltered spot on the coast and make your way on muleback to the Carthaginian border . . .' Philistus shifted on his seat with an apprehensive gesture, but Dionysius seemed not to notice, and continued: 'There you will contact the Campanian mercenaries in Himilco's service who garrison the Carthaginian province and offer to hire them . . .'

'What? You're talking about the animals that massacred the Selinuntians and the Himerans! They're bloody beasts . . .'

'They are war machines, not men. They would have slaughtered the Carthaginians in the same way had they been fighting for us. We've already spoken about this and I've told you what I think. Now listen well: the Campanians must be bored to death sitting there guarding the provincial borders, and would jump at the chance of delivering a good pounding. Well, we'll give them the opportunity. Offer them whatever you want, as long as you bring them over to our side. As soon as you have made the deal, inform me and I will send an officer to take command. Get ready to leave now. Trust me: we'll be out of this trap and will have turned the situation around before the end of the winter.'

'And if these missions should fail?' asked Heloris.

'Then we will fight to the end. We will fight with such vigour that when I fall no one will have any cause for celebration, so great will be the number of dead to mourn, burn and bury in this city. None of you are obliged to follow me. Whoever wants to can leave. I can take care of myself, especially if bad goes to worse.'

Philistus nodded solemnly. In his heart of hearts, he thought that it was all futile and that they would all end up dead, but he said: 'I'll leave as soon as I've gathered the money and had a ship prepared.'

Leptines left three days later and Dionysius accompanied him to the port. 'Have you ever seen that man again?' he asked his brother as he stepped on the gangway to go aboard the ship that would take him to Sparta.

'Which man?'

'The man who told you to follow me to Acragas.'

'No. I've never seen him since.'

'Who do you think it could have been?'

'I have no idea. I thought you had sent him; I figured you knew him. I didn't think about asking who he was. But why are you asking me now?'

'Because it's a mystery that I can't explain, and I don't believe in mysteries. Problems, yes, but problems can be solved . . . Go now. Do what I've asked of you and do it well. Have a good journey.'

Leptines put a foot on the gangway, then turned back. 'Listen . . .'

'What?'

'Do you really think we can make this work? I mean, wouldn't it be better if . . .'

'Just what has got into your head? What in Hades are you saying?'

'It all seems . . . useless to me . . .'

Dionysius grabbed him by the shoulders. 'Listen, by Heracles! Do you remember when we were lads and the gang from Ortygia shut us up in the warehouse down at the harbour and were getting ready to give us a thorough thrashing?'

'You'd better believe it!' replied Leptines.

'And wasn't it you, that time, who said we would never give up, for any reason?'

'True . . .'

'And how did it end up?'

'I climbed up on your shoulders and got out through the roof. I ran to call for reinforcements and . . .'

'So what are we doing now?'

Leptines shook his head. 'Right . . . But somehow I'm afraid the situation is a little different this time.'

'It's exactly the same. Only the proportions and the positions have changed. We're the bosses of Ortygia now . . . and we'll win, just as we did then. I'll prove that I'm the man destined to lead not only Syracuse but all the Greeks of Sicily and Italy against their mortal enemy. But I need to know that you believe in me. Every day and every night that I'm locked up in this fortress, inspecting the battlements, I have to be certain that you're on your way with reinforcements. That you'll be arriving at any moment, understand? Well then? What do you say?'

'Oh, sod the world, dammit!' exclaimed Leptines, using the same slang expression they would use as boys when they had stone-throwing fights with their adversaries from the well-to-do side of town.

'Sod the world,' agreed Dionysius. 'And now piss off.' He himself cast off the mooring line. The trireme slipped towards the centre of the harbour, then turned slowly around, driven by the oarsmen, and stood out to sea.

*

Philistus left the next day on a little trading vessel, carrying enough silver coins in the hold to pay for the enrolment of five thousand men.

Just in time: the joint Messanian and Rhegine fleet appeared soon thereafter, drawing up their battleships to blockade the Great Harbour and the small harbour.

Nicoteles's army entered the next day from the Catane gate, amidst an exulting crowd, and took up position on the isthmus midway between the city and Ortygia.

Dionysius was alone. Biton and Iolaus had been sent inland to keep the situation under control there. Heloris no longer enjoyed his esteem, and the young officers of the Company did not have enough experience or nerve to speak with him as an equal. He roamed the dark halls and corridors of the fort at every hour, and often went to check the warehouses down at the port and measure the stores, which were diminishing at a frightening rate, day after day, while the besiegers never let up, launching continuous waves of attacks from dawn to dusk.

His mercenaries began to desert, one at a time at first and then in small groups. Dionysius managed to catch two of them in the act, with Aksal's help. He had the fall-in sounded, illuminated the inner courtyard with dozens of torches, and had them crucified before the arrayed troops. But he realized that he could no longer hold them there by terrorizing them, that any little thing would likely provoke the dissolution of his army. And then they would tear him apart. He – the tyrant – would be killed and dragged out by the feet as Heloris had predicted, butchered like an animal, exposed to the scorn of the people, left unburied, prey to dogs and crows . . .

As he spent one long night up on the walls of the isthmus, wrapped in a heavy woollen cloak, he thought he saw a stocky, bald-headed man walking hurriedly in the direction of the port and he startled. 'Hey, you!' he shouted. 'Stop!' But the man continued walking as though he hadn't heard him and vanished into the darkness. He vanished completely, as if he had never existed. Dionysius thought he was seeing things; exhaustion, tension and lack of sleep were playing mean tricks on him. He thought of Arete, of Tellias, of Doricus and the people he had loved. All dead. It was his turn now. He thought of the wild girl who had perhaps returned to her shelter up there, at the source of the Anapus; she certainly had no memory of him. Or perhaps she'd lost her way, or been captured and sold as a slave . . .

His mind was straying, seeking distraction from an increasingly hostile reality that would have been best faced head-on. The Knights on the other side of the wall continued to garrison the isthmus, certain that it was only a question of time . . . and time was passing, without any sign of relief. Time was running out for Dionysius, day after day, hour after hour . . .

One morning as day was breaking, he received a message from Philistus, attached to the shaft of an arrow. He recognized his friend's handwriting immediately from the flounces on his sigmas and gammas. It began: 'You must let the Knights think that you are ready to surrender . . .' He was about to rip it up, but he went on reading, with growing interest in the mad plan it proposed . . . absolutely mad.

And yet . . . it might just work. What did he have to lose, after all? He called a herald and instructed him to take a proposal to the Knights. 'Tell them that I am ready to discuss surrender.'

'Surrender, *hegemon*? Have I understood well?'

'Perfectly well: you must negotiate the terms of surrender. Say that I'm willing to leave the city. All I want is five ships and five hundred men as my escort. No inspection on board.'

'I will do as you say, *hegemon*,' replied the herald. The gate was opened for him and he exited, holding the flag of truce, headed towards the guard post on the isthmus. The officer on duty met him, and he was soon brought before his commanders.

The negotiations thus began and went on for many days, as fatigue began to make itself felt in the besiegers' camp as well. The weather was particularly foul: it often rained, with even a dusting of snow at night. The hardships of the prolonged siege, and the continuous loss of men, began to sow tension and discontent among the members of the high command. In particular, the aristocratic haughtiness of the Knights was beginning to wear thin with the other officers, who were mostly middle-class small-property owners, merchants and port contractors. They finally went to Nicoteles, the Corinthian general, and demanded that the cavalry be discharged, claiming that horsemen were more useful on the open field and that they could be called back if and when they were needed.

Nicoteles, unused to such immobility himself, had taken to drink again, and he promptly reported the request of the other Syracusan officers to the Knights without the benefit of tact.

Offended, they stalked off furiously down the road to Aetna, indignant over this latest outrage. Although the position of the remaining officers regarding negotiations was uncompromising, they were so convinced that Dionysius had decided to abandon the field that they relaxed their vigilance. After all, their commander from their metropolis was hardly providing them with a fine example of discipline or temperance.

With the last moon of winter, many hoplites asked to be permitted to leave so they could prepare their fields for sowing, and their requests were granted. The isthmus was so narrow that holding it did not require a great number of troops.

This was what Dionysius had been waiting for. The next morning, he sent one of his men, disguised as a fisherman, out of the harbour on a little boat. The Rhegine and Messanian sailors searched the small vessel and let him pass; he sailed all the way around the Plemmyrium promontory until he found a landing spot on the southern coast. From there he made his way to a nearby farm and spoke to the owner, a livestock breeder, who climbed on to his horse and rode off to the north.

Before evening, Philistus had been informed that the isthmus was poorly garrisoned and that the northern gate of the city was open every day until dusk. He also learned that, according to reliable information, dusk was the time that found Nicoteles most heavily under the influence.

Philistus summoned the commander of the newly hired Campanian mercenaries, a half Etruscan, half Neapolitan cut-throat whose left eye was covered by a leather patch, and he entered into action immediately. As Philistus had suggested, they left all of their carts and baggage at one of the small inland villages, and advanced at great speed with mostly cavalry soldiers.

They burst through the northern gate, achieving complete surprise. They crossed the city at a gallop and rammed the line of siege on the isthmus with such force that most of the combatants were hurled into the sea. Nicoteles was found in his quarters with his throat slit; his murderer was never identified.

Dionysius greeted Philistus in the fortress's courtyard.

'Everything went just as you had foreseen,' said Philistus, hugging his friend. 'Isn't that incredible?'

'Incredible?' replied Dionysius. 'I never had a doubt.'

'I did,' said Philistus.

'I know. It was plain on your face . . . News from Leptines?'

'He should be back any day.'

'It won't be easy to force the naval blockade.'

Philistus smiled. 'I wouldn't say that. I've heard say that he's returning with Lysander in person.'

'What?'

'If my information is correct, that's the story. That son of a bitch has done it! Lysander is coming here to cut a deal with you. And they'll be followed by a thousand mercenaries, all Peloponnesians, the best. I don't think the Rhegines and Messanians will be up to challenging the power of Sparta. We have the situation back in hand, my friend. We have won.'

'I've won,' repeated Dionysius, as if he could not believe those words. Gripped by irresistible enthusiasm, he threw down his cloak and ran up the stairs to the highest tower of the fortress.

From there, he yelled those words over and over again at the top of his lungs, with a voice as shrill as a hawk's screeching and as thunderous as Achilles's shouting from the Scean Gates.

He finally stopped, panting. He looked at the sky, darkening with the approaching night, and at the city which lay mute, stupefied, at his feet.

19

LYSANDER'S SMALL SQUADRON arrived with Leptines's three warships a few days later, and entered the harbour with no problem because the Messanian and Rhegine fleets had already weighed anchor. No one wanted to face the Spartans, not even just a few of them, not even one of them, when that one was the winner of the great war.

Dionysius went to receive him at the wharf. Leptines was the first to come ashore, and Dionysius came forward to embrace him.

'You're back, finally!' exclaimed Dionysius. 'If I'd waited for you, I'd be dead and gone by now.'

'I did everything as quickly as I could, but it wasn't simple. And then I always knew that you would pull through.'

'I almost didn't . . . What's he like then?'

'Lysander? Don't ask me; I can never understand what he's thinking. He's . . . wait, what's the word? Evasive. He's a great commander, but he's not like any soldier I've ever met.'

'A son of a bitch.'

'Right, you've got it.'

'Then we'll get along just fine.'

'Careful, there he is, getting off.'

Lysander was descending just then from the gangplank of his trireme. He looked about sixty, with grey-green eyes, more grey than green, salt-and-pepper hair thinning a bit at the temples but rather long at the collar, in the Spartan manner. He was unarmed and wearing civilian clothing, but the ring he wore on his finger was much too showy for a Spartan, most likely a souvenir of his

Asiatic travels and a sign that he was strong enough to challenge the ire of the ephors, inflexible custodians of the rigid customs of Sparta, on his home ground.

'*Hegemon*,' Dionysius greeted him. 'Welcome to Syracuse.'

'*Hegemon*,' reciprocated Lysander. 'I'm happy to see you.'

Dionysius was gratified by his use of the title; it meant that his power was recognized by Sparta. He led the way to the fortress, where he had had dinner prepared. Aksal escorted them, armed to the teeth, completely similar by now to a Greek warrior. Lysander, instead, walked without a single bodyguard. Evidently he felt so strong that he did not need one.

Dionysius had him accompanied to his room so he could bathe and change, if he desired, but he returned wearing the same clothing he'd had on the ship. He had him sit at the head of the table and sat opposite him, at the other end. Leptines sat on the long side, equidistant between one and the other. There were no dining trays or couches. The table was a planed oak board, half a span thick; the seats were little more than stools.

'It's like Sparta, here,' said Lysander at once, and it wasn't clear whether his tone was congratulatory or hid a note of disappointment.

'We are simple people,' replied Dionysius, 'and we live a simple life. In any case, your black broth is too much, even for us. We've prepared fish for you.' He gestured at a serving platter which was just being brought in, along with some bread and a basin of warm water for rinsing their fingers.

'That's the way it should be for a true man-at-arms,' Lysander observed, and again it wasn't clear whether that was a compliment or a form of sarcasm.

'Son of a bitch,' thought Dionysius. Then, considering the civilities over and done with, he went straight to the core of the matter. 'It would be very helpful for me to know the reason for your coming here to Syracuse.'

Lysander stared into his eyes, suddenly serious, almost cold. 'Sparta has won the war, but that's no cause for celebration. We have lost many men and undergone much damage, and our allies have suffered the same. We have now established garrisons in all the cities of the old Athenian league, commanded by our officers, who also enjoy political power, but we realize that it will not be easy to maintain order as it now stands. The Persians helped us only because Athens has always been a threat for them; they might easily change their stance at any time. We need friends and allies everywhere. Sparta has always been Syracuse's friend; perhaps it is Syracuse to whom we owe our final victory. It was under these walls that the power of Athens was undermined in an irrevocable way. But on the other hand, you could never have managed it without our help.'

'Here, however . . .' replied Dionysius in a deliberately low tone of voice, 'we're not talking about the city as such. It is I who decide for Syracuse.'

Lysander cracked a grimace that might have been a smile. 'Allow me to be frank with you, *hegemon*. Dealing with one man alone is much easier than dealing with an Assembly. Have I made myself clear?'

'Perfectly so. And I obviously agree. My brother has said that we will be permitted to recruit mercenaries in the Peloponnese, and that the first contingent is already on its way.'

'That is true, but the initiative was his alone. We had nothing to do with it, and we are keeping out of it.'

'I fully understand,' replied Dionysius. 'And I ask for nothing more.'

'We have helped you to stay in power because at this time, it is in our best interests. I hope that's clear . . .'

'Very clear.'

'If things should change . . .'

'I'm on my own.'

'Exactly.'

'And what can I do to make sure things don't change?'

'Stay in Sicily.'

'I shall.'

Lysander gave a sigh as if all the weariness of his journey was suddenly upon him.

'Would you like to retire?' offered Dionysius.

'Yes, I will, soon,' replied the Spartan. His gaze fell on Aksal, who towered against the wall, immobile, at his master's back. He wore Greek-style armour, with a breastplate and greaves, but he had refused to remove his neckband or cut his moustache.

'What is that?' he asked.

'My bodyguard.'

'Where on earth is he from? He looks Thracian, but he's too big.'

'He's a Celt,' Dionysius said. 'I bought him at the market.'

'A Celt, is he? Are they all like that?'

'He says his brothers are even bigger.'

'I've heard that they live on the shores of the northern Ocean and that when the high tide invades their villages on the coast, they enter the water and raise their shields against the billows as if they could hold them back! They must set great store by their strength. If they wake up one day and notice the beauty and wealth of our lands, they could turn into quite a problem. Difficult to keep in check . . .' He eyed the Celt again. 'By Zeus, he's a real titan! Have you ever noticed a weak spot?'

'Yes, the sun. He can't stand the sun, and his skin burns. But my doctors have discovered that a mix of olive oil and walnut shells prevents this.'

'Interesting,' commented Lysander softly. 'Truly interesting . . . Your fish was good. Now I'll go to rest if I may. The strain of the war has left its mark on me. I'm not what I used to be.'

A servant came to take away the empty platter, which now revealed a brightly painted fish on the bottom, and another accompanied the guest to his bedroom. Dionysius nodded to Aksal and he left as well.

Only Leptines remained; he had said nothing all evening. He spoke now: 'It went well, didn't it? He was very clear: he said—'

'He said nothing,' Dionysius cut him off. 'He came only to see what kind of a man I am.'

'And do you think he knows now?'

'I think so, yes.'

'But he's interested in an alliance with us.'

'Not at all.'

'Well then?'

'There's only one thing that interests him: undermining Corinth. She's too powerful and unruly an ally. Corinth has taken a beating in this Sicilian venture and that is very convenient for them. That's all. And if we help him get rid of a bunch of stragglers by enrolling them in our army, that's even better. All things considered, the Spartans are folks that don't like the unexpected. They don't seek out adventure and above all, as true soldiers, they do not love war. Lysander came here to make sure that everything is under control and that I don't have any funny ideas in my head. He'll be leaving soon, you'll see.'

*

He left three days later and never again set foot in Sicily.

Dionysius dedicated himself to the preparation of his true plan: to annihilate the Carthaginians in Sicily and to avenge the massacres of Selinus, Himera, Acragas and Gela. Before setting off on a similar endeavour, there was much to be done. For three consecutive years he conducted a series of campaigns employing both the city militia and the mercenaries, in appropriate proportions.

He took Aetna, stronghold of the Knights, his staunchest opponents, and razed it to the ground. From there he advanced inland to subjugate the Sicels. He occupied Herbita, then continued up to Henna, high on the mountains and surrounded by woods, at the very centre of the island.

There stood the most venerated sanctuary of all Sicily: the Temple of Demeter and her daughter Persephone, the maiden who was forced to wed Hades. The virgin had been carried off as she picked flowers with her friends on those meadows, and dragged down into the dark reign of shadows, into the desolate abode of the dead.

There was a spot that everyone avoided, even the shepherds, a cave that led to the underworld. It was the grotto where Hades' chariot – drawn by black, flame-breathing stallions – had plunged into the ground with Persephone aboard and was swallowed up into the abyss. It was there that Orpheus had descended to seek Eurydice, his beloved bride. His song had so charmed the lady of the realm of shadows, the beautiful but sterile Persephone, that she had made a pact with him: Eurydice could follow Orpheus out to the kingdom of the living as long as she remained one step behind him and as long as he, the sublime poet, never turned around until they had reached the surface of the earth and seen the light of day. If he turned, she would vanish, for ever.

Orpheus thus began his climb up the dark passage, trying to imagine the light step of his beloved behind him, trying to feel her cold breath at his back, thinking of when the sun would warm her, dreaming of when her bloodless lips would take on the moist hue of a pomegranate and open like a flower for his kisses. But belief failed him and the suspicion that he was being deceived grew until, as soon as he could see a hint of sunlight, he turned around.

He saw her, heartbreakingly lovely and sorrowful, for just an instant, and then all he could hear was the sound of her screams as she was sucked back down into Erebus.

Dionysius was determined to go there, although everyone tried to dissuade him. He wanted to be initiated into the mysteries, to drink the red liquid whose origins were known only to the temple priests. Leptines accompanied him, as Teseus had accompanied Pirithous, but at just a few steps from the cave, he – who feared nothing in this world, who had recklessly faced danger and death – grew pale and broke into an icy sweat. 'Stop,' was all Leptines could say. 'Don't go. There's nothing down there, nothing to see.'

But Dionysius did not heed him and advanced alone up to the mouth of the cave. It was dusk, and the shadows were lengthening on the high plain. Slender tongues of fog crept out of the forests like tapering fingers to obscure the green light of the meadows.

He began to descend all alone towards the point at which it was said that once a year, on the night of the spring equinox, the ashen face of Persephone appeared as she rose to visit her mother.

Dionysius, who believed in nothing, believed that Arete could see him from the sad place she was in. He thought that she could hear him as he called out her name with cries so loud, so desperate that the entire grotto boomed with them.

He finally collapsed, exhausted, drained of strength. But then he began to feel a subtle yearning, a diffused chill creeping through his body, starting from his limbs. Was this Arete's kiss? Was this her way of being close to him, of letting him sense her? He did not have Orpheus's gift and he would never be able to move Persephone and black-veiled Hades to pity, but a song came to mind, the melodious air of that old serenade, the hymn of the singer of Acragas that she had loved so much and which had filled their hearts with joy on the night of their wedding. Oh, why hadn't he thought of it? Why hadn't he brought a soft-voiced singer, skilled at playing the lyre, so that song could reach her through that narrow chasm?

Cold sleep seized him; he forgot his breathing as though it were no longer important, and his mind was lost in a dream: Arete took on the semblance of the wild girl who had loved him in the spring of the Anapus. She had her eyes and her skin, the taste of her lips was the same . . .

He felt his heart pounding, and he saw her!

The wild girl was in front of him, draped in a gorgeous dress, a wonderfully light and transparent peplum like those that the maidens of Ortygia offer to the goddess each year at her temple on the acropolis. Her hair was gathered at the nape of her neck with a blood-red ribbon. Her lips were moist and red, her eyes as deep as night. What marvellous transformation was this? How possible unless she was a creature from another world? He felt lost in her arms, cold as he had never been yet burning with fire at the same time. He heard her speak, for the first time in so long, she spoke with her voice and finally called him by name.

'Take me with you, if you cannot come back,' he told her, and he heard those words echoing inside of him as though he had thought them and not said them aloud, as if they had been said by the man he wanted to be and was no longer. Then her face and her body vanished into the shadows. Her peplum fluttered like fog in the evening air.

He awoke in the dead of night in a quiet place near a crackling fire. He opened his eyes and saw Leptines's face.

'I saw her. I'm certain it was her. I've always known it was her. But this time I'm sure.'

Leptines did not answer. He helped his brother into a sitting position and rubbed his shoulders, his neck and his arms at length until he'd regained his colour and warmth. Then he said: 'Let's go now. The stars that have protected you are about to set.'

*

Having succeeded in subjugating the Sicels, as Gelon, victor over the Carthaginians at Himera, had done so many years before, Dionysius turned to the Chalcidic colonies of Naxos, Catane and Leontini. He was firmly convinced that the Sicilian Greeks must form a single coalition against their natural enemy, setting aside internal strife. Given that that was impossible to achieve peaceably, he had decided to accomplish his objective through force, as he had already done in his own city. He summoned Philistus and told him: 'I don't want a massacre while we are laying the grounds for a great pan-Hellenic undertaking. These cities must fall by treason.'

Philistus, who thought he had heard everything, was amazed. 'What are you saying?'

'You don't agree?'

'Treason is hateful for both the betrayer and the solicitor.'

'You never cease to surprise me, my friend. You continue to cultivate ethical concepts in your soul; you're obviously still under the influence of that old big-nosed, buggy-eyed sophist who puts strange ideas into the heads of the young Athenians.'

'Socrates is not a sophist.'

'I say he is. Isn't he the one who said: "The true wise man is he who knows he knows nothing"? And is that not the most deceitful and at the same time the most clever of sophisms? That old son of a bitch is not only convinced that he's a wise man, but also that he knows more than anyone else around—'

'Tell me what you want,' Philistus cut him short.

'Every man has his price. Find out who the most approachable characters are in Catane and Naxos, pay them whatever they ask, and let them turn over the cities to you. Later they'll thank us. There's no need to tell you that in order to comply with our request, they'll need some justification to make them feel less despicable than what they are. Find something. The pan-Hellenic cause, for example – now there's a fine justification. As far as the money goes, try to pass it off as an indemnity, an offer to propitiate the gods, a legacy deriving from an old hospitable pact, whatever comes to mind . . . Let me know, at the end, how much it's cost you. No blood, Philistus, if possible.'

In one month's time, Arcesilaus handed over Catane and Procles betrayed Naxos, the oldest Greek colony in Sicily, so old that the statue of the founder at the port was so corroded by wind and salt that it was unrecognizable.

Leontini remained alone, and surrendered without putting up any resistance. Dionysius decided to transfer all of the city's inhabitants to Syracuse.

The year after that, Rhegium and Messana, which were also Chalcidic colonies, imagining that it would be their turn next, fitted out a fleet and an army which marched south to engage battle with Dionysius's forces. Leptines proposed facing off on an open field and exterminating them to take care of the problem at its root, but Dionysius stopped him just in time and instead summoned Philistus once again.

'Do you think it will work with an army?'

Philistus shrugged.

'Don't make a fuss here. Will it work or won't it?'

'I think it will.'

'Then proceed. Those warriors may be marching at our sides next year against the Carthaginian provinces. I don't want them to die, and I don't want ours to die either. And tell me something:

if it does work, which action is more ethical – mine, based on perfidy, or the one your philosopher suggests, based on moral rigour?'

'You can't reason that way,' objected Philistus. 'The question is simply posed in incorrect terms. If you start from mistaken assumptions, there's no doubt that—'

Dionysius shook his head. 'Ah, philosophers! I avoid them like dog shit on the street.'

Philistus sighed. 'Is there someone in particular you have in mind, or must I find him?'

Dionysius passed him a sheet with a couple of names scribbled in charcoal. When Philistus had read it, he rubbed his thumb over it to blacken the sheet and make it illegible. Then, as his counsellor was leaving, Dionysius added: 'It's sowing time. That should make it easy for you.'

Philistus reached his quarters and summoned the men he had working for him. Before three days had passed, just a few hours apart, two high officers in the Rhegine and Messanian armies, both members of the general staff, asked that an Assembly be called and spoke with such vehemence in favour of ceasing hostilities, condemning the irresponsible behaviour of their respective commanders-in-chief, that when it came time to vote, the motion which proposed immediate withdrawal of the army obtained an overwhelming majority.

Dionysius was exultant. Not only was he the indisputable leader of his city, he would soon be the leader of his nation as well. He re-entered Syracuse between two cheering wings of the crowd, and shortly thereafter convoked Leptines, Philistus and a couple of friends from the Company. Old Heloris was ailing and no longer took part in the councils held in the Ortygia fortress.

'The time has come for me to marry!' he began.

Philistus and the others looked each other in the eye, completely taken by surprise. They all wore such an astonished expression that none of them obviously had been forewarned of his intentions.

'Who is she?' asked Philistus.

'You mean "they".'

' "They"? Why they?'

'Because I will take two wives.'

Leptines burst out laughing, as did some of the others.

Philistus jumped up: 'What's to laugh about? I've never heard of anything so foolish. What's the point? If you've got such an itch, find another way to scratch it.'

'You don't understand. My dual marriage will have symbolic significance . . .'

'Listen well,' Philistus interrupted him. 'Up until now, the people, in one way or another, have followed you. They respect you for your intelligence and determination and for your past as a heroic combatant, but if you start pulling stunts like this they will ridicule you. You're acting like a character from a comic play!'

Leptines and the others could not contain their laughter.

Dionysius pounded his fist on the table, shouting: 'That's enough!'

They all fell silent.

'If you want to know why I intend to marry two women on the same day, I'll tell you. Otherwise, I'll do it anyway, but the first one of you that cracks the slightest hint of an idiotic smile won't even have the time to be sorry about it. Is that clear?'

Philistus tried to make amends. 'I didn't mean to offend you, but that doesn't change the way I feel about this: it's a mistake. In any case, I am curious to know why you want to do such a thing.'

Seemingly appeased, Dionysius went on. 'I will marry two girls: a Sicilian and an Italian, to symbolize my position as chief and leader of both lands. The Sicilian girl will obviously be from Syracuse. I was thinking of Rhegium for the Italian girl, as a gesture of friendship. There must be any number of beautiful virgins from well-to-do families in Rhegium. You, Leptines, will go to ask for my bride's hand in Syracuse, while you, Philistus, will go to ask for the Italian girl's hand in Rhegium.'

Leptines raised a finger. 'Are questions allowed?'

'If they're not idiotic.'

'That depends on your point of view.'

'Then speak and stop breaking my balls about it.'

'Let's imagine that the two brides get along with each other and accept sharing you between them. Just how will you handle it in private? I mean, are you going to build a three-place bed or what? And which one are you going to fuck first, the Italian or . . .'

Dionysius punched him in the face, sending him rolling to the ground. Then he got up and left, slamming the door behind him.

'I'd say you were looking for that one,' observed Philistus, helping Leptines to get up.

20

THE RHEGINES DISCUSSED Dionysius's proposal to marry one of their daughters at length in the Assembly, while Philistus, who had brought the official request, waited patiently.

Opinions differed: some asserted the importance of having such a powerful ally as the tyrant of Syracuse, others thought the proposal too risky precisely because he was a tyrant and adventurer, and because if he fell, he would drag into ruin everyone who had become part of his family. Furthermore, the fate of Naxos and Catane had given a dire example; after all, they were Chalcidic colonies like Rhegium herself, peopled long ago by the inhabitants of the metropolis of Chalcis in Euboea.

Others still were furious over the request, which they judged impudent and shameless, and they proposed sending a prostitute as his fiancée to give him an idea of the consideration they had for him. In the end, the more moderate idea prevailed: to refuse his proposal without insulting him.

Philistus, on his return journey, felt ill at the idea of informing Dionysius of their response, which would certainly fail to make him happy. When he was received, he was relieved to see that Leptines was present as well, a sign that the two brothers had made peace and that the storm had passed.

Dionysius did not seem to react with particular disappointment. He only said: 'They'll regret it.'

'I'm sorry,' added Philistus.

'It's not your fault. I'm sure you did your best ... Did you mention that I'd be marrying another girl as well?'

'I had no choice.'

'No, you didn't, did you?'

'Are you so sure you wouldn't be happy with just one wife? There are lots of other girls who would be pleased to provide you with a little variety in bed ... you are the most powerful man west of the Ionian Gulf.'

'That's not the point. I made a decision and I don't change my mind once it's made up, you know that. I want two wives: an Italian and a Syracusan. You'll be leaving again soon.'

'Going where?'

'Locri. What do you say to Locri?'

'Right: the city of women.'

'They've always been our friends. I'm sure they'll accept.'

'I hope so. And if they give me a choice? What type of woman do you prefer?'

'Blonde, brunette?' prompted Leptines.

Dionysius lowered his head and thought to himself, 'Arete ...' then raised his eyes to meet Philistus's with a strange expression. 'Dark ... I'd prefer she had dark hair ...'

'Nothing else? I'm sure the Locrians will introduce me to their most attractive young women.'

'High flanks, fine breasts ...' said Dionysius. 'Do I have to tell you everything? No ... it's not very important, as long as she's from a good family and has an adequate dowry.'

'Naturally,' nodded Philistus.

'You'll leave in exactly twenty days.'

'Twenty days? Why, what's happening in twenty days?'

'What's happening is that something will be ready ... come on, I want you to see yourself,' and they left the room together.

'A gift? A special present?' asked Philistus as he followed him down the stairs along with Leptines and the ever-present Aksal.

'Wait and see.'

Dionysius walked at a quick pace towards the entry to the dockyards, while Philistus tried to guess from Leptines's expression what on earth he might be meaning to show him in that noisy, smoke-filled place. They reached a dock fenced off by a palisade and guarded by armed men. Two of them opened a gate and had them enter. Philistus stood open-mouthed with astonishment.

'A quinquereme,' said Dionysius, smiling and indicating a formidable battle vessel, propped up on bilge blocks in the middle of the shipyard and almost ready for launching.

'A quinquereme? What does that mean?' asked Philistus.

'It means a ship with five modules. Manned by one hundred more oarsmen than a trireme and equipped with a three-ram rostrum made of solid iron and weighing five talents, twice as heavy as any used until now. A beauty, isn't she? I designed her myself.'

'It's the biggest warship ever built anywhere in the world,' commented Leptines. 'The *Boubaris*.'

'She's the ship that will take you to Locri to fetch my betrothed,' added Dionysius, walking along the flank of the mighty ship. 'Imagine the amazement of the people as they see her sail into port, her aplustre and figurehead all decked out in gold and silver, her standards waving in the wind. Imagine how swiftly the news will spread, how the sailors in every port will be talking about her, giving rise to all sorts of rumours about her size and magnificence. And just imagine when you return! I've planned everything. As soon as the *Boubaris* is sighted, a chariot with four white horses will depart from the house of my Syracusan fiancée. At precisely the moment when the girl steps off the ship, here at the dockyards, the other bride will arrive from the opposite side of the square on a resplendent quadriga . . .'

Philistus heaved a long sigh. 'Nice ceremony, no doubt about it.'

'But that's not all!' added Dionysius, leading his guest to a platform from which he could see the entire dockyards. 'Look, twenty-nine more galleys like this one, already under construction.'

'Gods!' exclaimed Philistus, speechless, letting his eyes roam over the expanse of gigantic hulls around which hundreds of shipwrights, caulkers, carpenters, rope-makers, armourers and blacksmiths scurried.

'And it's not finished here,' continued Dionysius. 'There are more marvels to see. Follow me.' He left the platform and headed towards the side wall of the fortress, where they entered through a secondary door that led to one of the two inner courtyards.

Philistus followed him, struggling to keep up as he chatted with Leptines along the way. '*Boubaris* . . . what a curious name! Where did he fish that one up?'

'I was the one who thought of it,' replied Leptines. 'When we were boys, we had a duck in the farmyard that was so big and heavy they called her *Boubaris*: heavy-as-an-ox.'

'A duck!' said Philistus, shaking his head. 'A duck . . . my word!'

They entered the courtyard and Philistus was even more bewildered and amazed: three gigantic machines had been assembled in the middle of the yard, each of them surrounded by a dozen busy artillerymen. Some manoeuvred the arm of a winch connected to an enormous bowstring, in order to draw it taut. In response to a curt order, the slider was released and the string loosed a heavy dart of solid iron which struck a ten-inch-thick board with a dull thud, running it through from back to front.

'We've called it "ballista". If it is aimed at an infantry formation, it can cause a massacre. If it hits the side of a ship, even beneath the waterline, it can sink her from a distance of one hundred feet. And take a look at that.'

He pointed at a machine whose long, flexible wooden arm ended in a spoon which held a weight of perhaps one hundred pounds. A winch system pulled it taut, almost to the breaking point, then loosed it all at once. The weight was hurled at a wall made of large hewn blocks of lava stone and pulverized it. 'We've called this one a "catapult".'

'You designed these as well?' asked Philistus in astonishment.

'I did,' replied Dionysius. 'I've been working day and night, first on the plans, then on scale models built by architects, and finally on these working models that you see here. They function perfectly. We're building fifty of each. Himilco's rams will seem like toys compared to these!'

'You're preparing for war,' nodded Philistus.

'That's right. I'll finally drive the Carthaginians completely out of Sicily. I'll gather the survivors of Selinus, Acragas, Himera and Gela under my standard, I'll muster mercenaries from everywhere and I'll march all the way to Motya and Panormus.'

'All this is incredible,' murmured Philistus, looking over at the mechanisms drawing back the crossbows with a series of sinister creaks.

'You haven't seen anything yet,' said Leptines. 'If you're not too tired, we can take a walk through the city; you won't believe your eyes. The walls have been lengthened by seven stadia to include Epipolae, which has always been our Achilles' heel. What's more, we're building a castle at the top, an impregnable fortress called Euryalus. A line of bastions to make the Athenian Long Walls pale! It will be the most impressive fortified complex ever seen.'

'Let's go, then,' replied Philistus. 'I still can't really imagine what you've been up to in this city.'

'Leptines will go with you,' said Dionysius. 'I have to remain here for the testing of my machines. I want them perfect when it's time to line them up at the front.'

They crossed the Ortygia isthmus and proceeded to Achradina, following the line of walls which seemed to be growing before their eyes. Philistus couldn't believe what he was seeing. In the two months he'd been gone, the length of the walls had nearly tripled, and the city had become a gigantic building yard. Thousands and thousands of stone-cutters, porters, labourers, masons and master-builders were working simultaneously along the entire line.

'Dionysius has invented a system that works miracles,' explained Leptines. 'He divided the entire perimeter into one-hundred-foot sections and has assigned each section to an independent team, led by a building foreman, who is responsible for the execution and the progress of the works. Each team is paid on the basis of the length of the wall section they manage to build, and the faster the wall goes up, the higher the pay. So everyone works to his maximum potential. The slaves have even been promised their freedom, and this has driven them to quite unimaginable feats. They work in shifts, day and night, never stopping, under the supervision of inspectors who are directly accountable to Dionysius, so that their very lives are at stake if he doesn't find the work satisfactory!'

They walked for nearly an hour before they reached Epipolae and the Euryalus fortress, surrounded by trenches. From there they could take in the whole city in a single glance: the new districts, the long snaking walls, the two harbours and Ortygia.

'In three months' time, the entire circle of wall and the fortress will be complete. Syracuse will be impregnable.'

'I believe it,' replied Philistus. 'But all this won't go unobserved. They'll find out in Carthage and adopt measures to counter ours.'

'That's not said. The Carthaginian quarter here in Syracuse is completely surrounded by mercenaries. No one can enter or exit without permission. We'll arrest and imprison them on the slightest suspicion. We'll use torture, if necessary.'

'The first unhappy effects of the war,' commented Philistus. 'Those people have always lived amongst us, trading and carrying on business to our mutual advantage. Now all of a sudden they've become our sworn enemies, so dangerous they must be locked up, persecuted . . .'

'Well, they started first, didn't they?' objected Leptines.

'No one knows who started first, believe me. This war will become a clash of the two different races, us and them, and it will not abate until one of the two has been completely wiped out.'

'You're strange,' observed Leptines. 'Whose side are you on?'

'Do you need to ask? The fact is that the preparations I've seen worry me. Dionysius is tossing enormous resources into the furnace of war; he's sure of winning, but on the other side of the sea there's a shrewd and evasive enemy, a great naval power capable of cutting off our supply and trade routes . . .'

'But Dionysius also wants to marry . . . he wants an heir. That means he's looking towards the future, doesn't it?'

'Right, the two wives. And who might the chosen one be here in Syracuse?'

'Aristomache,' replied Leptines, suddenly serious.

'Hipparinus's daughter? I can't believe it.'

'He's always been a member of the Company, one of the most important.'

'Yes, but he's always been an adversary of Heloris, Dionysius's adoptive father.'

'Heloris will have to get used to the idea. His daughters are all as ugly as can be. Aristomache is gorgeous. You know, I've known her ever since we were children; we used to play in the courtyard together. When I went to ask for her hand for my brother, I couldn't believe my eyes: she's become as beautiful as Aphrodites! High, firm breasts, hands that were made to caress a man's body and . . .'

'That's enough,' Philistus cut him off. 'I don't even want to think about hearing those words. Let's say I've never heard them. Your brother would slit your throat if he knew.'

'You're right . . .' admitted Leptines. 'He'd probably slit my throat.'

*

With the return of spring, the *Boubaris* majestically went to sea, parting the waters with her rostrum like a plough does the earth and raising two symmetric waves as she passed. Dionysius was impatient to test her out and had had a Carthaginian ship captured on patrol near Selinus towed offshore to be used as a target. On board were Philistus and Leptines, along with his future father-in-law Hipparinus.

At a gesture from the navarch, the drummer started to pound out the rowing tempo, getting progressively louder and faster. Dismasted, the *Boubaris* was launched on to the waves with impressive force, helped along by a light, favourable wind.

At the navarch's order, the oars were pulled in with absolute synchrony and the pointed rostrum ran through the side of the target with a huge crash and split the Carthaginian vessel in two.

Dionysius and his friends had a firm grip on the railing, but the moment of impact was incredible. The ropes cut into their clothing and rubbed their skin raw, and Philistus nearly broke his back.

The two halves sank in a matter of moments. The *Boubaris* plunged forward and then put about, steered by the stern rudders, as the oars plunged back into the sea.

A cry of exultation rose from the crew and Dionysius ran to the stern to behold the flotsam from the wreck afloat on the foaming waves. '*Nike! Nike!*' he shouted. 'We won! The quinquereme is the most fearsome ship to ride the waves in our day!'

They all congratulated each other, but Philistus couldn't help but think that the Carthaginians would certainly not sit there like the target had, waiting for five talents of iron to tear into them, and that things might be very different indeed in battle. But he didn't want to spoil the mood, and so he too joined in the ovations. The *Boubaris*, after all, would soon be his means of transport for Locri, where Dionysius's Italian fiancée was waiting.

'Why did you call Locri the "city of women"?' asked Leptines as they were returning. 'Remember? After you came back from Rhegium.'

'Of course I remember. And if you weren't so ignorant, I wouldn't have to explain it to you. We know from ancient accounts that when the Locrians from the metropolis were in battle, the women became so tired of being at home alone that they went to bed with their slaves and had children by them. When their husbands came back from the war, they repudiated their wives, who took to the seas and sailed with their offspring to Italy, where they founded Locri. Women are still considered the heads of their families in Locri, and it is the women who hand down their names and their inheritance. That's why Locri is the city of women . . .'

Leptines grinned. 'If that's the way the city was founded, I don't know whether he's so lucky to be marrying a Locrian, but if he's happy . . .'

'Right: if he's happy . . .' shrugged Philistus.

The *Boubaris* entered the dockyard again, and the naval architects who had built her crowded around to inspect the vessel down to the last nail. They had to check that the rostrum hadn't suffered any cracks, and that the tension cable below deck hadn't lost any of its tautness. Everything was in perfect order; even the keel, which was almost twenty feet longer than usual, had held up well under impact. The first quinquereme ever built was about to become the queen of battles.

She set to sea again a few days later to take Philistus to Locri. Dionysius's betrothed had been chosen by the most influential family of the city, who had offered their noblest and most beautiful daughter: Doris.

She was not dark at all, as Dionysius had suggested. She was blonde, instead, with blue eyes, hair as fine and shiny as threads of gold. Her high breasts were so firm that the Ionian peplum she wore – as light as air and so soft as to reveal every curve of her body – fell with supreme elegance.

She knew very well that she would be sharing her husband with another woman, and yet she was very happy to be going to Syracuse; she seemed a little girl eagerly awaiting a party. Philistus imagined that her family must be very rigid and strict indeed if passing from the authority of her father to the authority of her husband was such a relief for her, but then he remembered that it was the women who headed the households in Locri. Perhaps female traditions took no notice of the idea of exclusive possession, typical of men obsessed by the thought of domination. Maybe she was happy because she would have children, or because she would lie with a man who everyone raved about, and was not bothered about anything else. After all, Dionysius's fame was such that he was certainly worth any other two men.

Philistus participated in celebrations and ceremonies of all sorts for three days. During the festivities, he delivered the groom's wedding gift: an ancient golden necklace, set with drops of amber, crafted by a great artist. He then took aboard the girl, her mother, and her vast dowry of coins, garments, furnishings, jewels, pets, fabrics, perfumes, paintings, statues, tableware both new and antique, and the sacred images she would worship in her new home.

Among all this, Philistus was struck by a little statue of Athena. It was rough and primitive and not lovely in any way, but extremely fascinating; quite strangely, it portrayed the goddess with her eyes closed. 'What is this?' he asked her.

'It's a reproduction of the Palladion, the sacred image of Athena that made the city of Troy invincible, stolen away by Odysseus and Diomedes. The night of the fall of the city, our national hero Ajax Oileus raped princess Cassandra at the foot of the Palladion. The goddess closed her eyes so as not to witness the abomination. Since then, in expiation for that rape, our city sends two virgins to Troy from our best families every year, to serve in the Temple of Athena of Ilium.'

'And have you been, my lady?' asked Philistus.

'No, but I would have liked so much to go! To see the armour of Achilles, his tomb and the tomb of Patroclus . . .'

'You are very well educated.'

'I know, you Dorians think that it's a scandal to educate women, but here it's the norm. It is we women who dictate the laws of society, and we have a much fairer and more sensible way of life.'

'And you're not afraid of ending up in the bed of the most terrible of these Dorians, the one who everyone calls "the Tyrant"?'

'No,' replied the girl, with a hint of a smile in her blue eyes. 'On the contrary, I'm curious to see whether he'll live up to his repute.'

They spoke at length during the journey, and became friends. Philistus thought it was only fair to warn her about what her life would be like in Syracuse. 'You know what awaits you,' he said. 'Dionysius has had two bedchambers built adjacent to his own bedroom, and he will sleep with both of you in turn. But the three of you will dine together, unless one of you is not well and prefers to remain in her apartments. But I would not recommend feeling ill more than once or twice in an entire year!'

'I understand,' said Doris as she leaned on the ship's railing, caressed by the wind of Zephyr until Philistus startled her by saying: 'Look: Syracuse!'

*

Aristomache arrived on a chariot drawn by four white horses, driven by a charioteer wearing a tunic shot through with purple threads. Her hair was raven with violet reflections, and she wore a flame-coloured peplum gathered at the waist with a golden belt.

Doris arrived from the port on a litter borne by eight slaves, including an Ethiopian who aroused the curiosity of the onlookers. But the crowd's applause went to the Syracusan, and they hoped deep down that she would be the one to give an heir to Dionysius, who the people had come to accept as a monarch and the founder of a dynasty.

They simultaneously crossed the thresholds of the eastern and western gates of the Ortygia fortress, following a protocol the master of ceremonies had practised again and again with the aid of actors.

The date had been selected so that neither of the two girls had her menstrual period on that day.

The groom was wearing a very simple, floor-length white chiton. His iron bracelet was adorned with a single red stone, said to have been forged with the iron of the dagger that had killed the murderers of his first wife, Arete.

A long wedding ceremony took place, followed by a lavish banquet laid for ten thousand people, to which both foreigners, including the mercenary officers, and citizens of every rank and social position had been invited. The adoptive father of the groom, old Heloris, was notable for his absence; he had felt so offended by Dionysius's exclusion of his daughters that he had gone into exile in Rhegium. There he would later put himself at the head of the Syracusan Knights who had fled or survived the distruction of Aetna and were organizing a sort of armed resistance against the tyrant in the city.

After the official banquet, the two brides were conducted each into her own bedchamber, where they were undressed and had their hair combed by their handmaids. A group of singers struck up first a Syracusan, then immediately after a Locrian, wedding hymn.

Dionysius entered Doris's room first. He contemplated her tenderly in the lamplight, for she lay completely nude on top of the covers, displaying her glorious curves to her husband's gaze. Her mother had instructed her well, and had taught her how to move her hips to give pleasure to her man and to induce him to spill all his seed into her womb, so that none would remain for the Syracusan bride.

But Doris added her own lascivious innocence to her mother's teachings and prolonged their intimacy at great length, gratifying her groom with enticing words, and flattering his vanity in every way.

When it was the Syracusan's turn, Dionysius knew he would find her ill-disposed by her long wait and perhaps vexed by the thought that he had no more seed for her. And so he was especially lavish in his attentions and his tenderness, and he satisfied all her senses to the utmost. He kissed her on the lips, then her breasts, her stomach and all over her body until he finally penetrated her, but he did not find the rapture in her body that he had expected. Doris, who was listening in from her own room, was surprised and rather pleased by all that silence. Was Aristomache so timid, as all the Dorian girls were said to be?

Dionysius promised the Syracusan that the next night he would lie with her first, and he was still holding her in his arms when the door opened gently and Doris appeared with a lantern in hand. She smiled at both and said: 'Can I stay with you? I'm afraid to sleep alone.'

Aristomache was about to react, but seeing Dionysius's amused expression, she held her tongue. Doris slipped into bed and began first to caress Dionysius, awakening the virility exhausted by that long night of love, and then Aristomache as well. The Syracusan stiffened, but did not push her away so as not to irritate her husband, who seemed delighted by the game.

Doris was the first to become pregnant.

21

Dionysius decided to wait until the crops had been harvested before beginning the war, to avoid defections on the part of the allies due to the demands of their farms. In the meantime, he sent an envoy to Carthage with an ultimatum: the prisoners must be released without ransom, and the city government must recognize the independence of the Greek cities destroyed in the previous wars. Dionysius knew from his informers that the Punic capital had been greatly weakened by the plague, but he underestimated his enemy's pride.

In Carthage, the government met to discuss – and almost immediately decided to reject – the arrogant impositions of the tyrant of Syracuse. Himilco was once again appointed to the supreme command and charged with waging war using every means possible. Word of Dionysius's preparations had reached them, and their greatest fear was that after conquering Sicily, he would attempt to land in Africa. He had to be destroyed before he became too dangerous.

In the meantime, the Italian allies had arrived in Syracuse, while the Rhegines and Messanians were maintaining an attitude that alternated between indifference and hostility. It was feared that Rhegium might even ally with Carthage, if that's what it took to humiliate Syracuse's hateful dynast.

Everything was ready: two hundred battle ships, including thirty quinqueremes fresh from the dockyards, all under Leptines's orders. Standing proud at the bow of the *Boubaris*, he reviewed the immense fleet that was weighing anchor to sail for Drepanum, in western Sicily. The fleet was followed by five hundred transports carrying food, water and the yet-to-be-assembled parts of the new siege machines.

The ground force was made up of forty thousand foot soldiers and three thousand horsemen, and the fleet carried nearly as many. Among them were many of the survivors of Selinus, Acragas and Himera, and the refugees from Gela and Camarina.

None of them had forgotten.

Dionysius addressed the arrayed troops after having mustered all of them at the city's western gate. 'Men!' he shouted. 'Sicilians and Italians of the Hellenic cities of the West! The moment of revenge has finally come. Much time has passed, nearly ten years, from the days in which you saw your cities die, your children butchered, your wives raped and killed!' His voice seemed to crack as he said those last words. 'I promised many of you then that I would bring you back home, that I would rebuild your cities, that I would avenge your dead.

'I would have done this long before now, believe me! I know well what you went through, because my flesh and my blood have borne the same pain. I was the first to come to the aid of the Selinuntians, I was at Himera and at Acragas and I suffered bitter defeat at Gela, not by my own fault, but through the adversity of fortune and the perfidy of treason.

'Those of you who were then twenty are now thirty, those of you who were thirty then are now forty, but I'm certain that your hatred and your thirst for vengeance have never abated over all these years. I know that you will fight without sparing your strength. I know that once you take up your shields and your swords, nothing will stop your onslaught.

'This is not a war like any other. It is not like the bloody conflicts that have been fought between brothers out of narrow-minded rivalry, out of selfish commercial interests. This is the war of Greeks against barbarians, like at Marathon, like at Thermopylae and like Salamis. Like at Himera, at Cumae eighty years ago! All of Sicily will be Greek, as is right and just. It was our ancestors who reached this land from beyond the sea, who created marvellous cities, who opened harbours and markets, who planted olive trees and sowed wheat, who raised glorious temples to the gods. These temples have been sacked and destroyed, the tombs of our ancestors profaned, our families devastated, our children sold into slavery.

'Enough now! The day that I promised you has come. Unleash your rage, men, remember what you've suffered, remember the cries of your violated women, remember the torment of your children, cut down on the streets and in your homes, their throats slit in the cradle . . . Avenge your honour!

'We will not stop until the last of our enemies has been thrown into the sea, until the hateful race that has destroyed our cities has been completely annihilated.

'I will be at your side, marching with you, I will be eating the same food and facing the same hardships and I swear to you, upon the infernal gods and upon my most sacred memories, that I will have no peace until I have brought this undertaking to conclusion, even if it should cost me my life!'

A roar greeted Dionysius's words, the din of spears rhythmically, obsessively pounded against bronze shields.

But he signalled that he had more to say and the uproar died down until there was silence.

'The barbarians employ,' he thundered, 'a handful of Greek traitors, mercenaries who have decided to combat against their own blood in exchange for money. I say to them: "Abandon your masters, join us as free men and redeem your shame. If you do not do so now, your punishment will be horrible, much worse than what we have in store for the barbarians. Beware, for here we come!"'

At the sound of these words, which were evidently meant as a signal, bugles blared and drums rolled to sound their departure and to mark their marching rhythm.

The great army surged forward between two wings of Syracusan citizens and inhabitants of the inland cities, who had come from everywhere to witness this superb spectacle. Dionysius rode a black horse identical to the one he had mounted in his first battle against the Carthaginians; he advanced at the head of the army covered by shining armour, flanked by Aksal and by his father-in-law Hipparinus riding a glossy-maned bay.

Behind him were three thousand horsemen lined up five-across, and behind them the heavy line infantry, divided by city, each group carrying its own standard and insignia, amidst a storm of applause and cheers.

Alongside the column, the naval squadron paraded on the foaming waves, led by the gigantic quinqueremes that ploughed through the sea with their huge three-rammed rostrums, each point sharp as a spear's tip.

*

Himilco realized immediately that this was a challenge to the death, and his first move was to try to force Leptines's fleet to turn back and defend Syracuse. He mounted a night assault with a dozen light ships on the Laccius port and the docks. They arrived completely unexpected, set fire to the shipyards and the vessels under construction and attempted an assault on the Ortygia fortress, but the Peloponnesian mercenaries remaining on guard at the stronghold reacted with great courage and determination and forced them to retreat. The Syracusans promptly sent a fast galley to notify Leptines that the enemy had been repulsed and that they did not require assistance.

Dionysius had in the meantime reached the place from which he planned to launch the attack on Motya. The fortified Carthaginian city stood on an island at the centre of the bay of Lilybaeum and was connected to the mainland by a long causeway. This causeway had been built in a north-south direction so as not to interfere with navigation in the lagoon surrounding the island, and as soon as the inhabitants of Motya heard that enemy forces were on their way, they began demolishing it to disallow access to their walls.

Between the bay of Lilybaeum and the open sea was another long island with a curious shape that had given it its name of 'Goat Shin'. It was separated from the mainland by two narrow straits. Entering the lagoon around Motya was relatively easy from the southern straits, where the depth of the sea was sufficient to allow the passage of big warships, but it was practically impossible from the north, where the water was too shallow, with shoals and sandbanks that only the local Phoenician and Carthaginian sailors knew about.

Leptines stopped at Drepanum, the port of Eryx, a city north of Motya peopled by the Elymians, who were in the habit of welcoming anyone they were incapable of fighting off. There he divided the fleet into two parts: the transports were anchored much further south, near the promontory of Lilybaeum, while the war vessels entered the lagoon and were moored near the northern promontory, not very far from the start of the causeway that connected Motya to Sicily, which the Motyans had already partially demolished.

Dionysius assigned the navy the task of rebuilding the causeway and assembling the siege machines, while he himself – at the head of the ground troops – moved east to invade the territory of Panormus and Solus, laying waste to the countryside and sacking the farms. He tried as well to storm the Elymian cities of Segesta and Entella, also allied with Carthage, but did not succeed. He thus decided to return to Motya and take command of the operations personally.

In the meantime Himilco, who was cruising offshore, was kept constantly informed of the progress achieved by the Motyan defenders. He learned that Leptines had beached his ships in order to put their crews to work rebuilding the causeway, and he decided the time was ripe to launch his fleet into an attack.

He met up first with the transports in the Lilybaeum area and sank a good number of them, but in so doing ruined the element of surprise. Leptines was informed of the approach of the enemy fleet and sounded the alarm to muster his sailors. The ships were swiftly towed back into the water and the crews managed to take their places on board before Himilco could fall upon them.

Leptines sent out a couple of light reconnaissance craft, and the news they brought back cheered no one. 'They are fanned out with their bows pointed north and they've closed off the southern mouth of the lagoon. We're trapped,' reported the scouts.

'Not yet,' replied Leptines. 'Where's my brother?'

'The commander is at headquarters.'

'Take me there.'

Leptines lowered himself into the dinghy towed by the *Boubaris* and raced to their headquarters at the mouth of the northern straits to report on the situation.

Dionysius darkened. 'I would have kept a contingent of the fleet outside this blasted lagoon. Now what do we do?'

'We'll launch the quinqueremes and split them in two.'

'No, we won't. That's exactly what they want. They've drawn us into this swamp to make it impossible for us to use our numerical superiority to advantage. I don't want to risk our new units in such a disadvantageous situation. The quinqueremes need space to manoeuvre.'

'You're telling me? I'm the commander of the fleet!' burst out Leptines.

'And I'm the commander-in-chief! Have you forgotten that?' shouted Dionysius even louder. 'Why is it that you always have to charge with your head down like a bull? One wrong move and we are all fucked. Don't you remember how things went in Gela? It was all preordained, all planned, and in the end we lost. We have the biggest fleet and the biggest army that the Greek nation has ever put together: we cannot fail, understand?' He continued as if speaking to himself, fretting: 'It had to happen just now that the causeway was almost ready . . .'

'Well, let's hear how you think you'll get out of this one, *hegemon*,' shot back Leptines, giving the title an ironic twist, 'seeing that there's no way out to the north; if any of the ships runs aground, the others will be shut off.'

Dionysius pondered his words for a while, then said: 'We'll go overland.'

'What?'

'That's right. We'll build a slide, grease it well and drag the ships over it one by one, until we can lower them into the sea on the other side of the promontory.'

Leptines shook his head. 'And that seems like a good idea to you? We'll only be able to put one ship at a time into the sea. If the Carthaginians realize what we're up to, they'll sink them one by one as soon as they put out to sea.'

'No, they won't,' replied Dionysius. 'Because they'll find a surprise waiting for them.'

'A surprise?'

'Have a screen of wicker and branches built along the shore of the open sea, three hundred feet long and twenty tall. You'll see.'

The project was begun immediately: as a group of sailors raised the screen, hundreds of carpenters set to work building the slip, two parallel guides made of pinewood beams, which crossed over the promontory from the shore of the lagoon to the open sea on the other side. Others melted pig fat and ox tallow in huge cauldrons to spread over the guides to ease sliding. The ships were positioned on the slide and then dragged over it with ropes, each ship by its own crew, with five hundred men on each side.

Construction of the slip was not visible from Motya but, when the ships began to be towed over the promontory, the sentries realized what was happening and sent news to Himilco that the mouse was fleeing the trap. The Punic admiral gave orders to man the oars and hoist the sails; they would advance in a northern direction and sail around Goat Shin island. This would keep them shielded until the last moment so that by the time the Syracusans saw them, it would be too late.

From the flagship, Himilco signalled for his ships to act in concert and stay together, so that the impact with the enemy fleet would be massive and synchronous. When the Syracusan warships finally came into sight, Himilco could count them: about sixty, making the ratio very favourable for him. He would destroy those, then go ashore and destroy the slip. At this point he would be free to blockade any ships which had been left behind in the lagoon, forcing them to rot or fight.

Having rounded the northern tip of the island, he turned

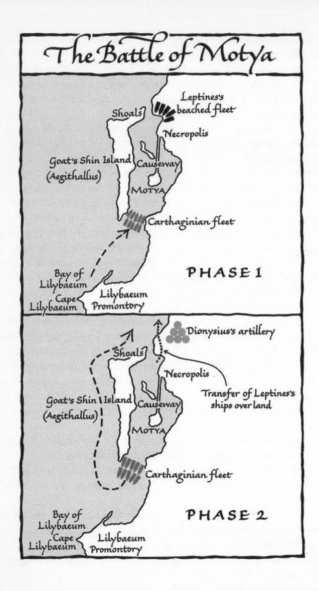

The Battle of Motya

PHASE 1

Leptines's beached fleet

Shoals

Necropolis

Goat's Shin Island
(Aegithallus)

Causeway

MOTYA

Carthaginian fleet

Bay of
Lilybaeum

Cape
Lilybaeum

Lilybaeum
Promontory

PHASE 2

Dionysius's artillery

Shoals

Necropolis

Transfer of Leptines's
ships overland

Goat's Shin Island
(Aegithallus)

Causeway

MOTYA

Carthaginian fleet

Bay of
Lilybaeum

Cape
Lilybaeum

Lilybaeum
Promontory

sharply starboard towards the coast, and, when he was at a suitable distance, ordered the drummers to set a ramming tempo. At that point, the Syracusan ships, whose bows were turned west, put to starboard as if to make their way north, and Himilco mirrored the move. In doing so, his ships exposed their flanks to the coast, where a strange structure had now become perfectly visible: a sort of screen made of reeds, matting and even ship's sails. And then the unforeseeable occurred: the screen fell, segment after segment, revealing a long line-up of mechanical monsters never before seen, missiles already in place, manned by dozens of artillerymen in combat position. A bugle sounded and, one after another, the enormous engines went into action. Himilco's fleet was inundated by a hail of projectiles launched by the catapults. The ballistas, which had been adjusted to aim low, let loose a swarm of massive iron darts that broke through the keels under the waterline and swept away the decks, sowing death and terror. The machines had been timed for alternating launches: first the ballistas and then the catapults, as the former were reloading.

Meanwhile, the Syracusan vessels which had been pulled across the promontory put about in a wide circle to create a ramming formation. Leptines was, instead, still in the lagoon and headed south; he swiftly succeeded in breaking through the southern straits, overwhelming the meagre forces left there to garrison the outlet. His thirty quinqueremes, followed by the other ships, set out to close Himilco's fleet in their trap.

The Carthaginian admiral, who had been warned by signals from the Motyans, put about, escaping the deadly attack of the artillery and put out to sea, just barely escaping entrapment between the contingents of Dionysius and Leptines.

Himilco thus abandoned Motya to her fate; such was the Carthaginians' gratitude to those who had saved them from total disaster.

Cries of exultation exploded from the decks of the Greek ships and from the shore, where the formidable new siege engines had achieved such excellent results.

From the towers of Motya, the city's defenders watched in

anguish as the Carthaginian fleet disappeared at the horizon while, on the opposite side, the huge machines that had sent their enemy running were being dragged to the causeway, which now once again connected the mainland to their island. They knew they would all die. It was only a question of time.

*

One clean, clear morning at the end of the summer, after a night of wind, Dionysius gave orders to attack, and the siege engines lumbered down the causeway, squeaking and creaking.

The ballistas and catapults were the first to enter into action from the end of the causeway, targeting the city's battlements and massacring her defenders. They were then hauled into position at the north of the island, where there was more room. There they were joined by the assault towers and battering rams.

The people of Motya knew full well what was in store for them. Many of them had taken part in the massacres of Selinus and Himera, and now they readied to defend their city to the last. They too had prepared a number of effective countermeasures. Long cantilevered planks were extended over the sides of the battlements from the wooden towers; caissons hanging from the ends of these boards held jars full of flaming naphtha and oil, which were hurled by the soldiers at the besiegers' machines. The attackers reacted by covering the engines with newly-flayed skins, and put out any flames using buckets of water passed from man to man with great speed.

The walls were battered by the siege machines for five consecutive days, until finally one of the rams succeeded in opening a breach on the north-east section of the wall. The assault towers came forward and gangplanks were lowered so the Greeks could rush through the opening and penetrate the city, but the Motyans were advantaged by their narrow maze of streets. They offered furious resistance, fighting with grim determination house by house, alley by alley, raising barricades and hurling anything that could serve as a missile from the tops of the buildings, which were three or four storeys high, practically as tall as the towers.

Combat became fiercer and bloodier as the days went on. The assaults began at daybreak, continued relentlessly the entire day, and stopped only when darkness fell, but despite these constant attacks, the besiegers made little progress. Within that tangle of winding streets, amidst the towering buildings, they could not make their numerical superiority and the power of their weapons work to their advantage.

In the end, Dionysius had an idea. He gathered the leaders of the Selinuntian, Himeran, Geloan and Acragantine refugees in his tent, along with his brother Leptines and the commander of the assault troops, his old friend Biton.

'Men,' he began, 'the Motyans have become inured to our daily attacks and they have sufficient time at their disposal to set up new forms of resistance. Their barricades built in the city's narrow streets between the high walls of the houses are practically insurmountable. The Motyans know to expect our attacks by day from the assault towers positioned at the only breach, because they know there isn't sufficient room to position them at other points of the walls. We must surprise them . . .'

He had one of his guards pass him a spear and used the tip to draw out his plans in the sand.

'We will attack at night, using ladders, at a completely different point. Here. Biton, your assault troops will carry out the operation. Once you're up on the walls, you should have no problem ridding yourselves of the few sentries that are usually posted in that area. You'll use the ladders as footbridges to put you on the terraces of the houses nearest the walls. The men will enter through the roof windows and surprise the inhabitants in their sleep. More warriors will follow and take control of an increasingly vast area of the walls. An incendiary arrow will be the signal that you've succeeded in the operation, and at that point we will launch an assault from the breach with the bulk of our forces. The Motyans won't know what to defend first, panic will spread and the city will be in our hands. Are you up to it, men?'

'We're raring to go!' came the reply.

'Fine. Leptines will transport the raiders with small flat-bottomed boats, painted black. You won't need heavy arms; peltasts' gear for everyone, cuirasses and leather shields. We'll attack this very night; there's a new moon and by moving quickly we'll also ensure that word doesn't get out. Men, the time has come to take your revenge. May the gods assist you.'

'Will they succeed?' asked Leptines when they'd left.

'I'm sure they will,' replied Dionysius. 'Go now. I'll wait here for your signal.'

Leptines went to the naval base to prepare the boats and ladders, then took the geared-up raiders on board. They were led by Biton, Dionysius's trusted friend and a member of the Company.

Leptines put them ashore at a spot where the walls were almost lapped by the sea; they were far away from the breach and so the area was poorly guarded. The first group of raiders placed their ladders and climbed up in silence. After a short time, two of them leaned over and gestured for more to come up. The route was clear. In a matter of moments, fifty warriors were on the walls. They found no more than a few sentries on a stretch of about one hundred feet of the battlements, and easily took them out. Several were wearing the armour of the murdered Motyans and took their places. They were Selinuntians who spoke the language.

The men continued to urge their comrades up the ladders until there were about two hundred men gathered on the walls. They split into two groups: fifty of them remained to guard the point of ascent, where more warriors continued to arrive in a continuous stream from Leptines's boats. The others laid out the ladders horizontally to reach the terraces of the houses closest to the wall and began to climb on to them, using the ladders as bridges. Then they opened the ceiling windows and dropped inside.

Surprised in their sleep, the inhabitants were massacred. Twenty men remained to garrison the terraces, as the ladders were extended to more houses and the assailants proceeded with their deadly mission. When the alarm sounded, the Motyans grabbed their arms and swarmed down into the streets, yelling loudly to wake up their comrades. Some of the houses had already been set aflame and many others were occupied by the attackers. More of them continued to pour over the walls, while others kept the breach under surveillance.

Biton launched the signal they'd agreed upon and Dionysius, already in position on the causeway, had the assault towers advance. Thousands of warriors invaded the city through the breach, easily overwhelming the one hundred or so defenders stationed there as guards.

Before long, contrasting rumours regarding multiple attacks at various spots of the circle of walls spread utter panic within the city, and the Motyans scattered in every direction, many of them defending the barricades that closed the entrances of the streets where their own families lived. When the common barrier was shattered, each of them fell back to the single barriers, until many found themselves – as had the Selinuntians so many years before – defending the doors to their own homes. It was the Selinuntians who were most murderous, and with them the Himerans. The shrieks of torment that reached their ears reawakened other screams in their minds: those of their dying wives and children, of their comrades massacred and tortured. Foaming with rage, out of their minds with bloodlust, excited by the mounting flames, they gave themselves over to merciless slaughter and to the sacking of that prosperous city, the hub of flourishing commerce between Africa and Sicily.

Dionysius, who had hoped to capture many prisoners to be sold as slaves in order to pay for part of the war expenses, realized that he had stirred up the men excessively and tried to take measures. He sent out heralds who enjoined the Motyans in Phoenician to take shelter in the temples that the Greeks respected: the temples of Heracles-Melqart, Hera-Tanit and Apollo-Reshef. Many lives were thus spared, and many more saved when the officers began to order their men to take the prisoners alive.

By dusk the city was completely under control. The prisoners had been amassed in the squares, tied and chained, to be carried off to the Greek camp on the mainland. Among them were a good number of Greek warriors who had fought for the Motyans. Many were residents who had lived peacefully with the inhabitants of the city for years, carrying out the activities they excelled in; they had been craftsmen, architects, sculptors, bronze-workers, decorators and weavers. One of them, an Italian sculptor from Medma, had been engaged by a rich merchant to execute a magnificent marble statue that represented a charioteer in typical Punic garb. Seeing that the Greeks were raging against all the images and statues that represented Carthaginians or Phoenicians, he had dragged his creation – in the heat of the battle – behind a wall near his laboratory and buried it in great haste under a heap of refuse, unable to bear the idea that his marvellous work would be hacked to pieces by the fury of war.

He was captured soon afterwards and hauled off with the others to camp.

One of the Motyan Greeks stood out above the rest: their commander, a certain Deimenes, who was taken to Dionysius's presence.

The Syracusan dynast ordered all the others to leave and gave the man a seat. He was bleeding from a number of wounds, his face had been blackened by the smoke, his skin burned by the flames, his feet were riddled with sores.

'What must I do with you and your men?' began Dionysius. 'Greeks who have chosen to fight alongside the barbarians against your own blood?' And he quoted a phrase of Herodotus from his *History*: '*Medizein . . . hellenes eontes.*'

'We fought for our city,' replied Deimenes in a faint voice.

'Your city?' screamed Dionysius.

'Yes. We've lived at length here in peace and prosperity. Our children were born here. Our work was here, our homes and our friends. Our wives come from this people, and their families, to whom we are tied by deep bonds. Our homeland is the land we live in, that our loved ones live in. We've betrayed no one, *hegemon*, we've done nothing but defend our families and our homes. What would you have done?'

'What about the people of Selinus and of Himera?' shot back Dionysius. 'Weren't they perhaps living in peace when they were savaged by your barbarians? They were people who spoke your same language, who believed in your same gods . . .'

The continuous dripping of blood from his wounds had created a large red stain at Deimenes's feet. He replied, ever more weakly: 'Eighty years ago Selinus fought alongside the Carthaginians against Acragas and Syracuse. Common gods, language and customs are only called upon when it is convenient to do so, and you know that well. When there are other interests at heart, no one mentions them. Spare us, *hegemon*, show us mercy, and you will be remembered as a magnanimous man.'

Dionysius remained in silence as the bloodstain on the floor continued to widen, and was transformed into a stream that ran, due to the inclination of the ground, towards his feet. 'I cannot,' he said finally. 'I must give an example. And it must be a terrible one.'

Deimenes was crucified on the causeway, and with him all the other Greeks who had fought in defence of Motya. The others were sold as slaves.

22

DIONYSIUS WENT BACK to Syracuse before the weather turned. Biton was left to garrison Motya with a unit of the mercenaries, and Leptines remained with one hundred and twenty ships of the fleet, with the task of intercepting and sinking any Carthaginian ship that attempted a landing. Dionysius's plans were to return the following year with a new expedition and to attack the remaining Punic cities on the island – Panormus, perhaps, and Solus – and he wanted to ensure there would be no help forthcoming from Africa.

Philistus came to greet him at the entrance to the city with a small cortège of notables, but the true welcome was given him by the people as he passed down the streets and through the agora, headed for Ortygia. They cheered him like a hero and he felt finally satisfied, gratified at achieving everything he had desired and pursued for so many years.

'Things went as you wanted,' said Philistus that evening, entering his private apartment.

'So far. Let's hope Leptines doesn't get himself into trouble. He is too impetuous, he doesn't reflect enough on the situation. And in war you pay a dear price for any error, no matter how small.'

'That's true, but that's the way he is and you've always known it. It was you who named him supreme commander of the fleet.'

'Who else? He's my brother.'

'Exactly. That's the problem for a man who governs alone. He can't trust anyone, so he can only hope that his closest relatives –

who are inevitably destined to become his closest collaborators –
are up to the task.'

'I can trust my friends from the Company; there's Biton, I've
left him in charge of garrisoning Motya . . .'

'And there's Iolaus . . . Doricus, too,' added Philistus, 'before
they killed him.'

'And there's you, if I'm not mistaken,' said Dionysius. 'I'm
sure you're happy now that you've delivered your tirade about
the solitude of the tyrant. You're right, some of my best friends
are dead, but I'm still not alone: I have many others, and you
yourself saw how the people greeted me today.'

'The people . . . will rip you to pieces and throw you to the
dogs as soon as fortune turns her back on you, or if you run out
of money to pay the mercenaries. You know that well.'

'But this is where the great innovation lies, can't you understand that? The mercenaries know that their generous salaries and
their privileges depend on me, and I know that my safety depends
on them. It's a relationship based on convenience and interest.
The most solid there can be.'

'I see you've named me last on your list of friends,' interrupted
Philistus in a mocking tone.

'You are here,' replied Dionysius. 'Isn't it obvious that you are
with me?'

'Certainly, of course. But I see you changing every day, and
not for the better. You had the Greek residents of Motya
massacred.'

'They gave me no choice!' he bellowed. 'They knew they
could have come over to our side. They asked for it!'

'You asked for it,' insisted Philistus, impassive.

'Blast you!' shouted Dionysius. 'Still under the influence of
that Athenian sophist . . .'

'Socrates is dead,' replied Philistus curtly. 'And he was not a
sophist.'

'Dead?'

'Right. Has been for a while. Hadn't you heard? He was
sentenced to drink hemlock.'

'Ah,' replied Dionysius. 'And what was he accused of?'

'Corrupting youth and introducing new divinities. It happened after Trasibulus took power in Athens.'

'What a strange accusation. There must have been something else underneath. In any case, your philosopher was condemned by a democratic government. As you see, a democracy can be as intolerant and destructive of liberty as the government of one man alone. Worse, I'd say. I don't kill philosophers, even if I can't stand them.'

Philistus said nothing and Dionysius changed the subject. 'So, tell me what has happened while I was away.'

'Everything's in order. The works have been finished here in the city and at Fort Euryalus as well, the people are calm, the exiles in Rhegium are not being taken too seriously for the moment.'

'Anything else?'

'Yes, you have a visitor.'

'Who is it?'

'An Athenian called Xenophon. He's about your age. He was a pupil of Socrates's . . .'

'Then tell him he can fuck off.'

'He's carried out an absolutely amazing endeavour, actually. He led the retreat of the Ten Thousand.'

'Him? The one who got all the way to Babylon, and then . . .'

'Him.'

Dionysius sighed. 'I wanted to spend this evening with my wives. I imagine they want to see me, and I them.'

'Why don't you invite him? The girls will be very amused to hear about such incredible adventures. They don't have much to distract them here . . .'

'They've got me, by Zeus!'

'You are not a distraction.'

'Right. But then you have to stay for dinner as well.'

Philistus nodded. 'Gladly. I don't want to miss a word of his story. It's the greatest adventure of all times, from what I've heard.'

*

'You are an Athenian yet you choose to live in Sparta and are a personal friend of King Agesilaus. The Spartans have defeated and humiliated your city. What must I make of you?' Dionysius asked his guest.

Xenophon considered him with an impassive expression. He was an attractive man with an athletic build, wide shoulders, a well-trimmed beard, and thick, very dark hair which was neither too long nor too short, elegant but not stylish. In a single word, a conservative. 'It was the recklessness of the demagogues that brought my city to ruin. We conservatives had always sought an understanding with Sparta, and if it had been for us, this war would have never happened. I admire the Spartans, and I share their values of frugality, honour and moderation.'

Dionysius nodded in satisfaction, then glanced over at Aristomache and Doris and realized that the talk of politics was boring them. 'It seems that you have experienced an incredible adventure. If you are not too tired of repeating your story, it would give us pleasure to hear about it.'

Xenophon sipped a bit of wine and began. 'When the democrats, led by Trasibulus, regained power in Athens with a military coup, I found myself fighting on the wrong side. I was just twenty-seven years old but I no longer had any hopes for a political future in my city, and so I accepted the invitation of a friend who had enlisted as a mercenary officer under the orders of Cyrus, the younger brother of the Persian emperor. Cyrus wanted to overthrow him and become emperor in his place, and he asked for help from the Spartans.

'The temptation was strong. Sparta had won the war against Athens thanks in part to the money that Cyrus had been supplying in continuation. If he succeeded in becoming king in his brother's place, he would be beholden to those who had helped him win the throne. On the other hand, the Spartan government was officially allied with the Great King and could not be found helping his younger brother in an attempt to usurp his power. And so they had to find a way to throw the stone and hide their hand, as it were.'

Dionysius interrupted ·him. 'Let me guess: the Spartans let Cyrus know that there was a mercenary army to be had, and as he was recruiting them, they looked the other way.'

'You're right there, but there's more to the story. The commander of this mercenary army was a tough number named Clearcus. The story was that he was officially wanted for homicide in Sparta, while in reality he was a Spartan agent.'

'A stroke of genius!' commented Dionysius. 'And they say that the Spartans are inept.'

'But then, when we were nearly in Syria, they sent a regular officer by sea, a battalion commander named Chirisophus.'

'I've heard my mercenaries speak of him. An excellent officer, they say.'

'He is my dear friend . . . the best I have ever had.' Aristomache and Doris exchanged whispered comments, probably about their guest's looks, as he began to tell his story again. 'The objective of our expedition was absolutely secret, but when we arrived in the Syrian desert, the soldiers began to baulk; they said they would not go on another step unless they were told where they were going and what they would be doing. Cyrus was forced to reveal his plan: he told them the truth and promised great riches for all of them as long as they lived. It was easy to convince them, and so we ventured into that vast country. We would often go hunting: ostriches, gazelles and antelopes, bustards. Animals of every species . . .'

'Were there lions?' asked Doris.

'They are said to live there, but we didn't meet any. I'm afraid they're being exterminated by continual hunting parties. But the things we saw were extraordinary: the Karmanda pitch spring, which flows all the way to the Euphrates, towering palms with huge, succulent dates and many other trees bearing strange fruits.'

'Did you see Babylon?' asked Dionysius.

'No,' replied Xenophon. 'We weren't far from there, but one morning, near a village called Kounaxa, the army of the Great King suddenly appeared. There were hundreds of thousands of foot and horse soldiers from every land: Persians, Ethiopians, Egyptians, Carduchians, Assyrians, Medians, Mossinecians, Armenians. They lifted a wide cloud of dust four or five stadia wide, clear across the plain. As they got closer, the fearful horde materialized, weapons and shields glittering, wild cries sounding in all those languages, drums rolling. The scythed war chariots raced towards us, built to mow down men as if they were heads of wheat. It was a frightful sight . . .'

'And you?' asked Dionysius, personally filling his guest's cup.

'What about you?' echoed Doris.

'Cyrus wanted us to attack at the centre so we could kill the king.'

'His brother,' commented Dionysius.

'Exactly. It's normal for them to settle dynastic questions that way. But Clearcus refused, and we attacked the advancing line head on. We managed to break through, and we returned that evening to the battlefield thinking we had won, but instead we found Cyrus's body, decapitated and impaled.'

Doris and Aristomache both gasped.

'Perhaps it is better that the ladies retire,' suggested Philistus, who had not spoken until then. 'I imagine that the story can only become more upsetting from this point on, and one of them is pregnant.'

Aristomache, the one who wasn't, lowered her head, then proudly said: 'I can stay.'

Dionysius nodded his agreement and Doris was taken to her apartments by a handmaid.

Xenophon resumed his story, narrating the interminable retreat that he had led, in the middle of winter, through Armenia and the Caucasus.

The mute listeners were treated to images of terrible and grandiose landscapes, dead cities, swirling rivers, lofty, snow-covered peaks that pierced the heavens, and then more combat to the death with ferocious savages, scenes of torture, pillaging, summary execution, hurried escapes . . .

Xenophon was a formidable story teller, and as he spoke his

eyes changed expression and colour, it seemed, as if he were reliving the experiences he told of. He described their endless wandering in a vast desert of snow, his men dying of frostbite, others blinded by the sun at that altitude, the dead left unburied, the wounded and sick abandoned.

And he finally reached the epilogue of that desperate march. 'I was bringing up the rear with my cavalry squad when I heard an uproar coming from the head of the column. I thought they'd been attacked and jumped on to my horse, spurring him on at full speed, followed by my men, and as we advanced we saw the most extraordinary scene: our comrades weeping, shouting, throwing their weapons into the air as if out of their minds with joy. And their cry was increasingly louder and closer, and it echoed through those snowy peaks: "The sea! The sea!"' Xenophon sighed. 'We were saved. Or at least that's what we thought . . .'

They listened to him until late that night, when they all finally retired, weary after such a long evening. Dionysius had his guest accompanied to his quarters and then went to Aristomache's room. It was her turn.

The next day, he dined with Xenophon and with Philistus.

'I was told that you eat three times a day!' said the guest. 'But I thought it was just hearsay.'

'And we never sleep alone,' added Dionysius, smiling. 'That's how we do things here in the West. I know that in Sparta they're happy with their black broth for dinner and nothing else. I wonder how they find the strength to march and to fight.'

'Their bodies have been accustomed for years to squeeze all the energy from such a poor, simple food. It costs very little to maintain them. You know, no one knows the recipe for their black broth. No one knows what it contains.'

'I've also heard that they only sleep with their wives a couple of times a month in all. Is that true?'

'Perfectly true,' confirmed Xenophon.

'Ah! That's no life! I have two wives, as you can see; I keep them both company, and no one's complaining.'

'It would be more correct to say that no one dares to complain,' observed Philistus wryly.

Xenophon made a face that could have been a smirk or a smile.

'I know,' Dionysius continued, 'you from the metropolises consider us from the colonies to be half-barbarians. But you're mistaken. This is the future of Hellenism. Here we have resources, men, innovative ideas. You should see our ships, our war machines. Today Philistus will show you our fortifications. When you go back to Sparta, you can tell them what you found here.'

'I will certainly do so,' replied Xenophon. 'You know, your customs may be surprising for some, but not for me. I've seen so much you can barely imagine. The Mossinicians, for example, do in public what we do in private: they couple, they relieve their bowels . . . And they do in private what we do in public: they speak only when alone, for instance.'

'Fascinating,' commented Philistus.

'What do you have to say about King Agesilaus?' interrupted Dionysius, bringing the subject back to topics he was interested in.

'He is a valiant, honest man who has the destiny of the Greeks at heart, wherever they may be found.'

'Then he must surely appreciate my efforts against the western barbarians.'

'Most certainly. I have no doubt about it.'

'If I should need more mercenaries . . .'

'There are many in the Peloponnese, men who can do naught else but fight. I know them well. They are the best, nevertheless: courageous to the point of temerity. They are tied to no one and are ready to follow whoever promises them money, adventure, risks. When a man has experienced such intense emotions, he can no longer adapt to a normal existence.'

Philistus broke in. 'What about you? Can you adapt to a normal existence?'

'Oh yes, of course,' replied Xenophon after pondering his

question for a few moments. 'I didn't go out looking for adventure. It was she who came seeking me. I've done my share. But now I want to devote myself to my studies, to my family, to hunting and farming. My dream is to return to my homeland as an honourable man, but at this moment that's not possible. They have killed my master and they may want to kill me as well . . .'

'Will you write an account of your expedition?' asked Philistus.

'I took many notes during our journeys. Who knows. Perhaps one day, when I have time . . .'

'He's asking you that because he's writing a history of his own,' intervened Dionysius. 'Isn't that so, Philistus? A history of Sicily, in which he even speaks of me. I still don't know in what light.'

'You'll know in due time,' promised Philistus.

The Athenian guest stayed a few more days, during which he visited the marvels of the city. He was not shown the *latomiae*, the stone quarries where so many of his compatriots died. Although he lived in Sparta and was an exile, he still remained an Athenian.

*

The rest of the winter passed tranquilly, marked by Leptines's dispatches, rather bored in tone, which reported to Dionysius on the stagnant situation in western Sicily. There were no Carthaginians to be seen, and it was unlikely that any would turn up before summer, according to their spies.

Dionysius's informers kept him up on how Leptines spent his time amusing himself with beautiful women, refined wines and foods, parties and orgies. But that was just in his nature, after all.

Doris had her baby at the end of spring.

A boy.

The wet nurses brought him to his father immediately. He was a beautiful baby, healthy, flawless.

Dispatches were sent to Sparta, Corinth and Locri, Doris's homeland. The world had to know that Dionysius had an heir that bore his name.

Much discussion went on in Syracuse about the primacy of the Italian wife, who was now the mother of the heir and had thus become, by force of circumstance, the first bride. But much of the talk was criticism of her mother, Dionysius's Italian mother-in-law. It was that witch who had intrigued to make sure that Aristomache would take second place! Perhaps she had even secretly given her potions that had prevented her from becoming pregnant. At least not right away, not before her own daughter.

Then Aristomache also became pregnant and had a boy as well, who was called Hipparinus after her father.

Leptines wrote a letter of congratulations from the headquarters of the fleet.

Leptines to Dionysius, Hail!

You are a father!

Making me an uncle. Uncle Leptines!

What will these tots have to say to me when they learn how to talk? 'Uncle Leptines, bring me a present, Uncle Leptines, buy me this, buy me that! Take me to the races, take me fishing in your boat. Let me kill a Carthaginian.'

I just can't wait. So how are you feeling?

You have heirs, descendants, by Heracles! Something of you will live on anyway, even if it's not your fame.

How will you bring up your first-born, the child who has your same name? Will you make him a warrior like us? An exterminator of enemies? I think not. It won't be possible. Don't delude yourself, it won't ever be the same thing.

We grew up in the middle of a street, brother, bare-footed and half naked. He won't be able to.

We threw stones and had fist-fights with the lads from Ortygia. We'd make our way back at night full of scars and bruises, and then we'd just get more at home. Remember? The street is a great teacher, there's no doubt about it, but your boy is Dionysius II, by Zeus!

He'll be raised by a host of nurses and governesses, tutors, trainers, fencing masters, equitation experts, Greek and philosophy teachers.

They will be the ones to encourage him, to punish him, to tell him what he must and must not do. You won't have time. You'll be too busy watching your arse here at home to protect it from our fellow citizens, and slaughtering those fuck-faced Carthaginians abroad.

You'll be getting statues raised to your left and right, making under-the-table deals with your allies and enemies, collecting taxes, recruiting mercenaries.

But if you should ever find a little time, take him on your knees, your little boy. Even if he is not Arete's child. Take him on your knees and tell him the story of another lad who believed in loyalty, in honour, in valour and in glory; a boy who hoped to achieve greatness by taking the most difficult path, and then mislaid his very soul in the intricacies of power, resentment and hate. He forgot all about what he believed, and he arrived at such a level of presumptuousness that he married two women, who managed, nonetheless, to be faithful and loving wives.

Doris is the mother of the heir. Aristomache is not. And it is she who knows better than anyone that no woman will ever be able to oust the memory of Arete from your heart. Give her a little affection too.

I'm just about soused and if I weren't I wouldn't be saying what I'm about to say: do you remember the apparition in the grotto at Henna? The girl with the peplum who was the same as the creature you saw at the spring of the Anapus?

She is not Arete. She is the girl who impersonates Persephone every year at the rites of spring. The priests keep her hidden the rest of the year at the rock necropolis at the source of the river. When she gets old, they'll replace her with a new one.

Arete is dead.

You have avenged her.

Enough.

Dedicate what is left of your mind or your soul, however you want to call it, to those who have remained to you.

Many of our friends have died fighting your wars. More

will die . . . think of them sometimes and you will be different. You will feel better surrounded by the memory of those who loved you, rather than by those ugly mugs of your Campanian lancers.

If this letter ever arrives on your table, you'll have my balls cut off by your thugs. That's why I won't be sending it. If you do receive it, it means that once I was sober, I felt exactly the same as when I was drunk.

23

THE APPOINTMENT WAS in Motya, at the house of Biton, the commander of the stronghold. Dionysius arrived from the causeway on horseback, the sea lapping at his steed's shins; Leptines was brought to land on the *Boubaris*'s dinghy. The flagship was even more impressive than when Dionysius had last seen it. The prow had been sculpted into a silver-clad bull's head, the sail was edged in purple, and painted at its centre was a gorgon's head with fangs bloodied and tongue protruding in a fierce grimace. The rowlocks on each oar were covered with brightly polished bronze, the head of the mainmast with golden laminae. On either side, six greased ballistas were lined up, loaded with lethal darts.

'Isn't she stupendous?' said Leptines, jumping to the ground opposite his brother and waving a hand at the massive vessel behind him.

'No doubt about it. But isn't she a little . . . ostentatious?'

'Ah, I want those bastards to crap in their pants as soon as they see her. They must understand that there's no place to run from the steel jaws of my *Boubaris*.'

Biton arrived with a dozen mercenaries and welcomed both brothers.

'News?' asked Dionysius as they made their way towards the governor's residence.

'All is calm for the moment,' replied Biton, 'but I'm afraid it won't last. I know that they're up to something in Carthage. They're said to have hundreds of warships, three or four hundred, some say five. The admiralty's shipyard is full of them. And I'm told that there's an even greater number of transports.'

Leptines's mood seemed to wane momentarily. 'I need more quinqueremes,' he said, 'at least double the number I have now. How many are under construction?'

'Ten,' Dionysius replied curtly.

'Ten? What am I supposed to do with ten?'

'They'll have to suffice. I can't give you any more, for the time being. Where's the rest of the fleet?'

'At Lilybaeum,' replied Leptines. 'It's a good spot to lay an ambush. As soon as those bastards show up, I'll sink them to the bottom.'

'Let's hope so,' commented Dionysius. 'But stay on your guard. Himilco is crafty. He won't attack until he's sure of winning. Understand? Don't let yourself get drawn into a trap.'

'How are my sisters-in-law?' asked Leptines.

'Well. Why do you ask?'

'No reason. The last time I saw Aristomache she seemed a little sad.'

'Women's affairs. No cause for worry.'

'Little Dionysius? And the other little lad?'

'They're well, growing up fast.' He changed the subject. 'You, Biton, how are you planning to hold this place in case of attack?'

'I've set up a signalling system from Lilybaeum that will warn me if there's danger in sight. The breach has been repaired and there are enough stores in the warehouses for three months of siege.'

'Good. This will be the greatest challenge of our lives. We cannot and must not lose. Do you both understand that well?'

'Of course I understand,' replied Leptines, 'but if only you had sent me those quinqueremes I asked for . . .'

'It's useless to recriminate. Keep your eyes open. I must convince the native Sicans that we're the strongest and that they had better stay on our side. So I'll be going inland.'

They had dinner together and then, as night was falling,

Dionysius returned to the mainland and Leptines returned aboard the *Boubaris*.

*

Himilco didn't make a move until much later, when the summer was almost at an end. He put to sea under cover of darkness with the ships' lights screened so they would not be seen. They sailed offshore and were effectively invisible from the coast.

He then sent out his convoy of transport vessels, and Leptines took the bait. When he saw them, slow and heavy, parading at dawn in front of cape Lilybaeum, Leptines jumped on to the *Boubaris* like a horseman on his steed. He plunged forward at great speed, dragging along all the ships whose crews were ready at that hour of the morning. He sank about fifty enemy vessels, four of them rammed by the flagship herself, and captured twenty more, but the rest of that immense convoy managed to escape to Panormus undamaged and to join up there with the combat vessels which had followed a wider route on the open sea.

When he learned about what had happened, Dionysius flew into a rage. 'I had warned him, damnation! I told him to stay on his guard!'

The messenger from Selinus who had brought the news was struck dumb, not knowing what to reply. '*Hegemon*,' he started off weakly, but Dionysius silenced him.

'That's enough! And where is he now?'

'Our navarch? At Lilybaeum.'

'Too exposed. You'll bring him this letter, immediately.' Dionysius dictated a message which was promptly brought to destination. He then continued inland to wrap up his campaign against the Sicans.

Himilco, who had recruited more mercenaries in the meantime, attacked by land and by sea. He took Drepanum and Eryx, where he installed, at the highest point of the mountain, a light signal that transmitted messages to Carthage at night; the signals were reflected by a couple of repeaters set up on floating platforms hingeing around the island of Cossira.

Just as Leptines was about to go out and engage the enemy fleet, he was fortunately reached by his brother's coded message.

Dionysius, Pan Hellenic *hegemon* of Sicily,
to Leptines, supreme navarch, Hail!

I congratulate you and your men for sinking fifty enemy vessels. I have first-hand information from Panormus. Himilco's fleet has a crushing numerical superiority over us of at least three to one. You have no hope for success, and would only be uselessly risking our fleet.

Retreat. I repeat: retreat.

Go to Selinus, if you like; leave scouts behind to inform you of the moves of the Carthaginians.

This is an order. You have no choice but to obey.

Stay in good health.

'Stay in good health?' howled Leptines when he had read it. 'Stay in good health? How in the name of Zeus can I stay in good health! He says we're to sneak off like cowards and let that son of a bitch win without a fight? What about Biton? We're to leave him here in the middle of the lagoon alone, like an idiot? What the fuck am I going to tell Biton? That I have to obey orders?'

The messenger attempted to put in a word. 'The commander told me it is essential that you carry out his orders, navarch, and—'

'Shut up!' shouted Leptines with such vehemence that the man didn't dare open his mouth again. 'And now get out!' he yelled even louder. 'Out of here, all of you!'

He ate no food nor took a drop of wine that entire day. Then, after dark, he called an orderly. 'Have the dinghy prepared. We're going out.'

'Going out? At this hour?'

'Move. I don't have much patience.'

The man obeyed and, soon after, a hooded Leptines entered the dinghy and had the helmsman point the bow north.

He landed at Motya in the middle of the night and got Biton out of bed.

His friend came to receive him wrapped in the sheet he had been sleeping in. 'You're mad to go out so late at night in that walnut shell! You'd make a tasty morsel for a Carthaginian scout ship. What a lucky strike it would be to catch such a big fish in their net!'

'The fact is that there's something I have to tell you in person. I hate people who send messengers when they don't have the guts to say something to someone's face.'

'What on earth are you on about?' Biton took a jug from the table, with two ceramic cups. 'Drop of wine?'

Leptines shook his head. 'I don't want anything.'

'Well then, what's the matter? Who are these people who hide behind messages?'

'Him.'

'Dionysius?'

Leptines nodded.

'What has he said?'

'He's ordered me to retreat, to abandon Lilybaeum. He said the fleet is too much at risk here. He wants me to take it to Selinus, but in doing so . . .'

'You'll leave me completely alone. Is that why you've come here in the middle of the night?'

Leptines nodded again. 'He hasn't said anything to you?'

Biton shook his head.

'See? He hasn't even bothered to warn you. This is too much. It's absolutely unjustifiable!'

Biton tried to calm him. 'My message will be getting here tomorrow, or the day after. Communications are always precarious in time of war, you know that.'

'That may be, but it doesn't change matters any.'

'What's his reason?'

'He says we're outnumbered three to one.'

'That's a good reason.'

'And for this reason I should leave my friend with no one covering his arse?'

'You have no choice, Leptines. We are officers of the Syracusan army before we are friends, and Dionysius is our supreme commander.'

'In the Company, we've always covered each other, and helped each other in every way. When we were lads and one of us was attacked by one of the other gangs, we'd run to help, at the price of having our faces bashed in. This has always been our rule, and I've never forgotten it.'

Biton sipped a little wine, then put the cup on the table and leaned back into his chair. 'Those were the days, my friend,' he sighed. 'We've come a long way since then. We've enjoyed many privileges at Dionysius's side: beautiful women, beautiful houses, beautiful clothes, the best food and drink, power, respect . . . Now he's asking us to do our part for the successful outcome of this war and we must obey him. He's right. If you stayed here, you'd only be massacred. You must save the fleet, save it for another more favourable circumstance. It's only right. We're soldiers, by Heracles!'

'But why doesn't that bastard have you leave as well?'

'Because it took so much money and so much blood to conquer this island that giving it up without a fight would be an admission of complete ineptitude. Dionysius can't afford that. Motya will fall, but after heroic resistance. We can do no worse than her own inhabitants; we defeated them, didn't we?'

Leptines couldn't say a word; he was biting his lip.

'Go now. It will be light soon, and you've got to set sail as soon as you can. The sooner you leave, the better.

Leptines hesitated, as if he just couldn't make up his mind to go.

'Clear out, admiral,' Biton encouraged him. 'And let me sleep another couple of hours. I have a lot to do tomorrow.'

Leptines got to his feet. 'Good luck,' he said, and left.

*

Himilco showed up at Motya seven days later with one hundred and fifty battleships and thirty thousand men. Biton had only twelve ships and two thousand men. They were overwhelmed after four days of strenuous resistance. His body was impaled on the causeway.

Dionysius, who risked being cut off from Syracuse, had no choice but to withdraw from his inland campaign. He reached the city after fourteen days of forced marches and found the fleet already at anchor in the Great Harbour. Leptines, who had arrived some time before, remained aboard the *Boubaris* and would not come to shore.

An explicit order from Dionysius finally summoned him to the Ortygia fortress.

'I've been told that in my absence you've visited Aristomache. Is that true?'

'Not only. I visited your son as well.'

'Is it true or isn't it?'

'Yes, it is,' admitted Leptines. 'You don't trust me?'

'I don't trust anybody.'

'No, you don't, do you? Not even Biton, right? You couldn't even trust him. But he stayed behind in that stinking hole to guard Motya for you and to die for you. They impaled him, did you know that? They left him there to rot until the crows and the gulls had picked his bones clean. You didn't trust him, did you? Answer me, by Heracles! Answer me, blast you!'

'Don't you ever dare see my wives again in my absence.'

'Is that all you have to say to me?'

Dionysius ignored his question and continued. 'Himilco has left Panormus directed east, towards Messana. I believe he wants to cross the Straits and attack us from the north. Take the fleet out as far as Catane. Stay offshore, and do not let yourself be drawn into a fight. You will attack only on my orders.'

Leptines stood and walked towards the door.

'I've had five more quinqueremes built for you.'

Leptines stopped a moment without turning, then opened the door and went out.

Dionysius covered his face with his hands and remained alone, in silence, in the middle of that vast room.

*

Leptines met Philistus at the harbour, where he was taking his leave of a delegation of foreign guests that was returning home. He barely nodded at him.

'Where are you going in such a hurry?' protested Philistus.

'Leave me alone,' replied Leptines.

'If you're angry with me, tell me why.'

'I'm not angry with you. It's that damned bastard of my brother. You've created a monster.'

'We, if anything. We have created a monster. Dionysius has risen to power thanks to all of us. But I don't think you want to discuss the corruptive effects of power.'

'No, I'm hungry. He didn't even invite me to dinner.'

'I'll invite you.'

Leptines hesitated a moment. 'Was it you who told him I'd gone to see Aristomache?'

'Yes,' replied Philistus.

'Is that any way to tell me?'

'You asked me a question. I answered.'

'Why did you tell him?'

'Because it would have been worse if he had learned it from someone else.'

'I would have told him myself.'

'I doubt it. I can see the look on your face when you speak of Aristomache.'

'I don't want to talk about it any more.'

'Will you come to dinner though?'

'If you don't ask me any more questions.'

'All right.'

They went to Philistus's house and the servants brought water for washing, and cool wine. Dinner was served on the terrace because the weather was still quite good, despite it being late autumn.

'He gets worse every day,' said Leptines suddenly.

'I wouldn't say so,' replied Philistus.

'You wouldn't say so? What are you saying? He left Biton

alone at Motya, without any reason in this world for doing so. Our lives matter nothing to him, all he cares about is staying in power. And as far as Aristomache is concerned . . .'

'You said you didn't want to talk about that . . .'

'I've changed my mind. As far as Aristomache is concerned . . . I feel that marrying two women at once was an act of extreme arrogance that can only provoke humiliation and frustration in both and . . .'

'I wouldn't have said you were so tender and sensitive. I'm sorry to disappoint you, but I don't feel that is true at all,' retorted Philistus. 'Dionysius is very attractive, he's strong as a bull and he's one of the most powerful men in the world. Women find these things appealing, believe me. And if you want my advice . . .'

'I don't.'

'I'm going to give it to you anyway. Heed my words well. Women get bored when they're closed up in their own quarters, it's only normal. Imagine being shut up between four walls for most of your life . . . And so they instinctively seek out distraction, and when they find someone to converse with, they tend to exaggerate their feelings and problems, making them bigger than they are. While in reality, they may be bothered by nothing much at all. Those two girls have everything a woman could desire: a husband who's like a god, who has more than enough strength and virility for both; they have a beautiful home, jewels, children, food, handmaidens, readings, music. When they appear in public they're at the centre of attention of thousands and thousands of people, they're admired like divinities . . . there's nothing that flatters a woman more than the admiration of others.'

'Aristomache is unhappy,' retorted Leptines. He turned away, pretending to watch a pair of triremes which were docking at the shipyard.

Philistus fell silent, apparently concentrating on the roasted bass he had been served. Even Leptines did not open his mouth for some time.

'Tell me something,' Philistus finally said. 'Was something

going on between you and Aristomache before Dionysius asked for her hand?'

'You think I'd tell you, if it were true?'

'Why not? Have I ever hurt you?'

'We'd play together, when we were children, in the courtyard between our houses. Dionysius was away that year, he'd gone to my uncle Demaretus's house in the mountains to be cured of an insistent cough.'

'That's all?'

'That's all.'

'How old were you?'

'Eleven. I was eleven, she was nine.'

'And you promised each other eternal love.'

'Something like that.'

Philistus sighed. 'By Zeus, you're the second most powerful man in Sicily, you command a fleet of nearly one hundred and fifty battle ships and twenty-five thousand men. You've killed hundreds of people in your life and wounded countless others, you've fucked hundreds of females of every size, shape and colour . . .'

'Let it go,' interrupted Leptines. 'It's better this way . . . I . . . have to go. Thank you for dinner.'

'It was a pleasure,' replied Philistus. 'Will I be seeing you?'

'No, not for a while. I'm leaving with the fleet.'

'Good. That's less dangerous than cultivating certain thoughts.'

'What do you mean by that?' asked Leptines.

'You know very well what I mean. Good luck.'

Leptines gave a little nod of his head, then went down to the harbour and boarded the *Boubaris*.

*

Himilco moved on to Himera, and her inhabitants surrendered spontaneously. Less than one-fifth of the original population had been restored, and they had no intention of attempting to resist such a fierce, implacable enemy.

The Carthaginian army proceeded towards Messana and

pitched camp about twenty stadia outside the city. The Messanians evacuated their wives and children, sending them to the mountains when they had relatives or friends there, or to their farms in the country. They then drew up their forces at a narrow pass between the mountains and the sea, determined to bar their enemy's way. But Himilco sailed beyond that point and landed the army directly in the harbour. The city was practically undefended and fell without a fight to massacre and pillage. Only about fifty able-bodied men in all managed to escape by swimming across the Straits to Rhegium. This feat appeared so extraordinary that it would later become an athletic competition held on every anniversary of the first crossing, accompanied by a ceremony in honour of Poseidon, the god of the sea.

Himilco took personal command of the ground troops and led them south towards Catane, leaving the command of his immense fleet to his admiral, Mago.

Not even a violent eruption of Mount Aetna managed to hold them back. A huge flow of lava stretched all the way down to the sea, raising a column of steam even more awesome that the plume of smoke that rose from the volcano. Himilco claimed that he feared nothing and had the army pass behind the fiery mountain, reaching the coastal road near Catane and joining up there with the fleet.

Dionysius decided to go forth and meet the enemy. He gathered all the available forces and recalled Leptines's fleet. Before leaving, he stopped to say farewell to his wives, both together, to avoid jealousy. But he knew that his Syracusan wife Aristomache was pregnant again and he showered her with loving attentions. 'Take care of yourself, I'm very eager to see our child.'

'Are you?' she replied, smiling. 'Are you eager to see him? I've already felt him move.'

'When is the birth expected?'

'In six months at the most.'

'Then he will be born in peace time. If the gods heed my pleas.'

Doris, the other wife, brought little Dionysius for a kiss from his father, and she whispered in his ear. 'I'm sure that Aristoma-che's child will look as much like you as he does.'

Dionysius looked at her with a strange expression and Doris lowered her eyes.

He kissed both of them on the mouth, then tried to kiss the child, but the little one burst into tears. 'Why does he cry whenever he sees me?' asked Dionysius, irritated.

'Because he never sees you,' replied Doris. 'Because of your beard and your armour.'

Dionysius nodded in silence and left, escorted by his mercenaries.

He called the first meeting of his staff in his tent, at a short distance from enemy lines. His father-in-law Hipparinus took part, along with Iolaus, who commanded a division of assault troops, Philistus, Leptines, who had returned from Catane, and the commanders of the Italian allies.

'I've decided to attack,' he began. 'We must inflict so much damage that they will be forced to return to Carthage for the winter. Their fleet plays a crucial role here. Without transports, such a huge army cannot survive.' He turned towards Leptines. 'You will attack the fleet from the open sea. Attempt to sink as many vessels as possible, but do not get carried away. Think through each move attentively and attack only when you are sure of succeeding. Above all, do not allow your forces to disperse, for any reason. We will draw up on the beach so as to give Mago the impression of being crushed between land and sea. But in this phase, you will be the one to engage the enemy. And don't forget, there's still a great disparity between their strength and ours.'

Leptines bristled under those orders and recommendations. He was the commander-in-chief of the fleet and he knew what he was doing.

Dionysius insisted. 'Keep your ships in a compact formation, don't let their numerical superiority give them the upper hand.'

'I understand,' replied Leptines, barely able to keep the irritation out of his voice.

'Fine then,' replied Dionysius curtly. 'Good luck.'

The day after, Leptines was at the head of a group of thirty quinqueremes cruising south of Catane. The rest of the Syracusan fleet, one hundred and ten triremes, followed five-across in a long column. All at once, they spotted the van of Mago's fleet advancing along the coast in the opposite direction. There were about fifty units in all. In the distance, they could see the glittering spears of Dionysius's warriors arrayed on the shoreline, across a front nearly one stadium wide.

Leptines called the second-in-command and ordered him to signal to the rest of the fleet to form two lines of combat. Obeying the signals from the flagship, the commanders of the single units began to manoeuvre in order to draw up in a line with their bows pointing towards land.

Leptines had noticed, in the meantime, that the Carthaginian ships were spaced rather far apart and were apparently having trouble with the ebbing waves along the coast. He realized that this was an unrepeatable opportunity to sink them and squash the enemy's superiority. He ordered the quinqueremes to follow him.

The second officer attempted a dismayed protest. 'Commander . . .'

'You heard my orders,' shot back Leptines. 'We're attacking. The others will follow.'

'Commander, the others have not drawn up into formation yet, and our orders were to keep the ships together. I . . .'

'We're at sea here and I'm the one giving orders!' shouted Leptines. 'Ramming speed!'

The officer obeyed and signalled to the drummer who accordingly accelerated the rowing tempo, striking the drum with great mallet blows. The *Boubaris* surged forward, ploughing through the waves with her three-pointed rostrum, followed by the other units.

A look-out soon reached Dionysius. '*Hegemon*!' he shouted. 'Leptines is attacking the Carthaginians with the quinqueremes!'

'No, you're wrong. That can't be,' replied Dionysius, growing pale with rage.

'Come see for yourself, *hegemon*.'

Dionysius spurred on his horse and followed at a gallop to the top of a hill. As soon as he reached the top, his doubts vanished.

'That bastard . . .' he growled under his breath.

24

LEPTINES'S QUINQUEREMES PLOUGHED into the Carthaginian ships at full speed, shattering them to pieces. The *Boubaris* clove an enemy ship in two before it could manage to turn its bow seaward, then swung around in a wide circle and turned back, shearing off all the oars on the left side of another ship. Immobilized, all it could do was wait for the next blow, which struck the bow so violently that the timbering that supported the rostrum was stripped off completely. It sank in a few moments, taking all the crew down with it.

From the shore, a roar arose from the Syracusan troops taking in the incredible clash as if it were a show at the theatre. But Dionysius was furious. To his left he could now see Mago's fleet, advancing with an aft wind, decidedly intent on wedging itself between Leptines's squadron and the rest of the Syracusan fleet, which was still far behind. He called Iolaus. 'Signal for him to disengage, damnation! Have him disengage!'

Another roar exploded from the crowd below as the troops frenetically cheered on the third and most formidable ramming by the *Boubaris*. Leptines charged like a bull, in his usual manner, forgetting all else.

A bronze mirror flashed several times to signal Dionysius's order, but Leptines must have been blinded by the raging battle, by the glare of so many weapons and by the reflection of the sun on the waves. Or perhaps he simply did not want to obey and pretended not to have seen.

'Bugles!' shouted Dionysius. 'Use the bugles, sound the alarm, he'll understand!'

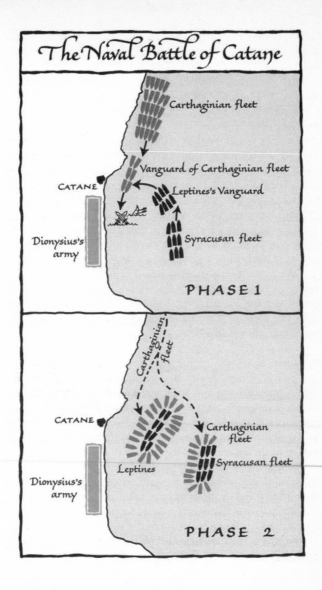

The Naval Battle of Catane

Carthaginian fleet

Vanguard of Carthaginian fleet

Leptines's Vanguard

CATANE

Dionysius's army

Syracusan fleet

PHASE 1

Carthaginian fleet

CATANE

Carthaginian fleet

Syracusan fleet

Dionysius's army

Leptines

PHASE 2

The bugles blared and from the ground their sound seemed earth-shattering, but they were nothing in the din of battle out at sea.

'Retreat!' yelled Dionysius, infuriated, from the top of the hill. 'Retreat, you bastard! Out of there! Get us out!'

But it was too late. Mago's naval armada was unfurling all of its vast power between the attacking vanguard of the Syracusan fleet and the rest of the ships still lagging behind. The Carthaginian admiral had so many vessels that he could divide his contingent into two fleets, one of which attacked the Syracusan ships still at sea, while the other ships fanned out like pincers, headed towards Leptines's squadron, still busy sinking the last Carthaginian galleys.

At that point, Leptines realized he was in a trap. The circle of enemy vessels was already closing in and his quinqueremes were being crushed in the vice. There was no room to manoeuvre, and the sea battle became a ground battle, with soldiers jumping from one ship to the next, joining in violent combat with the adversary crews and infantry aboard. Leptines fought like a lion with his sword and axe, throwing overboard anyone who dared to climb onto the flagship. 'Get out of my ship, you dirty bastards,' he screamed. 'Off my ship!'

The desperate struggle raged on, and, although the little Syracusan squad was completely surrounded, Leptines managed to open a passage. His men took control of an enemy vessel placed crosswise and sank it from the inside by hacking the keel to pieces with their axes, so that the *Boubaris* could slip out of the opening and rapidly pick up speed. The other surviving ships managed to stay behind her, actually sinking another three enemy vessels in the process. But the outcome of the battle was sealed. The rest of the Syracusan fleet was forced to fight in conditions of sharp inferiority, and the crews were demoralized by the flight of their admiral and by the absence of a flagship leading them.

Leptines himself narrowly escaped capture by racing out to sea and making a wide turn outside of the sights of the enemy. The Carthaginians won an overwhelming victory, but, not content with this success, they launched a number of light craft full of men armed with harpoons who ran through all the sailors who were trying to swim to the safety of the shore.

Dionysius helplessly witnessed the disaster. He saw his fleet chopped to pieces, his men massacred as they floundered amidst the bloodied waves. By dusk, the coast was full of cadavers and wreckage.

The losses were enormous: over one hundred ships and twenty thousand men.

Leptines arrived in the middle of the night and was brought to his brother's tent, where a stormy meeting of the general staff was going on.

Dionysius would have liked to strangle him, but when he saw him spattered with blood, wounded in the right shoulder and left thigh, his face bloated with an eye swollen shut, his skin blackened by smoke and flames, his lips split, panting, his features contorted and nearly unrecognizable, he could neither move nor say a word.

The other officers stopped speaking as well, and for several long moments there was a tomb-like silence in the tent of the high command. Philistus approached Leptines with a jug and poured him some water; only then did they realize that no one had so much as offered a drink to the supreme commander of the fleet who had fought like a hero the whole day long and had returned in the middle of the night to take his place among the other combatants.

Leptines gulped down the water, then collapsed to the ground. Dionysius gestured to Aksal, who picked him up and carried him to his tent.

Dionysius went to call on him before dawn. He was burning with fever and his face was even more swollen, but he managed to whisper: 'I'm sorry . . . I wanted . . . I wanted . . .'

'I know,' replied Dionysius. 'You've always been this way, and you'll never change. I'm the stupid one, the one who keeps trusting in you. I should murder you, I should have you executed for insubordination . . .'

'Do it,' replied Leptines with difficulty. 'I don't care about dying.'

'I've already lost Doricus and Biton,' said Dionysius, 'I can't lose you too. Sleep now. Try to get better . . .'

'What have you decided?' gasped Leptines.

'The allies think we should attack Himilco's army.'

'They're right.'

'They're wrong. If we are defeated, Syracuse will be lost. We'll retreat back behind our walls.'

Leptines said nothing, but Dionysius could hear him weeping as he left.

Indignant at their chief's decision not to fight, the Italian allies decided to return to their cities. In any case, it was hardly possible for so many thousands of warriors to be sheltered within the walls of Syracuse for any number of months.

Philistus did not sleep that night. He retired to his tent and wrote until dawn.

Dionysius found a city in mourning: the laments of the women who had lost their sons rose from the houses, black palls and leafy cypress fronds hung from the windows. Disparaging writings on the walls condemned the tyrant. In just a few hours, the memory of the dazzling victory of the year before had vanished. Now there was only the bitterness of defeat, the fear of an uncertain future, the searing grief for their young men lost.

Philistus returned to the city and withdrew to his house near the harbour, where he feared he might soon be seeing Mago's fleet advancing unhindered to blockade the harbour and the shipyards. He sat at his table and began once again to write.

It was the worst disaster which had ever occurred in the history of Syracuse. The city had lost most of her fleet, and many of her citizens had perished among the waves, harpooned one by one like fish. Upon his return, the rumour went out that Dionysius had deliberately exposed the city's troops to a risky battle at sea against such a superior force, while he hadn't risked the life of a single one of his mercenaries. The men of Syracuse were free men, after all, who could have sooner or later demanded the return of democracy, while the mercenaries were the pillar upon which he had built his power.

Dionysius reacted swiftly and mercilessly, arresting all those who were merely suspected of spreading such rumours, even if the charge had been made by a single informant. Despite the military setbacks and the enormous sacrifices that he imposed on his citizens, Dionysius remained firmly convinced that he must remain their irreplaceable leader in the battle against their mortal enemy. At such a crucial time, with the city's very survival at stake, internal dissidence must be struck down without hesitation. His brutal purges included quite a few members of the Company. The powerful association – which had always supported Dionysius in his climb to power – did not fail to send a warning in return: eight of his mercenaries were found murdered in different parts of the city, and two more inside the Ortygia barracks. All ten had been pierced through the heart by arrows bearing the image of a dolphin on their shafts, as if to say that the Company could arrive anywhere. Furthermore, the number of dead mercenaries was exactly equivalent to the number of Company members who had been eliminated.

Iolaus brought up the matter with Dionysius. 'Beware,' he admonished him, 'they want you to know that you can't touch them or they'll make you pay. They wanted to prove to you that they can strike however and whenever they like.'

Dionysius said only: 'I'll settle up with them another time.' He was in a foul humour and had no desire to talk about it; he realized that Iolaus was right, but wouldn't admit it. The only sign of hope that he'd had in such a dark moment was the birth of Aristomache's second child; he named his son Nysaeus.

The next day at dusk, Philistus left his work table and walked towards Ortygia to pay a visit to Leptines, who was still feverish and bedridden. He strode through the corridors of the fort, dimly lit by a few lanterns, until he reached his friend's quarters in an isolated part of the southern wing. He approached the door to Leptines's room and saw that it was half open. He cautiously drew closer, and heard the voice of a woman speaking softly.

'Why do you always throw yourself into danger that way?' she was saying.

'Because it's my duty. And because I have to prove to him that I don't need him to . . .'

'But you could have died!' protested the woman's voice unhappily.

'I wish I had. My men all ended up at the bottom of the sea as food for the fish.'

'No, please, don't say such things . . .' continued the voice.

Philistus moved away into another empty room that was being used for storage. He left the door open a crack and soon saw Aristomache leaving the bedroom. He recognized her despite the hood she wore to cover her face and head. He waited a while, and then entered Leptines's room. 'How are you feeling today?' he asked.

'Better,' Leptines lied.

'I'm glad. We need you back.'

Leptines's mouth twisted into a grimace. 'An admiral without a fleet? I don't think I'd be very useful.'

'Stop feeling sorry for yourself. What happened was completely your fault. You may not like following your brother's orders, but he was right this time, as he always is. The *Boubaris*, if you're interested, is nearly intact. They're fixing her up in the dockyards.'

'How many ships are left?' asked Leptines.

'Thirty, sixteen of which are quinqueremes, including yours.'

'Next to nothing.'

'You're right, unfortunately . . . Has the surgeon been by today?'

'Yes, and he tortured me at length. I think he hates me.'

'He's a good doctor. He'll have you back looking for trouble again in no time.'

'I don't feel like joking.'

'Neither do I, but we mustn't give up. We still have a chance. No one has ever succeeded in storming Syracuse.'

He stopped a moment on the threshold as he was leaving. There was something he wanted to say, but he didn't dare. He thought it would be useless at that point. He said only: 'Be careful, my friend, if you can manage it,' and left.

★

Mago's naval armada appeared the next day at dawn and the entire city hurried up to the walls to behold it. It was truly an extraordinary sight: hundreds and hundreds of vessels paraded past, making the sea boil with their oars, their sails snapping in the wind, their standards waving at the bows. Light signals flashed between the ships like a mysterious language which kept that huge host united in perfect order, like an array of soldiers. The world's greatest navy had put its power on show to throw the besieged city into dismay, to give them the sensation that any effort at defence would be futile.

They passed off the shore of Ortygia, then turned west, directed towards the Great Harbour.

Dionysius, Hipparinus and Iolaus were together on the tallest tower, dressed in their armour. Philistus arrived as well. 'They're going to drop anchor between Plemmyrium and Dascon,' he said. 'That means that the ground troops will settle in that area.'

'Good,' snarled Dionysius. 'In the tomb of all the armies that have ever besieged Syracuse.'

'I wouldn't count on it,' observed Iolaus. 'They have unchallenged dominion over the seas; they can provision their ground forces when and where they want. They have a three-to-one superiority over us on land, and the fleet outnumbers us one hundred to one.'

'We have our walls,' retorted Dionysius. 'They have never let us down.'

'That's true,' commented Iolaus. 'But our most powerful weapon is another: Arethusa.'

'Arethusa?'

'Of course. Why do you suppose the oracle ordered our ancestors to found the city around the Arethusa spring? Because it is she who guarantees our well-being.'

Their conversation was interrupted by the arrival of a messenger. 'Hegemon, Himilco's army is circling to the north of Epipolae and is headed towards the Anapus.'

'See? What was I saying?' said Dionysius. 'They're going to the same place as last time.'

Philistus intervened. 'Tell me something: why do you think they're doing that? Because they're stupid?'

'No, I don't think so,' admitted Dionysius. 'Himilco is a fox. They simply don't have a choice. There are no plains in the vicinity large enough to accommodate so many troops. They know full well that the Athenian commanders witnessed the ruin of their army from there ten years ago. They must be planning to storm Syracuse in the winter. That's why they're not afraid to pitch camp in that cursed place.'

No one answered because none of them had ever considered that an army might keep up a siege during the whole winter, during the most inclement months of the year.

Iolaus neared Dionysius. 'How is Leptines?'

'His fever will not break. I don't know if he's going to make it,' he replied, with deep discouragement in his voice.

'Can I see him?'

'Of course. His friends can always see him.'

Iolaus nodded and went down into the courtyard, headed towards the southern wing, where Leptines was housed. He dismissed the surgeon and took over the patient's care personally. Leptines began to improve day by day, slowly at first and then much more visibly, until his fever disappeared.

'How did you manage it?' Philistus asked him some time later.

Iolaus replied with a smile: 'I can't tell you.'

'Are you familiar with the natives' method of healing; the medicine that saved Dionysius at the spring of Anapus?'

'No.'

'Then you must know Pythagorean medicine. You studied at Croton, didn't you? I've always wondered how, up to a century ago, the Crotonian athletes always won all the Olympic games.'

'So what have you come up with?'

'There must have been a secret. Some mysterious, initiatory medicine that cures bodies with the energy of the mind and the resources of nature.'

Iolaus said nothing.

'A secret that I thought had been lost; but evidently there are still some who possess it.'

'Perhaps. It depends on the teacher, and on a fortunate encounter between teacher and pupil. In any case, it wasn't easy with Leptines. He was turned more towards death than towards life.'

'I had the same impression. But why?'

'It's obvious, isn't it? Being defeated in such an important battle, before the eyes of the entire army and of his brother in particular. His men found themselves without a leader and were massacred . . . And yet there was something else, something that escaped me . . . something like . . .'

'Like a love without hope?'

Iolaus stared at him with an enigmatic look and nodded. 'Yes . . . maybe something like that . . . Sometimes the strongest and most courageous men hide the soul of a child, with unsuspected sensitivities. But don't say anything else, Philistus, not a word. Not a word.'

And they parted.

*

Himilco's intentions turned out to be as Dionysius had predicted.

The inhabitants of Syracuse witnessed the progress of his plans from atop the walls. The first thing he did was to occupy a rural sanctuary, dedicated to Demeter and Persephone – the goddesses most venerated in Sicily, even by the natives – stripping it of all its adornments and precious objects. He carried off the two gold and ivory statues and dismembered them to sell off their parts. It was a sacrilege that horrified the people, who were genuinely devoted to those divinities. Dionysius was outraged as well; his experience in the grotto of Henna was still vivid in his mind.

Then Himilco began to build a fort at the tip of the Dascon

promontory, to control access to the stretch of shore where he had beached some of his ships and anchored the rest.

Meanwhile the Iberians and Mauritanians demolished the great monumental tombs which stood along the road to Camarina, and used the materials to build a reinforced camp meant to defend a second naval base at Plemmyrium, the southern promontory of the bay.

Their attempt to blockade the northern harbour failed, however, because the catapults deployed by Dionysius at the end of the wharf prevented any ship from coming closer than one hundred feet without the risk of being sunk. The Laccius harbour thus remained open to allow Syracuse to maintain her contacts with the outside world.

The enemy's awesome preparations spread a sense of great apprehension and impotence among the inhabitants of Syracuse. It seemed that catastrophe was drawing nearer with each passing day. Dionysius realized that something must be done to shake them from their deadly resignation; he had to restore their morale and his own prestige as well. He called on Philistus. 'You must leave,' he said. 'You'll go to Corinth, to our metropolis. It's not that I need much, but the people must realize that we are not alone, that we are still capable of obtaining aid, alliance, help. When Syracuse was besieged by the Athenians, the arrival of a small Spartan contingent turned out to be enough to raise the people's morale and convince them that victory was possible. We need ships. Those we have are insufficient for organizing effective operations. You'll leave tomorrow. Leptines will keep a passage open for you and you'll be escorted out to the open sea by a couple of quinqueremes.'

'I'll do my best,' replied Philistus, and he went down to the harbour to make agreements with Leptines and to give instructions for loading his baggage, which always included a rather voluminous crate of books.

Leptines received him at the admiralty's residence, near the dockyard.

'You're looking well,' said Philistus.

'You're looking well yourself,' replied Leptines.

'Have you heard that I'm going to Greece?'

'I know. He deigned to notify me.'

'Don't talk that way. Dionysius is fond of you and esteems you.'

Leptines changed the subject. 'When do you think you'll be ready?'

'Tomorrow night.'

'Good. We'll avoid being seen.'

Philistus managed to escape Carthaginian surveillance as Leptines manoeuvred to create a distraction. He reached Greece safe and sound, stopping first in Sparta and then in Corinth. Sparta gave him a sole officer in the role of military consultant, while Corinth saw fit to send a squadron of thirty ships complete with foot soldiers and crew; they reached Syracuse early that spring.

Leptines went out to meet them on the open sea in a small boat, and had them enter the harbour one moonless night. Sheltered docks had been prepared – practically invisible from both the sea and the city – to hide the small Corinthian fleet and hopefully allow them to catch the enemy unawares.

Once anchorage was accomplished, he held the first general staff meeting at his residence in the admiralty. After welcoming the Spartan officer and the Corinthians, he began to lay out his plan: 'I learned this morning that a convoy of nine Carthaginian triremes is due to arrive tomorrow evening with supplies and money to pay the mercenaries. With your help, I intend to intercept them.'

Those present stared at each other in alarm and perplexity. Had Leptines thought up this idea himself or was Dionysius's approval behind it? No one dared to ask.

The Spartan officer, whose name was Euridemus, replied: 'It seems like a good idea, but it will take considerable skill to carry it off.'

'That's right. That's why I need pilots and crew capable of navigating at night,' said Leptines.

'All of our pilots can navigate at night,' replied the Corinthian officers. 'We were navigating at night when you didn't even know how to navigate by day.'

Leptines did not allow the comment to annoy him; the Greeks from the metropolis were always quite arrogant, and it wasn't worth it to challenge their ideas of superiority. He said only: 'Very good. That's what we need. We'll use twenty ships: ten of ours and ten of yours. I want the men at their oars and the crews at the rigging when the bugle sounds the second guard shift. The task of the mission will be communicated by the commanders once the ships are in the open sea. I will sail at the head. The rest of you will follow the *Boubaris*.'

The following day, the squadron left the harbour at midnight with their lights out and slipped silently into the open sea.

25

LEPTINES HAD DONE everything in his power to make sure the night assault would be successful. Several boats had been posted at intervals one stadium apart, with navy officers on board disguised as fishermen apparently intent on fishing with lanterns. As soon as the outermost boat spied the looming bulk of the Carthaginian ships, it sent a signal, and the Syracusan fleet fanned out with their bows to the sea and the wind at their sterns. The flagship flashed another light signal and the attack was on.

The Carthaginians were so sure that the ships were friendly vessels come to escort them into the harbour that when they realized the truth they had no time to react. Two Syracusan ships drew up on either side of each of their triremes and hundreds of attackers flooded on board. Many of the Carthaginian soldiers were still sleeping when they found their enemies' swords at their throats.

The combatants who attempted resistance were killed, the others were simply disarmed; the ships were towed into the harbour and the rich bounty was unloaded and put in safe keeping.

Dionysius, who was waiting on the wharf, went forward to meet his brother and embraced him. 'Well done, by Zeus! We needed a victory, even a small one: tomorrow you'll be celebrated as a hero!'

'Small?' replied Leptines. 'Just wait and see: we're not even half finished.'

'What are you saying?'

Philistus arrived out of breath, still wearing his nightclothes. 'What's happening here? You could have told me that—'

'Himilco's expecting these ships tonight, is he not?' said Leptines.

'Yes . . .' agreed Dionysius.

'And he'll have them.' He turned to the officers gathered around them. 'Each of you switch your clothing and your weapons with those of the prisoners, transfer the oarsmen to the Carthaginian ships and be ready to set sail!'

'Brilliant,' commented Philistus. 'Absolutely brilliant: a plan worthy of a great strategist.'

'I'm coming with you,' said Dionysius.

'No,' replied Leptines. 'It's still a very risky undertaking. One of us is more than enough; it's best that you stay here in the city. You have a family, while I have no one. It's gone well so far, hasn't it? Let me take care of things this time.'

Dionysius stared straight into his eyes: 'I could have killed you at Catane . . .'

'I know.'

'And I would have committed a great error. I sometimes ask myself which of us is truly the better man.'

'Me, obviously,' replied Leptines. 'Give me the password, you bastard!'

'Sod the world!' laughed Dionysius.

'Sod the world!' repeated Leptines, and he jumped on the deck of a Carthaginian ship.

Philistus was moved by their banter; he realized that Dionysius's deepest feelings were still alive beneath the crust of power that got harder with each passing day. He continued to hope – or perhaps he was only fooling himself – that the man would finally win over the tyrant.

The squadron left Laccius and turned to starboard, keeping in the lee of Ortygia as far as possible, until they found themselves directly opposite Plemmyrium, on the side facing the Great Harbour. They veered right again towards Dascon, where the lights of the Carthaginian guardhouse were glittering; they could soon make out the surveillance units.

The look-out soldiers saluted the standards of Tanit on the

ships parading by and they were greeted in response in their own language. A Carthaginian officer had been convinced, by a sword digging into the small of his back, to reassure them with the familiar sound of his voice. The small fleet was free to move now, and Leptines guided it to the end of the roadstead, where fifty or so warships were riding at anchor.

The attack was as fast as it was violent: immobile as they were, ten vessels were rammed and sunk in the initial strike. The others went up in flames under a shower of incendiary arrows.

A second wave of fiery arrows came down on the tents and deposits, while shouts exploded from every corner of the camp and prolonged bugle blasts sounded the alarm.

The confusion was such that Leptines managed to hook up half a dozen enemy ships and tow them out into the bay. At dawn, his squadron entered the Laccius harbour triumphantly, greeted by a cheering multitude.

Leptines felt reborn in the embrace of the crowd and in that of his brother Dionysius, but then his glance fell on the fortress walls, and he saw a slender female figure on the tower bastions. She seemed to be waving her arm and he knew deep down that it was Aristomache, so small in the distance, so far away and unattainable.

Emboldened by their success, the Syracusan navy under Leptines's command launched a series of attacks, sinking a great number of transports and more than a few warships. The Carthaginians were furious over their losses, and decided to drive their adversaries from the Laccius port and destroy their bases through a massive attack.

This time Dionysius was aboard the *Boubaris* as well, and in the furious fray that followed the two brothers were seen fighting at each other's sides with incredible daring, leading the assault troops as they had when they were twenty.

Supported by catapults drawn up on the two promontories that curled around the entrance to the harbour, the Syracusan fleet were in a favourable position in the restricted area of Laccius, and they inflicted heavy losses on the enemy, forcing them to withdraw in the end. Ten ships were captured and repaired, so that the available force now amounted to more than fifty units, in addition to their own.

On the ground, the cavalry was no less triumphant, carrying out dozens of raids, attacking the Carthaginian patrols roaming the countryside in search of food and forage, wiping out the military units reconnoitring the territory, and often threatening Himilco's own outposts on the Anapus plain.

These constant skirmishes continued throughout the spring, and then came summer, burning hot, sweltering and humid.

And with the summer, plague broke out in the Carthaginian camp. The dead were thrown into the lagoon with stones tied to their ankles, sowing contagion through the hidden veins of water.

The brutal heat had dried many wells inside the walls, but the Arethusa spring continued to flow clear and pure. Philistus recalled the words of Iolaus, when he had said that the fount would be the salvation of the city, and he ordered the Syracusans to drink only the water of the sacred spring until the war was over and the rains had returned.

During those endless days, blinded by a fierce sun, Dionysius often caught himself thinking of the wild girl who lived in the rocky valley at the Anapus springs and the day he had made love to her on the shore. He wondered whether she was still alive and whether she ever thought of him.

Neither his Italian wife – an artful administrator of her charms, inclined to give only when she could have something in return – nor his Syracusan wife, so melancholy and reticent, had ever given him so much pleasure. Not even the birth of her sons, Hipparinus and Nysaeus, had removed the veil of sadness that always shadowed Aristomache's face.

For some time now Dionysius had avoided occasional encounters with women he did not know, for fear of putting his life at risk. He even saw his friends – or those who claimed to be so – infrequently. His solitude increased and all of his thoughts were concentrated on his strategy for war and his political design for the great State of Western Greece, to which he dedicated all his energy. He asked himself how many Syracusans loved him and how many hated him, how many admired him and how many dreaded him.

All of these thoughts only nursed the suspicions that were growing inside, and with them the fear that someone might attempt to take his life. All his efforts would be thwarted, the enormous toll of human lives would have been for naught. Perhaps he was the only one left to believe in his dream of greatness. The words of Heloris, his adoptive father, sprang to mind: 'The only way to get a tyrant to abandon his place is to pull him out by the feet.' The image obsessed him, and yet he could not share his fears with anyone. He could not afford to seem weak and vulnerable, not even with the few real friends he had left: Iolaus, Philistus and his brother Leptines.

Only Aksal the giant, his inseparable bodyguard, gave him a sense of reassurance, like the armour that covered his chest in battle. Aksal was both powerful and blindly faithful, ready at his beck and call.

On one occasion, as they were discussing a plan of attack with the officers in the barracks courtyard, Leptines took a spear from one of the Campanian mercenaries; he had wanted to use its tip to sketch the lines of action on to the sand, but Dionysius started. Leptines saw the rage and terror in his brother's expression for just an instant, and he couldn't believe his eyes. He handed the spear back to the warrior and walked off in silence.

Dionysius ran after him and stopped him. 'Where are you going?'

'I can't believe you're asking.'

'You don't understand . . . The men have orders to never let anyone disarm them, and I can't let . . .'

'Are you still capable of a sincere answer?' asked Leptines, staring straight into his eyes.

'What do you mean by that?'

'Are you capable of answering me?' he shouted.

'Yes.'

'Then tell me: did you think I wanted to kill you?'

Dionysius's head dropped for several interminable moments, and then he said: 'I thought so.'

'Why?'

'I don't know.'

'I'll tell you why: because you'd be capable of it if you were in my place.'

'No,' he replied. 'You're wrong. The reason is that perhaps I hate myself more than anyone else can hate me.'

Silence fell between the two brothers. They looked each other in the eye without being able to say a word.

'What must I do?' asked Dionysius finally.

'Attack. Lead your men on the front lines. The Syracusans, not the mercenaries. Send the hirelings out on their own. Show that you are one of us, that you're ready to die for what you believe in.' He said nothing else, and walked away, down a corridor. Dionysius listened to the sound of his steps fading into the distance.

*

They waited to attack until Himilco's troops seemed on their last legs, and the stench of unburied cadavers became unbearable. Dionysius decided to put the battle plan which had failed him at Gela back into action.

'We will attack with three army corps,' he announced at the meeting of the high command. 'I'll be at the fore of the central unit, which will head directly for the fort at Dascon. Euridemus will lead the second division with the mercenaries, from the west. Leptines, you will lead the assault from the sea, putting ashore the third contingent. The decision of when to deliver the final attack will be made then and there, on the ground, when the three divisions are in position at the fortified camp and our situation is clear. The password will be "Apollo, leader of troops!"'

The two land divisions set off under cover of darkness, after Leptines had left the port with the fleet. Dionysius proceeded directly to Dascon, taking the fort by surprise. He occupied the position and established his headquarters there. He signalled for

Euridemus to send forth his mercenaries just as Leptines was rounding the southern promontory of Ortygia. The Spartan ordered the attack.

Although their numbers had been decimated by the plague, Himilco's Iberians and Campanians reacted with great vigour, driving back the mercenaries led by Euridemus and inflicting heavy losses. But in the meantime, Leptines had set ashore his division of assault troops and Dionysius was approaching with the bulk of the force, leaving only a garrison behind to hold the clearing in front of the fort of Dascon.

The fortifications of Himilco's entrenched camp appeared too strong for a frontal attack, and Dionysius decided not to risk it. He launched his troops instead against the naval camp. Caught between Leptines's men and the two ground divisions, the Mauritanians and the Libyans posted in defence of the ships were soon overwhelmed and thoroughly beaten. Many of the lighter Carthaginian ships had been pulled aground, and Dionysius ordered for them to be set on fire, transforming the camp into a huge blaze. A violent land wind pushed the flames out to sea, and a number of the transport ships caught fire as well and were devoured. The crewless triremes anchored three rows out were destroyed in part and towed in part to the Laccius harbour. Less than a third of them managed to escape out to sea, with greatly reduced crews.

A vast crowd had formed up on the city's walls, drawn by the spectacle of the raging fire; the people were out of their minds with joy at seeing the enemy fleet destroyed, and they loudly cheered on the soldiers they could see quite plainly in the fields below. Many of them, especially the old men and boys, seeing the huge quantity of Carthaginian vessels drifting in the roadstead, went out with anything that would stay afloat to take possession of them and tow them to port. So many vessels were recovered in this way that there was no room left at all in the shipyards, and the ships had to be anchored at the centre of the gulf or along the northern shore.

That evening, a victorious Dionysius entered the city at the head of his troops, amidst the frenzied applause of the crowd. He officiated a solemn sacrifice at the Temple of Athena on the acropolis. Both his wives were present, dressed in beautiful gowns, Doris holding little Dionysius by the hand, and Aristomache with Hipparinus and tiny Nysaeus as well.

The fortified Carthaginian camp was nonetheless still intact, as was Himilco's army, although his fleet had been largely lost. Only about sixty battleships and transports had escaped, out of more than five hundred that the great armada had boasted of at the start.

The destiny of the war had been completely overturned.

Two days later, a dinghy approached the Ortygia castle from the open sea after dark, and the boatmen called out to the sentries: 'A message for your commander.'

Iolaus was immediately notified by his guards and went in person to meet the man on the boat. He took him to Dionysius, who was dining with Leptines and Philistus. The nocturnal messenger was bearing a message from Himilco.

'Speak,' said Dionysius. 'This is my brother and I consider the others likewise.'

The man removed the hood covering his face and proved to be the same ambassador who had come during the last war to negotiate peace.

'Things have changed since we saw you last,' observed Dionysius in a nonetheless conciliatory tone. 'What can I do for noble Himilco?'

'My lord has a very reasonable proposal to make you, that I hope you will accept.'

'That depends on how reasonable it is,' replied Dionysius.

'To begin with, he offers you three hundred talents in silver, eighty per cent in coins and the rest in bars.'

'Promising beginning,' scoffed Leptines.

'In exchange, noble Himilco requests that you allow him to leave with the Carthaginian troops. Ten thousand men in all.'

'What about the mercenaries? And the natives?' asked Iolaus.

'We do not have sufficient ships for them. You can do with them as you please. If you accept, the sum will be delivered tomorrow morning at an established spot near Plemmyrium. What do you say?'

'Leave us now,' replied Dionysius. 'We must discuss this. You will be notified.'

Aksal led him out of the room and the four men began to discuss the terms.

'You can't intend to accept!' protested Leptines immediately. 'He must surrender unconditionally. At the very most, you could allow him to slip off on his own and save his own skin. We'll get the booty anyway when they've finished rotting in that hole. After all, they have no way out. We'll close them off by land with the cavalry and block them at sea with the fleet. We're stronger than they are now. We even have the quinqueremes.'

Dionysius held up his hand to stop his brother's ranting. 'Desperation can perform miracles. Men who have nothing left to lose can find an unimaginable amount of strength.'

'That's true,' agreed Iolaus. 'There's a hidden store of energy inside every human being, a kind of buried treasure that comes to the fore when he is threatened. It is the last resource that nature gives us for our survival.'

'One thing is certain,' said Philistus. 'We need those three hundred talents. War expenses have been enormous, we've fallen behind in paying the mercenaries and we also have to compensate the families of the Syracusans who have fallen in battle. What's more, we have to rebuild the fleet and make payment to the contingent sent by the metropolis.'

'That's not all,' intervened Iolaus. 'The longer these people stay here, the greater the chance that the plague will spread to us as well. If we let them go, they'll spread it back at home. It has happened before. I know how that kind of disease spreads.'

'I'm convinced of it as well,' approved Philistus. 'Well then, what shall we do?'

Leptines was furious. 'You're all mad! We finally have the chance to exterminate every last one of them and you want to let them go for three hundred talents?'

'It is a pretty sum,' admitted Philistus.

'Listen, if it's about the money, I swear to you that I will find it myself and bring it here to you. I'll blockade the camp so that not even a fly will be able to get out.'

'I've listened to your opinions,' interrupted Dionysius at that point. 'Have the ambassador come back in.'

Aksal brought Himilco's messenger back into the room. 'We have meditated on your proposals and I would like to make one myself . . .' began Dionysius.

'Excuse me, supreme leader,' interrupted the ambassador politely, 'but a short while ago as I was waiting outside, without meaning to, I heard one of you, whose voice was quite loud . . .' Dionysius shot an irritated look at his brother, who was still flushed with anger. 'I thought I heard, I was saying, that you intend to set up a blockade so that the treasure cannot leave the fortified camp. The fact is, my friends, that the money . . . is not in the camp and, if these negotiations fail, it will be immediately dumped into the sea, at a depth that no one will be able to reach. A true waste, wouldn't you say? When a reasonable decision could satisfy both you and us.'

Dionysius sighed.

'Well then, may I know your decision?'

'Tell your lord that I accept. The exchange will take place at sea, halfway between your camp on the Anapus and the southern promontory of Ortygia. As soon as I've seen the money, the first ships can set sail. This will all take place at night, with the utmost secrecy.'

'That is agreeable to us,' confirmed the ambassador. 'When would you like to proceed with the transaction?'

'There is a new moon tomorrow night,' replied Dionysius. 'You'll bring the money at the beginning of the second guard shift. Three light signals on our side and three on yours.'

'Very well, *hegemon*. Now, if you will allow me to do so, I shall return to tell my lord of the happy outcome of my mission and reassure him of your good intentions.'

'See?' said Dionysius to Leptines as soon as the ambassador had left. 'You think you can screw a Carthaginian? When dealing with money, above all? I've made the right decision. And now let us go to bed. A long day awaits us tomorrow, and most likely not an easy one.'

His guests took their leave, but Dionysius called Leptines back.

'What do you want?'

'I reflected on your proposal. There was some good in what you said.'

Leptines looked surprised. 'Don't mock me.'

'I'm not. Listen well: after the money is delivered, imagine that someone in Ortygia should notice strange goings-on at the mouth of the Great Harbour . . .'

'I can see where you're going,' replied Leptines. 'But that means that you're precluding any future possibility of an honest agreement between them and us.'

'That wouldn't be true if, for example, the Corinthians attack. We can't give orders to the navy of our metropolis. And the Carthaginians know that as well.'

'I wish you hadn't said anything to me. I don't like deceit, even if it's used against my worst enemy. If you need me for anything else, you know where to find me. Rest well, brother.'

Leptines left.

The following night, at the hour agreed upon, Dionysius went out on a dinghy and met up with a trireme that was waiting for him at a stadium's distance from land, on the open sea. Then the warship slowly advanced towards the harbour. Two small reconnaissance units were stationed at both sides in a forward position, at about half a stadium's distance from the trireme, to guard against surprises or ambushes.

Everything went as planned. As soon as they had reached the spot agreed upon, the ship was approached by a Carthaginian vessel and, after an exchange of signals, the transfer of the money was begun.

The ambassador who had conducted the negotiations was on board. '*Hegemon*,' he said immediately, 'I would ask to have the count done as soon as possible. Our fleet is already near Plemmyrium, ready to put out to sea.'

Dionysius nodded and his administrators, ready with their lever scales, swiftly weighed the money and gave the go-ahead. 'You can tell your lord that he may leave,' he said to the ambassador, 'and tell him never to come back. You see, Sicily is like a delicious fruit with a very hard pit inside, which anyone would break their teeth on. Syracuse is the pit. Farewell.'

The boat sailed off and Dionysius saw it sending off light signals, probably to Plemmyrium where Himilco was waiting with the fleet.

'How will he have managed to deceive the mercenaries?' asked Iolaus.

'It probably wasn't difficult. He may have said that he was preparing a night raid. The Carthaginians are the only sailors who navigate well at night, so no one would have been surprised that they were the only ones aboard. Let's make our return; there will be a lot going on around here in a short time.'

Iolaus nodded and motioned to the pilot to turn towards Ortygia.

The treasure was unloaded at the base of the cliffs below the castle, where a secret passage led to the underground chambers of the fortress. Dionysius and Iolaus entered the same way, and went straight to their apartments.

Some time passed before they heard bugle blasts rending the night. '*Hegemon! Hegemon!* The Carthaginians are escaping! The Corinthians have spotted them and are going out with their ships. What must we do?'

'What do you mean, what must we do?!' he shouted. 'Sound the alarm, by Zeus! Call my brother, all the crews to their ships! Move!'

Great turmoil ensued, but the only ones who managed to get out in time were the Corinthians, who intercepted the tail end of the Carthaginian fleet and sank a dozen ships.

Himilco got away. When he arrived in his homeland, he publicly confessed his mistakes to the people and the Council, in the Semitic manner, and then he killed himself.

26

HIMILCO'S DEATH AND the spread of plague in Africa set off a revolt of the peoples subject to Carthage, the inland Mauritanians and Libyans, and the city had to use all her residual energy to ensure mere survival.

Dionysius thus found himself with a free hand in Sicily. He occupied the northern coast of the island all the way to Solus, an ancient Carthaginian settlement near Panormus, and consolidated his authority over the Sicels. He realized that in order to achieve an entirely Greek Sicily – at the centre of all the seas and lands – the resources he had at his disposal were not sufficient. He would have to extend his own dominion first and create the great State of Western Greece that he had so long yearned for: a personal domain with Syracuse as its hub, extending all the way to the Scylletian isthmus, the point at which the peninsula opposite Sicily was at its narrowest, between the Ionian and Tyrrhenian seas. This would give him control of the Straits, the waterway from which the most dangerous threats had often come.

The main obstacle to be dealt with was Rhegium, so close to Messana that her temples could be seen from Sicily, and her lights at night. The city had always been hostile to him. She was home to Heloris – the adoptive father who had repudiated him and who had been his relentless enemy for years now – as well as all of the exiled Knights. These old aristocrats had raised their children to fiercely hate the tyrant who had stripped Syracuse of her freedom and them of their homeland. They never missed an opportunity to spread the most negative propaganda about Dionysius and the most shameful slander, loaded with disgraceful anecdotes.

Dionysius paid them no heed whatsoever and continued with his preparations for war, in agreement with the Italian families of Locri who were bound to him by family ties.

There was one last endeavour to be completed in Sicily before he marched on Rhegium: he must conquer Tauromenium, the formidable 'Hill of the Bull' held by the Sicels allied with Carthage. They considered the city a sort of sacrarium of their nation, protected as she was by a practically inaccessible position at the top of a rocky cliff. Tauromenium dominated the coastal road that connected Syracuse to Messana and to the Straits. The dreadful convulsions of Mount Aetna as she erupted could be seen from there, as could the snowy peak of the volcano turning red before dusk on a tranquil winter evening.

Dionysius attempted a night attack, leading his troops in person in the middle of winter, as a snowstorm raged on the mountain. He and his raiders climbed up the cliff on the side where it was steepest and hence most carelessly guarded.

The venture came close to success, but once the Sicels realized what was happening, they rushed to the spot en masse and engaged in furious hand-to-hand combat with the assailants, who soon found themselves heavily outnumbered.

Dionysius, who was fighting at the head of his men, was injured, and only Aksal's might managed to save him from death. The giant Celt decapitated his adversary with one fell swoop of his axe, threw his head into the midst of the dumbfounded enemies and launched a savage attack against them all alone, roaring like a beast and slaying them in great number. Dionysius was carried off and taken behind the shelter of a wall. Iolaus led the retreat, rallying the men in a compact group.

Aksal lowered his wounded master with a rope, as other warriors hurried down to retrieve him at the first accessible shelf on the cliff's side. They managed to save him, but many of their comrades perished in their precipitous descent under the hail of stones and every sort of projectile that the Sicels could hurl at them from up on the walls.

Carthage had not forgotten the humiliation suffered at Diony-sius's hands, and as soon as her people had recovered from the plague, she recruited Iberian and Balearic mercenaries, Sardinians and Sicans, and managed to crush the resistance of the Libyans in short order, subduing them again in just a few months' time. Then Admiral Mago was assigned the task of responding to the arrogance of Syracuse.

The fleet was greatly reduced in number, and equipment was scarce, but Mago succeeded nonetheless in advancing unchallen-ged all the way to Cephaloedium. From there he headed south towards Agyrium, where a local tyrant, friend to Syracuse, ruled. Dionysius went forth to meet him with the army and drove the Carthaginians back twice in partial victories. But when his general staff and allies demanded that he inflict the final blow, he refused; he felt that their supremacy had already been established, and that risking the forces in a frontal attack was not worth the trouble. He still had his expedition against Rhegium in mind and did not want to lose a sole man in what he considered nothing more than one of the thousands of trivial episodes of conflict with the Carthaginians that would resolve nothing.

But his generals were indignant over his remissive conduct and could not bear the idea of being considered cowards by the barbarians. As much of the army was made up of citizens of Syracuse, they decided to abandon Dionysius and march home.

Iolaus followed them in order to maintain control over the situation which could have fallen apart at any time in the absence of a high authority, while Philistus and Leptines remained with Dionysius, who still commanded his personal guard and a contin-gent of Peloponnesian mercenaries.

They managed in the end to re-enter Syracuse without prob-lems, although Dionysius was anxiety-ridden at the idea that his city might attempt to overthrow his rule in his absence and that the city's troops might occupy Ortygia. None of this happened, which was practically a miracle.

Mago considered himself satisfied with having forced Dionysius to withdraw, and he returned with his army to the confines of the Carthaginian provinces. From there he sent an ambassador to propose a peace treaty.

If Dionysius agreed to give up Solus and the other centres of the north he had so recently conquered, Mago in exchange would recognize his dominion over the Sicels, including those of Tauromenium. The conditions were advantageous for both and peace was stipulated.

Commerce flourished once again, traffic and the flow of trade opening up from the Pontus Eusinus to the Adriatic Gulf, from Spain to Africa, from Greece to Gaul, Asia and Egypt. The two harbours of Syracuse teemed with vessels from all over the world, with craftsmen and merchants, labourers and dockers who unloaded timber from Italy, iron from Etruria, copper from Cyprus, papyrus from Egypt, silphium from Cyrene, and loaded up on wheat, olive oil, hand-crafted goods of every sort, horses and weapons for exportation.

Dionysius's wounds healed and he couldn't help but recall Aksal's strength and bravery. 'If we had several thousand mercenaries like him,' he said one day to Philistus, 'no one would be able to stop us. They would be invincible combatants.'

'Beware,' replied Philistus, 'they could easily become a threat. There's an invasion under way in the north. I've learned about it from our Venetic informers, who have just come from Adria with a load of amber. There are many tribes descending from the other side of the Alps, with their families. A true migration of peoples. They've engaged the Etruscans in bitter fighting between the Apennines and the Padus, and the natives of these lands have appealed to their brothers who live in their original homeland, between the Arnus and the Tiber, for help.'

'If they're all like Aksal, the Etruscans have no hope,' observed Dionysius.

*

The pretext for taking action against Rhegium was offered by a border skirmish between Locri and the cities of the Straits, which soon turned into full-blown war. Doris, Dionysius's Locrian wife, was very worried; many people dear to her still lived in the city.

'Your city has nothing to fear,' Dionysius reassured her. 'On the contrary; when this war is over she'll be all the richer and more important. Those who are my friends can only stand to benefit.'

'Then remember, as soon as you land in my city, to offer sacrifice to our national hero, Ajax Oileus.'

'I will certainly do so, even though I doubt your Ajax will be coming to pull me out of trouble.'

'Don't say that! Don't you know that the Locrians always leave a space in the front line so he can take his place in battle?'

Dionysius smiled, and seemed to be curiously watching his little son who was playing with a wooden horse.

'Really?' he said distractedly. 'I didn't know that.'

'Certainly. More than a century and a half ago we fought a dreadful battle against Croton, near the Sagra river. The Crotonian commander noticed that opening in our front lines and saw his chance to break up our formation, but he was cut down by an invisible arm and immediately taken out of action. The wound would not heal, although his doctors did all they could to cure it, cauterizing it again and again; it gave off a terrible stench and caused him piercing pain. The Crotonians consulted the oracle of Delphi, who responded: "The spear of a hero has inflicted the wound, the spear of a hero will heal it."

'The priests interpreted the prophecy to mean that he should go to the Maeotide swamp at the northern bank of the Pontus Eusinus, where Achilles's spear was preserved, on a little island. The Crotonian commander undertook this long journey and, once he reached that sanctuary at the ends of the earth, he laid the hero's rusted spear against his wound and was healed.'

'That's a beautiful story,' said Dionysius. 'You'll have to tell it to our son.'

'Will you take me with you?' pleaded Doris.

'I wouldn't dream of it. Our child is still young, he needs his mother, and war is war. One day, perhaps, when this is all over, when peace and prosperity reign at last, I will take you to Locri. We'll have a beautiful house built there and we'll spend time in it every now and then.'

'Are you serious?' asked the girl. 'Just you and me, alone?'

Dionysius darkened. 'You know you mustn't speak that way! Aristomache is like a sister to you. You should be asking me to take her along with us.'

'I've tried to be her friend. I even shared a bed with both of you, our first night, remember? I would have done so again, but she's always so jealous, so melancholy . . . even now that she has children of her own. I don't know how you can stand her . . .'

'That's enough!' stormed Dionysius. 'I know where you're going with this. You should be content with the way things are. No woman in the world could ask for more!'

Doris turned to her handmaid. 'It's late, put the child to bed. Dear, give your father a kiss.'

The little boy timidly kissed his father without letting go of the maid's hand; she took him off to bed.

'Will you sleep with me tonight?' asked Doris as soon as they had left the room.

'You know that it's Aristomache's turn.'

'But Aristomache has her period. I don't.'

'There's nothing that escapes you.'

'It doesn't take much. Once you know, all you have to do is keep count.' As she said these words, she loosed the belt of her gown and let it slip off. Doris's nude body was radiant in her proud, harmonious femininity.

'You are terrible,' said Dionysius, letting his eyes run over his bride's sensual curves. The lantern cast a golden halo on her pure white skin.

She drew close and embraced him, her breasts close to his face.

Dionysius kissed her passionately and dragged her to the bed. 'But afterwards,' he said, 'I'll be going to sleep with Aristomache.'

*

'The Celts have taken Rome!' exclaimed Philistus, entering Dionysius's apartment at a near run.

'What?'

'It's true! The Romans tried to make a stand, but they had such a fright as soon as they saw the attackers that they took to their heels. Many jumped into the river, others fled to the allied cities nearby.'

'How did you find this out?'

'The Etruscan merchants from Cuma told me that they had learned about it from their compatriots in Tarquinia. It was a disaster. The city was sacked, the senators who decided to stay behind were massacred. The acropolis held out for a while, but then they were forced to surrender, and to pay a high ransom to win back their freedom.'

Dionysius turned to Aksal. 'Have you heard what your brothers are up to? They have burned down one of the most powerful Etruscan cities of the Tyrrhenian.'

'No one can resist us,' the Celt commented laconically.

'I'm starting to believe that myself. What I'd like to do is send you up that way one day with Philistus, to see if any of them would like to combat in my service.'

'If you command, Aksal go.'

'Good. But by Zeus, I've been saying for years that someone should teach this creature a little Greek!'

'The truth is,' replied Philistus, 'that no teacher has lasted more than a few minutes. I'm afraid you'll have to keep him as he is. It's not a man of letters you want, after all; you need a beast who will keep everyone else at bay. He's perfect, I'd say.'

'What do we know about these Celts?' asked Dionysius. 'We've spoken about this already, but I suppose you must know more by now.'

'Not much, really. They live in the north, divided into tribes commanded by chieftains. Some say they are the Hyperboreans spoken of in myth. Others say they descend from the union of a certain princess Galata with Heracles upon his return from Spain with the oxen of Geryon.'

'Fables . . .' commented Dionysius.

'They live in fortified villages, they venerate Apollo, Ares and Hephaestus as we do, they practise human sacrifice, they stand by their word and they always tell the truth . . .'

'They're barbarians, in other words,' concluded Dionysius.

'What did you expect? You've had a sample here for years.'

'For what I have in mind, the more barbaric they are the better. But I would like you to start thinking about something . . . If I ever manage to recruit a good number of them, you'll have to see whether there isn't a version of some myth that connects them to Sicily.'

'I would say decidedly not.'

'Well then you'll invent one. People who are transferred to foreign lands need to find something familiar.'

'These Celts are highly unstable, and they've already made their way very far south. Be on your guard.'

'My friend, there is nothing and no one who will be able to threaten us when I've accomplished my plan. I will draw a wall from the Ionian to the Tyrrhenian and my fleet will dominate the Straits unopposed. Syracuse will be the greatest city in the world and the mighty of this earth will have to reckon with us and contend our friendship.'

'So now you'll attack Rhegium.'

'They have assailed my Locrian family and allies . . .'

'Who had provoked them into it.'

'That is immaterial.'

'You have considered, I hope, that Rhegium is part of the League that unites most of the Greeks of Italy. If one city is attacked, the others are bound to come to her aid.'

'I know. And I know what I'll do. You will remain here to command the Ortygia fortress.'

Philistus nodded slightly, quite embarrassed by the honour bestowed upon him.

'Leptines will have as always the supreme command of the fleet. Do you know where he is now?'

'Where do you think? He's on the *Boubaris* having the rowlocks, figurehead, stern ornaments and mastheads polished. There's no wife he could love as much as he does that ship.'

'Then let him know that I will be his guest for all the operations at sea.'

*

Dionysius drew up in front of Rhegium towards the end of the summer of that year with a powerful army: twenty thousand men, one thousand horses and one hundred and twenty battle-ships, including thirty quinqueremes. They set ashore east of the city and set about sacking and devastating the territory. It wasn't long before the League responded. Sixty ships from Croton entered the Straits to bring help to the threatened city, but Leptines had been vigilant, and his entire fleet fell upon the squadron while they were still at sea.

The Crotonians, seeing the crushing superiority of their enemy, sought escape landward and tried to beach their ships in order to protect them. The Rhegines came to their aid in great numbers.

Leptines came so close that his keels almost touched bottom. He had harpoons thrown in an attempt to secure the Crotonian ships and tow them offshore. A bizarre tug of war ensued between the Crotonian crews on land as they tried to hold their ships back by anchoring them to the ground using ropes and stakes, and the Syracusans who were trying to pull them out to sea by dint of their oars.

The grotesque contest was interrupted by the explosion of a storm announced by a sudden gust of Boreas which hit the Syracusan galleys broadsides, sending them into a frightful roll. Leptines gave the signal to desist and withdraw to the harbour of Messana, but the wind continued to pick up with every passing moment, the waves swelled and boiled with foam and the threatening roar of thunder could be heard in the distance. The commanders ordered the ships to strike sail and dismast, but more than a few had been surprised with their sails to the wind and were overturned. The shipwrecked crews had no choice but to swim towards the Italian coast, where they were immediately captured and imprisoned by the Rhegines.

The rest of the fleet fought bravely against the gale for hours and hours. When the *Boubaris* entered the harbour of Messana last of all at midnight, many of her oars were broken and her hold was full of water.

The weather was against them so late in the season, and Dionysius was forced to return to Syracuse, furious over the reverse.

He locked himself up in the barracks at Ortygia at length, and would not be approached even by his closest friends, who knew better than to pester him and sat back to wait until the storm had passed. Then, one day, he summoned Philistus. 'I need you,' he began as soon as his friend had entered.

Philistus took a sidelong look. Dionysius had dark circles under his eyes, surely a sign that he wasn't sleeping, and his face was ashen. 'Here I am,' he answered.

'You must leave for a diplomatic mission. You have to stipulate an alliance for me.'

'With whom?'

'The Lucanians. I have to bring Rhegium to her knees, along with the entire Italian League, if necessary. And I intend to conclude everything by the end of this year. The Olympics will be held next year and my plans must be accomplished by then. I will present myself as . . .'

'The Lucanians?' Philistus interrupted him. 'Did I hear you well? You want to ally with the barbarians against a Greek city? Do you realize what you are saying?'

'I know full well what I'm saying. And don't annoy me with this foolish nationalism. The Spartans entered into an alliance with the Persians against the Athenians in order to win the Great War, and the Rhegines themselves were allied with Carthage against us at the time of Gelon . . .'

'But when the Persians tried to assert their dominion over the Greek cities of Asia, King Agesilaus of Sparta landed in Anatolia and attacked them at full strength . . . Dionysius, all of this is relative. It's the change in you that is terrible, that saddens me and pains me. What has happened to the young hero I once knew? The champion of the poor against the aristocrats? The intrepid combatant, the defender of the Greeks, the implacable enemy of the Carthaginians. The avenger of Selinus and Himera?'

'I'm right here, in front of you!' shouted Dionysius. 'Wasn't I fighting the barbarians until just a few months ago? Isn't my body still aching from the wounds I received at Tauromenium? Haven't I served my homeland, my city? Haven't I made her greater and stronger, more feared and respected? The Athenians court us, and so do the Spartans: we are envied for our wealth and our power and just who has achieved this? Answer me, by Zeus! Who achieved all this?'

'You, of course, but also your brother Leptines, who has risked his life a thousand times to follow your orders, and Iolaus as well, who has never abandoned you and has always believed in you, and Doricus, murdered in his tent, and Biton, executed at Motya, and me. Yes! Me as well! I who have sworn to follow you to Hades, if necessary. But don't ask this of me, Dionysius, don't ask me to stipulate an alliance with the barbarians against the Greeks. It's against me, it's against what I believe in. And it's against you as well, can't you see that? Your autocracy is already a scandal for the Greeks. It's been tolerated until now because you appear as a champion of Hellenism against the barbarians. But if you ally with the Lucanians to attack Rhegium and the Italian League, they will turn and spit at you. You will become a monster in their eyes!'

'So be it! I have no need for their consideration.'

'Yes you do. No one can live without the esteem of their fellow men, remember that!'

Dionysius, who had been pacing back and forth across the floor of the fencing hall, stopped all at once in the middle of the room and shot a troubled look at Philistus. 'I can do this myself. Winning is what's important. If I am successful, I will be acclaimed and everyone will need me. And I will win, with or without your help. I'm waiting for your answer.'

'Without,' replied Philistus. 'You'll win, if you can, without my help.'

'Fine. Now I know who I can count on. Farewell.'

Philistus dropped his head, then looked at him for an instant with a pained expression. 'Farewell, Dionysius,' he replied. And started for the door.

'Wait.'

Philistus turned, as if he hoped Dionysius's mind might still be changed.

'Leptines must know nothing, for the moment. Do I have your word?'

'My word? It's been a long time since you believed in words or oaths.'

'In my friends' words, I do,' he replied in a softer voice.

'You have my word,' said Philistus, and left.

27

THE TREATY OF alliance that Philistus refused to negotiate was nonetheless concluded by a Messanian emissary on behalf of Dionysius. The following summer, the Lucanians sent a marauding force to Thurii, a Greek colony founded half a century earlier at the spot in which Sybaris had been destroyed. Meanwhile, Leptines had been deployed with the fleet in the Tyrrhenian sea near Laos. Dionysius had told him to wait there for allied troops coming from the east, over the mountains; together they would trap the forces of the League that had invaded the territory of their friend Locri.

The Thurians reacted with great resolve to the Lucanian attack and when they saw the marauders retreating towards the mountains they chased after them, instead of waiting for the bulk of the League's army who were marching in from Croton.

They climbed the Carax valley until they reached the ridge of the mountains and, finding no one to hinder their way, continued down the other side in the direction of Laos, which was located on the coast. But when they arrived at the brief plain between the mountains and the sea they met with a bitter surprise. The Lucanians were not ahead of them, but at their backs. There were tens of thousands of them, the entire might of all of their tribes put together, and they were hurtling downhill shouting and shaking their arms. The Thurians realized they were completely entrapped and drew up into a phalanx, prepared to resist to the death. But the numerical superiority of the enemy was so great that the battle was transformed into a bloodbath.

A group of about four thousand warriors managed to withdraw

to a hilltop, where they continued to drive back the barbarian assaults. One thousand more, completely surrounded on the beach without a chance of saving themselves, suddenly saw a Greek fleet appear behind them. They tossed aside their weapons and swam out to the ships.

It was not the Rhegine fleet, as they had hoped, but the Syracusan fleet, arriving just in time to close off the trap from the sea. But at the sight of those wretches bleeding and floundering in the water, trying desperately to reach safety, Leptines gave a start. He realized that it was a barbarian army massacring the Greeks of Thurii on the beach, and in his mind's eye he saw the horrible scene of the Carthaginian crews at Catane stringing up his sailors as they tried to swim to the coast. He yelled, with all the breath he had: 'Save those men! Hurry!'

His officers were shocked. 'But *hegemon*, those are our enemies . . .'

'They're Greeks, by Heracles. Save them, pull them up, I said!'

The order was signalled to Iolaus, in charge of the right wing, and to the rest of the squadron, whose officers had no doubts about misinterpreting the command when they saw the flagship hoisting aboard all the survivors they could find.

As soon as he had set foot on the *Boubaris*, a Thurian officer asked to see the commander. He was taken to the bow, where Leptines was posted.

The man was disfigured by the blows he had taken and by the immense strain of the crossing. He was trembling and he could barely get out a word.

'Give him dry clothes,' ordered Leptines. 'Move, by Heracles, what are you waiting for?'

'*Hegemon*,' the man managed to blurt out. 'What will you do with us?'

Leptines looked at him and had no doubts. 'You will be treated with the regard that all brave combatants deserve. And you will be . . . returned to your families.'

The second officer looked at him in amazement; he felt as if he had ended up in the wrong place, or in the wrong war.

His commander's voice recalled him to duty: 'We'll go to shore now.'

His second-in-command gave the order and, as the other ships continued in the rescue operation, the flagship approached the beach until her rostrum practically stuck into the sand. From the ship's bow, Leptines had already had a nearly complete vision of the battlefield and he was disgusted. Before him lay the worst carnage he had ever seen in his whole life, a massacre of monstrous proportions. Cadavers lay in piles everywhere, the ground was completely soaked with blood, collecting in little trickles which reddened the waters of the sea. Ten, perhaps fifteen thousand men had been killed in a space of just one stadium, caught between the mountains and the sea, like animals in a slaughterhouse. Most of them had already been savagely maimed, plundered and stripped. Many had been hacked to pieces, the better to slip off their armour, great heaps of which were being accumulated at the edge of the field by the Lucanians.

Leptines staggered through that horror as if he were living a nightmare: bodies of ephebic boys, just out of adolescence, the muscular bodies of mature men, all stiff in the pallor of death. The severed heads of bearded veterans stuck on to pikes regarded him with glassy eyes, their mouths open in a mute, grotesque laugh. There was an obsessive buzzing of flies, everywhere.

All at once, the echo of the battle still raging at the top of the hill reached Leptines. He shouted to Iolaus, who had remained aboard ship, to send him an interpreter. He then made his way towards the spot where the tribal chieftains had gathered in anticipation of another massacre when this contest was over.

He turned to the one who seemed to be the commander-in-chief. 'I am Leptines, brother of Dionysius, lord of Syracuse and your ally. I ask you to put an end to this fighting. You've already won,' he said. 'Allow me to negotiate the surrender of those men.'

'No,' replied the chief. 'We have been at war for a long time with this people, who have unrightfully occupied our territory. We want them exterminated.'

'You'll be much better off if you spare them. I'll pay a ransom for each and every one of them. I'll give you . . . twenty drachmas of silver a head. No, thirty . . . wait, a mina, there, I'll give you a silver mina for each one of them. Do you accept?'

Leptines's second-in-command had arrived just in time to hear this proposal. He grabbed his arm: '*Hegemon*, do you know how much that will cost you? At least one hundred and fifty talents – it's more than half of what we have on board! We need the money to pay for war expenses . . .'

'This is a war expense,' retorted Leptines. Turning towards the interpreter, he insisted: 'Will you ask this goat whether he accepts my offer, blast it?'

The interpreter translated and the chief nodded gravely, with condescension, as if conceding a great favour.

'Finally!' exclaimed Leptines. 'Now tell him I have to reach the men on the hill.'

The chief shouted out something and the bulk of the Lucanian warriors halted their attack, then started slowly to retreat. They finally allowed an opening for the Syracusan admiral to pass through. He made his way slowly up the slope until he found the four thousand Thurian warriors before him, exhausted, wounded, panting, parched, covered with bloody sweat. They looked at him in silent shock. The only sound to be heard was the suddenly deafening buzz of the cicadas on that sun-scorched hillside.

Leptines spoke: 'I am the supreme navarch of the Syracusan fleet and I am your enemy, but I had not been told that these barbarians had orders to totally wipe you out. The slaughter has been consummated now, there's nothing to be done. But although I am your enemy, I am still a Greek. I speak your language and worship your gods, and I'll do whatever I can to save you. I have offered a ransom for your lives and if you surrender I give you my word that no harm will be done to you. You will return to the families that await you. Your comrades who dived into the sea thinking that the Rhegine fleet had come to rescue them have been pulled to safety and cared for. They too will be allowed to return to the city.'

The men stared at him in astonishment, not knowing what to

think. Some yelled out unreasoning, incoherent phrases, others fell to their knees, still others burst into tears.

'Throw down your arms and follow me,' said Leptines. 'No one will harm you. If anyone attacks you, I will order my own troops to defend you.'

Upon hearing those words, the warriors on the hillside threw their swords and shields to the ground one after another and, beginning with the oldest, set off after Leptines, passing between the files of armed barbarians still lusting for blood.

They advanced in silence, staring off into a void, until they reached the beach, where they collapsed on to the sand.

The Lucanian chieftain had them counted one by one. He then boarded the ship and counted those survivors as well, and added up the sums.

Leptines paid over one hundred and seventy talents in silver coins without batting an eye, then personally negotiated a peace settlement between the barbarian tribal chieftains and the most highly ranked surviving officers representing the city of Thurii. He ensured the Greeks' right to gather the dead and burn them on pyres.

At dusk he reboarded the *Boubaris* and ordered them to point the bow in a southward direction, towards Messana, where Dionysius awaited him, and, perhaps, the most difficult encounter of his life.

*

Dionysius knew everything. He received his brother at his headquarters in Messana, his back turned to him.

'I know what you're thinking . . .' began Leptines, 'but you should have been there; you didn't see the carnage, those heaps of cadavers mangled and hacked to pieces, the blood staining the land and the sea . . .'

'I've never seen massacres?' roared Dionysius, turning all at once. 'I've seen nothing but massacres all my life! And so have you, by Zeus! You can't tell me this is the first time you've seen blood.'

'But they were Greeks, damn it! Greeks slaughtered by barbarians who were doing it for us! You had spoken of an agreement with the Lucanians, of strategic support, skirmishing, you never said you'd give them free reign in exterminating an entire city!'

'That's enough!' shouted Dionysius, even louder. 'Enough, I say! You have committed a serious act of rebellion. You signed a peace settlement which goes against my political design and against my military strategy. You have dissipated an enormous sum of money that was to serve for operations of war. Do you realize what this means? High treason, insubordination, collusion with the enemy on the field of battle!'

Leptines dropped his head, crushed by the harsh reaction of his brother as though he hadn't expected it. When he raised his eyes and saw the bloodshot eyes before him, the face purple with rage, the veins in his neck swelling as he yelled out still more accusations and insults, he felt that he had a stranger in front of him, a cruel, inhuman being.

He waited until his brother had finished and, as he was still panting with the rage of his unchecked ire, Leptines replied: 'I know, and I am ready to pay the consequences. But there's one thing I must tell you first: when I saw all that horror, I suddenly realized what a Greek city is; I had nearly forgotten. I'm not talking about Syracuse or Selinus or Catane, I'm not talking about friends or enemies. I'm talking about any city whose people descend from a fistful of wretches forced years ago to cross the sea in search of a little fortune. They arrived here with nothing more than their lives and their hopes. Not to build empires; all they desired was the semblance of their original homeland: a little spot with a harbour for trade, a hill for their gods, fields for wheat and for olives. For every one of the cities that found a future, many others were never born. For every group that managed to find a place to land, many more finished up on the bottom of the sea, in the jaws of fish. It's true, we've fought each other many times in useless wars over stupid rivalries, but I will never again permit savages to annihilate a Greek city through any fault of my own. I did what I did because I believed I was right.'

Dionysius turned his back to him again and said: 'As of this moment, you are dismissed from command of the fleet and are under arrest. You will be taken to Syracuse and held under custody in your quarters at the Ortygia barracks, pending my definitive decision. And now free me of your presence. I never want to see you again.'

Leptines left without saying a word. As soon as he crossed the threshold he found two guards who took him into custody and escorted him directly to the port.

He asked for a last look at the *Boubaris* and his wish was allowed. He left her, passing a callused hand over the shiny railing of the stem from which he had led so many battles; a final caress for a friend.

Those who were close to him could see the tears in his eyes.

*

Dionysius made Iolaus commander of the fleet and proceeded with operations as if nothing had happened. He had mustered an impressive army: twenty thousand foot soldiers, three thousand five hundred horses and fifty brand new warships, which were added to the others already at anchor in the port of Messana. He set sail as soon as the wind was favourable and landed his troops on the Ionian coast of Italy, a little north of Rhegium. He began to march north.

In the meantime, the Italian League had united all her federal forces and put them under the command of Heloris, the old aristocrat who had once been Dionysius's adoptive father and was now his most relentless adversary. They marched for five consecutive days until they reached the banks of a little river called the Eleporus, which flowed between bare, sun-scorched hills. The army stopped here, but Heloris decided to push forward with his advance guard, made up mostly of Knights anxious to come into contact with the enemy and perhaps to succeed at some surprise attack. In doing so, they distanced themselves nearly two stadia from the bulk of the League forces.

Dionysius's native scouts had already been posted everywhere, on foot and horseback, hidden amidst the brushwood and the groves of pine and holm oak, so that the command was immediately informed of the situation.

Dionysius did not wait an instant, and personally guided the attack with selected troops in a series of rapid waves: first the archers, then the assault troops and last, the heavy line infantry. Heloris and his men were overrun and slain before their requests for help even got back to the army that was camped on the other side of the river.

The commanders of the various divisions of the federal forces decide to engage in battle nonetheless, but they were attacking without their generals and were demoralized by the loss of their vanguard contingent, and they were soon overwhelmed. A good number of them, about half of the army, managed to withdraw in closed ranks and reach the top of a hill overlooking the narrow Eleporus river.

Dionysius surrounded the hill, preventing any access to the river. He would not need to do anything but wait: the baking sun and the absolute lack of water would do the rest. Iolaus landed before dusk, had a horse brought and reached the ground army command before the sun set behind the mountains. He beheld the battlefield strewn with dead bodies and the arid hill on which the survivors of the Italian League had dug themselves in. He felt as if time had stopped. What he found before him was the same scene that he had already seen at Leptines's side just a few days before at Laos.

Dionysius noticed how shaken he was by the sight and said: 'You seem upset. It's certainly not the first time you've seen a battlefield.'

'No, it isn't,' agreed Iolaus. 'It's that I've already seen this very scene.'

'I know,' replied Dionysius.

'I imagine you must have already made your decision.'

'That's right.'

One of the guards entered just then. '*Hegemon*,' he said, 'the Italians want to negotiate. They are outside.'

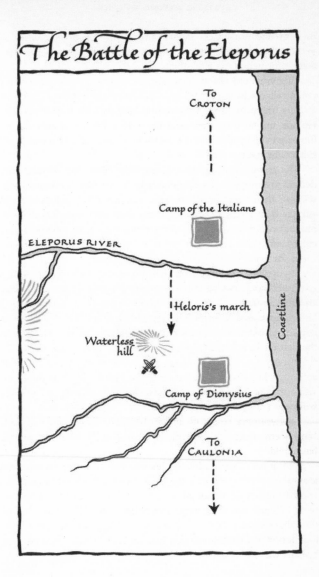

The Battle of the Eleporus

To Croton

Camp of the Italians

ELEPORUS RIVER

Heloris's march

Waterless hill

Coastline

Camp of Dionysius

To Caulonia

'Have them come in.'

Four Crotonian officers entered the tent and approached Dionysius, who received them on his feet, a sign that their meeting would be short.

'Speak,' he said.

The oldest of them, a man of about sixty with a deep scar on his face, began to speak. 'We are here to negotiate an agreement. There are ten thousand of us. We are well armed and we stand in an advantageous position. We can still . . .'

Dionysius raised his hand to interrupt. 'My point of view,' he said, 'is very simple. You have no way off this dry, barren hill and as soon as the sun rises, the heat will become unbearable. You have neither food nor water. And so it doesn't seem to me that you have a choice. All I can accept from you is an unconditional surrender.'

'Is that your last word?' asked the officer.

'It is,' replied Dionysius.

The officer nodded solemnly then gestured to his comrades and left the tent.

Iolaus bowed his head in silence.

'Go to sleep,' said Dionysius. 'It's going to be a long day tomorrow.'

*

The sun rose over a desolate landscape, illuminating the land all around the Eleporus, still cluttered with corpses. Swarms of green flies buzzed over the death-stiffened bodies, and the monotonous song of the crickets had already given way to the harsh screeching of the cicadas.

There was not a breath of wind and the rocks on the river bed were soon red hot, making the air quiver and creating the illusion of shiny pools of water where there was naught but sand and stones. There was not a single tree to cast a bit of shade on top of the hill, not a shelter where one could seek a little relief from the merciless blaze of the sun.

The shrieks of crows could be heard in the midday heat; they had come to feast on that field of death. A little further over, big black-and-white-winged vultures with long featherless necks were swooping down from the tree branches.

Below, under the camp pavilion, Dionysius sat reading the reports of his informers, and waited. A servant fanned him with a flabellum and poured water into his cup and into a basin where he could wet his wrists every now and then.

Iolaus sat just a short distance away under the shade of a lentisc.

Much of the day went by thus, without anything happening. Then, towards mid-afternoon, they could see something going on at the top of the hill. The echoes of voices, seemingly raised in anger, reached them, and then a group of unarmed men began to wend their way to the valley, walking towards the pavilion. They were the same men that Dionysius had met the day before and they had come to offer the unconditional surrender of their troops.

'I'm glad you have come to the right decision,' replied Dionysius.

'We beseech your clemency,' began the man with the scar on his cheek. 'Today fortune is on your side, but one day you could find yourself in our condition and . . .'

Dionysius interrupted him with a characteristic wave of his hand. 'Tell your men that they are free to return to their homes without paying any ransom. There will be no retaliation on my part. All I ask is that a peace treaty be drawn up between us and signed by the authorities of the Italian League.'

The man looked at him in amazement, incapable of believing what was being said.

'Can you guarantee that the League will sign?'

'I can guarantee it,' replied the officer.

'Then go. Return to your cities and never raise your arms against me again.'

The officer did not know how to answer. He mutely searched the gaze of the man before him to find an explanation for behaviour that contrasted so completely with anything he'd ever heard about the tyrant.

'Go,' repeated Dionysius. 'I will gather up your dead.' And he took his leave.

They passed, armed, through the ranks of Syracusan soldiers who held their spears lowered as a sign of respect.

Ten days later the Thurians sent the signed treaty to Dionysius, with a golden crown.

Iolaus picked it up. 'A sign of gratitude. It happens rarely. Clemency is the greatest merit of a leader, especially when he has won, and this gift has been given in recognition.' Dionysius did not answer; he seemed absorbed in reading the document that the League had sent him. Iolaus waited until he had finished, then spoke again. 'Can't you really understand Leptines? You've done the same thing he did; I'm sure you must understand. If the sight of that massacre moved you to mercy, why can't you pardon your brother?'

Dionysius placed the roll with the treaty on the table and replied: 'My gesture has ensured the neutrality of the League, if not her friendship. It has freed my hands to take Rhegium; the city is now completely isolated.'

Iolaus could not hide his disappointment.

'What did you think?' asked Dionysius. 'That I would give up my plan for sentimental reasons? Is it possible that you know me so little?'

'Few people know you better than me, but it's difficult to resign myself to the fact that what I have always loved in you no longer exists.'

'Time changes everyone,' replied Dionysius in a monotone. 'You could have refused this position. Instead you accepted and you have taken Leptines's place.'

'It's true. I'm the supreme commander of the fleet but there is a reason . . .'

'Certainly. You want power, and you know you can have it only if I stay in power. If I fall, all of you will follow me into ruin. You might as well support me then, and not waste too much time on useless nostalgia.'

'There is some truth in what you say,' replied Iolaus. 'And yet that is not the explanation. You forget that I am always capable of finding within myself a good reason for living, reasons that I have learned from my teachers and never disavowed.'

Dionysius regarded him with an enquiring expression.

'The reason why I accepted his position,' continued Iolaus, 'is not because you asked me. It's because Leptines asked me.'

He did not wait for an answer. He left the tent and rode his horse down to the sea, where the *Boubaris* awaited him, ready to set sail.

28

PHILISTUS ENTERED THE east wing of the barracks and approached the door to Leptines's apartments, guarded by two Arcadian mercenaries. 'Open it,' he ordered.

'No one can enter: orders of the supreme commander.'

'I have command of Ortygia when he is absent and I assume complete responsibility for my actions. Open the door or I'll call the officer on duty.'

The two warriors gave each other a look, then one of them drew the bolt and opened the door, allowing him to enter.

Leptines was lying on a cot with his back against the wall, his arms crossed and his gaze fixed on the wall opposite. He said nothing, nor did he turn. His eyes were red, his lips dry, his beard and hair unkempt.

'You can't go on like this. Just look at you, you're a mess.'

Leptines did not answer.

'I know what you're thinking, and I feel no better than you do, but letting yourself go like this doesn't serve any purpose. You must react! The Company has met and they are indignant over the way your brother has treated you, and I'd say they're ready to . . .'

Leptines started. He turned slowly towards Philistus and said: 'You shouldn't have. There was no reason for you to do so. I disobeyed orders and I'm suffering the consequences.'

'I don't agree. You were right, and I feel the same way you do. For years and years we stuck by him in his plans for an entirely Greek Sicily. We tolerated execrable operations because we envisioned a future of peace and prosperity, but now things are totally out of hand. He is taking openly hostile action against the Italian Greeks and I say no, this is no longer tolerable. I refused to negotiate the alliance with the Lucanians.'

'And why didn't you tell me?' asked Leptines.

Philistus took a stool and went to sit next to the cot. 'Because he didn't let me. Maybe he thought I would convince you to see things my way, and he didn't want that to happen. He had the negotiations carried out by men who never say anything but yes to him, and he never told you the whole truth. It was all done by the time you got there; you found a horde of barbarians massacring Greeks and you reacted as any civil person would have done. Leptines, for what it's worth, you can still count on all my esteem and my friendship. And not only mine . . .'

He lowered his voice and continued. 'The people are tired of these continuous wars, of seeing foreign mercenaries growing rich beyond measure and obtaining privileges that are not even granted to citizens. He continues to demand sacrifices in the name of a radiant future that keeps getting further away rather than closer. And with every passing day he becomes more gloomy, suspicious and intractable. He has an heir but he barely looks at the boy, even when he is at home. He says the child trembles as soon as he sees him, that he's a little coward . . . do you see what he's become?'

Leptines sighed. 'I thought I'd bring the lad with me to the countryside, teach him to raise bees and chickens. I wanted to take him out fishing, but my brother is too jealous of him, he doesn't want his son influenced by anyone but the tutors he has chosen. The problem is they're brainless and heartless. They're turning him into a wretch who will be afraid of his own shadow . . .'

Philistus took an apple from his pocket and put it on the table at Leptines's bedside. 'Eat this. Looks like they've been starving you here.'

Leptines nodded and bit into the fruit. 'What is he doing now?' he asked between one mouthful and another.

'He has laid siege to Rhegium, but the city won't give in.

Iolaus is returning with part of the fleet, but he is remaining. That's what I've been told.'

'Iolaus is a good soldier.'

'Yes, he is. And it seems that Dionysius wants him in charge of our participation in the Olympics next spring.'

'That seems like a good idea.'

'Terrible. Not because of Iolaus. Because of the way our participation is being organized. We'll make a laughing stock of ourselves. The Olympics are a pan-Hellenic celebration, but they are being held just as the Persians are laying claim to the Greek cities of Asia. And then we step in with our alliance with the barbarians against the Greeks. Does that seem wise to you?'

Leptines didn't know what to answer.

'I had a reserved meeting with the leaders of the Company, as I was saying,' continued Philistus. 'They are looking for a radical change. They are tired of this situation of perennial uncertainty, of the atmosphere that has taken root in the city. They are fed up with never being allowed an exchange of ideas with the person in command. Anyone who expresses a point of view which is different from his is immediately branded an enemy, a suspect to be followed, watched, even imprisoned. Many of them are much more favourable towards you. What you did at Laos is seen as a sign of the humanity that your brother has lost.'

Leptines tossed the apple core and turned away. 'I won't betray him, if that's what you're trying to suggest.'

Philistus bowed his head. 'Do you see me as a traitor?'

'You are a politician, a man of letters, a philosopher. It's in your nature to examine all the options. I'm a soldier: I may not agree, I may be undisciplined, but my loyalty is never in question.'

'But what we're talking about here is loyalty towards your people. Doesn't that count for you? Dionysius's power is justified only if the people will be repaid in the end for their sacrifices, for all the tears and blood they have shed.'

Leptines didn't answer.

Philistus walked towards the door, but before leaving, he turned. 'There's a person who wants to see you.'

'It's not as if I can move from here.'

'She would come to you.'

'When?' asked Leptines, getting to his feet, visibly agitated.

'Tonight, at the second change of the guard. You can trust the two men I'll have posted outside. Remember . . . that I still love him as you do. Nothing has changed as far as I am concerned. I would still be ready to give my life for him if I had to. Farewell, my friend. Reflect on what I've said.'

*

Shuffled steps could be heard outside, low voices, then the sound of the bolt sliding and the door opened.

A woman appeared, her head and face covered by a veil.

Leptines took a lantern from the wall and held it close to her face. 'Aristomache . . .' he murmured as if he could not believe his eyes. 'It's you.'

The woman removed the veil and revealed her pale skin, huge black eyes, perfect nose.

'Why have you come? It's too dangerous . . .'

'I can't think of anything but you, here, alone, closed up like a thief. You who have risked your life so many times, suffered so many wounds, you who have always been at his side . . .'

'He's my brother and my supreme commander.'

'He is unworthy of you. He has become cruel and insensitive. All he cares about is staying in power.' Leptines turned towards the wall as if he didn't want to hear those words. 'Long ago, you told me you loved me . . .' whispered Aristomache.

'We were children.'

'I was telling the truth, as you were. I've never forgotten, and neither have you.'

'You are my brother's wife.'

'And so you scorn me?'

'No, you're wrong. I respect you . . . I worship you as if you were a divinity, as if . . .'

'I'm nothing but a miserable wretch. I accepted an absurd proposal of marriage because my family obligated me; power was the only issue, even then. I have had to share my husband's bed with another. No free woman, even the most unfortunate, has ever had to submit to such humiliation. Leptines, I've always felt your eyes on me. Whenever you were close, but even when you were far away. The eyes of a good man, a courageous man, who would have loved and respected me.'

'It just wasn't possible, Aristomache. Life has decided otherwise and we must accept this, resign ourselves.'

'But I love you, Leptines! I have always loved you, since the first time I saw you with your tousled hair and skinned knees, punching it out with the boys from Ortygia. You've been my hero since then. I dreamt of you for my future, Leptines. I would have wanted a child from you, a boy, who looked like you, who had your light in his eyes . . .'

'Say no more,' said Leptines. 'I beg of you. You know it's not possible.'

Aristomache fell silent for a few moments as if she didn't know quite how to continue, or didn't have the courage to speak.

'What is it?' prompted Leptines.

'There is a way. I know I seem crazy, but . . . have you talked to Philistus?'

Leptines considered her with a perplexed expression. 'He started to say something but I didn't let him finish. I have the impression that you listened to him all the way through. What is it then?'

'Many people in Syracuse would like to see you take power. And for me, it would be the only hope of . . . can't you see what I'm trying to say?'

'I understand too well,' replied Leptines. 'And I do not approve of anything you are thinking, even though I do love you. Believe me, it would be madness. It would end up a bloodbath, a disaster. I'm not the right person for this sort of thing. I would never join a plot against my brother. Do you know why? Because such a plot always aims at the physical elimination of the enemy. Can you see me murdering my brother?'

'No, that's not true. You would save his life and turn him into a human being again.'

'You're wrong. An uprising can easily get out of hand; we've seen it happen time and time again. Just the thought of betraying him disgusts me. But there's one thing you can be sure of: my love, my devotion, my respect. I would give anything to have you, Aristomache, but not that, I can't do that. Go now ... go before someone discovers you're here.'

He took her arm gently to lead her out, but she turned towards him and threw her arms around him, sobbing.

At that same moment, they heard the sound of the bolt being pulled and the figure of a man dressed in full armour appeared at the doorway: Dionysius!

'She has done nothing,' said Leptines immediately. 'Do not hurt her.'

Dionysius shot him an enraged look but did not speak a word. The light of the lantern cut his face in two, carving out his features and deepening the creases on his forehead. He gestured to one of the guards, who took Aristomache by the arm and led her away. With another gesture, the door was shut again.

Leptines stormed the door with his fists, shouting: 'Stop! Listen! Listen to me, don't go!'

There was no answer but the pounding of the hobnailed boots of the mercenaries along the corridor.

The following day, the two guards that had let Aristomache pass were executed in the barracks courtyard, in the presence of the entire garrison. Leptines was seized and taken to the harbour, where he was put aboard a trireme.

The commander of the ship was a member of the Company, an officer named Archelaus who Leptines knew well.

'Where are you taking me?' he asked.

'I don't know,' he replied. 'Our destination will be communicated by one of my men when we are in the open sea. But I won't learn his identity until then. I'm sorry, commander.'

The ship put out to sea, headed east.

That same day, Philistus received a visit from Dionysius.

'Betrayed by my brother and my best friend, the man to whom I had entrusted my family and given the keys to my fortress.'

'Betrayed by yourself, Dionysius. By your own unbridled ambition, by your recklessness, by your selfishness. How many people have died for you, seeking to follow you on your mad endeavours? No, I have not betrayed you, and Leptines is only the first of your victims. He loves you and has always been true to you. And as for Aristomache, there is nothing between them but an innocent childhood love. Leptines is an upright man; he has never so much as touched her. And now, who knows where you've sent him to. Tell me: one of your henchmen is on that ship, isn't he? With the order to murder him and throw him into the sea when they are far enough out, so that his body will never drift to shore and be recognized. Isn't that true?'

Dionysius did not answer.

'If it is true, you will have committed the most heinous of crimes. Have that ship followed, now, and stop this atrocity, if you're still in time. As for me, I'm still trying to save you from yourself, from the destructive fury that possesses you like a demon. I could never have hurt you. It's true Dionysius, I promised to follow you all the way to Hades, but I imagined glorious exploits, not this incessant massacre, this bloody, unending sequence of horrors.'

'Shut up,' said Dionysius. 'I don't want to listen to you any more.'

'You will listen to me! Haven't you wondered why your best friend no longer wants to follow you in your suicidal folly? Have me killed as well, if that's what you've decided. I don't care. But who will you be able to trust? Iolaus remains, but he's wavering as well. The core of the problem is that you've formed a void around you. You can't count on anyone any more, there won't be a single person you can trust.

'This is just what I had wanted to save you from, because I know that solitude is the worst of punishments. I don't know what destiny you've reserved for me, although I will surely soon find out. But our roads separated long ago, Dionysius, since the time I refused to negotiate an alliance with barbarian populations against Greek cities. Now, unhappily, our quarrel has peaked. You have troops, weapons, power . . . I have only words, and not even those any longer, since I have nothing left to say to you. The outcome of such an unequal struggle is no contest, I'm afraid. Let me just ask one thing of you: do not seek out other culprits, because there are none. Punish me. There is no one else to punish.'

'I will,' replied Dionysius. 'Farewell.'

Instead, many Syracusans – including many members of the Company – were hunted down, interrogated, imprisoned. Some, it was said, were put to death in secret. But this time there was no violent response. Apparently no reaction. Some assumed that the Company had become afraid of Dionysius, but those who knew the association well knew that they would not forgo revenge. It was just a matter of time.

Philistus, on the other hand, realized that he was being followed, but nothing more. Until one evening a messenger from the Ortygia fortress came and told him to pack his things.

The very next day he was put aboard a merchant ship laden with wine and oil, commanded by the ship's owner, a wholesale dealer named Sosibus.

Their voyage lasted nearly a month, and ended in a remote locality at the extreme tip of the Adriatic Gulf, within a vast lagoon, at the city which gave the gulf its name. Adria was a settlement of Venetics to which a Greek colony had been added over the course of the years, and later an Etruscan colony as well. It was a humid, sultry place, surrounded by swamps and infested by mosquitoes even by day. Dionysius had installed a trading colony there, which exchanged agricultural and metallurgic products with amber and war horses.

Philistus settled in a little house not far from the sea, in the Syracusan quarter. There were no soldiers, but the place was crawling with spies and informers, and he knew that his every move would be kept under strict surveillance.

At first life was terribly hard for Philistus, because Adria was made up mostly of wood and straw huts and had none of the characteristics that made a Greek city so appealing. There was no theatre, not a single library, there were no schools nor porticoes, no fountains or monuments of any kind. Even the sanctuaries were shabby and barren, looking much like the other huts. The ground was so wet and soft that it could not support the weight of stone buildings.

The coming of winter made it even worse; a thick fog rose from the surrounding swamps and the lagoon and swallowed up everything. The damp penetrated to the very bone, causing fierce pain in his joints.

The desolation of the place, the uncertainty of the future and the total lack of any news about Leptines's fate plunged Philistus into a state of profound consternation. He paced the seashore for long hours, listening to the melancholy cry of the gulls, and he spent sleepless nights racking his brains for a way out of the solitude and misery he found himself in. He sometimes thought of begging for Dionysius's forgiveness, pleading with him to call him back from this abhorrent place at the ends of the earth, but then he would find the strength to grit his teeth and hold out. He knew that a man of learning must not bend to power, he knew that both independence and dignity could only be found in the strength of his own mind.

The coldest part of winter slowly passed and with the coming of spring he began to find some pleasant aspects in the land he inhabited. He began to wander inland and found no one hindering him, and he realized that perhaps Dionysius had not locked him in a true prison. He had imposed this bitter exile upon him, but he had left him a certain liberty of movement.

It was a land very different from Sicily, low and flat, rich with forests and with water. The lagoon was visited by a great number of vessels, coming mainly from the east, but also from the west. He saw the huge river which the inhabitants called Padus; according to the Greeks, it was the mythical Eridanus.

As time passed, some news began to trickle through; friends

from the Company had not forgotten him and sent him word when they could, always by mouth.

He thus learned that Leptines had not been murdered, but was confined to a little island on the Illyrian coast called Lissos, where Dionysius had established another colony.

Early the following summer, Sosibus, the merchant who had brought him into exile, returned to Adria, bringing more news. 'Our participation in the Olympics was a total failure. The Syracusan pavilion was too luxurious, too showy. Gilded stakes, purple curtains, Egyptian linen ropes; the Greek sensibility was greatly offended.'

Philistus had him sit down, and said: 'Wasn't there anyone who could advise him? The metropolitan Greeks are so presumptuous – they think they're like gods. The Athenians are the worst of all! They think of beauty as the essence of simplicity; has no one read Thucydides, by Zeus? Exaggerations of any sort are seen as manifestations of barbarism.'

'That's not all,' continues Sosibus. 'The literary contest went no better. I believe that Dionysius decided to participate in order to create an image of refinement and sensitivity. One of the very best actors recited his work, but it was met by catcalls and a chorus of laughter, because, they say, of the poor quality of his poems.'

Philistus couldn't help but feel gratified at this news. 'Had I been there,' he said, 'that never would have happened. I would have advised him not to participate, or to have the verses written for him by a fine poet. I imagine that he must be surrounded now by sycophants who certainly praised the quality of his poetry, and he obviously fell for it.'

'Something like that,' admitted his guest.

'What about the sports competitions?'

Sosibus snorted. 'A disaster! Our two quadrigas collided during the chariot race, creating a terrible entanglement; two charioteers lost their lives and others were badly maimed. But that's not all: a great Athenian orator, Lysias, made a public speech inciting the Greeks to overturn the tyrant of Syracuse who had allied with the barbarians to annihilate the Greek cities of Italy and was still besieging Rhegium, openly violating the sacred truce that imposed peace among the Greeks for the entire duration of the games. The pavilion was attacked by the mob who wanted to drive the Syracusans from the Olympic grounds. But now,' he continued, 'the worst news of all: Iolaus, who was leading the return expedition, ran into a storm in the Gulf of Taras and went down with his ship.'

'He's . . . dead?' asked Philistus.

Sosibus nodded. Philistus wept: he had lost the last of his friends. The last of those who had seen the golden years of Dionysius's ascent to power. They had always remained faithful to him, each one of them, to the very end.

'When are you leaving again?' Philistus finally asked the merchant.

'In three days' time, as soon as I've finished loading.'

'Could you get a message to Leptines for me? Is he still on Lissos?'

Sosibus warded off his request. 'It's too dangerous. But if I should meet up with someone going that way, I'll let him know that you're alive and well. What do you say?'

Philistus thanked him. 'I appreciate it greatly. We are good friends and I know he'd be pleased to have news of me.'

They said their farewells three days later, at the harbour. Sosibus already had one foot on the gangplank when he turned around. 'I forgot the most interesting bit,' he said, 'the Plato story.'

'Plato?' repeated Philistus, widening his eyes. 'Are you talking about the great philosopher?'

'Yes, him all right. He was visiting Italy this spring and he made a stop in Sicily and at Syracuse. He received many invitations, as you can imagine, from all the most prestigious circles in the city, and from some members of the Company as well. Well, he set out by saying that our luxury was deplorable: our habit of eating three times a day, of sleeping with our wives every night, of having sumptuous houses. Not happy with that, he started going on about the vices, corruption and depravation of social institutions under tyranny. He said that, if it were impossible to remove this curse, the only alternative was for a philosopher to educate the successor of the tyrant, in order to make a philosopher – and hence a worthy ruler – out of him. Can you believe it? He was offering himself as a tutor for young Dionysius!'

'That took courage,' commented Philistus.

'Courage! Pure folly, I'd say.'

'But the two of them – Dionysius and Plato, that is – did they ever meet face to face?'

'Not in your dreams. When he'd been told about all those nice proposals, Dionysius convinced the captain of the ship that was taking Plato back to Greece to sell him to the pirates.'

'By Heracles!' gasped Philistus. 'To the pirates?'

'That's right. Plato's disciples had to pay a pretty ransom for him at a market in Aegina before he ended up who knows where.'

Philistus couldn't help but laugh as he remembered Dionysius's line: 'Philosophers! I avoid them like dog shit on the street.'

Sosibus departed and Philistus returned to writing his history of Sicily, which was particularly difficult now, due to the scarcity of information.

During the following year, he was engaged by the people of Adria, among whom he enjoyed great esteem, to take on a grand project: the opening of a canal which would connect the northern-most arm of the Padus with their lagoon, in order to make the city an even greater and richer trade and transit centre. And so Philistus set to work.

29

PHILISTUS SPENT FIVE more years in Adria, under conditions which were unusual from many points of view. His exile allowed him almost complete liberty. The only thing that was forbidden to him was returning to Syracuse. He accepted this limitation – even though it was anything but painless – when he realized that, in reality, Dionysius had sent him there with a mission, albeit non-declared: to lead the Syracusan colony that was settling there.

Work proceeded on the grand canal that connected the northern arm of the Padus with the lagoon of Adria, and Philistus often supervised its progress personally, staying at the work yards for days, and sometimes months. He was slim and tanned, and even seemed younger. When the huge project was finished and the gates were raised, allowing the water to flow through the canal, it was a thrilling spectacle.

The canal harnessed the waters of the great river and created a new route inland, allowing contact with vast lands, rich with every kind of natural resource: livestock, skins, wheat, timber, as well as wine, oil and metallurgical products from Etruria. A project for peace and, finally, prosperity. The people of Adria were so grateful to its designer that they dedicated an inscription to him in the local sanctuary, and called the new canal the 'Philistina Channel'. Philistus was moved, and thought that perhaps that canal would have a greater chance of perpetrating his fame than his historical writings, which he continued to work on with great assiduity.

Adria was not the only Syracusan settlement in the area. Another colony was founded on an elbow-shaped promontory on the western coast and was called Ancona. In the meantime, the Celts, who had burned down Rome eight years earlier, had definitively settled into the territory of the Umbrians, not far from the new colony on the promontory, which became the base for recruiting them as mercenaries in Dionysius's service.

One spring day a warship, a trireme named *Arethusa*, docked at Adria. Philistus had seen her many a time at anchor at the Laccius dockyard; she was mainly used now for diplomatic missions. A visitor was soon announced, and who should Philistus find before him but Aksal, Dionysius's Celtic bodyguard! A few white hairs had appeared, and he was quite a bit heavier, but all the more imposing for it.

'Aksal!' he exclaimed. 'I never thought I'd see you here. What brings you to this place at the end of the earth?'

'Boss want my brothers as mercenaries and say you come with me to make contract.'

'Actually, I've received no message or instructions from him about this, and I think it's better that I stay here. I'm sure you can handle it well on your own. Your Greek hasn't got much better, but I imagine you speak your own language quite well.'

Aksal insisted. 'Boss say you don't want to come, I take you with me anyway,' and he stretched out two hands as big as bear's paws.

'Good boy, all right,' Philistus reassured him. 'I'll come. But give me the time to prepare . . .'

'Tomorrow we leave.'

'I understand. But I have to find someone who will take care of my books, my personal things . . .'

'You take all,' said Aksal.

Philistus's heart skipped a beat. 'All? What do you mean? Explain yourself, you beast.'

'All your things. You no return again to this hole.'

'No? And where are you taking me then?'

'Aksal no say.'

'I understand,' replied Philistus, resigned. But he didn't dare imagine the final destination of that voyage. He thought that

Ancona would be a good step forward; at least she was said to be a city in the true sense of the word.

They reached Ancona after six days of navigation. The first two, along the coast of the lagoon, were quite relaxing, while the last four were anything but tranquil, due to a westerly wind that tended to push them away from the shore and made the *Arethusa*, no longer so young, drift leeway in a worrisome way. Aksal was often agitated, despite his long sailing experience, and when a big billow hit he would let out a guttural yell, perhaps to relieve some tension.

Ancona was in fact a true city, from every point of view. It had a beautiful harbour, sheltered from Boreas, with havens for the transports and warships, and a striking acropolis on top of the mountain that overlooked the gulf. The magnificent temple that Dionysius had had built there could be seen from a great distance. Below it was the agora, with porticoes that skirted the harbour, which was visited by a great number of vessels. The multicoloured market attracted Greeks from the colonies and the metropolises, Picenians from the interior with their picturesque embroidered wool garments, Umbrians, Etruscans and Celts, men and women in great numbers. Philistus was struck by the beauty of the Celtic women: they were tall, with slim legs and supple breasts and blonde, waist-long braids. Some carried babies in their arms and shopped at the market stalls using Syracusan coins. The men were astonishing: very tall and muscular, they were bare-chested except for the *torques* at their necks. The wool trousers they wore were narrow at the ankle and their long swords hung from belts of wool or embossed metal plates.

The recruitment point was inside the harbour; there were many Greek mediators who spoke Celtic, but above all a great number of Celts who spoke a Greek not much different from Aksal's. Philistus felt reborn: he was finally breathing the air of a *polis*, admittedly a bit cross-bred.

Before seven days were over he had signed twenty or so work engagements and made advance payment, and the *Arethusa* had taken to the seas again.

Philistus was impressed by the Syracusan presence so far from Sicily. Dionysius must have realized that, since the markets of the eastern sea were in the hands of the Carthaginians, the Adriatic was an area where he could expand his trade interests and establish colonies.

Philistus learned more interesting news from the ship's commander. The opening of new markets and the stability of recent years had brought great prosperity to all of Dionysius's dominions. His wives had given birth to more sons and daughters. The last, a little girl born of Doris, had been given the name Arete by Dionysius's express desire.

When he heard that name, Philistus thought that the tyrant must still have some feelings deep down after all. He thought of poor Aristomache, forced to give him children although she loved another man, but then he consoled himself by the thought that, in the end, time heals many wounds and allows us to bear the misfortunes and difficulties of life with greater courage.

One day, Philistus realized that the ship was turning east, and he imagined that his final destination would be at some lonely outpost among the infinite islands and inlets of the Illyrian coast, where Syracuse was settling new colonies. Then, suddenly, like a stroke of lightning, he thought: Lissos! Perhaps they were going to Lissos!

They landed there, not without difficulty, the evening of the third day after setting sail from Ancona. Shortly thereafter, under Aksal's amused gaze, Philistus met up with an old, dear friend, once mourned for dead. 'Leptines!' he shouted as soon as he saw him.

'Philistus!'

They embraced, tears in their eyes.

'You bastard!' said Philistus. 'You're still in one piece! What a joy to see you, by Zeus! What a joy!'

'I can't believe it's you, you old wisecracker!' exclaimed Leptines with the hint of a quiver in his voice. 'Look at you, you're as good looking as a whore from Ephesus! The climate of the Adriatic has done you well! Where did you end up?'

'In Adria, to be precise.'

'Adria . . . where's that?'

Philistus pointed a finger north. 'At the very end of the gulf. The mosquitoes ate me alive at first, but then they left me in peace, or maybe I just got used to them. How long has it been, by the gods! How long . . .'

They walked arm in arm in the golden light of sunset down a lovely paved road that led to the little city until they reached Leptines's house. It was a grey stone building with an inner courtyard surrounded on three sides by a colonnaded portico. A well decorated with floral motifs stood at the centre.

'You've set yourself up well here,' commented Philistus.

'I can't complain.'

'So your brother hasn't treated you too badly?'

'No,' replied Leptines somewhat dryly. 'What about you? How's it been for you?'

'I could move around. I even had governmental responsibilities, in a way. I guess you could say I was living in a state of conditional freedom. Did you notice where Aksal went?'

'No, I can't say I did.'

Philistus turned. 'He was right behind me . . . You know, your brother put me in charge of recruiting Celts on the Ancona market. Or at least that's what Aksal told me. I haven't heard a word from him directly. Have you?'

'No, neither have I.'

'Aksal ordered me to pack up all my things because I won't be returning to Adria. Maybe they'll let me stay here. I quite like the place. The climate looks good, and there are no mosquitoes. We could play a game of knuckle bones every once in a while, go fishing together. You know, now that I'm not in politics any longer, I can't say I miss it. A world of madmen . . . What about you?'

'Me?' replied Leptines. 'I don't know . . .' his voice trailed off.

'Right,' commented Philistus, 'you're a combat animal, aren't you? You must feel like the *Boubaris* in a washbasin.'

'More or less,' admitted Leptines. 'You're my guest,' he said to change the subject. 'I have fish for dinner. Is that all right?'

'Is that all right? I'd eat a crust of dry bread to stay in the company of my old friend!'

They ate together in the internal courtyard, reclining on couches with dining tables and slaves serving them. They lingered until late that night, drinking wine and remembering old times. Philistus realized that Leptines knew nothing of what had happened in Syracuse and in the metropolises over all the years. He had been kept in a kind of isolation. 'Has your brother ever written to you?' he asked.

Leptines shook his head.

'Sent word by messenger?'

'No.'

'I see. Do you think he'll let me stay here?'

'I have no idea. I hope so. It would make me very happy.'

When they took leave of each other, Philistus remained to watch the full moon illuminating the roadstead and the few ships at anchor there. A marvellous sight. There was a little bit of Greece here as well. A temple had been built, a square, a harbour; the language, customs and religion of the Hellenes were spreading inland.

The shrieks of the gulls woke him early the next morning, and he heard a bit of an uproar at the main door. He went to see what was happening and found Aksal there. 'What's wrong?'

'We leave now,' replied the Celt.

'We who?'

'We: Aksal, you and commander Leptines.'

'By Zeus, you don't mean that . . . Where are we going?'

'To Syracuse. Ship go with tide. Hurry.'

Philistus ran up the stairs, panting and burst into Leptines's room. 'We're leaving!' he shouted.

'What are you saying?'

'Aksal has just told me: we're going home, my friend, we're going back home!'

Leptines was stunned by those words; he didn't know what to say. He paced back and forth across the room, looked out the window.

'You have to hurry,' Philistus insisted. 'Aksal wants to take advantage of the tide.'

'Aksal doesn't understand a thing. The harbour is so deep that we don't have to consider the tides. We have all the time we want.'

'Hey, are you happy or not? You look so glum . . .'

'Oh yes, sure, I'm happy. But I'm already thinking about when I'll have to face up to him.'

*

There was no one waiting for them on the wharf and no one seemed to recognize them when they disembarked the *Arethusa*, as if they were ghosts. They stared in wonder at all the changes they could see: buildings, people. Everything looked new and different, and they felt somehow like strangers. Leptines suddenly lifted his eyes towards the repair docks and he couldn't hold back his tears.

'What's wrong?' asked Philistus, who hadn't noticed anything.

'Nothing,' replied Leptines, and started walking off, but Philistus took a look in that direction and saw that the *Boubaris* was out of commission. Her huge skeleton, still bearing the unmistakeable figurehead, seemed a sun-bleached whale carcass.

They stumbled on behind Aksal, and the animated buzz of the port in the evening hour became a distant hum, like that of a beehive.

Ortygia.

Dionysius's austere fortress had remained the same, as had the sullen faces of his mercenaries. They crossed the courtyard, went up the stairs – always behind Aksal, who never said a word – and found themselves in front of the audience chamber. The door was ajar, and the Celt gestured for them to enter.

Dionysius was sitting on a stool in the corner and his back was turned to them. The seat he used to receive foreign delegations was empty.

He turned at the sound of the door closing and got to his feet. Not one of the three managed to get out a word and the hall seemed a hundred times bigger than it was in reality.

'You've called us in . . .' said Philistus finally. He spoke as if they'd come on foot from a local quarter and not from the ends of the earth, after years and years of separation.

'Yes,' replied Dionysius. Another interminable silence followed.

'We . . . I mean to say, your brother and I, are happy that you've called us back,' spoke up Philistus again. He tried to lighten up the leaden atmosphere with a witty remark: 'I was getting a bit bored, to tell you the truth, in that lagoon in the middle of all those mosquitoes.'

'And you?' Dionysius turned to Leptines.

Leptines's head hung low, his eyes were on the ground.

'Won't you even greet me?' he insisted.

Leptines walked up to him. 'Hail, Dionysius. You are looking well.'

'I find you in good form as well. You weren't so badly off there.'

'No. Not so badly off.'

'I need your help.'

'Really?'

'I'm preparing the last war against the Carthaginians. The last one, understand? And I need you. Iolaus is dead.'

'So I heard. Poor lad.'

'Lad . . . we're still using that word after all these years.'

'We are, aren't we.'

Philistus observed them and felt something breaking inside, tears crowding his eyelids. He could feel the intense emotion between those two men, both marked by such hard lives, emotion so powerful that it shattered the layers of ill feeling, of suspicion, of fear, of reason of State, politics and power. The emotion of a deep, heartfelt bond, wounded and offended and perhaps made even more intense by just that reason.

'What is your answer?' urged Dionysius.

'What do you expect from me? You confined me to that rock for five years without a word, without a message. Five years . . .'

'Maybe it's better not to dig up the past,' Philistus broke in unhappily, but his voice immediately died down as he realized how stupid his comment was.

'I could not forgive what you had done . . .'

'I would do exactly the same thing, the same, identical thing, if I found myself in that situation,' retorted Leptines. 'So you can send me back right now.'

Dionysius sighed. He was torn between remnants of a distant rage and the emotion of finding himself once again in front of the most loyal and generous man that he had ever known in his life. 'I need your help,' he repeated, and he took another step towards him. They stared at each other at close range and neither would drop his eyes. Philistus felt like hiding.

'Let it be clear,' replied Leptines, 'that you called me back. I didn't ask to return.'

'All right,' replied Dionysius. 'What else?'

The tension was such that Philistus felt shivers under his skin, but this time he did not speak a word.

'Oh!' exclaimed Leptines. 'Sod the world!' and he left.

Dionysius waited until he had slammed the door and repeated with a grin: 'Sod the world!'

'Do you need me as well?' asked Philistus.

'Yes,' replied Dionysius. 'Sit down.' He pulled over a stool and began speaking as if only hours had passed since the last time they'd seen each other. 'Listen well. The peace treaty with the Carthaginians recognized their right to demand tribute from Acragas, Selinus and Himera.'

'True.'

'These cities have sent emissaries saying that they would be willing to pass over to our side if we are ready to protect them. But they made it clear that they were not willing to trade one subjection with another.'

'I understand. And what do you want me to do?'

'You'll meet with the governors of those cities to negotiate a formula of . . . annexation that respects their autonomy and does not offend their dignity. Is that clear?'

'Perfectly,' replied Philistus.

'That's all.'

'That's all?' repeated Philistus.

'Why? Have we got other things to discuss?'

Philistus lowered his head. 'No,' he replied, 'I suppose not.'

He walked out and found Aksal waiting to accompany him home.

When he entered he found the house in perfect order: the walls had been freshly painted, the furniture and objects were in place as if he had never left.

He sat down, took a tablet and a stylus, drew a long breath, and said: 'Let's get back to work.'

★

Leptines came by a few days later. He was in the blackest of moods.

'What did you expect?' asked Philistus, putting aside his papers. 'That he'd throw his arms around you?'

'Not in the least.'

'Well, you're wrong, because that's what he did, in his own way. He asked you to help him: that's like getting to his knees in front of you.'

'Because he's as lonely as a dog. There's no one he can trust.'

'Exactly. In theory, he can't even trust us. The last time we saw each other, the situation was anything but clear.'

'In your case, not in mine.'

'True. In fact, I'm sure that his feelings for you haven't changed at all. As for me, I don't think he'll ever forgive me, and do you know why? You failed him with your heart, but I with my mind. But he needs me. He's never found anyone as good as I am in diplomatic relations. But that's enough for me. It's enough for me to be back at his side, I admit it.'

'What about those plans for change that you talked to me

about, that you wanted to involve me in? Is that all over? Is everything all right now?'

Philistus sighed. 'Men of letters should keep away from action. We're just not cut out for it. That awkward attempt of mine was a huge mistake, and trying to involve you an even worse one. But I did it in good faith, I swear to you. Have you taken a look around in the city? Have you seen what the mood is? No one cares about politics any more. The administrative system is running well, the citizens' council can rule on any number of economic questions, on public order and urbanistics, our confines are guarded with an iron fist, trade is blooming, and there's plenty of money in circulation. Syracuse is a great power that can deal with Athens, Sparta, even Persia, as her equals. I just hadn't realized. And they say that he's even become a better poet! A miracle, if it's true.

'He has built a system that works, and the facts are in his favour. The age of heroes is ancient past, my friend. We're dealing with a middle-aged man now – who is very capricious and often intractable, but who's still capable of conceiving incredibly daring strategies. If he wanted to, he could happily enjoy a tranquil old age at this point: receive foreign ambassadors, preside over public events and theatrical representations, hunt and raise hounds. No, he's preparing an expedition against Carthage. The last, he says. After which all of Sicily will be Greek, and will have become the centre of the world, the new metropolis. You know, if you think about it, it's our natural vocation, wouldn't you say? Positioned at the centre of the seas, halfway between the Hellespont and the columns of Heracles. It's a great vision that he has, understand? Unfortunately there's a fundamental problem that makes the whole operation futile.'

'What's that?' asked Leptines.

'It's simple: there will never be a second Dionysius. Your brother has always been too detached from his first-born son, who I hear has become even more timid and retiring. Everything rests on Dionysius, like the sky on the shoulders of Atlas. The best of tyrants cannot be preferable to the worst of democracies. He is not replaceable, and when he falls, his construction – no matter how great and powerful he has made it – will fall with him. It's only a question of time.'

'But then,' said Leptines, 'if it's all useless, why did we come back?'

'Because he called us,' replied Philistus. 'And because we love him.'

30

Someone knocked at the door.

'Come in,' said Leptines, and opened it.

He found Aristomache before him, as beautiful as when he had last seen her, but paler. It took him a little while to recover, as if he had met with an apparition. 'Come in,' he repeated.

Aristomache removed her veil. 'We've been apart for so long! I'm so happy to see you.'

'And I as well. I thought of you every day I was in exile. Now you're here . . . I never would have hoped it. Has he sent you?'

'No. I asked him if I could see you and he agreed.'

Leptines didn't know what to say.

'It's a generous gesture,' said Aristomache.

'Do you think so?'

'Well, what do you think?'

'Perhaps he thinks you can convince me to help him in the upcoming war.'

'Oh, no. It's not that. You're free to do as you like. Your privileges have been restored. Your properties are intact and have been well kept up in your absence. You could choose a tranquil life and no one would blame you. He least of all.'

'How do you know?'

'He told me.'

'You've spoken of me?'

'Every day, since your return. Sometimes . . . even before then. He never wanted to admit it, but your absence was the worst punishment for him.'

Leptines wiped his hand across his forehead. 'And what . . . what did he say about me?'

'You are the most important person in the world for him. More than me, more than his children, more than his other wife.'

'Words . . .'

'More than words. Feelings,' replied Aristomache with a quiver in her voice. 'The most precious of our possessions; the only things that make life worth living. If I could, I would convince you to choose a life of tranquillity. You no longer have to worry about governing or commanding. You've paid a high price for your courage, your valour and your honesty.'

Leptines looked at her at length in silence, listening to the pounding of his heart. He wasn't used to such strong emotions. He felt that her urgings – although they were coming from the woman he loved – went against his natural inclination. He answered: 'I'm afraid that kind of life isn't for me. For five years I stood on that windswept rock and I did nothing but watch the sea, day in and day out. Inactivity is unbearable torture for me. I'll have time to rest for an eternity when I'm closed up in a tomb. Tell my brother that I am willing to take up my sword and fight for him, but only against our old enemy. And that he should call upon me for this and this alone.'

Aristomache stared at him with moist eyes. 'So you'll go back to fighting.'

'If necessary, yes.'

'I will pray to the gods that they may protect you.'

'I thank you, but I don't think the gods care much about me. Your thoughts will be of much greater comfort to me.'

'You will always have my thoughts, at every moment of every day and night. It has been a great consolation for me to see you again. Take care of yourself.'

She brushed his lips with hers and left.

He never saw her again, alone.

★

Preparations lasted three years, during which Dionysius extended his hegemony to the most important centre of the Italian League, Croton, even though the city was allied with Carthage. The massive use of Celtic mercenaries had secured his victory.

The alliance between the League and the Punic city had in reality never become operative, because Carthage had been struck once again by plague and had had to put down another revolt of the native Libyan tribes. In the meantime, Dionysius decided to refill the empty coffers of his treasury in view of a new war and teach a lesson to the Etruscan pirates who were venturing ever further south. He launched a bold foray all the way to the very heart of the Tyrrhenian, where an assault contingent took and plundered the sanctuary at Agylla which the Greeks called 'the Towers'.

The raid brought in over one thousand talents and the abhorrence of philosophers, who once again branded Dionysius as a monster who didn't even respect the gods.

Philistus had managed to conclude new treaties with Acragas, Selinus and Himera, including them in Dionysius's Greater Sicily. Carthaginian territory was reduced to the far western corner of the island, with a few cities still in Punic hands.

Leptines did not participate in his brother's campaign against the Etruscans, in keeping with his promise, but he was preparing in every way he could for the decisive match with the Carthaginians. He spent hours each day in the palaestra with Aksal, training with shield and sword, wrestling and boxing. When the two of them moved to the centre of the arena, all activities in the gymnasium were abruptly stopped as the others thronged around the ring to watch the battle of the titans. The gleaming sweat on their bulging muscles and the convulsive panting of their gaping mouths made the encounter extraordinarily realistic; only the lack of blood marred the impression that they were watching a duel to the death.

*

When Dionysius returned from Italy he invited his brother to dinner.

There were only the two of them, and they dined in military camp style, with a planed table and folding stools.

'See? The Italian League had allied with the Carthaginians. They don't seem to mind making pacts with the barbarians.'

'You're playing with loaded dice: you know that things aren't quite that way. There are some who consider freedom the highest good, more important even than ties of blood or language. And I understand them.'

Dionysius nodded solemnly. 'And yet you've accepted to fight the coming war with me.'

'I have.'

'May I ask you why?'

'No.'

'All right. Can I trust you?'

'Yes.'

'Like . . . I used to trust you?'

Leptines lowered his eyes. That phrase had sufficed to set off a turmoil of memories and emotions.

'I had to send you away, keep you in exile, because seeing you and thinking that you could betray me would have caused me insufferable pain.'

'You're still capable of suffering?' asked Leptines. 'I wouldn't have said so.'

'Like any human being. Like any mortal man. And now that I'm approaching the threshold of old age, I'd like for things to be the way they once were between us.'

'What about my betrayal?'

'I've had time to think about it. Everything requires time, but mine is running out, day after day. I want to say one thing: if I should . . . die, in this war, you will be my successor and you may marry Aristomache. She won't say no to you. I'm certain of it. You are the best man I know. There have always been very few men like you, and I don't think there will be more in the future.

If I fall in combat, you will arrange for my ashes to be united with those of Arete. Promise me that.'

'I promise you,' said Leptines.

Dionysius stood and walked to where Leptines sat. He did not give him time to get up: he grasped his brother's head close against his chest, while Leptines, in turn, embraced him tightly around the waist.

They wept in silence.

*

The Carthaginians made their first move that very summer, when Mago decided to advance from Panormus towards Messana. Dionysius called a meeting of his high command and laid out his plan. The fleet would not leave the harbour. The ground troops would go out alone to intercept the enemy army to the north and destroy it. The Celtic mercenaries would hold the centre under his direct command, the Syracusan militias would occupy the right wing commanded by Leptines, and the Campanian and Peloponnesian mercenaries would be on the left with their unit commanders. The cavalry would remain in reserve and be launched at a second stage in pursuit of the fugitives.

The battle took place ten days later at a native village in the centre of the island called Cabala, and Dionysius's secret weapon proved to be a triumph. The sight of the gigantic Celtic warriors with their long white manes and tattooed chests and arms threw the adversaries into a panic and at the moment of impact, their extraordinary power sent the enemy into a ruinous rout. Leptines launched his militias from the right, leading them in person with unrestrained impetus, advantaged by the slope of the land. He circled around the enemy in a sweeping manoeuvre, herding them towards the centre as the Campanians and Peloponnesians were doing the same from the left.

The Punic army was annihilated: ten thousand were slain, including their supreme commander, Mago, and five thousand were taken prisoner. Five thousand others – nearly all Carthaginians – managed to take up a defensive position on a hill behind an old wall where they could dig in for the night, under the command of the son of the fallen general, a valiant young man who bore the fated name of Himilco.

Before the sun set, they had sent a delegation to negotiate their surrender, but Dionysius, who was feeling invincible, imposed very harsh conditions: immediate withdrawal from all of Sicily and payment for war damage as well.

Himilco's messengers communicated that in order to make such a decision they must send a messenger to Panormus to consult with their superiors. They promised an answer within four days, and asked for a five-day truce.

Dionysius and Leptines, still covered in sweat and blood from the battle, retired to their tent and held council. 'What shall we do?' asked Dionysius.

'We do have five thousand of them in our hands, but you've advanced a proposal that they'll find difficult to accept. They'll want to play for time, which is what they're doing. Let's close the circle around the hill, to be sure we're safe from their tricks. We will let no one through but the messenger.'

'You're right. That's what we'll do. Tell them they can come in.'

The envoys listened to the terms of the truce with visible satisfaction, then they respectfully took their leave and returned to their makeshift camp.

Leptines immediately sent the cavalry and the Peloponnesians with the Syracusan officers to close in around the hill and set fires all around. The messenger arrived at one of the road blocks when darkness had fallen and was allowed to pass. He galloped off in a rush.

The rest of the night and the next day were tranquil. The dispatches from the guard posts that Leptines would receive now and then did not report any news. The third day, towards evening, he began to become suspicious; the messenger had not returned and it didn't seem possible that there was no movement whatsoever on the top of the hill. He took command of a group of light infantry and advanced on foot towards the peak, fanning his men out. As he made his way up, a terrible premonition wormed into his mind. Suddenly certain that he was not mistaken, he loosed his men at a run towards the wall. He soon arrived at the top, panting, and let out a bitter laugh: the place was deserted.

'Search everywhere!' he shouted. 'Turn over every stone! They can't have vanished like this. Find them, I said!'

Dionysius himself arrived and was appalled at the sight of the abandoned camp. Pale, his jaw clenched, he was trembling with rage and frustration.

'*Hegemones!*' shouted a soldier. 'This way, quick!'

Leptines and Dionysius rushed over and found themselves before the entrance of a cave, one of many that dotted that bleak landscape. It was a natural cavern that descended into the depths of the earth, wound on for a distance of nearly three stadia and finally ended up in the open countryside; the aperture was hidden by thick scrub and brambles. Bloodstains on the thorns and on the trodden earth left no doubts.

'Blast them!' cursed Dionysius. 'Follow their traces!'

'They're too far ahead by now; they will have marched at full speed. We'll never catch them. Destiny has mocked us by robbing us of a definitive victory. But we have defeated them nevertheless and we can be happy with that for the time being. Let's go back now.'

Three days later a Carthaginian messenger brought word from Himilco; he was sorry, but he would have to reject the conditions of surrender.

'How dare he ridicule me!' roared Dionysius.

'It's his right to do so, I'd say,' commented Philistus philosophically after joining them.

'Oh! Sod it!' swore Dionysius and rode off at a gallop.

*

It took Dionysius the rest of the year to prepare for resuming the war; his informers had told him that the Carthaginians would almost certainly attempt another attack. In fact, the armies set off once again at the beginning of the summer.

Dionysius and Leptines, accompanied by Philistus, advanced from the south; Himilco from the north. After testing and provoking each other at length through a series of feints and skirmishes, and after long observation of the opposite camp by reconnaissance squads, the two armies finally faced off at a place in western Sicily that the Greeks called Cronium. Dionysius was bitterly surprised to see that the Carthaginians had added on a massive contingent of Celtic mercenaries, probably enlisted directly in Gaul, or through their bases in Liguria.

The battle began in the late morning. The Syracusan forces, alerted by blaring horns and the shouted password, attacked the enemy with great vigour, encouraged by their success the previous year. At first the outcome of the clash was uncertain as each of the two armies alternately fell back and gained ground under the merciless rays of the sun. Towards midday, the Celts that Dionysius had lined up at the centre, wearied by the heat, began to lose ground, baring the flank of the right wing where Leptines was fighting with unflagging fury. Dionysius realized what was happening and ordered his adjutant to send reinforcements to cover his brother, but Himilco's Celts and Balearics had already wedged deep into the opening. They managed to almost completely cut off the right Syracusan wing which suddenly found itself in crushingly inferior numbers.

Submerged by a multitude of enemies, Leptines did not lose heart: he plunged into the heart of the fray roaring like a lion. He struck cleaving blows, mowing down one foe after another for as long as his strength sustained him. He finally collapsed, his chest, his belly, his neck run through.

When he fell a cry of exultation rose from the enemy ranks and dismay invaded the Syracusans, who began to retreat without breaking their formation. But their withdrawal soon turned into an open rout. News reached Dionysius almost immediately, and his heart sank. He saw his men falling left and right, the enemy charging in pursuit, determined to spare no one on their path. He was about to turn his sword upon himself when Aksal arrived on horseback, screaming like an infernal fury and brandishing an enormous axe. He chopped down all those who got in his way then leaned over the side of his horse, grabbed his master by the arm and hoisted him on to the steed's back. He sped towards a little hill located at a distance of about one stadium, where a rear observation post had been sited, garrisoned by Philistus who was waving a Syracusan standard.

Aksal leapt to the ground, turned Dionysius over to the men of the meagre garrison and blew hard on his horn. The long lament echoed through the valley, flew over the field of the massacre and rallied the scattered soldiers.

Dionysius remained on his feet under the standard for hours to gather his men, to bolster their spirits and to draw them up in a square formation for the final defence. Only when darkness fell did the slaughter cease, and at that point, strangely, he heard the Carthaginian war horns sound the retreat and saw the victorious army withdraw well beyond the line of battle.

Only then did he let himself go, and he crumbled to the ground, unconscious.

When he opened his eyes again, he sought Aksal, but no one knew where he had gone. Philistus had his men search everywhere for him. They called out his name with all the breath they had, combing the countryside all around, without success.

He appeared just before dawn, on foot, staggering with fatigue and covered with blood, holding the corpse of Leptines in his arms.

The men ran towards him and helped him lay the commander's lifeless body on the ground before his stunned brother.

Aksal approached Dionysius and said: 'Carthaginians go away.'

'What are you saying?' asked Philistus. 'That's not possible.'

'Yes. They going away.'

It was true. Himilco's army, after winning a crushing victory were inexplicably withdrawing.

Dionysius ordered a pyre to be built, and had his brother's body washed and laid out. Then he drew up the troops for their last salute.

When their shout had died down he dismissed them. 'Go now,' he said in a firm voice. 'Leave me alone.'

The soldiers lined up and marched off in a column. A small group remained behind under Philistus's command to protect him. They withdrew to a certain distance.

Dionysius took a torch and lit the pyre. He watched the flames licking at the wood, stoked by the dry branches. They crackled louder and louder and surrounded the body of the fallen warrior in a blazing vortex.

Philistus, who hadn't dared watch at first, now turned his eyes to the fire raging in the darkness. In the light of the flames he saw a shadow, a man on his knees, bent in half and sobbing into the dust.

31

PHILISTUS RECEIVED THE terms of the peace proposal twenty days later. The message, which came from Panormus, was drawn up in Greek and bore the signature of Himilco and the Great Council of Carthage. It said:

> Himilco, commander of the army of Carthage and
> governor of the Epicraty of Panormus, Lilybaeum,
> Drepanum and Solus,
> to Dionysius, archon of Sicily, Hail!
>
> Our two peoples have fought too many wars, causing each other only bloodshed and devastation. Neither of us has the strength to destroy the adversary; let us thus resign ourselves to accept the situation as it stands. We won the last battle and you still have five thousand of our citizens in your hands. We thereby ask, as was formerly the case, that the city of Selinus be acknowledged as ours, along with the territory of Acragas up to the Halycus river, while the city of Acragas itself will remain yours.
>
> You will return our prisoners and pay one thousand talents for war damage.
>
> You will recognize our borders as definitive, and we shall recognize yours, as we shall recognize the authority of Dionysius and his descendants over the territory defined in this treaty.

Philistus took the dispatch and asked to be announced at the Ortygia fortress, where Dionysius had been closed up for days, refusing to see anyone.

Aksal barred his way. 'Boss no want anybody.'

'Tell him that it's me, Aksal, and that I must absolutely speak with him. It is a matter of the utmost importance.'

Aksal disappeared inside and reappeared after a short time, gesturing for Philistus to enter.

Dionysius was sitting on the audience seat. He had dark circles under his eyes, his skin was ashen and his beard and hair were dishevelled. He looked as though he'd aged ten years.

'I am sorry to disturb you,' said Philistus, 'but I have no choice. The Carthaginians propose peace.'

Dionysius reacted to those words. 'Of their own initiative? You didn't make the first offer?'

'I would never have taken the liberty without informing you first. No, the proposal comes from them.'

'What do they want?'

Philistus read him the message, saw that he was listening attentively, and continued: 'I would say it's a very reasonable proposal, given our current state of inferiority. We can discuss the war damage. The Carthaginians are always willing to haggle over money matters. But the most important thing is their official recognition of your authority and your claim to this territory, extending to your descendants. This is fundamental; you mustn't miss this opportunity. Think of your son. You know well that he doesn't resemble you, or his uncle. If you leave him a solid state, with recognized borders, life will be much easier for him, wouldn't you say?'

Dionysius let out a long sigh, got to his feet and walked towards him. 'Yes, perhaps you're right. Let me read it through one more time.'

They sat together at a table. Philistus placed the sheet in front of him and waited as he read it.

'You are right,' Dionysius said finally. 'I will follow your advice. Prepare the official protocol and enter into negotiations for the war damage. We don't have all that money.'

'Maybe we could make concessions as far as territory is concerned. Inland, perhaps one of the Siculian districts that's not vital to our economy.'

'Yes, that is a possibility.'

'Well then . . .'

Dionysius was silent, absorbed in thought.

'Well, then, I'm leaving,' said Philistus, and seeing that he wasn't getting an answer, rolled up the sheet and headed towards the door.

'Wait,' Dionysius called him back.

'Yes?'

'Nothing . . . nothing. You can go.'

Philistus nodded his head and left. For a moment he thought he was about to say something personal. But perhaps he still needed time . . .

*

Three years passed, during which Dionysius seemed little by little to resume his old habits, dedicating himself to government matters and to the political training of his first-born son, with very little satisfaction in truth. The young man preferred to organize parties with his friends, inviting artists, courtesans and poets, and he always seemed embarrassed when his father summoned him.

His mother Doris, who had become quite heavy over years of inactivity, tried to defend him. 'You've always been too harsh with the boy; you frighten him.'

'I'm trying to make a man of him, by Zeus, a man of state, if I can manage it,' replied Dionysius.

'Yes, but how are you trying? Never a gentle word, never an affectionate gesture.'

'You can worry about simpering over him. I'm his father, by Heracles, not his mother! You've succeeded in making him a spineless, incapable . . .'

'That's not true! He has good qualities, and if you gave him a task to accomplish, any kind of responsibility at all, he could prove it to you. Anyone can see that all your affection goes to Arete, the daughter of that . . .'

'Shut up!' ordered Dionysius. 'Not another word! Arete is my child like all the others. She's just the youngest and she is an adorable little girl. I have the right to have some satisfaction from this brood!'

Their discussions invariably ended up in quarrels, with Doris bursting into tears and closing herself up in her rooms for days with her maids and lady companions.

Philistus, on the other hand, became his intimate adviser and, although Dionysius would never completely admit it, his friend. The only one he had left to him.

Having definitively settled the western borders and their relations with Carthage, Philistus began attending to relations with Sparta, which had always been Syracuse's protecting power. When she once again waged war against Athens, he sent ten ships to take part in operations in the Aegean, with Dionysius's approval. It was an act of duty, not an intervention with expansionistic ambitions.

Dionysius seemed increasingly interested in literature, an old juvenile passion of his, while he continued to remain hostile towards philosophy. He had the city theatre enlarged and had his plays performed there, usually to great applause. Knowing who the dramatist was, the public was eager not to offend him.

The expedition in the Aegean had a terrible outcome: the Athenians sank nine of the ten Syracusan ships and the admiral leading them preferred to take his own life rather than sail back to Laccius with a single ship.

Politics in Greece had become so complicated that it was difficult to guess how things would develop from one season to the next, let alone from one year to the next.

The Thebans had introduced a new military formation called the 'oblique' array – invented by two of their generals named Pelopidas and Hepameinondas – that was so effective that they managed to defeat the invincible Spartans, once their allies, at a place called Leuctra. Startled by a similar success, which was wholly unimaginable, the Athenians passed over to the side of Sparta, their old enemy, in an effort to contain the Thebans.

Things were going badly, and would have got much worse if

it had not been for Dionysius's intervention. The massive use of Celtic mercenaries and of his siege machines had great success and overturned the situation. Athens went so far as to dedicate a golden crown to him. Rumour had it that the king of Sparta, Agesilaus, after having seen Dionysius's ballistas and catapults in action for the first time, exclaimed: 'By the gods, a man's courage is no longer worth anything nowadays!'

The bestowal of the golden crown provided Dionysius with a unique opportunity: he obtained Athenian citizenship and, through Philistus, laid the basis for a treaty which bound his State in an alliance with Athens, ending belligerency that had lasted virtually fifty years, from the time of the Great War when the Athenians had besieged Syracuse.

Dionysius was accepted now with great honour in all the metropolises, recognized and celebrated as the champion of western Hellenism against the barbarians. His slips in the past in this regard were eclipsed or forgotten. He returned to Syracuse in the autumn of that year, the sixtieth of his life, and was resolutely determined, this time, to dedicate himself to preparing his son to succeed him.

Dionysius II was twenty-eight years old now, and a grown man. Up until that moment he had never proven himself in a challenging situation. He had always lived in luxury, giving himself over to the pleasures of wine, food and sex, and he had never enjoyed his father's esteem. He was cultured and well educated, but feeble and irresolute.

Philistus tried to defend him as well. 'You mustn't judge him so severely,' he said to Dionysius. 'Any son of a father like you feels crushed by the comparison. He grows up feeling inadequate and incompetent, and this continually puts him in a bad light. He realizes that, but at the same time he feels less and less capable of showing what he's worth. It's a vicious circle that has no end.'

'So what should I do?' asked Dionysius. 'Give him kisses and pat him on the head? By Zeus, if he doesn't want to become a man I'll force him, by fair means or foul!'

But these were only words. In reality, Dionysius was convinced that no one could succeed him, that no one was up to such a task. Philistus was tempted at times to suggest that he restore the government to the people, but he held his tongue. He knew full well that, although a democracy might be capable of governing a city, it would never be able to handle a State of such dimensions, with outposts all the way in Epirus, Illyria, Umbria and Padusa. It was respect and fear towards one man alone that held together the complex. A government of citizens would never be likewise feared nor respected by other citizens' governments in subjugated cities.

Perhaps the situation would have remained stable, with the political, economical and cultural equilibrium that Dionysius had managed to create, had news not come from Africa that threw him into a state of great agitation.

Philistus was urgently summoned and he rushed to the fortress. 'What's happened?' he asked as soon as he was in the door.

'Plague has broken out in Carthage.'

'Again?'

'And this time it seems to be exterminating a good number of those bastards.'

'I understand how that may please you.'

'That's not all. The Libyans are in revolt.'

'That's not new either. Why are you so excited?'

'Because it's our opportunity to finally chase them out of Sicily.'

'You said you wouldn't be trying again.'

'I lied. I intend to try again.'

'You signed a treaty.'

'Only in order to gain time. A man like me can never give up his plans. Never, understand?'

Philistus lowered his eyes. 'I imagine it would be useless to remind you that Carthage has been debilitated by plague and rebellion many times in the past, and each time she came back stronger and more determined than ever.'

'This time is different.'

'Why is it different?'

'For two reasons. First of all, those curs killed my brother and they'll have to spit blood until I say "Enough". Second, I'm sixty years old.'

'That should make you sensible and dedicated to wise administration. War is always bad business.'

'You don't understand. I mean to say that if I don't carry through with my plans now I never will. As far as my son is concerned, it's best you don't even mention him. I've made my decision. We will attack next spring with our army, fleet and artillery. We will attack with the greatest army that has ever been seen and we'll tear them to shreds.'

'And where are you counting on finding so much money?'

'You worry about that. Must I always teach you everything? Borrow the treasures from the temples: the gods will apply a reasonable rate of interest, I'm sure. Tax the Company. Ours here in Syracuse and in the other cities as well. They have plenty of money.'

'I wouldn't try either of those options, if I were you. You'll come out looking sacrilegious. And as far as the Companies are concerned, you know full well how powerful they are. There's the risk that they'll make you pay this time. Even here in Syracuse. They may have pardoned your purges, or they may be temporarily overlooking them, but when it comes to money they don't make allowances for anybody.'

'Do you want to help me find this money or not?'

'All right,' said Philistus. 'But don't say I didn't warn you.'

'This time we've been given our golden opportunity! This time we will carry it off, believe me, and all of Greece will honour me. They will raise statues to me at Delphi and Olympia, dedicate inscriptions to me in public places . . .'

He was dreaming. Now that he had been accepted at the highest levels by the metropolises, he – the one from the colonies, treated with scorn and arrogance for years, ridiculed for his awkward literary endeavours – wanted to crown his life's achievement by becoming the leading man in the Greek world.

Nothing could dissuade him. By the beginning of the summer

he had mustered an enormous army: thirty-five thousand foot soldiers, five thousand horsemen, three hundred battle ships and four hundred transports.

★

His army swept through Sicily: Selinus and Entella welcomed him as a liberator, Eryx surrendered to him, as did Drepanum, where he stationed the fleet. But he had to stop at Lilybaeum. The Carthaginian fortifications were so imposing, their defences so tough, that any attempt at an attack would have ended in failure, or worse, in defeat.

The season was drawing to an end and Dionysius prepared to return to Syracuse. He intended to leave almost the entire fleet at Drepanum to head off any possible attack from Africa, but he received a piece of news that made him change his mind: a secret dispatch announced that a fire had broken out at the island of the admiralty in Carthage and had nearly destroyed the shipyards.

The partially artificial island of the admiralty was one of the wonders of the world, the only structure that Dionysius envied his great rival. Perfectly shaped in a circular form, in the middle of a vast lagoon, its covered docks could host more than four hundred battle ships. At the centre was the admiralty building which gave the island its name. It was said that the most jealous secrets of the Carthaginian navy were conserved there: the routes of gold and of tin, and those that led to the remote Hesperides, at the extreme confines of the Ocean.

The legendary trophies of the most daring exploits of navigation were displayed there, even those from the journeys of the caravaneers who had gone so far as to cross the sea of sand that led to the land of the Pygmies. Some claimed that the maps of lost worlds were preserved in those inaccessible archives. It was even rumoured that most of the Carthaginian harbours were designed to reproduce the ancient capital of Atlantis.

If the island had truly burned down, then Carthage had lost her heart and her memory.

'The gods are with us,' he said to Philistus. 'See? I'll leave a hundred ships at Drepanum; that should suffice. And next spring, as soon as the weather turns good again, we'll be back to deal the decisive blow. We'll concentrate all our efforts on artillery; we'll build more machines, I'll have new ones drawn up . . .' His eyes shone as he spoke, brimming with enthusiasm, and even Philistus began to believe that the venture that had occupied forty years of his life might at last be happily concluded.

Dionysius was so sure of himself at that point that he spent the winter working on the last draft of his tragedy *The Ransom of Hector*. He had an actor recite excerpts in Philistus's presence to have his opinion. In the meantime he had sent a delegation to Athens to enter his tragedy in the competition held at the Lenaean festival, the solemn celebrations in honour of the god Dionysus. Dionysus had given Dionysius his name, and this seemed an excellent omen.

When the day arrived, he asked Philistus to accompany him. 'You must come as well. You have been of such great help to me in perfecting my work.'

'I would come very gladly,' replied Philistus. 'But who will remain here to see to preparations for the new expedition?'

Dionysius sighed. 'I have reflected upon the situation at length. I'm sure that the Carthaginians will still be quite occupied repairing the damage to their dockyards. What's more, our navy officers in Drepanum are a good lot, and very competent. In the third place, I've decided to invest my son with a few limited supervisory responsibilities to see how he manages. So I would say you can leave with me. Now don't imagine that I'm doing this just for literary glory! What I'm most concerned with is drawing up a protocol with the Athenians and signing the treaty that will confirm our place among the great powers of the world. Our weak spot has always been the navy, whereas the Athenians have at least as much experience as the Carthaginians; we could learn much about their techniques and expertise in the field of naval warfare.'

The reasons Dionysius laid out were certainly convincing but not entirely reassuring; nonetheless, in the end Philistus agreed to leave with him. There was a kind of uneasiness gnawing at him, an anxiety that kept him awake at night. The stakes were too high, the risks too great; too many uncertainties in a winter so uncharacteristically mild that it was even favourable for navigation.

They reached Athens midway through the month of Gamelion and they found the city in a flutter over staging the performances. They lodged in a beautiful house with a garden that they had bought near Ceramicus, and they threw themselves into preparations, sparing no expense: they hired the actors and chorus, had the costumes made up, chose the masks, had the stage machines built. Announcements had already been posted in the theatre, on the acropolis and at the agora but Dionysius, at his own expense, had more announcements put up all over the city, in the most frequented spots, under the porticoes and in the libraries. He was sure that his name alone would draw the crowds.

He personally supervised the rehearsals, and did not hesitate to dismiss any actors who were not up to his standards and to engage others. He did the same with the chorus and the musicians, making them repeat the dances and songs that would accompany the tragedy countless times.

And the great day arrived.

The theatre was packed. Dionysius and Philistus sat in their reserved places among the city magistrates and the priests from the various colleges. The tragedy was performed in an impeccable manner, with certain parts even expressing considerable intensity, revealing the author's long experience in matters of war and in the exhausting negotiations for the liberation of hostages and prisoners. The scene in which old Priamus got to his knees to kiss Achilles's hands, and the mournful chorus of the Trojan women pleading for the return of Hector's body, moved the public to tears. Even Philistus was surprisingly moist-eyed; could Dionysius have felt real emotions? And felt them strongly enough to communicate his feelings to the people gathered in the theatre?

The question was unanswerable: Dionysius was and would always be a sphinx, an enigma, for all his days. And yet Philistus, in watching those scenes, recognized many aspects of his personality, witnessed many fragments of his past life, many moments of both glory and abasement. Dionysius had recited his role in life like an actor; he had often concealed, feigned, deceived; he had hidden his human feelings, if he had any, behind the harsh mask of the tyrant.

The finale met with applause, not overwhelming, perhaps, but not merely polite, either, considering that that theatre had hosted the works of Aeschylus, Sophocles and Euripides, and that the Athenian public was the most demanding in the entire world.

At the conclusion of the festivities, rather surprising the author himself, Dionysius's tragedy was awarded first prize. Many claimed that the other contestants were chosen from among poets so modest that even a mediocre poet like Dionysius could win.

No matter; Dionysius celebrated his victory with great solemnity and magnificence, laying on a sumptuous banquet in a garden at the foot of Mount Hymettus, inviting all the dignitaries and notables of Athens.

Just before dinner, Philistus was told that a messenger had arrived with an urgent message from Syracuse. He received the man personally, fearing that the news he brought might have ruined the party. He was not mistaken.

'The Carthaginian dockyard never burned down,' reported the messenger.

'What do you mean, it never burned down?'

'I'm afraid not; it was a trick. The Carthaginians are masters at this sort of thing. We should have imagined it.'

'That's not possible!' protested Philistus. 'Our informers assured us they saw smoke and flames rising from the island.'

'True. It was all part of the staging. They set fire to some old laid up wrecks while the fleet was anchored at a number of secret landings along the northern coast.'

'Stop dragging this out and come to the point. What has happened?'

'The new Carthaginian admiral invaded the port of Drepanum

at first light with two hundred battle ships. Our fleet was greatly outnumbered, and had the worst of it.'

Philistus dismissed the messenger and lingered for a while all alone to meditate on what had to be done. In the end he decided not to tell Dionysius anything for the time being, so as not to spoil the festivities. He stretched out at his place, ate and drank, apparently enjoying himself.

That same night, after the guests had gone, towards the third guard shift, Dionysius fell ill. Aksal rushed to awaken Philistus. 'Boss not well.'

'What are you saying, Aksal?'

'He very sick, you come now.'

Philistus hurried to his room, where he found Dionysius in a terrible state: shaken by convulsions and retching, soaked in sweat but cold as ice, ashen-faced and dark-nailed.

'Go call his doctor, Aksal, run! Three blocks from here, towards the agora. Run, by all the gods! Run!'

As Aksal rushed down to the street, Philistus tried to lift Dionysius to a sitting position and help him breathe. He dried his forehead and dampened his parched lips. The bed stank of sweat and urine.

Dionysius seemed to rally for a moment, to regain his strength. 'It's finished,' he whispered. 'It's all over, my friend.'

Philistus was moved by that word that he hadn't heard for so many years, and he clasped his hand tightly. 'What are you saying, *hegemon*? Your doctor is coming. You'll get better. You drank a little too much, that's all. Take heart, you'll see that . . .'

Dionysius cut him off by wearily raising his hand in his habitual imperious gesture. 'No, I'm not wrong. Death is cold . . . feel it? Fate mocks me! I've always fought on the front lines, I've been wounded five times, and here I am dying in bed, pissing myself . . . like a man worth nothing. I'll never see the dawn of the new era I've dreamed of all my life . . . Sicily . . . at the centre of the world . . .'

'You will see it! We'll go back home and finish up this war, once and for all. You will win, Dionysius. You will win, because you are the greatest.'

'No . . . no. I sent all the friends I had to their deaths: Doricus, Biton, Iolaus, my own Leptines. I've spilled so much blood, for nothing.'

The steps of a lone passer-by could be heard from outside. Dionysius lit up. 'Arete!' he said, straining to hear. 'Arete . . . is that you?'

Philistus lowered his tear-filled eyes. 'Arete's here,' he answered. 'She's come – she's here for you.'

Dionysius collapsed with a long gasp. He whispered again: 'Remember what you promised. Farewell, *chaire . . .*' and then nothing.

The doctor burst into the room all at once, short of breath and accompanied by Aksal, but it was too late. All he could do was verify his death.

Aksal stiffened at the sight. His face hardened into a stone mask. He struck up a mournful dirge, the harrowing lament that his people sang to accompany the last journey of great warriors. Then he closed himself off in an impenetrable silence. He mounted armed guard over Dionysius's body, day and night, neither eating nor drinking. He never abandoned him, not even when the coffin was placed on the ship that would carry him back to his homeland.

In Syracuse, Philistus personally saw to the funeral rites. He had a gigantic pyre built in the courtyard of fort Euryalus at the top of Epipolae so that the whole city could see his soul rising in the vortex of fire and sparks that would push him towards the sky. Dionysius's body, dressed in his most splendid armour, was set on the pyre in front of the drawn-up army. Twenty thousand warriors from every nation shouted out his name ten times, as the flames rose roaring towards the winter sky.

Late that night, Philistus and Aksal went to gather his ashes. Together they went to Arete's tomb and joined his ashes with hers in the urn.

When they had finished this simple rite, Philistus dried his eyes and turned towards the Celtic warrior, frightening in the gaunt severity of his fasting, grief hollowing his face and blackening his eyes. 'Go back to your quarters now, Aksal,' he said, 'and break off your fasting. Your master doesn't need you any more . . . We do.'

They left, and the tomb remained dark and silent.

But when the sound of their steps had died away completely, a solitary song rose from the darkness, the heart-rending melody that accompanied the first night of love for Arete and Dionysius.

And the last.

EPILOGUE

'No one was ever able to explain the cause of his death. They said that Philistus had seen the sign of the dolphin carved into the bottom of the cup that his lord and master had drunk from the night of the celebrations. He remembered how Dionysius had ordered the deaths of many members of the Company during the last great purge, and how he had unceremoniously taxed Company members in other cities to finance the coming war, heedless of any warnings.

'Some attributed his death simply to the revelry that followed his victory in the Lenaean tragedy contest. Others saw the long arm of Carthage in his decease; how else could they have hoped to destroy such an obstinate enemy?

'I signed the peace treaty, as soon as I had the power to do so, and I tried to uphold it. But I struck fear into no one's heart, and even the philosophers were lining up to teach me how to govern . . .

'In ten years' time, all that my father had managed to build up was in ruins and would never be revived. An ageing general sent by the metropolis, Timoleon, defeated the Carthaginians and deprived me of my powers. I was exiled here to Corinth . . . the place from which our founding fathers set off so long ago . . .'

*

'Maestro! What are you doing? Talking to yourself?'

The schoolmaster rubbed his eyes and looked around. The asses and their minder had disappeared; lounging against the wall on the other side of the road was one of the three brutes who had rescued him the night before, one of the inseparable bodyguards that the city had charged with his safety.

Standing in front of him was the tavern keeper, a cup of steaming milk in hand. 'Drink this,' he said. 'It will put you back on your feet.'

The maestro took a look at him, and then at the sun that was emerging at the horizon, setting off a thousand golden reflections on the street still shining with the night's rain. He stuck a hand in his satchel and felt for the scrolls. They were still there; he breathed a sigh of relief.

He got up with some difficulty, stretched his aching limbs and rubbed his eyes again, as if he could not quite awaken from a dream. 'That's all right,' he said. 'Another time.'

He walked off unsteadily, and the tavern keeper stood for a while watching him bemused, until his figure dissolved in the glare of the dawning sun.

Author's Note

The story of Dionysius I of Syracuse is so complex that I've chosen at times to simplify some of the historical figures, as well as the events themselves.

I've purposely left out the tyrant's numerous offspring, except for the first two, Dionysius II and Hipparinus, and little Arete. The figure of Dionysius's young brother-in-law Dion, so noteworthy in the ancient sources that Plutarch dedicates one of his biographies to him, has been completely removed. To introduce and develop such a character more than halfway through the novel would have created narrative problems. The figure of Iolaus also embodies Dionysius's younger brother Thearides, who thus does not appear in our story.

Apart from these considerations, the story of Dionysius I substantially reflects the accounts given in the ancient sources, especially Diodorus Siculus, who draws from both Timaeus of Tauromenium and Philistus himself, who readers will be familiar with as one of the protagonists of this novel.

The theme of the Company, which rather explicitly echoes the modern Sicilian Mafia, is not fabricated; the *hetairiai* were somewhat secret associations of citizens – attested to in historical sources – who often used intimidation or even physical elimination of their adversaries to attain their means. Such associations also existed in Greece, but it seemed to me that the extent of this phenomenon in Sicily, in such ancient times, was particularly significant.

As far as the names are concerned, I've used the Latin spelling where a consolidated use of such names exists; I've used the Greek (or Carthaginian) spelling only for rarer and less well-known names.

Some readers may be surprised that I've used 'Italians' and

'Sicilians' instead of 'Italiots' or 'Siceliots', but I've preferred to eliminate terminology which is too specialistic or academic in favour of more suggestive terms, bearing in mind that the terms I've chosen are the literal translation of the original words. Obviously, the words 'Italy' and 'Italians' always refer here to the southern tip of the peninsula, the area we call Calabria today.

The use of language in slang expressions, in cursing and dialogues, has been derived from theatrical comedies, which have conserved such colourful everyday expressions.

The political perspective mirrors the point of view of the story's protagonists, and could not be otherwise, although in various cases and situations, secondary characters express values which differ from those of Greek civilization, especially regarding the politics of the Greeks of Sicily.

Dionysius emerges as the great protagonist that I believe he was. His substantial failure appears to be a consequence of the basic error he made in running the State: absolutism.

Valerio Massimo Manfredi